Praise for
Sloan Parker's Other Books

"Sloan Parker is an amazing writer. Her work is beautiful and touching and emotional. If you haven't read any of her books, I suggest you run out and do so!"

—*Sadonna at The Armchair Reader*

"…an emotional and sensual blockbuster."

—*Joyfully Reviewed on MORE*

"…I loved everything about this story—especially the level of intensity and connection that crackled between Grady and Mateo. I'd sum up my reading experience with this book in one word—unputdownable!"

—*Hearts on Fire Reviews on I SWEAR TO YOU*

"…I have loved every one of Sloan Parker's books and this one is no different. …exciting, suspenseful and most importantly, romantic. The love story between Walter and Kevin is so sweet and real. They have a connection that can't be denied by either one of them."

—*Literary Nook on HOW TO SAVE A LIFE*

"I loved both of the heroes… and found myself easily rallying for their relationship to grow from being best friends to developing a loving, romantic relationship together that lived long within my heart long after the story was over."

—*Night Owl Reviews on TAKE ME HOME*

"So sweet and romantic and incredibly well done in such a short format."

—*Joyfully Jay on SOMETHING TO BELIEVE IN*

OTHER TITLES BY SLOAN PARKER

More Than Most
(More Book 2)

SLOAN PARKER

MORE THAN MOST (More Book 2)
Copyright © 2015 by Sloan Parker

ISBN-13: 978-0-9911212-8-1
ISBN-10: 0-9911212-8-7

Cover Design: Copyright © 2015 by Sloan Parker
Cover Photos: licensed through shutterstock.com and fotosearch.com.

Published by
Sloan Parker Press
www.sloanparker.com

More Than Most

Prologue

Fifteen years ago...

"Don't do it, Richard." Joe Mason shook his head, his shocked expression laced with concern. He had offered his warning loud enough for several of the men and women seated nearby to hear, even over the drone of music from the twelve-piece orchestra.

I laughed as I leaned forward, my elbows resting on the linen-covered tablecloth. "Why? What's he going to do to me?"

Despite my playful tone, my friend shot me another warning look, whispering this time as he said, "I don't want to know what *he's* capable of. He's one mean old bastard." Joe swirled the Chivas Regal in his glass and watched the amber liquid for a moment. Then he lifted his gaze and studied me. He ditched the glass on the table with a *clink* as if he just realized I really did have every intention of talking to the old man.

Leaning forward Joe jabbed a finger my way. "Richard Marshall, you be careful. You get on his bad side, and he'll fuck with you for the fun of it. Men that wealthy get bored easily."

That they did.

I met Joe's concerned stare. "Don't worry, Mom." I gave him a wink and stood. "I'll be careful."

He shook his head again in exasperation and threw me a grin. "Good luck. Although I doubt you ever need that."

Sure I did. I'd never gone after a property owned by someone of Edward Harrison's stature. I gave Joe a nod and headed across the crowded ballroom of the exquisite Harrison Estate.

The worst thing Old Man Harrison could do that night was make a scene. That didn't scare me. Regretting that I didn't take the chance at all would bother me a hell of a lot more. I lived with worse regret every day of my life. It was the kind that forever changed a man—and the person he hurt most. I wasn't about to add to that regret because of my work.

As I wove in and out of the tables in the ballroom, I gave Joe's words more thought. Was he right? Should I be doing this?

I owed Joe a lot. Not only had he taken me under his wing when I first joined the real estate investment firm where we both worked, he and his wife had also invited me into their family, giving me a home to go to when I couldn't make it back to New York for the holidays. I didn't want to let him down by taking a chance he thought was too risky.

But I also didn't want to disappoint myself. I'd been dreaming of this project since I first got a look at the Harrison Estate two years earlier. The historic stone house, with its tall, elaborate chimneys and gothic arches over the doors and windows, along with its famous, mysterious history, had captivated me. And very few properties, or people, completely captured my attention like that. If the Harrisons no longer planned to own the estate, I wanted to be involved in preserving the house and its beauty.

I glanced across the ballroom at Edward Harrison, the white-haired old man who'd loaned his family's home to the hospital for their Annual Children's Charity Ball—and the man Joe had been warning me about all night.

Harrison wore a perfectly tailored five-thousand-dollar tux and leaned on a carved wooden cane. At his side was a woman at least forty years younger. She hung on his arm, and his every word, while he looked as disinterested in her as if she wasn't there at all.

I'd seen Harrison around at other functions, but I'd never had an opportunity to talk with him. I was pretty sure he had no clue who I was.

That was all about to change.

I wasn't missing my chance. I'd already started thinking through the plans, knowing exactly how far back in the home's history I wanted to go with the restorations.

Landing the famous Harrison property—either as my personal investment or one for the firm—would be a career-defining acquisition.

Time for me to make my move.

The woman who'd been hanging on Harrison had finally given up and was off on her next millionaire conquest. I smoothed the front of my tux jacket and approached before anyone else could engage him.

When I was two steps away, he spoke.

"Back off, boy."

Boy? I had at least fifty pounds of muscle on him and stood almost a foot taller, even if he got rid of the hunch that came with old age. He looked like a stodgy businessman who spent his days watching his investments from behind a desk. I looked like a pro football player who hung out in a weight room. That usually worked to my advantage when it came to my business.

"You might as well not even try," Harrison added. He waved his hand in the air, flashing an ostentatious diamond cuff link, dismissing me as he leaned on the cane at his other side for support. "I have no interest in doing business with the likes of you."

Too bad. I wouldn't be dismissed by anyone.

Without another moment's hesitation, I covered the last steps separating us.

The old man reached for a glass on the tray the server standing at his side held out for him. He swallowed a mouthful, discarded the glass, and then lit a cigar. "Let me guess." Still without looking my way, he blew a puff of smoke directly into my face. "You've heard I'm leaving the estate after tonight, that I'm considering selling, and you want to get your hands on my family's home."

So maybe he had heard of me. Had I or my reputation impressed him? Not likely with the way he was speaking to me.

He didn't wait long enough for me to say a single word in response.

"If I decide to sell, it'll be to someone much more respectable." He paused and examined the second-floor ballroom around us as if to emphasize that point. "Someone who would live here. Raise their children in this house. Make it into a home again." He huffed on the cigar once more and took his time exhaling the plume of smoke. "You are so far beneath worthy of this property, it's a joke. And a sign of how bored I am at this function that we're even talking."

Talking? Hadn't he noticed he'd been the only one doing that? Maybe he spent his days conversing with himself, surrounded by servants who never said a word.

I wasn't one of his servants.

I stood taller, folded my arms across my chest. "You have no idea what I would do with this place."

"I don't want to think about it. The disgusting things a *faggot* like you could do in my family's home... Generations of Harrisons buried in the family cemetery out back would turn over in their graves if I so much as considered you."

My jaw clenched. Every muscle in my body went tight. There

wasn't a man in the world who called me a faggot to my face and got away with it.

I wanted to lunge for him.

My business sense kept that instinct in check. This wasn't the time or the place. Not when I hoped to someday leave the firm to start my own company. I'd need a slew of wealthy investors like the men and women seated nearby.

The party had grown quiet around us, most people pretending they weren't listening, but they'd likely caught every word. Even the orchestra had softened its tune.

A skittish, miserable-looking young man wearing an ear piece that indicated he wasn't a guest approached. "Is there a problem, Mr. Harrison?"

I'd seen the ear-piece man at various functions. He was Edward Harrison's personal assistant. He usually spent his time completely invisible until Harrison required something. Then he was there without a word or a look his way.

Harrison motioned to me with the cigar. "This boy here was just leaving, and I think he needs someone to show him the door."

The assistant gestured across the room, indicating the way for me.

When I didn't move, Harrison glared at the assistant as though he'd run down his favorite prized hunting beagle instead of merely failing to get me out of the house.

I held still for a moment more. "You're right." I took a step and halted in front of the old man. "I do want this property, and someday it'll be mine."

Harrison laughed, an unnerving malevolent sound that gave credence to Joe's warnings. Then he looked me in the eye for the first time. "Over my cold. Dead. Body."

I grinned at him through my own laugh, letting my humor last long enough to clearly irritate him. "Well, you're what? A hundred and five?" More like seventy-five, but despite his vast wealth and resources, he looked a hell of a lot older. "Shouldn't be too long until you're pushing up daisies in that family cemetery out back and I'm signing the paperwork on this place."

I didn't give him a chance to get in a last word. I turned my back on him and sauntered toward the exit, grabbing a bottle of champagne as I passed by the bar. I stopped and faced Harrison. He still had that steely gaze locked on me. I tipped the bottle his way and downed a long chug. With a smirk, I slammed the bottle on the nearest table and walked off.

When I was certain I was out of Harrison's line of sight, I paused at the top of the staircase leading to the main foyer and glanced back into the open doorway of the ballroom, then to the house's entranceway below. The white marble flooring in the grand foyer was the original that had been installed when the house was first built. So was the hand-carved woodworking of the arched doorway leading into the dining room. Every facet of the house illustrated the great attention to detail that had gone into its construction. I wasn't easily impressed by wealth or extravagance, but it was that painstaking thoughtfulness that had first drawn me to the estate.

Despite what I'd said to Harrison, I wondered if I was getting my last look at the place.

I sighed and started down the steps. When I reached the middle of the staircase, someone approached behind me. I kept going, and the assistant scrambled to my side. Apparently I was getting an escort out of the house.

At the front door I asked the valet to call a cab. As I waited, I faced the assistant, removed one of my business cards from my wallet, and held it out for him. "If you ever want to work for a boss who'll actually respect you, give me a call."

He stared at the card but stopped short of taking it. Slowly he met my gaze and searched my face as if he didn't know if he could trust my words. Like a wounded dog that had been kicked around too much to know there was a better life out there if he could just summon the courage to take off.

"I'm serious," I offered. "A person with your attention to detail would make a great assistant. If I don't have a position for you, I can find someone who does."

The assistant glanced at the card again, then accepted it and quickly pocketed it in the tux he wore. "Thank you," he whispered.

I gave him a nod and headed out the front door to wait on the cab.

A half hour later my ride dropped me off at the Haven, a membership-only gay sex club.

I didn't hesitate once inside the club. I went straight for the bar. Sitting on a stool was a young man in a dark sleeveless shirt with black tribal tattoos circling his biceps. He leisurely raised a beer to his lips as he watched me cross the room. I almost approached him and asked if he wanted to go for a drive, crash a fancy party, and fuck someplace where we'd be able to hear the boring, stuffy chatter in the ballroom, but I held back.

The first time I spent the night with someone inside the Harrison Estate, it wasn't going to be with a one-night stand.

It would be with someone special.

And the next time I walked into that house, this *faggot* was going to own the place.

Chapter One

I shifted the car into park and glanced at our town house through the falling snow. Three weeks of nonstop meetings all over the country—Seattle, New York, Atlanta, San Francisco—and I was finally home.

I couldn't wait to see my men. Occasional text messages and rushed phone calls before bed—with hardly time for more than *hello, how are you, talk to you tomorrow*—hadn't been enough.

Nowhere near enough.

I grabbed my keys, my bag, and threw open the car door. The whirling gusts of snow smacked me in the face, knocking the breath from my chest. We were in the middle of the worst series of winter storms in decades, and the snowfall amounts were approaching record levels, even this early in the season.

Raising the collar on my coat, I rushed to get inside, then shoved the door closed behind me before the heavy flakes of snow pelted the entire foyer floor. No matter how much I loved our house—loved living there with Luke and Matthew—it wasn't the first time that winter I'd wished I'd bought a place with a garage so I could park inside.

Not that it mattered. The snow. The cold. Nothing could dampen my good mood.

I was home.

Leaning back against the door, I stared off down the hall toward the doorway that led to our kitchen. A lone light was on inside. That—along with the news I couldn't wait to share—had the tension I'd been sporting for weeks fading away.

Before this latest business trip, I hadn't been home for dinner in far too long.

Hell, forget dinner. More often than not, with all the networking and meetings, I hadn't gotten home before they went to bed. The three of us hadn't even had sex in...

I wasn't sure how long.

Which meant I had some serious making up to do.

Yet it wasn't just the sex I'd been missing. I needed them. In a way I'd never let myself need anyone before them. I wanted nothing more than to head toward that light and lose myself in my two lovers—in the peaceful bliss of what I had hoped our lives would become after Luke's father had pleaded guilty to the charges the feds had brought against him eight months earlier.

My chest tightened as I thought about it once again. It wasn't the money his father had stolen from my business in an attempt to coerce Luke to leave us that still got my blood boiling. It was his threat to kill Luke and Matthew—it was the loaded gun he pointed at Luke, and the knife his henchmen had pressed against Matthew's throat—that had me wishing the former senator's sentence had been longer than the few years he'd gotten.

I pushed aside the anger. I wouldn't let anything that man had done to us taint our lives. Or the night I was about to spend with Luke and Matthew.

I shrugged off my overcoat and suit jacket, then set the house alarm I'd had installed a few months back. Working my tie open, I headed for the kitchen, ready to get back to enjoying my nightly ritual of watching them make dinner together—or more precisely watching Matthew make dinner and Luke do his best not to get in the way as he groped and teased.

Several scenarios of what I wanted with them flashed through my mind. Luke's hands and mouth all over me. Slowly, teasingly using his tongue to stroke the skin of my chest and abs, those serious blue eyes looking up at me, never glancing away as he loved on every part of me.

Added to that were Matthew's lips and tongue on my neck as he caressed my body with his. I'd push him to the bed, straddle him, and sink into that beautiful mouth, all the while feeling Luke at my back, burying his cock inside me.

I gave a good rub to the back of my neck.

It had been far, far too long.

Which gave me a thought.

The Haven.

A night out at the club where we all met would be the perfect way to show them how much I'd missed them.

If only it weren't snowing like a beast outside.

I sighed and stepped into the kitchen, but the room was empty, the stove top and kitchen table bare. I checked the living room and the rooms upstairs. Nothing. Every other room in the house was dark and quiet. Too quiet.

I returned to the kitchen. The empty space mocked my earlier thoughts of how I wanted to spend the night with them.

They knew what time my plane landed, and it wasn't like them to come home late without at least sending a text. Even Luke had gotten pretty good about letting us know what he was doing and when he'd be home.

Maybe they'd decided to head to the store to stock up on essentials before the storm got any worse. Or maybe Luke had gone to the library with Matthew to keep him company while he studied. Matthew's finals had to be getting close. Or had I already missed those? Which had me feeling like an even bigger ass about my recent work schedule.

Then I heard them.

Or more specifically, I heard Luke. His laughter eased the last of my tension.

I ditched my tie on the kitchen counter and followed the laughter down the back staircase toward the basement, my anticipation increasing with each step.

Luke's laughter grew louder, and he said, "It's not going to stay in there."

"Yes, it will." That was Matthew, the frustration evident in those three words.

"No, it's too big."

"It's not."

Their voices carried through the closed door of the makeshift bedroom I'd set up as a playroom—complete with a spanking bench and metal loops on the walls and floor for bondage play—when they'd first moved in. The loops were gone, and we didn't use the ropes or cuffs any longer, not after Luke had confessed he'd been asking us to tie him up as some kind of punishment he felt he deserved. But we still liked to mix things up and spend time in the basement when the mood struck any one of us.

Although that was another thing we hadn't done in a long time.

I slowly pushed open the bedroom door, so damn curious at what I'd find them up to.

Luke lay on his stomach across the width of the bed, his chin propped on his folded arms as he stared down over the edge of the mattress. His brown hair was a little longer than he normally wore it, and the snug black T-shirt and faded jeans perfectly showcased his lean runner's build and long legs. A gap was visible between the bunched-up T-shirt and the jeans, exposing his lower back. I wanted to run my hands over that skin, over every inch of him.

I held back. For now.

I couldn't see the best part of him. His eyes. Ever since that first night when I'd caught him staring at me from across the dining room at the Haven, those expressive blue eyes always told me what he was feeling or thinking—even when the rest of him was lying his ass off.

Now he lay there watching Matthew, who sat on the floor beside a giant cardboard box. Matthew held a squirming puppy in each hand. Both were mutts, some kind of German shepherd/Labrador mix from the look of them. One pup was black and brown. The other was the same but smaller with white at the tips of its paws and a white stripe along its belly. Matthew set the pups into the box right as two more popped their heads over the side, claws digging into the cardboard. They hung there, wiggling and whining, trying to get their plump little bodies over the edge.

"See." Luke pointed at the escaping puppies. "They're too old for a box."

Matthew stood and flopped onto his back on the bed, letting out an exasperated sigh as if he'd given up.

Luke got on all fours and turned to straddle him. "Admit it." Leaning over him, he tickled Matthew along his sides. "I was right."

Matthew laughed and squirmed under Luke's teasing, but despite Matthew's firm build, he was shorter and smaller than Luke and had no hope of getting the upper hand.

Then, as if Luke couldn't stand tormenting him any longer, he stopped and swept two fingertips across Matthew's forehead, wiping aside his dark hair. Then he traced an invisible path down the side of Matthew's face.

I was still as amazed as ever at how tenderly Luke touched either of us. It reminded me yet again how lucky we were that he hadn't run. He had fought himself and every fear he had to be with us.

There wasn't much I wouldn't do to be worthy of that.

Luke leaned down and planted a kiss on Matthew. He ran a hand through the back of Matthew's wavy dark hair, and lifted him off the bed, tugging him closer. The kiss deepened, their limbs mingling as their bodies came together.

Leaning against the doorjamb, I slowly unbuttoned the cuffs of my dress shirt and rolled up my sleeves. Then I froze, my breath hitching as I caught sight of Matthew's tongue pressing into the kiss. I wanted to be a part of that. I wanted to feel both of them against me, reach out and sink into their warm embrace, into that kiss, but I was enjoying the sight of them too much to interrupt. They were as beautiful together as that night the three of us first met.

My body started to respond.

It felt good to let the desire build. Not to rush to stroke myself in the shower so I could get off fast before I had to leave for work, or before collapsing into bed at night where they lay already asleep.

Their kiss ended, Matthew breathless. He raised his head farther off the bed and parted his lips for more.

"Hey!" With urgency Luke rolled off him and onto his side. "Don't slobber on my hair." A pup had managed to crawl up the blanket and was on the bed with them.

I pushed away from the doorway and approached. "Guess you need a bigger box."

Matthew bolted upright, a huge smile on his face. "Richard. You're home." Then his mouth dropped open, and his gaze swung to the box beside the bed. Before I could say anything, he spoke again. "It's just temporary."

I rescued Luke from the pup, carried the wiggling ball of fur to the box, and settled it inside. I returned to stand beside the bed and placed a hand under Matthew's chin. "It's cute."

"Yeah," he said around a delighted sigh that I knew had more to do with me touching him than anything about the dog. "She is, isn't she?"

I shook my head. "Not her. That look on your face." I leaned in, and he released another breathy exhale right before our lips met.

I took my time, enjoying the slow, sensual press of our mouths, the little whimper he let out as the kiss deepened and our tongues met. I grabbed him by the waist and heaved him up onto his knees, needing to be closer, needing to feel all of him against me.

He wound his arms around my neck and whimpered into the kiss again. I wasn't the only one who'd missed this connection.

Another minute of that amazing contact, and Matthew drew back. "My friend from school, Erika... She just needs someone to watch them for a few weeks. Her dad died, and she had to take time off from school to head back east."

That he wanted to help a friend with the puppies wasn't a big surprise. That was pure Matthew. He was a full-time student in a veterinary technology program, worked part-time cleaning kennels at a nearby clinic, and also volunteered at the Clark County Humane Society, lugging homeless cats and dogs to every Pet Place Palace and Artie's Animal Shop all over the city for adoption days.

"Uh-huh," I said as I gripped the bottom of his T-shirt and drew it over his head, then tossed it aside.

Luke laughed from where he still lay sprawled across the bed.

Matthew continued. "She said they weren't able to get out of the box at her apartment."

"Sure they weren't." I brushed my lips along the base of his throat, then up the side of his neck, taking in the faint scent of him—and Luke's cologne—on his skin, breathing in the combined aroma of my two lovers.

Matthew rested his hand at the back of my neck and tilted his head to give my mouth more room. Breathlessly he said, "I figured..." A slight moan escaped him as I added my tongue to the explorations. "I figured they wouldn't get into too much trouble down here in the basement."

"Uh-huh." I traced another line up the side of his neck to his ear and let my hands wander down his back to his ass.

"I'm thinking—" He stopped for a moment as if he needed to catch his breath. "I can put up some kind of barrier and keep them confined by the washing machine."

I gripped his jean-covered ass cheeks and forced him tighter against me.

That had him quiet. His lips met mine again, and he kissed me deeper, harder. Then he tugged me down to the bed so I was on top of him, the two of us lying beside Luke.

Matthew clutched my arms, my shoulders, my upper back, anywhere he could reach as he kissed me over and over. "God, I've missed you. That trip was way too long."

"Tell me about it." I pulled back and took in the sight of him lying there before me, those wide dark eyes watching me in return, that hungry, trusting look he always gave me when we were in bed together.

I had missed that look, missed him, missed them both beyond words.

I met Luke's stare. He searched my eyes and threw me a slow grin that told me he felt the same. Then he watched as I ran my hand down Matthew's bare chest and stomach, tracing the thin dark line of hair that disappeared into his jeans. I followed that same path with my lips and tongue, breathing in his scent, all while I stared up at Luke. His grin faded and desire overtook him. Fuck, how I'd missed this.

I sat up and planted my knees on either side of Matthew's hips. "What have you two been doing without me?" I popped open the top button on his jeans.

Matthew licked his lips. "Huh?"

I knew they hadn't fucked without me there. We still kept that one rule, but I wanted to hear every single thing they'd been doing together while I spent all my time working.

"What did you do last night?" Without undoing the zipper, I slid my hand into his jeans and stroked him through his underwear.

His lips parted, and he gasped. He was already hard. Had probably been that way from Luke's kisses. I knew just how amazing it felt to kiss them individually. Put them together, and it was explosive.

"Did you suck Luke off? Did he do that whimper thing right before he came?" I moved my hand faster, and Matthew arched into it. Moisture was gathering at the tip of his cock, wetting the fabric of his underwear. Without moving the briefs out of the way, I spread his precum around the head of his dick with my thumb. "Did he lick your ass and jack you off at the same time?" Matthew loved that one.

He didn't answer. He rolled us and pushed me onto my back so we were closer to Luke. Then he kissed me again, his tongue seeking out mine while Luke spoke.

"I found him on the couch, rubbing himself through his sweatpants, watching that video we made of our trip to New York. He'd just gotten to that part in the hotel room where he was testing the video settings on his new phone and you teased him with all that dirty talk."

That was the best night of our trip east.

We'd gone to New York to visit my parents not long after Luke confronted his father—the night his father had threatened to kill him.

When we'd first gotten to the hotel, Matthew had been a nervous wreck, anxious about meeting my parents, and Luke had been stressed for his own reasons, not the least of which were the constant calls from the press wanting to talk to the son of the recently incarcerated US senator. There had been a lot of attention paid to the fact that we were three people in a relationship. That night in the hotel room when we'd captured the video using Matthew's phone had us all feeling relaxed like we hadn't since before the trouble with Luke's dad.

"Did you like listening to me tell you how I was going to lick and finger and fuck that sweet ass of yours all night long?"

Matthew nodded and leaned down to kiss me again. The soft, wet, sensual slide of that tongue on mine was exquisite.

"Yeah," Luke said. "He came down my throat as soon as he heard you say that part on the video."

At that, I jerked my hips off the bed, wanting the friction of Matthew's body rubbing against my dick. I was more turned on than I had been in a very long time from just Luke's words and Matthew's kisses.

Matthew straddled me, pressing his ass against my erection. Then abruptly he stilled and held my face in both hands, looking at me like he was drinking in the sight of me, like he couldn't believe I was there. "God, I've missed you." He stroked my lower lip with his thumbs. "How was the trip?"

I sucked in a deep breath and found my voice. "It was very productive. In fact…"

His eyes widened. "You got the estate?"

"I did."

"Oh my God." He lunged forward and hugged me. "Congratulations."

"Thanks." I returned the embrace, equally relishing his excited touch and his elation at my news.

He sat up again. "I can't believe it."

Neither could I, really. After fifteen years, Edward Harrison had finally decided to sell me the property, and then he'd gone and died shortly after that. Fortunately, his grandson had agreed to honor the deal after Edward's passing.

"While I was still in California," I said, "I got the last of the funding I needed and signed the paperwork. Since everything was prearranged, I was able to officially take possession of the house yesterday."

"So it's a done deal?" Luke asked as he propped himself on his arm beside us.

"Yeah. I stopped to get the keys on my way home. Even called yesterday to get the security company on board so they can at least keep an eye on the place until I can have an alarm system installed."

Matthew stared down at me. His excited expression had faded, and he once again sported the lust-filled look he'd had a moment ago.

"And," I said as I cupped his cheek. "I know just how I want to celebrate."

Matthew bit his lower lip and worked on getting my shirt unbuttoned. He only made it halfway before he was tugging on me. "Sit up." He pulled my dress shirt over my head in a fluid motion. With a hand to my chest, he pushed me back down to the bed and rubbed us together in a blatant, passionate slide of body against body. No one moved like him. He pressed his lips to the base of my throat and whispered, "Please say you don't have to work tonight."

"Not tonight."

I needed to talk to Joe. He'd offered to give me a hand and was contacting the people who'd expressed interest in investing in my plans for the estate, but I had no intention of worrying about that until later.

Much later.

Matthew sat up and shifted to my side opposite Luke. He reached across me and encouraged Luke forward so I was pinned between them.

Luke made like he was going to kiss me, and then he leaned into Matthew instead. The two kissed over top of me, and I was once again captivated.

That sweet, slow way Matthew swept his lips over Luke's. The way Luke kept the contact going, holding Matthew by the back of the head as if he was afraid he'd lose him forever if he let go, like they were in a boat at sea and there was a chance Matthew might tumble over the edge into the dark, stormy waters below.

Over the years I'd witnessed countless men together at the Haven, but I'd never seen anyone display as much passion in a single moment as the two of them did every time they touched.

Without breaking the kiss, Luke slid a hand over the front of my dress pants, cupping my cock. The fabric of my underwear brushed the sensitive skin below the head of my dick, and I hissed.

Luke chuckled into the kiss.

"Come here," I said. Despite the erotic thrill of watching them, I was done being an observer. It had been too long since I had Luke in my arms. I drew him down to me.

But the fucker still wouldn't kiss me. He ran his lips across my chest, right below the scar I got years ago. He was as fascinated by that scar as ever.

That one touch had me ready to go off, and he wasn't even using his tongue yet. He was loving on me, reveling in the contact as I caressed him everywhere I could reach.

Needing to feel all of him, I forced him up my body so we were plastered together. Only, he still had his clothes on and I still wore my damn pants.

The clothes would have to wait.

"Kiss me." I sounded even more desperate than a minute ago.

His eyebrows rose, and I knew my Luke was about to tease.

Maybe he wanted me to know how frustrated he'd been with my recent work schedule. Normally I would've encouraged him to tell me what he felt. But we both needed something else first.

"Luke, just kiss me already."

He smirked as he came forward, but that grin vanished when his lips met mine. Our tongues slid into the kiss, and Luke slowly made love to my mouth like there was nowhere else he'd rather be, no reason to hurry on to anything more. So different from the Luke I'd first met over a year ago.

I wrapped an arm around Matthew and drew him to us. Another long, deep kiss from Luke, and then Matthew's mouth was in the mix, all of us kissing as one. Three mouths, three tongues, their hands all over me, mine on them, their bodies coming in closer.

They felt so damn good in my arms. Like I was really home for the first time in months—as opposed to the three weeks I'd actually been gone.

They took turns next, one of them on my lips, then the other, trading places as if they shared an oxygen tank underwater and kissing me was all that was keeping them alive.

I wanted to savor every single moment, every touch and caress and—

A chime on my phone brought it all to a halt.

"Seriously?" Luke dropped back to the bed beside me. "If that's about your work, I'm gonna fuck up that phone."

I slipped a hand into my pocket with the intention of shutting off the phone and tossing it aside. Then I read the text.

"Shit." I sat up with a start, nearly smacking foreheads with Matthew in the process.

"What is it?" he asked.

"The security company found a trespasser at the estate." I'd officially owned the place less than forty-eight hours, and someone had tried to break in. "Sounds like they have it under control, but…"

"But what?" Luke scrutinized me with an angry intensity I hadn't seen directed at me in a long time.

"I need to head over there and check it out. The security guards are supposed to wait until they can give me a report."

He didn't seem pleased with that answer. Quite the opposite.

"You guys want to go with me?" I asked.

"Yeah?" Matthew bounded up and sat next to me, tucking his legs under him. "Definitely." He cocked his head to the side and watched me for a moment, his expression shifting from excitement to unease as if he was embarrassed about something. He looked to Luke.

Luke lifted up onto his elbows. "Matthew's been dying to see the place."

Matthew reached across me and smacked Luke on the arm. "You have too."

I wasn't surprised the abandoned mansion interested them. There weren't many people who didn't know about the place and its famous history, but I was disappointed I hadn't noticed how excited they were about it before then.

Matthew focused on me again. "We want to see what you've been working so hard on." He shrugged. "You're not usually so personally involved with all your properties."

He was right about that. "This one's..." I searched for the right word.

"Special," he said.

It meant a lot that he'd picked up on that. I gave a nod. "I'm glad you want to see it. We'll all go, then." I could hear the nervousness in my voice. I had no idea what they were going to think about my plans for the estate—or the other detail about the purchase that I hadn't told them yet.

Matthew was already off the bed, his T-shirt back on. He was gathering the pups that had managed to escape the box again. "I'll rig something up for these guys in the other room until we get home."

Luke fell onto the bed with a loud sigh. "We're seriously going right now?"

I rolled to my side and leaned over him. "I've got to go see what the security company found."

He stared up at me. It had been a while since I'd seen him looking so... frustrated, so disappointed.

I moved in and kissed the base of his throat, working my way up to his lips, inch by inch, one kiss at a time. "I'm sorry I've been gone so much lately." Sorry wasn't a word I said unless I meant it, and we both knew it.

When I pulled back, he gave me a nod of understanding. The way he watched me with those intense blue eyes... I wanted to say fuck checking with security, fuck taking them to see the estate, and instead stay right there in that bed with them.

Then something crawled across my left shin. Two of the pups were on the bed. One lay over my leg, biting the ear of the other. "You definitely need a bigger box. How many are there?"

"Seven." Matthew stood beside the cardboard box, staring down at two more puppies that were attempting to get out. "I swear it's only until Erika gets back. She's trying to find them all homes."

I extricated my leg from the dogs and turned toward him. "Did you actually think I'd be mad about it?"

"I don't know." He darted a look to the bed, where the pups were now climbing over Luke's legs. "Maybe."

That one word slammed into me like someone had taken the heel of his boot to my chest. I glanced at Luke.

"Well," he said, "you do like your house neat and orderly. Dogs aren't the neatest things."

Sure I did, but I wasn't a nut about stuff like that. I just preferred when—

"Wait. *My* house?"

Luke stretched with his arms over his head but said nothing.

I slid to the edge of the bed, reached for my shirt, and slipped it on as I got up. "I thought we established this place was *our* home. Do you still think of it as mine?"

"No." Luke tucked his arms behind his head. "Well, technically, I guess. You were the one who bought it. If we moved or something, you'd get all the money from this place."

I looked to Matthew. He stood beside the box, not making eye contact, not saying anything, which told me all I needed to know.

I crossed the room but stopped at the door, my back to them. The tension from earlier that week was returning, working its way down my body.

"Richard." Luke paused until I faced them. He still casually lay there on his back. "It's *our* home. Don't overanalyze it."

"I suppose you think I do that too much?"

"Yeah, and you're always talking instead of fucking. It's annoying." He threw me that cocky smile I had loved about him from day one. Because it wasn't cocky at all. It was Luke letting down his guard and trying to keep it up at the same time. Only, now there were less of the steel-reinforced walls he'd built around himself. There was more of the man underneath in that one smile.

I didn't want to ruin the moment or the rest of the night. There'd been too much distance between us lately.

I sauntered toward them as I gave Luke my best *you're totally fucked* look.

Matthew laughed, that uncontrollable giggle I'd grown addicted to.

I kept my movements slow and measured and stopped at the edge of the bed. With that confident expression plastered on Luke's face, I knew he thought he had me all figured out. So I waited, let my gaze wander to Matthew, and then I pounced. I had Luke pinned to the mattress in an instant. He squirmed and kicked, struggling to flip us, to get the upper hand. No matter how fit and toned he was, he was no match for me.

Matthew got in on the act, laughing as he yanked on my arm. Then he flung his weight at me, trying to roll me the other way.

I gave in, slackened my body, and let them have their victory.

"You know it!" Luke straddled my hips and braced himself with his hands on either side of my head. "We got you, old man."

I was about to remind him I was only five years older than him when Matthew got off the bed and tugged on Luke's arm. "Come on. Let's go."

Luke groaned again, but he rolled off me and got up. He never could resist giving Matthew what he wanted. Just like I couldn't.

Which I knew meant, in the end, we'd be keeping one of those pups.

I wanted to ask Matthew about it right then, but a part of me also understood it was time for me to let him share his wants and needs on his own when he was ready. He knew he could talk to us about anything.

Or did he? It wasn't like I'd been looking for the signs that he'd been holding back lately. Not with how little I'd been home.

"And when we get back," Matthew whispered as he encouraged me off the bed, "Luke's learned a new trick with his mouth. You gotta feel it."

Luke scoffed as he headed into the other room. "It was your idea."

"Yeah, but you were the one who perfected it."

At their words, my chest went tight. I really had missed a lot.

What else had I missed that had nothing to do with sex? Had they needed me, and I hadn't even noticed while I was busy working? It killed me to think I might've let them down in some way.

Chapter Two

"Damn, this place is something else." Luke stopped at the base of the grand wooden staircase that dominated the Harrison Estate's massive foyer. "I didn't realize it was so huge."

He started up the stairs, dust floating in the air behind him as his feet disturbed the thin layer that covered everything. He paused at the fifth step, aiming the beam of his flashlight toward the second-floor landing. Then he swung it across the ceiling, briefly lighting up the iron-and-crystal chandelier that hung above the open foyer where Matthew and I stood.

The chandelier sparkled, momentarily casting shivering slivers of light on the walls all around us, an odd contrast to the dark, abandoned state of the house. The power and heat were still off, and I was glad I'd thought to bring the flashlights. The heavy coats we wore didn't hurt either.

When we'd arrived there earlier, the two uniformed guards informed me they had chased off three teenagers who'd been trying to break into a back window where the locking mechanism was loose. After the guards offered their report, they left, and I gave Matthew and Luke a tour of the majority of the first floor, including the library with its floor-to-ceiling bookcases and the veranda that ran the width of the house along the east side.

We'd ended our survey of the first floor in the grand foyer. The main staircase was flanked by two doorways. One was an elegant archway that opened to the formal dining room, and the other was a set of double doors that led to the library.

Luke spoke again from the stairs. "I knew this place was big from the pictures, but I had no idea."

I gave a nod. "It's impressive." And it wasn't just the size of it, the number of rooms, the original woodwork, or the classical symmetrical style with elements of Chateauesque architecture. The three-story hand-cut stone mansion was located on the most beautiful stretch of land.

I started for the staircase, and Matthew moved with me, our wet snow-covered shoes squeaking on the marble floor. "Joe says I should turn around and sell it. I've had an offer already that would give me a sizeable profit."

"Sell?" Luke turned toward us. "You just got it."

"Apparently Joe thinks I'd be a fool to pass up this offer."

Luke almost seemed disappointed by my response. Then he flashed a smile. "Can we check out upstairs?"

"Sure. The place is in need of serious work, but the contractor I had take a look said it's structurally sound. The stairs and floors are in good shape."

Actually the entire house was in fantastic condition considering it had sat empty for fifteen years. None of the windows were broken. There were no signs of vermin. There was also no smell of mold or other foul odors. There were cobwebs and dust, but even those I had expected to be in greater supply.

Luke darted up the staircase again, and I followed, with Matthew continuing to keep close to me. He hadn't said a word since we'd pulled up outside. Maybe the rumors that the estate was haunted were getting to him now that we were inside the place.

For years people had spotted flickering lights through the windows of the house, the drapes would go from closed to open, then closed again, and there had been reports of occasional plumes of smoke pouring out the various chimneys. A handful of people had even mentioned the shrill screams of a man in the middle of the night.

I'd had no idea that kind of thing would freak Matthew out. Which bothered the hell out of me. I thought I knew everything about him.

I had also spent a fortune on the estate, and I hated that he no longer seemed happy with the purchase.

Maybe the ambience had him feeling uneasy. Every single room was still furnished. There were drapes on the windows, knickknacks on the end tables and mantels, tapestries on the walls, and ornate area rugs on the floors. There were even books still perched on the shelves in the library and a silver tea service sitting on the counter in the kitchen. It was like everyone had gotten up and walked out without packing a thing.

I was curious to see what Luke and Matthew would think of the main room on the second floor. It had been a shock, to say the least, when I'd toured the house weeks earlier after Edward Harrison finally put it on the market.

I continued following Luke up the stairs, using my flashlight to guide the way.

"Richard?" Matthew's voice was soft from where he trailed behind me.

I stopped and shone the light back at him. "Yeah?"

"Are you really thinking about selling this place?"

"No. I'd actually like to hold on to it."

"What will you do with it?"

Luke had paused a few steps above me. I moved to lean with the banister at my back so I could talk to both of them. "I'm going to restore it to what it was fifty years ago. Turn it into a resort, with a restaurant on the first floor. Rent out rooms for weddings, parties, fundraisers, corporate retreats, that kind of thing. It should be a great draw once the restorations are done."

"You're kidding?" Matthew stood there with his mouth gaping for a moment, and then he sprinted up the steps separating us. "You're kidding?" he repeated with an unmistakable squeal of excitement.

"No. I'm definitely not."

He lunged for me, wrapping his arms around my neck. "I was so scared you were going to tear it down or gut the place and make it all modern or something."

I held him in return, savoring how he clung to me and the excitement radiating off him. That open genuineness of his was what I'd missed most about being away from him lately. I said, "I didn't know that would matter to you."

He let go of me. "When I was in high school I wrote a paper about the Harrison family. I said someone should buy this house and turn it into a hotel."

"Seriously?"

"I did." He glanced at what we could see of the first floor in the darkness below, his expression more animated than when we'd toured the rooms. "Did you know it was designed by Clyde Urbanski?"

"Yeah." That was part of the draw for me. It was the only building left standing in the city—and one of the few in the country—that the famous architect had designed.

Luke descended and stood on the step above us. "That one movie star from the sixties used to live here, right? Griff Harrison. He won the Oscar for playing that World War II prisoner of war."

"That's right," I said. "Urbanski built this house for the Harrisons several generations ago, and they've owned it since." I grinned. "Until now."

"I can't believe you're gonna restore it." Matthew practically vibrated at my side. He looked to Luke. "Did you ever see any pictures from when Griff lived here?"

"I don't think so."

"Oh man. He had this really cool huge mural painted on the ceiling in the ballroom. And there's one that covers the entire wall behind the tub in the master bathroom. I've only seen pictures, but now we get to see the real thing." He grabbed Luke's hand and tugged him up the flight of stairs.

I hesitated for a moment, relieved they were on board with my plans for the place. Then I trailed up after them and into the second-floor ballroom.

Matthew and Luke had stopped just inside the doorway.

Luke shook his head. "Wow."

Matthew nodded. "This is freaky."

It was, and I'd already seen it once before during my tour with the real estate agent.

The room hadn't changed since that night I'd been there fifteen years earlier, except it was presently devoid of people and was dark and dust-covered, moonlight streaming in through the wall of windows opposite us. A sea of tables and chairs still filled the space, the tables covered in gold linens and the chairs draped in matching slipcovers. Long-stem candleholders served as centerpieces, the glass sparkling in the moonlight. The other end of the ballroom was set up with chairs where the orchestra had been situated during the party, and there was an empty space beside that for the dance floor. This room, even more than the others, looked like it had been frozen in time right after I walked out that night.

Except... It hadn't occurred to me before, but all the glasses and plates and silverware had been removed. The way I'd heard the story, Edward Harrison had fired his entire staff immediately after the party, before they managed to start any sort of cleanup. He'd sent those who were living at the estate to their rooms to pack their personal items, and then everyone was gone, Edward included.

So who had cleared the tables? Maybe the real estate agent had arranged it when she'd taken the job weeks ago to sell the house.

Although the amount of dust covering every surface told me that wasn't the likely story.

Luke meandered through the maze of tables and chairs, and Matthew followed. They stopped before the wall of floor-to-ceiling windows that overlooked the grounds. I crossed the room to them. The moon was bright, offering enough light to see the expanse of land surrounding the home. With the dense grove of maple trees that formed the perimeter of the property, the city beyond was barely visible, even with the trees missing their leaves in the dead of winter. A polished, glinting stone statue—an eagle with its wings spread wide as if in flight—served as the focal point of the courtyard. The frozen pond and the snow-covered walkways made the entire yard appear untouched by the world. Like a sparkling white veil of innocence had been draped over everything.

Luke whistled. "What a view."

"You should see it in the fall when the leaves turn colors." I stepped up behind him and wound my arms around his waist, resting my hands over his stomach. He leaned back against my chest, and I let my eyes fall shut, relishing the touch. I'd never tire of him giving in to a moment of intimacy that had nothing to do with sex.

I settled my lips over his ear. "What do you think?"

He had grown up in a large impersonal house with a live-in staff, and I'd been more than a little worried what he'd think of me owning a place that had once been quite similar to the life he'd run away from.

I added, "You think this is a good investment?"

He dislodged himself from my arms and turned to examine me. "What's up with you? You've never asked me for input with your business before."

I shook my head, surprised by his reaction. "Nothing's up. I just wondered what you thought."

Before I could read the look in his eyes, he faced the windows again. "It's a smart move. People have romanticized this estate since Griff's death. They'll be lining up to have their weddings and balls and boring parties here. And to catch a glimpse of the man's ghost if they believe all those rumors." He laughed at that. "You'll make a ton of money. Then if you ever do sell, you'll make even more."

Matthew nodded his agreement. "Renting out this room alone will bring in a small fortune."

I was betting everything on that exact idea.

Luke moved closer to the window. "Are those footprints?" He indicated a path leading away from the back of the house. It stretched beyond the pond to the private fenced-in cemetery at the rear corner of the property.

With the moon's brilliance, I could make out the snowcapped headstones peeking through the drifts. "Probably those kids who tried to break in. Or maybe some tourists wanted a look at Griff's grave." I really needed to get moving on better security. For the past fifteen years, Edward Harrison had kept an alarm system in place and hired a private security company to monitor the estate—which explained how the house hadn't been looted long ago, especially with all the interest the ghost rumor had generated. But his grandson had shut off the power and canceled the security the minute Edward had passed away. Since then, the house had sat dark and vulnerable.

"Look." Matthew pointed toward the graves. "One of the headstones is cleared off."

From this distance, it was hard to tell if that had been the result of the wind or if someone had deliberately cleaned the gravestone. But since it was the only one, that probably meant it had been intentional.

"That's Griff's grave," Matthew added.

I looked his way. "You sure?"

"Yeah. I saw pictures of the family cemetery when I did my report in school. His headstone was the largest and sat off away from the rest."

So probably not some young kids. Maybe it had been nosy tourists interested in the famous actor's old home.

Matthew seemed sad for a moment, and then he spun around and took in the full view of the ballroom. "It's so spooky how it's all still set up like this."

"I was at this party." I indicated a nearby table with a lift of my chin. "Joe and I sat there. In fact I talked to Edward Harrison that night about buying this place, but he had no interest in doing business with me and was quite an asshole about it."

"Then why did he end up changing his mind?" Luke asked.

"I honestly don't know. Maybe he knew he was dying and just wanted to be rid of it. See over there?" I pointed to the portable bar on the opposite wall near the doorway. There was no sign of the booze or glassware that had covered it during the party. "That was the bar. The last thing I did before I left was grab a bottle of champagne and take a swig just to irritate him. That was right after I told him I would definitely own this place someday."

Luke spread his arms out wide. "And here you are."

Matthew smiled at me. Then he grew serious again. "He should've sold to you back then. I mean, why did he leave it empty for so many years?"

"I have no idea. I don't think anyone does. Not even his only grandchild." The lone heir to Edward's fortune had moved away years ago and wanted nothing to do with his grandfather or his family's estate.

Matthew wandered the length of the room, checking out the cathedral ceiling above. The mural covered the entire expanse of the room's ceiling. It was one large ocean scene, painted to appear as if we gazed up through the water to the surface above. The sea life— orcas and dolphins and various tropical fish—were so realistic, it felt like we were actually standing on the ocean floor. The brilliant colors were a sharp contrast to the rest of the house's dark traditional decor.

With the moonlight streaming in through the wall of windows, we didn't need the flashlights to see the mural, or for Luke and me to follow Matthew's movements across the vast room. He paused at one corner to examine a portion of the mural above him in more detail. His obvious wonder at being inside the famous mansion had him looking even younger than his twenty-four years.

I lowered my voice so only Luke would hear. "He seems happy."

"Yeah. He found out he's on track for a 4.0 this semester."

It stung that I hadn't heard that yet.

Luke kept his gaze on Matthew, and his expression transformed, became uneasy, agitated. I opened my mouth to ask what was up but stopped short when Luke flicked on his flashlight and shone it in my face.

"He *is* happy. So don't go fucking that up."

Chapter Three

"What the hell?" I recoiled a step. "You know I'd never do that."

Luke shook his head as if he regretted his words, or maybe how he'd spat them at me. "I know that, but…" He ran his thumb over the switch on the side of the flashlight without turning it off.

My phone rang in my pocket. I ignored it and kept my focus locked on Luke, waiting for him to say more.

The ringing stopped, then started again. I pulled out the phone and checked the display. It was Joe. He'd promised he'd call when he had news about the potential investors.

"Just take the call." Luke turned away and stared out the window.

"No." I punched the phone off and moved to stand beside him. "Why would you think I'd fuck up Matthew's happiness?"

Luke wouldn't make eye contact.

"Hey."

He finally faced me. "It's just not like you."

"What?"

He gave me a pointed look. "Secrets."

"*Secrets?*"

He watched me for a moment, then gave a nod, but he held my gaze as if he wanted me to get his real meaning without having to offer more. He'd gotten used to me doing that, which meant I'd really been taking shortcuts for the past few weeks. Luke would probably always prefer me interpreting his nonverbal communication unless I pushed him for more.

I was about to press when he asked, "What haven't you told us yet?"

So maybe it wasn't just me who could read him.

Still holding the flashlight, he crossed his arms over his chest. "Just fucking say it, Richard."

Even with most of the light from the flashlight now pointed at the floor, it wasn't hard to miss that *I don't trust anyone* look he'd sported for such a long time when I first met him.

Matthew approached, his steps quiet as if he was afraid he was interrupting something he shouldn't. "What's wrong?"

"Richard has something to tell us. I'm guessing we're not going to like it."

I raised my hands in a defensive pose. "Hold on here. I'm not revealing some big secret. I'm excited about this. And one of the main reasons I asked you here tonight was because I wanted you to see this place. I wanted your input on what I'm thinking of doing with it. It matters that I have your support on this."

Luke's mistrusting gaze didn't falter.

I'd do just about anything not to have that look directed at me. I thought we'd long ago gotten past his trust issues.

And my own.

"Why now?" he said. "Why ask us about this project?"

"This one's different. I didn't take on any investors to make the purchase."

Matthew's jaw dropped. "You bought it yourself?" There was no missing the surprise in his voice. "With all your own money?"

"Yeah. That's why I took that trip. I was selling off my other assets to put together the financing for this place."

Their matching furrowed brows demonstrated their confusion. Which I understood. The house alone was worth more money than my accountant had expected I could afford. Add in the vast grounds within the city limits, along with the famous history and the architect behind the house, and even I'd been surprised I was able to swing it.

Luke turned to Matthew. "Did you know he had that kind of money?"

"No." Matthew looked about to panic, like he feared Luke would be pissed at him. Or that the three of us were about to have an argument that would forever change things. "I mean, he manages a lot of big investments, and I know he's put his own money into a few properties, but…" He shook his head. "I had no idea."

I hated how they were talking to each other as if I'd left the room. Had all that time they'd been spending together without me brought them even closer?

I didn't want to follow that train of thought, or the insecurity it had me slipping toward.

"It's not like I had the cash lying around. I had to liquidate all my personal assets, except the town house. I took a loss on several things so I could access enough money to put down for this place, but I was able to make it work."

Again, neither said a word. Then Luke's expression finally softened as if what I'd revealed had been nothing compared to what he'd assumed. "Is that a good idea? Financially, I mean."

"Probably not right away. Without my personal investments, I'll be losing money in the short term, but in the long run, this place is going to be worth it." I glanced around the ballroom again, and for the first time it felt real. The Harrison Estate was mine. Fifteen years I'd waited for this moment.

Maybe nothing would ever seem real again until I brought Matthew and Luke into it.

"I need to take on a few investors to afford the restorations, or else this house is just going to sit here losing money, but I'm hoping to buy them out as soon as I can get the estate turning a profit."

"Why?" Matthew asked.

"Why did I buy it?"

"Yeah."

"I've loved this place since I first saw it, and lately I felt like I needed..." I paused to find the right words for how I'd been feeling since Luke's dad fucked with my business.

Matthew studied me. "You're not happy?"

"That's not it. I just want to do something... I don't know. Something different. You think it was a bad call?"

Luke had been moving the beam of flashlight back and forth between Matthew and me. Now he stopped it on Matthew, who still sported the alarmed, almost confused expression. When he didn't say anything, Luke spoke.

"It's..." He trailed off. Despite those rare emotional outbursts of his, he still had a hard time sharing what he felt.

"Are you angry with me?" I asked. I would understand if they were. After all, I'd spent a sizeable amount of money without talking to them first. "I can turn around and sell this place." It would about kill me to do it, but I would. For them.

"No," Luke said. "I'm not mad. I'm surprised you didn't mention what was going on, but it's your money. You can do whatever you want with it." He looked to Matthew again as if wanting help to say more, or maybe he was trying to figure out what Matthew was thinking so he could verbalize it for him.

That unnerved me. Not exactly in a jealous way, but I felt like I wasn't doing my part in the relationship. I was the one who usually interpreted what they were thinking, and when I couldn't, I got them talking.

Matthew looked away toward a series of wrought-iron chandeliers that hung in a line down the center of the ballroom ceiling. Without the lights on, the iron chandeliers looked like a swarm of giant spiders about to attack the room. Or us. The disparity between the bright, lively mural above and the dark, daunting chandeliers unnerved me.

Or maybe what really bothered me was the lingering silence between us.

I waited for either of them to say something, but they didn't offer anything more.

"Matthew?"

He shrugged. "Luke's right. It's your decision. This isn't about us."

"My money's your money. We're family, remember?"

Then why hadn't I told them earlier? I'd made a huge purchase that had nothing to do with the real estate portfolios I managed for others without telling my partners. Why? Because there had been a good chance I wasn't going to be able to get enough cash together, and I would've had to take on other investors just to buy the estate. Or I would've lost it. I didn't want Luke and Matthew to see me fail. Not like that.

As if he could read my mind, the tension in Luke's body seemed to ease. "I think you buying this house was a great idea."

"He's right," Matthew said, a little too nonchalantly for my taste. He turned away and started across the room. When he spoke again, the nonchalance was gone. "I absolutely love that you're gonna restore it. And you're right about this place being a big draw. Just the fact that Griff Harrison lived here will bring in the tourists." He glanced around the empty ballroom. "Do you know what room it happened in?"

"Where Griff killed himself?"

"Yeah." Matthew's voice was soft, and with a sadness to it that I didn't like hearing from him.

I nodded toward the ballroom's doorway. "In the master suite on the top floor. They say no one's slept in that room since that night. Not even Edward Harrison." When that gem was revealed in the press, it had fed into the haunting rumors, most speculating that Edward had left the room untouched so as not to piss off his cousin's ghost.

"Can we see it?" Matthew asked.

"Sure." I gestured toward the hall again, and Luke led the way up the flight of stairs once more.

Despite that I'd toured the house weeks before, even I had to admit that traversing the dark staircase to the third floor of the abandoned mansion, with the wood steps creaking under our feet, was a little unnerving. I had never believed the ghost stories, but it would've been nice to have the lights on.

Halfway up the stairs, Matthew said from behind me, "He didn't kill himself."

I stopped and turned to him. "What?"

"Griff Harrison. He was murdered."

"You really think so?" Luke asked.

"Yeah." Matthew sprinted up past me until he was beside Luke. "The police didn't try too hard to find out the truth. They just ruled it a suicide and closed the case."

"So what do you think happened?"

"I don't know. But from what I read about him, Griff seemed too happy to have taken his own life."

"Yeah," Luke agreed. "He even had that gorgeous fiancée, the princess from Greece."

Matthew frowned at that. "But he didn't love her."

"No?"

"I don't think so."

We started climbing again and Matthew added, "I think all those rumors about him being gay were true. I think she was his beard, and he was in love with someone else. He just couldn't let people know about them. Not in Hollywood in the fifties and sixties. It would've ruined his career."

The certainty of Matthew's words had me smiling at his back.

Luke paused at the top landing, shaking his head. "Anyone ever tell you you're a sap?"

Matthew wrinkled his nose in response.

"Yeah." I patted Matthew's ass as I went by him, remembering how we'd often described him. "Sweet and addictive and a sap."

That had Matthew rolling his eyes. "Whatever."

Chuckling at his reaction, I got moving down the long hall of the third floor. All the doors to the guest rooms we passed were closed, and the hall seemed to narrow the farther we went. When we reached the end, I opened the door to the master suite but stopped short of going in. Matthew had halted a few feet away and was peeking into one of the other rooms where the door stood open a crack.

I seized Luke by the hips and brought him to me in the doorway. "Are we okay? What you said about me and him—"

He shook his head. "Forget I said that. I didn't mean it. You just haven't been home much and…"

"What?"

He drew in a deep breath like he didn't want to admit the next part. "It might be getting to me."

"Might be?" I teased, but there was something he wasn't saying.

With another shake of his head, Luke added, "You worry too much. You're gonna get an ulcer."

"What's your prescription, Doc?"

Matthew laughed as he approached. He slid in behind Luke and headed into the bedroom. "Uh, stupid question, Richard." His voice lowered a touch as he mimicked Luke. "Less talking, more fucking."

"Hey!" Luke made like he was going to chase Matthew down, but I held on to him, and Matthew laughed again as he checked out the room.

Luke gave up and leaned back against the doorjamb. The jeans he wore rode low on his hips, and the black flight jacket gave him a bad-boy look I was completely digging. He threw me the same expression he used whenever he wanted exactly what Matthew had said. "I'd resent that if…" In an oddly insecure move, he dropped his gaze and stared at the floor between us. The playful demeanor was gone, and something much more vulnerable had replaced it.

"If what?"

He glanced up at me. "If it hadn't been weeks since you've fucked me." He licked his lips, and I couldn't look away from his mouth.

The words Edward Harrison had said to me in the ballroom fifteen years earlier rolled through my mind.

"The disgusting things a faggot like you could do in my family's home."

I reached for Luke again and drew him to me. "Matthew, come here."

He didn't.

He stood by the fireplace across the room, his flashlight pointed at a pile of blankets. "What's all this?"

The master suite was the one room in the estate with barely any furniture. Just a lone red love seat positioned in front of a picture window. The hardwood floor, cathedral ceiling, and lack of any other furniture had our voices bouncing off the bare walls, creating an eerie echo.

Reluctantly I let go of Luke, and we joined Matthew at the fireplace.

I gestured to the blankets. "They're probably from a homeless person who crashed here at one time or another."

Matthew used the tip of his shoe to lift an edge of a blanket, and he flipped it back. Underneath was an oil-powered lantern, cans of oil, a backpack, a hardcover copy of *The Murder of Roger Ackroyd* by Agatha Christie, two cardigan sweaters, a framed picture, a box of saltine crackers, and six cans of vegetable soup. The photo in the silver frame was several decades old by the looks of the hairstyles and clothing. It was of a young couple with a daughter, maybe three years old.

I bent for the frame.

"Don't touch that," came a low voice from across the room.

The three of us spun around.

In the doorway stood a dark figure, his face hidden in the shadows. He spoke again in the same hoarse whisper. "I want you out of my house. Now."

Chapter Four

I raised my flashlight, but I was too late to catch a good look at the man. He'd turned and was taking off down the hall.

I went for the door, calling back to Matthew and Luke. "You two wait here."

"Fuck that," Luke said from behind me as I exited into the hall.

The man was nowhere in sight. If he'd been going for the staircase at the other end, there was no way he'd have made it that far already. I ran for the stairs anyway and shone the light over the railing. No one was there.

"Where'd he go?" Luke asked as he and Matthew caught up to me.

"He's still gotta be on this floor," I said. "In one of the other rooms." I pulled out my phone. "I'm calling the cops."

A door slammed shut down the hall near the master suite. Then another door. And another.

"Shit," Luke said under his breath. "How many people are in here?"

Matthew stepped closer to me. "This is creepy."

I started to dial the police but quit when I heard a scraping sound like metal on wood. Whatever it was, it was coming right for us. I tugged Matthew closer to me. "Luke, get back." I shone the light down the hall, but there was nothing. Another door banged shut.

The scraping continued, though it sounded much softer. It was definitely coming from near the master bedroom. The door to the room was now closed. I strode for it.

"Richard." Matthew sounded about to panic.

I could hear his and Luke's footfalls behind me as I kept moving toward the bedroom. "This guy is just fucking with us, trying to scare us off."

"Richard," Luke pleaded in a more forceful tone than Matthew's.

I gave in and froze ten feet from the door. I dialed 911 and immediately got a voice recording directing me to hold on the line. I handed the phone to Matthew. "You two go outside and wait in the car. When someone comes on the line, tell them we have a prowler."

Luke glared at me. "Stop telling us what to do."

"We should all get out of here," Matthew said in a hushed whisper.

A low creaking came from the master suite. All three of us shone our flashlights on the wood door, which was slowly opening. A bright flickering light was now on inside the room, casting the man standing in the doorway once again as a dark figure with no face, despite the light from our flashlights.

"Get out of my house." He raised an arm to shut the door.

I'd had enough.

I charged forward and rammed my foot between the doorjamb and the closing door, then shoved the door open. I could see him more clearly now. He had tousled gray hair and a wild look in his eyes. He stood with a slight hunch and had to be sixty-five years old, or older. Before my eyes could fully adjust to the new brightness, he lifted his arm again and something like a metal pipe or a fireplace poker slammed down on my shoulder. The force of the blow wasn't horribly strong, but it still stung and had me staggering backward.

That was it. I'd *really* had enough.

I went after the man as he scrambled into the corner of the bedroom.

Another fireplace poker sailed across the floor toward my feet. I jumped out of the way.

A third one came barreling at me. It hadn't come sliding along the floor. The old man had thrown it at my lower legs like a Frisbee, and right as I landed from the jump, it smacked into my shin. The pain wasn't too bad, but the blow knocked me off balance, and I went flinging sideways, landing on my right hip with a thud.

"Richard." Matthew was kneeling beside me in an instant.

"I'm okay."

He helped me up, trying to support my weight.

Luke advanced and had the stranger by the neck and against the wall by the time I stood on solid feet again. My ankle throbbed from where I'd twisted it, but I could put weight on it. My hip was going to have one hell of a bruise.

The old guy squirmed in Luke's grip. "Let go of me!"

I moved toward them. Matthew slid his arm around my waist once he spotted my slight limp. I shone the flashlight on the intruder. He'd lost some of his fight in Luke's clenches.

My estimate had been off. He couldn't have been less than eighty-five. He wore a checkered polo shirt buttoned to the top and a red wool cardigan sweater that featured tiny white reindeer running across the front in single-file lines.

"Ease up," I told Luke.

He let go of the old man, who immediately lunged at Luke.

Luke had him flattened to the wall again with no trouble, this time more gentle about it but still keeping him firmly restrained by the shoulders.

"Matthew," I said, "are you still on hold?"

He checked the phone's display. "We were disconnected."

"Call back and tell them we've caught a prowler."

The old guy shook his head. "No. This is my home." He had a crazed look in his wide eyes, like he might come unhinged at any moment. Or maybe he already was.

I signaled Matthew to hang on. "Who are you?" I asked the man.

He pursed his lips and glared at me, his eyes squinting below the bushy white eyebrows forming a single line across his forehead. I pointed the flashlight directly in his face. He blinked and attempted to shield his eyes but was unable to do anything with Luke pinning him to the wall.

"Why are you here?" I asked.

Nothing.

I decided to offer a little information, hoping it would get the old man talking. "My name's Richard Marshall. And this is Matthew Stewart and Luke Moore."

Finally he spoke. "I don't care who you are. You're trespassing. This is *my* house."

"Your house, huh? What's your name?"

"Dominic."

"Dominic what?"

He hesitated, then said, "Pesaro."

"And just why do you think this house is yours?"

"Because I'm the one who's taken care of it for sixty-five years. Even when no one lived here anymore."

I lowered the light so it no longer blinded him. I nodded at Luke. "Let him go."

As Luke released him, the man grabbed his right shoulder like he was in pain. Luke helped him stagger to the love seat by the window.

When he was settled, Luke asked him, "You okay?"

"Yeah. You're not that strong."

Luke scoffed at that. "How about you?" he asked me with more concern than he'd used with the old man.

"I'm fine."

Despite that, Matthew held on to me as we made our way to the love seat. The three of us stared down at Dominic Pesaro.

"Talk," I said. "I own this estate now. Explain to me why you're here."

"*You* bought it?" Those bushy white eyebrows now crawled up his forehead in surprise.

"I did. What do you mean you've taken care of this place? Did you work here?"

"I've lived here all my life. I took over caring for this house and the Harrisons after my father passed away."

Caring for the Harrisons? I could only imagine the kinds of things this guy had seen from the eccentric family.

"How did you take care of them?"

"I was the butler."

Luke snorted out a laugh. When I looked his way, he added, "The butler did it." He laughed again, then shrugged. "I'm guessing he's the one who's been *haunting* the place."

The old man shifted like he wanted to jump off the love seat and take Luke on again. But he stopped, perhaps realizing he was resigned to the limits of his body. He spoke with more vigor, though. "I wasn't just going to abandon my home because the Harrisons decided they didn't want to live here anymore. Someone had to keep people from breaking in all the time, keep the tourists from invading the place."

I opted not to tell him that making it appear as if the estate was haunted had probably done the exact opposite. Teens and college kids from all over the city dared each other to step foot onto the property, and the tourists came out in droves to see the home where the famous actor Griff Harrison had died—and where he was possibly still hanging around if they believed the rumors.

The old man pointed at me, a scowl on his thin lips. "And just because someone new owns it doesn't mean I will stop doing what I have to. This is my home, and I won't let anything happen to it."

Great. I'd purchased my own one-man security force along with the estate. "Listen, Mr. Pesaro—"

"Dominic." The minute he said that, he seemed like he regretted getting so informal with me.

"All right, Dominic, do you think you could answer a few more questions?"

He studied the three of us for a moment. I wasn't sure if he was trying to decide if he could trust us or was analyzing us in some way.

He gave a nod toward Matthew, then Luke. "I saw you touching them. Are you... intimate with both of them?"

"That's none of your business."

"Having sex with two people? Back in my day, we had a name for guys like you."

"Watch it," I warned. I never liked to hide that we were in a threesome—not anymore—but I didn't want this guy knowing too many personal details. "Will you answer some questions or not?"

His gaze darted to me briefly. Then he quickly glanced away. "Depends on the questions."

"If you don't, I'm calling the cops right now. They will remove you from this house, and you will have to answer their questions."

He crossed his arms over his chest in a move that had him looking like a kid who'd rather be outside playing soccer—or in his case, throwing fireplace pokers at people. "Fine. Ask."

I pointed at the blankets and supplies. "You've been staying here?"

"When I can get away."

"Away from where? Where do you live?"

He snapped his mouth shut and stared at the ceiling behind me. Finally he offered one word. "Around."

"Around where?"

He gestured toward the window over his shoulder like the answer should've been obvious. "Around out there."

"Are you homeless?" Although he didn't look or smell like he'd been living on the streets. His clothes were tidy, and he was well groomed.

"No!" That question irritated him, going by the way those eyebrows grew together to form one long bushy brow again. Then he rolled his eyes, obviously thinking I was either completely stupid or annoying. "How can I be homeless when this is my house?"

I sighed. "Well, you can't stay here anymore."

Dominic was shaking his head before I'd even finished.

I added, "Very soon I'm going to have a construction crew in here. It'll be dangerous."

All of a sudden he was on his feet, a fist clenched before him with one shaking finger pointed at my face. "If you so much as tear down one wall, I will kill you in your sleep."

I raised both hands before me. "Whoa. Hold on. First off, it is none of your business what I do with this place, and second, you have to leave. Tonight. Now, are you living with any family?"

He took a step back and lowered himself to the love seat, his jaw set, chin lifted, arms folded across his chest again. "I've escaped, and I won't go back."

I exchanged a look with Luke, who said, "Maybe his family kicked him out. He's already getting on my nerves."

Dominic threw him a nasty look like he could end him with that expression alone. "Let me guess. You don't get along with your father?"

Luke glared at the old man in return.

I wanted to pummel Dominic for that remark. Only the fact that he was old enough to be my grandfather kept that instinct in check.

Leave it to Matthew to end the tension. He asked, "When did you start working here?"

Dominic turned to him. "I helped my dad from the time I could walk. I took over for him after his heart attack. That was when I was twenty years old. He was gone two months later."

Matthew moved to sit on the love seat beside him. "I'm sorry."

"Matthew," I said in warning, stepping forward.

Luke tapped my arm with the back of his hand and whispered, "Let him talk to him."

I gave in but kept close to Matthew. Luke eased into the narrow space between the window and the love seat so he was behind Dominic. He'd be able to grab him if he made a move for Matthew. Or me.

Matthew spoke again. "So you worked here when Griff Harrison lived here?"

Dominic sat taller, turning more toward Matthew. "I did. Griff was a wonderful boss. He wasn't like the rest of the Harrisons. He treated the employees like family. Even when he was in Hollywood or off on location for a picture, he would remember every staff member's birthday and send us all gifts for the holidays." Dominic shook his head. "Not many wealthy people those days were as thoughtful. His father certainly wasn't. Or his uncle and his cousin. They didn't even come to my dad's funeral."

"His cousin was Edward Harrison?" I knew the answer but was curious if Dominic would offer anything else.

"Yeah. When that branch of the family invaded the house, everything was different. Of course, after Griff died everything was different for a lot of reasons."

"What really happened to him?" Matthew asked.

Dominic went perfectly still, a stone-cold look on his face. He turned to face me. "You asked about my family before."

"Is there someone who can come pick you up?"

"No." He looked around as if he'd just thought of something. "My picture." He made like he was going to get up.

Luke put a hand on his shoulder, stopping him. He went for the pile of blankets and returned with the framed photo. He gave it to Dominic. "This one?"

"Yes. My family."

Luke walked behind me and said in a low voice, "Check it out." He handed over a thin blue blanket that was stamped in the corner with the words *Legacy Village Nursing and Rehabilitation.*

Dominic was focused on the framed photo in his hands.

"Where are they now?" Matthew asked him.

"Gone." Dominic kept staring at the smiling faces of the woman and child in the photo. "For many years."

"What happened?"

"She didn't want to live here anymore. She took our daughter to her parents' farm south of the city. My daughter was still young then. After that I saw her every other weekend, and she would stay here with me for three weeks in the summers."

"Do you still see her?"

"No. She and her mother were killed in a car accident when my daughter was in her thirties. They were here in the city shopping, and a cab ran a red light, smacked right into the side of their car."

Matthew placed a hand on Dominic's arm. "I'm so sorry."

Dominic's loss had me feeling like an ass, but there was no way I was getting around having to kick him out of the estate.

He said, "I have a granddaughter, though. Isabella. She's a woman now. In her twenties. She was just a baby when they got into the accident, but..." He trailed off and went silent again.

"But what?" Matthew asked.

"My son-in-law took her away. He hated me and didn't want me anywhere near her. I think he changed her last name. I couldn't find her." He looked up at me. "So you see. I have no one. I have nowhere to go. So if you don't mind, I'd like to die in peace. In the only home I've ever known."

Matthew returned his hand to Dominic's arm. "Are you sick?"

"He's not dying," I said. He'd been far too spry when he was running from room to room and throwing fireplace pokers at me. He was in better shape than a lot of men half his age who never left their couches.

"Fine," he said, his arms locked across his chest. "I might not be dying tonight, but I'm an old man who's all alone. This place is all I have."

"Oh, please." Luke pulled out his phone and with quick jabs of his thumbs sent a text message to someone. "What's with you dads and not knowing how to do the right thing? You got a grandkid out there, go find her."

"I tried."

"Obviously not long enough or hard enough." Luke's phone chimed with a return message. He read it. "My friend Walter's a retired cop. He owns a security company and works with a lot of PIs. He says he'll be happy to help you track her down."

"I..." Dominic looked from Luke to Matthew, then to me. "Who are you people?"

I took a step closer to him. "I told you. I'm the one who owns this place now, and..." I handed him the blanket and pointed to the words *Legacy Village Nursing and Rehabilitation.* "I'm driving you back to your home."

Dominic grimaced. He pointed to Matthew beside him. "He's a sweet kid. I like him." He indicated the other way to Luke. "He calls it like he sees it. I gotta respect that." He pointed straight ahead at me. "You... I don't think I like you very much."

"Well, my hip and shoulder ache and my ankle's throbbing like a bitch, so you're not my favorite person right now either." I pointed at him in return. "You have two choices. Either I can drive you to your nursing home or the cops will. I'd rather do it myself."

Apparently he agreed. He clutched the blanket and the photo to his chest as he stood. Then he headed toward the bedroom door. Halfway across the room he stopped and without looking at us said, "This house is in danger, and someone needs to protect it."

"I won't do anything to hurt the house."

"I'm not talking about what you might do. I'm talking about the others."

"Others?"

He faced us. There was a resolve to his expression that had him looking years younger. "They have waited a very long time to get what they want, and now that they know the truth, they are not going to wait any longer."

"What others? What do they want?"

"This house. So they can destroy it." He hugged the blanket and frame tighter to him. "They were here many, many years ago. When Griff died. And now they're coming back." He started moving again, faster than I could think about chasing after him with my throbbing ankle.

Luke turned my way. "What's he talking about?"

"I have no idea. But you can bet your ass I'm going to find out."

Chapter Five

Dominic Pesaro refused to say another word on our drive to drop him off at his nursing home, and by the time we got to our place later that night, I was frustrated and sore all over. While Matthew went to take care of the puppies, I headed upstairs. I had hoped a hot shower would go a long way to easing my aching muscles and sour mood.

No such luck.

I dried off and slipped on a pair of jeans and a snug white T-shirt that I was pretty sure was Luke's since it was two sizes smaller than what I normally wore, but before the shower I'd been too distracted to notice I'd grabbed one of his. I dropped onto the edge of our bed and dialed my phone.

Joe answered, saying, "I've been trying to get ahold of you."

"Did you hear back from anyone?"

"Yeah. They've decided to go another way."

"Which one?"

"All of them."

"What?" It wasn't possible. Not every single person Joe and I had approached over the past several weeks. They'd all been excited about the plans I had for the estate. "What reason did they give?"

"Just that they'd changed their minds. They don't think the resort's a good idea. Said the rumors about the place being haunted make it too big of a risk."

Risk? I was the one taking all those.

Joe cleared his throat as if he didn't want to say the next part. "Maybe you really need to consider selling to Kinkaid. I hate to say it, but from the responses I'm hearing, I'm beginning to think you aren't going to get anyone interested in investing, and if you can't restore that place..." He didn't finish that thought. "No one else seems to think it's a smart move."

Bullshit.

It was a great idea. The best I'd had. At least when it came to my business.

"Listen," I said. "I appreciate all that you're doing to help me out, but it's too early for me to throw in the towel."

"Richard, you're going to lose a shitload of money if that property just sits there."

"I know." If I couldn't find someone to back me on it, I was going to lose everything I'd worked for. But I couldn't sell. Not yet.

And not to Terence Kinkaid, my biggest rival. I would never hand over the estate to him, no matter how much he offered for it.

I thanked Joe again for his help, and we said our good-byes. Clicking off my phone, I fell back onto the bed and stared at the ceiling of our bedroom. I couldn't help but feel like that call was a little too reminiscent of what had happened with my business when Luke's dad decided to intervene months earlier. Despite the fact that all the money he'd stolen had been returned, I'd taken a big hit with some of my regular investors, and my business was just rebounding from that. Perfect timing for Luke's dad to fuck with me again.

Although it was probably too soon to be thinking that as well.

I got up and made my way downstairs where I found two quiet, somber men on the couch.

"What's wrong?"

"That place was awful." Matthew scrunched up his nose like he'd had another whiff of the hallway leading to Dominic's room at Legacy Village. A fancy name for a place that offered its residents such a bleak existence and cared nothing for their legacy.

"Yeah." Luke groaned with a similar expression. "I'm not even sure I'd put *my* dad in a place like that."

Both Matthew and I stared at him.

"Okay. Maybe my dad but nobody else's."

"I hear ya." I started for the couch, and a twinge of pain shot through my hip. I sighed in relief as I sat between them. "It *was* pretty depressing."

"What did that nurse tell you?" Luke asked.

"That dear old Dominic is quite the troublemaker. Apparently he's always complaining and is notorious for getting the residents riled up about stuff."

"Like what?" Matthew asked.

"The staff ignoring their duties in favor of playing around on their phones, what the kitchen serves for dinner, how little time the residents get to spend out of their rooms." I paused and considered that. "He's probably just bored. He hasn't had a visitor in two years.

Not even the cousin—a young guy in his twenties—who put him in there."

Luke scoffed. "No wonder he didn't mention him as family."

I nodded and rubbed the tense muscles at the back of my neck. "She also said a few times a month Dominic walks out without telling anyone. The police usually find him wandering the streets with shopping bags full of canned food and cleaning supplies, probably headed to the estate. His disappearances have escalated in the past several weeks, most likely since Edward passed away and the security was turned off at the estate. She's not sure how much longer he'll be allowed to stay at the nursing home unless he stops taking off."

"Where was he before?" Luke asked.

"An assisted-living complex. He had his own apartment. When he started complaining about the staff and leaving in the middle of the night, his cousin had him moved to the full-time-care facility. Which is too bad. He's too healthy and mobile for a nursing home."

Matthew shifted around with one leg on the couch so he was facing us. He reached out and caressed the back of my neck, his fingers cleverly working away the tension. "You really think he's been the ghost of the Harrison Estate all this time?"

"After what he did tonight? Yeah. I think he's also been taking care of the place like he said. It's in too good of shape."

Luke chuckled at that. "He seems crazy enough to do the upkeep—and haunt the place—without a paycheck for fifteen years."

I laughed with him. "Maybe after I open the resort, I'll hire him to live there and continue with the ghost routine, keep the mystique going, drive up curiosity with the tourists."

"It'd be better than where he's at now." Luke threw me a pointed look. The condition of the nursing home really bothered him. Hell, it did me too. No one should spend the end of his life in a place that reeked of piss and mold.

Well, maybe Luke's dad. There were a lot worse things I could imagine doing to that man, things I *wanted* to do to him.

Matthew encouraged me to turn so he could reach both my shoulders. I leaned back into him and whispered over my left shoulder, "Thank you."

He kissed the back of my neck and started the massage again.

"In any case," I said. "I'm going to have another talk with Dominic, find out if his obsession with protecting the estate and everything he said about the house being in danger is just a lonely old man keeping himself occupied or if it's something more."

We were quiet for a while, Matthew continuing with the soothing strokes along my neck and shoulders.

"Well," Luke said, finally breaking the depressing silence. "That's one good thing about Matthew barely being old enough to shave. He can take care of us when we're old."

It was a rare occasion when Luke talked about our relationship as if it had no end. His words brought a smile to my lips. I turned to look at Matthew.

He wasn't smiling. He had stopped the massage, and his mouth was hanging open. He folded his arms across his chest. "I've been shaving for almost ten years."

Luke raised his hands, palms out. "Whoa. Ten years? You're gonna need a cane and dentures soon."

That did it. Matthew lunged over me to get to Luke. He straddled Luke's lap and tickled his sides. "Just for that, I'm gonna put you in a run-down, stinky home when you're old."

"Yeah?" Luke squirmed, bucking up, trying to dodge the playful touches. "Richard too?"

"Yes, both of you." All at once Matthew halted the tickling. He shook his head. "No. No one." He held Luke's face in his hands. "I'd never do that. To either of you."

Luke cupped the back of Matthew's head, and their lips met. A chaste kiss that lingered for a moment.

Then Luke gestured to me with a tilt of his head. "Why don't we go upstairs and see the damage on our old man's body?"

"Yeah." Matthew nodded. "We'll take real good care of him."

Luke planted another kiss on Matthew's lips, this one longer, deeper. "I'm thinking a full-body massage, and then…" He whispered in Matthew's ear, and Matthew nodded again.

Despite how old they'd made me sound, I wanted exactly what Luke had described—and I'm sure whatever he'd said to Matthew—but I also had something to take care of first. I breathed deep and stood. "You two go on up, and I'll be there in a few minutes. I've gotta check on something."

Luke dropped his head to the back of the couch and groaned, his tone even more irritated than he'd sounded in the basement earlier when I'd gotten the phone call about the break-in.

"I promise. I'll be right up."

Thank God for Matthew. He diverted Luke's attention with a kiss, and I slipped into my office. I knew I'd be distracted for the rest of the night if I didn't curb my curiosity on this one thing before heading upstairs. And once the three of us hit the sheets, I had no intention of focusing on anything else.

The online searches didn't take long, and the first few that came up were definitely about the right Dominic. Most of the articles were about the Harrison family and their famous estate, as well as Griff's death. Almost all of the latter indicated that Dominic had said only one thing after his boss had passed away.

That Griff had definitely not killed himself.

I then searched for two names together: Dominic Pesaro and Edward Harrison.

Several news stories about Edward's death displayed on the screen, all stating the same thing. The last person Edward asked to see on his deathbed was Dominic. The two talked alone for an hour. Then, less than half a day later, Edward was gone.

Was Dominic still working for the Harrison family, working for Edward Harrison?

Had Edward sent him to the estate to mess with me on purpose? Was that bit about the house being in danger even true? And what about Dominic's family? Was his granddaughter really missing? Or was that all a line of bullshit to play on my sympathies?

It would be just like the old homophobic Edward Harrison to know everything about my past, to utilize that against me.

Guilt hit me hard whenever that part of my life crawled into my thoughts.

Which meant there was one more thing I had to take care of. I got out my cell phone. The call wouldn't take long. It never did. I wouldn't let it. She didn't need me bringing this up in the first place, let alone dragging it out.

I selected her name on my speed dial. Phone in hand, I stood and faced the picture window that dominated one wall of my office. The usually impressive view of the city did nothing for me. Behind the high-rise buildings and the sparkling lights of downtown sat the home where I'd kicked out an old man and sent him back to his understaffed, reeking elderly prison.

I turned away from the window and forced myself to focus on the ring of the phone in my ear.

For the past year I'd managed to avoid asking the question I was about to ask—the question I'd repeated so many times before.

I regretted—seriously regretted—few things in my life, but not being there when she needed me the most, putting her in danger in the first place, definitely topped the list.

I dropped into the chair again and propped my elbows on the desk, holding the phone in one hand, my head in the other. A familiar groggy female voice answered, and I winced as I sat back. "Anne, I didn't mean to wake you. I wasn't thinking. Go back to sleep. I'll call you tomorrow."

"Richard? No, now's okay." I heard her push off the blankets and pad out of her bedroom, keeping her voice low so she wouldn't wake her husband. "What's the matter?"

"Everything's fine. I just wanted to check in."

"Bullshit. I can hear it in your voice. What's going on?"

I paused, knowing she wouldn't like the next part. "I need to hear you say it again."

"Richard…" The long sigh came across the line loud and clear. "Why now?"

"Just tell me."

"You know I don't remember. Just the first few minutes and the hospital. Almost nothing in between. It's like a dream. I don't really associate it with being real." I could hear her moving through her house. I pictured her trudging down the stairs to her kitchen, wearing those gold fuzzy Garfield slippers with the whiskers. I was pretty sure she still didn't wear anything like that, but there those cat slippers were, cemented in my memories of her.

She spoke again, sounding more awake and even more concerned. "You have to let this go. It's behind me. I don't ever think about it. I haven't for so long."

"Okay." I swung the chair around and stared out the window once more, the city lights blurring into one glowing sphere. "I've gotta go. You go back to sleep."

"Richard, talk to me."

When I offered nothing, she added, "If not me, then you need to talk to someone. It has been too long for this to bother you so much." She waited, and when I continued with the silence, she asked, "You haven't told them about it yet, have you?"

"It didn't happen to me."

"Really? You're more damaged because of it."

Damaged? Was I?

I never let mistakes or failures keep me down for long. I didn't let anyone or anything stop me from getting what I wanted.

So I needed her to remind me every once in a while that she was okay? Where was the harm in that?

Except… I was fooling myself. I should've said something to Luke and Matthew. No matter how long ago it had happened, it was a part of me. It was never truly far from my mind.

"Richard." Anne exhaled, the sound more one of concern than exasperation. "You need to share all of yourself with the people who mean the most to you."

I grinned at that. If she only knew how much I worked to get the three of us talking.

"Richard—"

"Listen, I've got to go. I'll call you next week."

It took her a moment, and then she said, "Okay."

After we hung up, I kept the phone clutched in my hand. Was she right? Had I purposely held back on saying something to Matthew and Luke?

And what did that mean if I had?

I trusted them, but would they look at me differently when they knew the truth?

Distracting myself from those rocky, vulnerable thoughts, I dropped the phone to the desk and glanced back at the web results on my computer screen. The anger and frustration worked through me again at the idea that Edward Harrison might be fucking with me from beyond the grave. Had he hated me that much that he'd go so far as to plan out some sort of torment for me while he lay on his deathbed? And if so, why had he agreed to sell me the house in the first place? Had that all been a part of his plan?

It seemed unlikely.

In any case, one way or the other, Dominic Pesaro was going to answer my questions.

The framed photo at the corner of my desk caught my eye. It was of Luke and Matthew. A candid shot I'd snapped on my phone one night when neither had known I was standing there. Matthew was asleep on the couch, sporting more facial hair than usual. He had his head on Luke's lap. Luke's legs were out straight in front of him, his feet propped on the coffee table. He was watching a movie, idly running his fingers through Matthew's dark hair. That was only a few minutes before Luke's dad had called our house. The next night, Luke had gone to the Haven in search of someone to hurt him the way he thought he needed—the way I wouldn't. That was the night we'd almost lost him.

If he had succeeded in being with another man... That was one thing I wasn't sure we could've gotten past. Some other guy touching him, kissing him, giving him pleasure... The mental images would've plagued my every moment with him. I had never been the kind of guy who could share the man in my life with anyone else. Which was funny considering the relationship the three of us were in. Because I had no issues sharing Luke with Matthew. And vice versa.

Even now, with how close the two of them had grown while I'd been busy working, all I still wanted was to see them together, to be a part of that closeness.

I glanced back at the photo of them on the desk. I wanted to climb into that picture, join them in that contented moment.

What the hell was I doing alone in my office?

Chapter Six

The bedside lamps were turned off, but the low light from the bathroom illuminated the bed enough I could see them.

They were facing away from me. Luke lay on his side, Matthew's ass pressed against Luke's groin, the sheet pulled halfway down their bodies. They both wore underwear and nothing else.

I rounded the bed to my side and stood there, taking another long look. The best part was the way Luke had his arm around Matthew, holding him close, his nose buried in Matthew's hair. Matthew always craved physical contact, but it hadn't been easy for Luke to accept sleeping like that, to open himself up to that level of intimacy.

Now here he was, touching Matthew, loving on him, even in sleep.

Or, in this case, mock sleep.

I worked the tight T-shirt over my head and waited, wondering how long they could keep this up and who would break first.

"I know you two aren't asleep yet."

Still they didn't move.

I gave in and knelt on the mattress beside them.

Where to begin? I wet the pad of my thumb and ran it over and around Matthew's right nipple.

Almost instantly he shuddered, and laughter poured out of him.

"Dammit, Matthew." Luke rolled onto his back. "You suck. How are we supposed to teach him a lesson about putting work before sex when you give in so easily?"

"Oh, is that what this is?" I climbed over Matthew and straddled Luke, pinning him to the bed by his wrists above his head. "Trying to teach me a lesson, huh?"

"Yeah. Somebody needs to."

That had me laughing. "You think you can handle a job like that?"

I was enjoying the teasing, but then abruptly Luke's body went tight beneath me, his expression stern.

"I'm sick of this bullshit." He fought my hold, and with the shock of that move, I let go of his wrists. He shoved at me with enough force I fell back onto my ass. He wasn't playing for Matthew's benefit.

He was seriously pissed at me.

Returning my hands to the mattress beside his shoulders, I braced myself over him. "I'm here now."

"For how long?"

"For as long as you want."

"Bullshit." He shoved me again. So hard I thought he might hurt himself if I didn't move. As soon as I shifted off him, he rolled away and flew off the bed. "I'm taking a shower."

I was about to chase him down when Matthew raced around the bed and beat me to it.

He caught up with Luke in the bathroom doorway. He spun him to face me and encouraged him toward the bed. "You don't want to do this."

Luke glanced over his shoulder back at Matthew. "I don't?"

"No. He apologized for being gone so much, and this was important to him. It seemed like it was something he had to do." He steered Luke to the far side of the bed and kept shoving until Luke lay in the middle of the mattress. Matthew crawled in after him so Luke was between us, each of us in a different location than we usually slept. That didn't sit right with me, or maybe it was how Luke lay there on his back, stiff as a board, staring at the ceiling, arms folded across his chest, like a stone sculpture had taken his place.

I moved in closer and propped my head in my hand.

He met my gaze, his steely eyes glaring at me. "And don't think this has anything to do with sex."

"I don't." If he was pissed about not getting fucked, he'd already have my dick buried in his ass. This was something else entirely. And it wasn't just about how much I'd been working either. "What is it?"

When he didn't answer, I looked Matthew's way.

"He's been having nightmares. About his dad."

Luke stiffened more, and his hands clamped down around his biceps. "It's not a big deal."

Right.

He'd needed me, and in typical Luke fashion he hadn't known how to say anything. That's why he'd lashed out at me at the Harrison Estate.

I had hoped confronting his father would've helped him put it in his past. Matthew and I had reassured him it was over, that his father wouldn't dare try to come at us again. The defrocked senator would be the first one suspected if something happened to us, and he wasn't man enough to face additional prison time.

Maybe Luke hadn't believed us.

And why would he? It was a fear I couldn't rid myself of either, no matter where his father was currently located.

I ran a hand down Luke's arm. His posture remained tight, arms locked across his chest. It was a rare occasion when I couldn't use physical touch to get him to relax.

He sucked in a sharp breath. "I just can't shake the feeling someone's watching me."

"That's understandable," I said. "His men followed you for years. He threatened to kill you. All because you were living a life he was too scared to live."

Matthew nudged Luke in the side. "Tell him the rest."

Luke rolled his eyes, and the tension in his body kicked up another notch.

"What rest?" I wasn't liking the sound of this. "Luke."

"He called. Left a message on the answering machine here at the house. He wants to see me."

It took everything I had to refrain from snapping out the word *no*. Even with his father locked down in prison, guards all around, there was no way Luke was going to be in the same room with the man who'd held a gun on him and threatened to kill him.

Luke glanced my way. "Relax. I'm not going."

"But…" Matthew looked to Luke, then to me. "Ever since then, he wakes up about half an hour after he falls asleep. He's kicking off the blankets, moaning, almost screaming. And he won't tell me what the dreams are about. Just that it's his dad." Matthew seemed beyond relieved to have the words out in the open.

I reached for him and cupped his cheek. "It's okay. We'll figure out how to help him."

"Great." Luke threw his arms out in exasperation. Then with a sudden urgency that I didn't see coming, he seized me by the back of my neck in both hands. "Thought we said tonight was all about the fucking." With jerky movements, he ran his hands over my shoulders, down my back. He gripped my jean-covered ass and dragged me in between his spread thighs. "Or have you forgotten how long it's been since you had a chance to let go inside either one of us?"

My Luke. Still using sex to avoid thinking or feeling.

I held myself up over him, not letting him pull me closer. "Do you honestly think that's going to work? You know me better than that."

He let go, and his hands landed on the pillow above his head.

Matthew moved in closer and curled along Luke's side, a hand on his chest.

It took a couple of minutes, but Luke finally spoke again. "The message said he'd like to make amends." He sighed, and I knew there was more.

With a hand on his chin, I forced him to look at me. "What else?"

"The call here at the house wasn't the only one. He called my cell after that. Left a similar message. I tried to call back. To tell him to fuck off, to leave me alone or I'm going to inform the press, the police, the parole board, and anyone else who will listen that he's harassing me if he doesn't stop. But the call went to the prison's main line. They said he's only allowed outgoing calls two days a week, one hour at a time."

"You think that's what he's doing? Using his call time to fuck with you? Or do you think he really wants to apologize?"

Saying those words nearly did me in, but Luke wouldn't admit to his thoughts any other way.

"I don't know." He dislodged himself from us, then slid off the end of the bed and went to the bathroom. A moment later he came back out, wearing a pair of jeans and chugging down a glass of water. He slammed the empty glass on the nightstand beside me. "All I know is I don't want to hear his excuses."

"Then you won't." I gestured for him to lie down with us again, but he shook me off and continued to the foot of the bed, where he just stopped like he had no idea what to do next. The jeans indicated he still felt the instinct to run, but the fact that he'd come to a halt in the middle of our bedroom spoke volumes. At least to me.

"If he calls again," I added. "We'll go to the police." I glanced Matthew's way. His brow was furrowed. His usually full lips were pursed into a thin line. I tapped him on the arm, then gestured to Luke with a tilt of my head.

Matthew sat up and asked, "What happens in the nightmares?"

The side of Luke's jaw twitched as he clenched his mouth shut. With agitated strides he crossed to the window opposite our bed. He stared out at the city lights for a minute, his hands shoved into the front pockets of his jeans, the muscles in his defined back and shoulders tight.

Without facing us, he said, "He's hurting one of you guys, and I can't get to you. I'm right there. I can see what he's doing to you, but I can't move. I can't stop it." He removed his hands from his pockets and scrubbed the top of his head in a frustrated move. "Fuck." He slapped the wall on each side of the narrow window, then kept his palms pinned to the surface like he had to hold up the wall or his entire world would come crumbling down. "I hate that I can't let this go."

I got off the bed and went to him. "He fucked with your head for a lot of years." I pulled him backward to lean against my chest, and he reluctantly dropped his hands from the wall. "It's not going to disappear overnight. Just because he pleaded guilty to the charges and is in prison does not make the worry and fear and betrayal simply disappear."

Matthew swept a hand over my back as he slipped past me to stand between the window and Luke. He searched Luke's face, and I knew Matthew wanted to do anything he could to wash away the pain. I held back on telling him that there were things that could never truly be erased. A man just had to learn to live with them, and Luke would.

"Your mom mentioned therapy," Matthew finally said.

I was glad he'd brought it up. Although talking about Luke's mom was probably not the best way to have this discussion. He was still reluctant to do things how she suggested.

"Maybe it's worth a try," I offered. "The therapist might know how to make the dreams stop."

At that, Luke tensed again.

"Just give it some thought," I added. "It's an option. That's the point. Your dad's not in control. You are. You have choices."

He didn't respond, but he seemed to be considering that. Then slowly, like he might decide to take it back at any moment, he nodded.

I asked, "Has he called again since those two messages?"

"No. If he had, I'd have gone to the cops. I'm not letting him harass me again."

"Good. See? You're in charge." I kissed his bare shoulder. "If he does call, I want to know right away. None of this keeping things to yourself. You call me at work or whatever. If I'm in a meeting, tell them they need to get me."

He shook his head. "Don't do your overreacting thing."

That had Matthew laughing.

Luke leaned in and kissed him, then faced me. The corners of his mouth were turned up in what was almost a smile. "Thanks. I'll think about what you said." His gaze dropped like he was giving it more consideration right then, but then he lifted a hand and traced the scar across my chest, starting at my right nipple and moving to my left underarm. He'd been fascinated by that old scar since we met, and even more since I'd told him how some homophobic assholes had given it to me one night at a college frat party.

I was fairly sure Luke still didn't understand why he'd always been drawn to it, but I knew. It amazed him that I held a physical reminder of a trauma that hadn't tainted who I'd become.

Or had it?

Had that night changed me?

Like that day I'd hurt Anne.

She was right. There was a part of me that was still fucked up about that.

Luke kept tracing the scar with his forefinger. Then all his fingers ran over my pecs, his attention no longer on the scar but on all of me. He met my stare as he reached up and gripped the sides of my neck in both hands. It was a tense, controlling grip, but I had no fear he would hurt me. This wasn't about me, but about what he was feeling—the frustration and lack of control where his father was concerned.

He pressed our foreheads together. "God, I've missed you." The words were barely a whisper against my lips.

So maybe this *was* about me.

"Come here." I pulled him to me.

There was so much I wanted to tell him. That no matter what his dad had done, Luke was the far better man. That I was proud of him for standing up for himself, and that I would always be there for him.

But those were all things I'd said to him before.

Sometimes words weren't enough.

I felt some of the tension melt away as he stepped into the kiss, as his lips parted under mine.

There was a longing to his touch, to the way he moved against me, but there was also something more to it. Something desperate and vulnerable.

I hated seeing him—feeling him—like that. I tried to focus on the fact that he trusted Matthew and me enough that he could show us this side of himself, that we were a part of his life—of him—in a way no one else had ever been.

I wanted to be everything he needed right then. I turned us and backed him toward the bed, never breaking the kiss until I had him lying in the middle of the mattress.

I straddled his hips and said, "Matthew."

"Yeah." Matthew's voice sounded strained. I glanced over my shoulder at him. He stood by the window where we'd left him, his dark gaze locked on us. He still wore only the briefs, the firming erection evident in the tight fabric. Just watching us always got him going.

"Come here."

He came toward the bed but stopped before climbing in.

"What's wrong?" I asked.

"Nothing. I just…" His Adam's apple bobbed as he swallowed. "I really missed this."

I reached out for him and pulled him onto the bed and toward me at the same time as I drew Luke up until we were all so close I felt their combined breath on my lips.

"Kiss me."

Without delay Matthew's lips met mine, and Luke's swept down the side of my neck. Then he licked and kissed a path along my chest, his tongue teasing one of my nipples. Their mouths had me hard and wanting and desperate in no time.

I glided my hand over Matthew's back, his ass, as I kissed him again and again. We savored the contact of lips and tongues as if that kiss meant more than any orgasm.

Then he let go of me and fell to lie on the bed like he couldn't keep upright any longer.

I held Luke by the back of the head and whispered in his ear. "Stand up and get undressed." I moved off him so I lay between them. "Kiss me again, kid." I wrapped an arm around Matthew and tugged him toward me until his lips were on mine. Sliding on top of him, I pressed our erections together, and even through my pants and his underwear, it was heaven.

I rocked against him, and he groaned, his warm, heavy exhales heating my lips.

It was then I realized Luke still lay beside us. I rolled onto my back and threw him a questioning look.

He shook his head like he'd lost focus and had no hope of it returning. "You two are…"

"Yeah?"

"Unreal together."

Apparently it wasn't just because of his dad that Luke had needed me there with them.

Something about the moment, though, had me wondering if he missed the spontaneity of sex with strangers.

Without asking the question, I was pretty sure he was giving me his answer on what sex with me meant to him. Because he stood, moving slowly, keeping those serious eyes focused on me as he popped open the button on his jeans. The Luke I'd first met would've sped through the getting-undressed portion of the night's events. Now he knew how much I liked watching him, how much I ached for him to slow it down and make the moment last.

Matthew sat up and crouched over me, kissing his way down my body. He stopped when his head was positioned over my crotch. He had his lips parted like he was ready to devour me. Cupping the bulge in my jeans, he licked those lips but then took things as slowly as Luke, carefully lowering the zipper on my jeans and parting the opening.

Luke kept his pants on for now. He ran the tips of his fingers down his bare chest, dipped his hand inside the jeans and briefs, gasping at the contact of his own hand on his cock, his gaze still locked on mine like I was the one touching him.

My breathing picked up right as Matthew mouthed my dick through my underwear. Between the two of them, I was going to shoot before we got the rest of our clothes off. I threaded a hand through the waves of Matthew's dark hair. "Kid…"

That encouraged him to up the intensity. The front of my briefs were soaked with his saliva as he tongued and sucked me through the fabric.

With his free hand, Luke lowered the zipper on his jeans. The hand inside picked up speed on his dick, his briefs still blocking the show. The action of that hand underneath the fabric of his underwear, combined with the lust-filled look in his eyes and the heavy pants that poured out from between his parted lips, was erotic as hell. I didn't want him to stop, but I needed to feel his body against mine.

"You're not undressing. You really want to come just standing there jerking off?"

Luke closed his eyes and slid his hand out. His ragged breaths matched mine. "I just…" His words trailed off. He swallowed hard. "I almost forgot how good you two look together."

Matthew turned Luke's way. "Come help me."

That was all it took. Luke ditched his pants and underwear and returned to the bed. Then the two of them worked on removing the rest of my clothes, peeling off my jeans and underwear in a series of graceful movements. There was such a synchronized rhythm to their actions, it was as if they'd practiced those moves for weeks.

Then they leaned over me, one on each side. Matthew ran a hand up my inner thigh, leaving a trail of goose bumps in his wake, while Luke grasped my dick so it stood straight in the air, looking desperate and feeling more alive than it—or I—had in weeks. He tapped the tip against his moist lips, and then he parted those lips so the sensitive ridge of my cock struck his tongue with each slap. Such a simple action, and it left me utterly desperate for him to take me all the way inside that beautiful mouth. There was always a vulnerability to Luke when he gave head that no other sexual moment with him matched, and I would never tire of seeing that open, determined focus in his eyes. Maybe that was another reason he'd been needing me there with them. Maybe he needed to be that vulnerable. After all, he'd always found it easier to be truthful with sex than words.

I wanted to show him we could all be that open and vulnerable together. Not that I could hold back my reactions. Not with them.

"Suck me," I said. Or more like begged.

Luke gave me a pointed look that said he had other ideas. "Stand up."

Stand up? I wasn't sure my legs would hold me just then.

I must have hesitated too long, not wanting to dislodge Luke's hand. He made the choice for me and pulled away. "We're going to show you that new trick. I've practiced on Matthew, but to get the full effect you have to have three people."

"Three, huh?"

"Yeah. Perfect number. And you have to stand up."

"All right." I got off the bed. "Just one thing first." I encouraged them to lie on their backs side by side before me, and then I stripped Matthew of his underwear, loving the way he shimmied his ass as the briefs slid down his legs. I knelt on the bed again, straddling a leg of each man, and set to tasting them one at a time, getting them nice and slick. I swirled my tongue around the head of Matthew's dick while pumping Luke's with my hand at the same time. Then I switched, sliding my lips down Luke's length and stroking Matthew's. I repeated the action again and again. Back and forth, alternating between hand and mouth as Matthew's encouraging words and Luke's little breathy sounds filled our room.

I kept at it, desperately wanting to see and feel them when they both came. It had been far too long since I was the reason for their release, for the desire and passion rushing through them, culminating in that moment of erotic bliss. But when Luke started with the whimpers, I reluctantly pulled off and stood, anticipation and need racing through me. "You said you had something to show me."

Luke's head hit the mattress. "Fuck. That was cruel."

Matthew stared up at me. The frustrated lines across his forehead were so damn adorable, I almost gave in and sucked him off.

Then Luke recovered. He shoved at Matthew. "Get up, kid. Let's do this."

Matthew laughed as he slid off the bed. When he was out of the way, Luke spun around and lay across the width of the mattress on his back, his head hanging over the edge of the bed. Matthew encouraged me to move to the side of the bed, and then he came in close behind me and positioned my body, legs spread so Luke's mouth was at the perfect angle. I understood what they had in mind now, and I was all on board.

With an arm around my waist, Matthew grasped my cock, and Luke gripped my ass, drawing me closer until he had his mouth on my balls, his tongue teasing my sac, sucking and swirling and wetting my skin. Watching him lying before me with his lips on that vulnerable part of my body was intoxicating.

Matthew took hold of my hand and guided it to my dick, helping me pump myself like he had to show me how I liked it, where to put pressure and when to add a twist, as if he knew my tastes better than I did. Maybe he did by now.

Eventually he left me to it and dropped to his knees behind me. Cool air struck my ass as their four hands spread me wide.

That act alone had me nearly losing it. Their mouths on me at the same time got me off faster than anything else.

With a hand on my back, Matthew forced me to bend forward. He traced a path with his tongue down my ass to the one spot where I wanted him the most. Then both of them were pleasuring me in those intensely intimate ways while I jerked my cock.

"Fuck."

I wasn't even going to make it to getting Luke's mouth on my dick.

I squeezed the base of my erection. I must've muttered something more, because Luke stopped the attention on my balls. His head fell into position over the edge of the mattress, mouth open. I leaned in farther and fed him my cock, pausing with just the tip inside him. He sucked the head repeatedly, rapidly, and then he pressed at the slit, just how he knew I liked.

These two were killing me.

"Luke." His name was barely a grunt escaping my lips.

He got my meaning. His hands clutching my ass, he brought me forward and swallowed my length. Watching him at that angle intensified his touch.

Everything felt more intense.

Luke had always been a master at deep throating, but this took it to a whole new level.

I fell forward the rest of the way, hands propped on the mattress on either side of him. I momentarily pulled out and let him catch his breath. Then he drew me back in, his throat milking the head of my cock as Matthew worked his tongue in and out and around the entrance to my body again and again. The last thing I heard before I lost it was the sound of flesh on flesh as they each jerked themselves off.

When I finally stopped groaning, I dropped onto the bed beside Luke, lying with my head at his feet. Without getting up, Luke spun around and tugged me to my side so we were face-to-face. He brought our mouths together, then pumped against me, his hand smacking my hip as he kept on stroking himself.

He moaned, and his heavy breaths poured out onto my lips. Then his release struck my skin. He trembled in my arms, kissing me one long last time.

When we parted, I collapsed onto my back again, panting like I'd been pushing myself on the treadmill for a half hour. "Oh fucking hell."

"Yeah," Luke huffed out.

Matthew still knelt on the floor. He hadn't come.

"Matthew," I said, "get up here."

He crawled up the bed and on top of me, bracing himself on his hands on the mattress beside my shoulders. I reached between us and grasped his hard shaft. "What do you want?"

"You." He hissed as my thumb circled the moist head. "Just like this."

"Like this?" I repeated the action, moving the pad of my thumb in slower strokes, and he rocked against me.

"Uh-huh." He licked his lips. We were so close, his tongue almost connected with my lower lip. "Please make me come. It's been so long since it was you."

I couldn't resist that beg, that desperate neediness in his tone. Luke had been right when he said I hadn't been home enough, but it wasn't just Luke that had been affected. I stopped the teasing and stroked Matthew harder, faster, kissing him deep and hungrily. With his lips pressed to mine, he groaned and his hips slammed against me as he came, his release mixing with Luke's on my stomach.

When Matthew stilled, I held him by the back of the head and kissed him again, unhurriedly, tenderly, showing him how much I'd missed being with him.

As soon as we parted, he plopped down onto me, his head on my chest, and he snuggled in like he had nowhere else he wanted to be, even with their cum drying between us.

"New rule." Luke breathed deep once more from where he lay beside us, and then he continued. "No more working so damn much that we have to wait that long again."

I laughed despite my complete agreement with him. "So you're making up the rules now?"

"Apparently you need them." He lifted his head off the bed. "I know your business is important to you, but when the sex is that good, you seriously gotta get your priorities straightened out."

He was right, but it wasn't just for the sex that I was going to do that. The entire night with them—the sex, the talking, Luke's confession at the estate, Matthew's desperate pleas for me to touch him—had demonstrated just how much we were meant to be three men together. Luke and Matthew needed me to be a part of them as much as I did. I'd been letting them down more than I'd imagined. All for what? To acquire an old, empty house?

Well, no more. I wouldn't let any project consume me to the point where I irreparably damaged our relationship.

No matter how long I'd waited to land the Harrison Estate, it wasn't more important than being there for them—for us.

Matthew laughed then as if Luke's words had just penetrated his blissful state. His body shook in my arms. "No. Don't do it, Richard. Don't straighten." Without moving off me, he reached up and tapped my cheek. "I like you as gay as one of those sing-alongs for *The Sound of Music*."

Luke snorted. "That was bad."

Matthew raised his head. "How about so gay he needs two men fucking him?"

"Damn right he needs two." Luke slid over on top of us and playfully humped against Matthew's ass, which had Matthew laughing again, his cock gliding along mine. He gripped my sides to keep from falling off me, and I winced as he grazed the bruise on my hip from where I'd slammed into the floor earlier at the estate.

"Oh God. I'm sorry." He scrambled off me, taking Luke with him in the process. "Are you okay?"

"You still hurting?" Luke asked.

"It's not bad."

I grabbed a few tissues off the nightstand, gave a quick swipe to my skin to clean up, and offered the same to Matthew. Then we all shifted around until we were in our usual places on the bed, Matthew between Luke and me.

I stretched and tucked my arms behind my head. "In fact, I'm more than fine. Haven't felt this good in weeks." Except I needed another shower, but not enough that I had any plans to move right then.

"Yeah." Luke's voice had slipped into its usual half-asleep mumble that always followed sex.

A few minutes later, when his deep, even breaths started up, Matthew turned to face me. "I'm worried about him."

"He'll be okay. It's just going to take time." Time I had every intention of being there for. I opened my arms, and Matthew moved into them, laying his head on my chest again.

I lived for those moments—the intimate, sensual contact following the sex. I wanted to feel them, connect with them in a way that getting off didn't allow. I loved to bring them pleasure in every way they needed, but the touching after, that was for me.

I ran a hand down Matthew's bare back and kissed him on the forehead. "Thank you for telling me about the dreams, for helping me get him to talk."

"I should've said something sooner."

"You did great." It was I who should've been there to pick up on what Luke had been going through long before then.

Matthew raked his fingers through the light dusting of hair on my chest.

I seized his hand in mine. "You know, I'm fine with the puppies. They can stay as long as they need to."

He turned his head and kissed the middle of my chest. "Thanks."

The scent of him, the feel of his warm skin against mine, being there together in the quiet, one of the two men I loved safe in my arms—it was perfection, like nothing could hurt him as long as I held him there with me in our bed.

That idea had me back to considering what Luke had said earlier about the house.

Did they see the town house the same as I did?

I cupped a hand over Matthew's cheek and embraced him tighter. He murmured something. All I understood was the word *love*, and then he was asleep.

It felt like I'd just drifted off when the muffled moans started.

I bolted upright. The room was still dark. I could hear the low intake of Matthew's sleep-filled breathing. He now lay beside me on his pillow. I waited, trying to decide if I really had heard something.

A low groan came from the other side of the bed.

Luke.

I threw back the covers and rounded the bed. I knelt next to him as I turned on the bedside lamp. He was asleep, but his upper body shifted with the slightest twitches. He moaned again, then mumbled, "No. No. Stop."

Softly I shook him by the shoulder. "Luke, wake up." His skin felt cold, clammy. I wanted to warm him. I wanted to take away all the pain and fear. My gut churned at the thought of Matthew waking up to this alone.

I gave Luke another shake, a touch harder this time. "Luke."

His eyes shot open. He blinked twice, then reached out and clasped my forearm. The panicked look in his wide eyes had my stomach even more in knots.

"It's okay. You were dreaming."

"Yeah." His grip relaxed, but he didn't let go.

"He's not going to hurt us."

"Right." Despite his agreement, he let go of me and flipped over toward Matthew, who lay on his side facing us, his dark hair a disheveled mass of waves on the pillow.

Luke swept the tips of his fingers along the side of Matthew's neck. When he spoke, his voice was tight. "He was choking him." Then Luke traced the curve of Matthew's mouth without touching him. "His lips were turning blue. He just kept clawing at my father's hands, staring at me like he was begging me for help, and I couldn't move." Luke paused, his fingers lingering above Matthew's lips. "If he ever—" He swallowed down whatever he was about to say.

I slid into the bed behind him and spooned him, an arm around his waist. "We won't let anything like that happen."

He nodded, but he had to be thinking the same thing. Even from prison, if Luke's father wanted to make our lives hell, he could. He could hire someone to get to us anytime, anywhere.

I kissed the skin between Luke's shoulder and neck. "Why don't we talk to Walter and see if there's more we could be doing here at the house for security?"

"Okay."

I continued to hold him, and he grabbed on to the arm I had wrapped around him. He looked back at me. The warm expression in his eyes told me that he knew I'd be there for him, no matter what. He knew I'd help him protect Matthew—protect all of us. He would never be alone in any of it.

"Okay," he said again, still clutching my forearm.

Chapter Seven

"I can do this all night." I glared across the small space at Dominic, then sank back into the uncomfortable plastic chair, the slats in the seat pinching my ass with that move.

He didn't say anything. Just kept his arms folded across his chest, kept that scowl directed at me from where he sat on his bed, exactly as he'd been twenty minutes before when I first arrived at the nursing home.

I'd found him lying on top of his blankets, wearing brown slacks and a green cardigan sweater that was open to reveal a T-shirt for Lake Front Amusement Park, which if I wasn't mistaken had closed in the 1970s. He'd been staring at the spinning ceiling fan that squeaked with each whirl, blowing cool air down onto him. I wasn't sure why the fan was on in the middle of winter, but I decided to skip asking. Probably one more thing he'd get worked up about when it came to how things were done at Legacy Village.

When he spotted me, he'd pointed down at the bed on each side of him. "Look. I'm here. So if there's been another break-in at the estate, you'll have to go harass someone else."

I grinned but didn't offer any other response, just took a seat in the chair at the foot of his bed and asked him to elaborate on what he'd meant about people coming after the house.

He'd said nothing to that.

And twenty minutes later, it was the same silence between us, combined with the occasional shuffle of feet in the hall as someone passed by. His room had a claustrophobic feel to it. Maybe it was because one half of the space was dark where a second bed was located for a roommate who wasn't there right then, and the curtains over the lone window were drawn closed.

I shifted in the ridiculous plastic chair and waited some more.

Finally he said, "I don't care how long you sit there. I'm not talking to you until you answer *my* questions."

"And I'm not going anywhere until you talk to me."

That got me nothing but another glare.

Time for a different approach. I stood and stepped around the bed to get a closer look at his side of the room. There wasn't much. Just a nightstand, a dresser, and a narrow wardrobe. On his nightstand he had the picture we'd seen him with at the estate, and there was another one of him holding a baby. He was older in that picture, so the child was probably his granddaughter, Isabella.

Dominic was intently watching me. "You're awfully nosy."

"I'll stop snooping as soon as you tell me what I want to know."

He harrumphed in response.

I continued with my examination. A haphazardly stacked pile of magazines, each with a sticker from the public library, took up most of the dresser. Multiple issues of *The Family Handyman*, *Reader's Digest*, and *Vegetarian Times*. On top of the magazines sat a paperback copy of *Murder on the Orient Express*. Behind all that, at the far back corner, was a tall gold statue. I got a closer look. An Oscar. The inscription indicated it was Griff Harrison's Academy Award for Best Actor.

"How'd you get that?"

Dominic stared at the award, the scowl locked firmly in place and his lips pursed shut like he had no intension of saying anything. Then surprisingly, that look was gone. "Edward gave it to me after Griff died. He said he didn't want it where he could see it anymore, and since I actually liked his cousin..." He shrugged.

"That sounds like him."

"You knew Edward?"

I returned to the chair. "Not well. He didn't care for me."

For the first time since I'd gotten there, Dominic seemed to be considering me with interest, not contempt.

Taking a chance, I asked again, "What did you mean about someone wanting to destroy the house?"

Nothing.

Civility and patience weren't working. Time for a new tactic.

I pointed at him. "Are those pants cutting off your ability to breathe? Is that why you can't talk all that much?"

Dominic unfolded his arms and glanced down at his brown trousers, clearly confused as to what was wrong with his wardrobe.

"They're cinched about six inches above your natural waistline. They've gotta be cutting off your air supply."

That time he rolled his eyes like it had been a lame attempt at best.

So much for angering him into talking.

This guy was too smart for his own good.

I was about to try a more forceful strategy when my phone rang. Joe's name flashed on the caller ID. He'd promised to contact a few of his more obscure clients who'd mentioned years ago they were interested in investing in the Harrison Estate, long before it had been put up for sale.

It didn't bother me that Joe was giving me a hand. I would've done the same for him. But it did bother me like hell that I needed the help.

I hurried to answer the call.

"Sorry, Richard. They're not interested."

"Dammit." I switched the phone to my other ear, got up to cross the room, and went out into the hallway, needing to move as the frustration I'd been feeling for weeks returned in full force. "Did they give you a reason?"

"Just said it was bad timing. Most have their money tied up in a number of other investments."

"Right."

There must've been something to my tone. Joe asked, "What is it? What are you thinking?"

I leaned back against the hall wall outside Dominic's room and lowered my voice. "This is beginning to feel a little too familiar. Like someone's messing with me."

"You think Luke's dad is coming at you from behind bars?"

"I don't know. Maybe."

I had spent the morning making calls to some of the most wealthy, influential citizens in the city, and I still hadn't been able to bring anyone on board for the restoration project.

Which made no sense considering the vast interest in the property when Edward Harrison had put it on the market. There was only one reason I could think of: someone was purposely blocking me. Someone with a lot of power.

"You said anything to Luke yet?" Joe asked.

Dominic exited his room, giving me a look of amused superiority as he sauntered by. If he thought he'd won simply by leaving his room, he was sadly underestimating me.

"No," I said into the phone. "Luke doesn't need me getting him all worked up over something that might not be true." Not with the nightmares he'd been having.

But even with his dad's recent contact, my gut was telling me it wasn't him who was coming at my business this time.

"Any way for you to find out for sure if this is his father?" Joe asked.

"Maybe. I'm probably overthinking this. Yesterday I actually thought—"

"What?"

"That perhaps Harrison wanted me to have that property, just so he could screw with me."

"What do you mean? Like he paid someone to make sure no one invested in the renovations after he was gone?"

"Maybe."

Joe laughed. "You really think Edward Harrison would go to all that trouble when he was dying?"

"Why not? You always say that wealthy people get bored easily."

"Well, he lived ten years longer than anyone would've guessed. There's a good chance he was pretty senile near the end." Joe laughed again.

I didn't join him. A man in a wheelchair passed by me, shuffling down the hall with his feet on the floor between the folded footrests of his chair. I kept watching him until he turned a corner and was gone.

"Richard." Joe's voice had taken on an astounded, almost amused quality. Very few people took that tone with me. "Tell me you know this isn't the old man."

"I honestly don't. What am I missing here?"

"Edward Harrison liked you."

That time I did laugh. "Bullshit."

"He admired your tenacity. I saw it every time I was at some party or charity function when he was there and your name came up."

That I really hadn't seen coming. Not that it would've changed my mind about the homophobic old bastard.

But it did have me curious. Was I seeing things accurately? Or was I overanalyzing everything? Like Luke had said I did far too often.

Over the phone, Joe sighed around a chuckle. "Anyone ever tell you, you worry too much?"

"Absolutely not."

"Right. I'm guessing it won't do any good to remind you that you always find a way to get what you want."

Not *always*.

Which also had me wondering... Was I in over my head with the Harrison Estate? Would I know when it was time—when it was the right move—to let it go?

After I hung up with Joe, I headed down the hall in the direction

Dominic had gone. I found him sitting at a table in what was labeled the *Recreation Room*. Although recreation seemed like the furthest thing that went on there.

A TV was on in the far corner, playing a talk show where the host was dancing through the crowd and then onto the stage. The only other person in the room was a man whose wheelchair was pointed away from the TV. He appeared much older and weaker than Dominic. There was no way he'd be able to use his feet to move like the man in the hall. His head was tilted to the side, and he stared up at one of the flat-panel industrial lights in the ceiling. Or maybe it was the cluster of dead flies in the bottom of that light that held his focus.

Was that the look of utter loneliness?

As if he just noticed I'd entered the room, the man looked at me in a slow, shaky turn of his head. I smiled at him, and he returned the gesture, but it wasn't a lighthearted expression. He went back to keeping vigil on the light.

Taking the seat opposite Dominic, I asked, "You ready to talk yet?"

He said nothing.

"I told you. I can wait as long as it takes."

He shrugged. "Visiting hours end at nine. They'll kick you out then."

I sighed and glanced at the other man again. From the occasional twitch of his lips that coincided with the audience's laughter on the TV, it was clear he was listening to the host do her monologue. Had whoever dropped him off bothered to ask if he wanted to watch the show?

I got up and went to him. "Would you like me to turn you around so you can see the TV?"

With jittery movements, he looked my way. "Yes. Yes. Thank you."

I undid the brake on his chair and got him situated. "You okay like this?"

"Yes."

"You want to check out a different show?"

"No. I like this one." His hands shook as he held them out for me. I took one in mine, and he clasped on to me with both hands as if that was the only way his trembling limbs could manage the gesture. "Thank you."

I gave a nod and crossed the room to Dominic. His eyes were wide like he was seeing me for the first time, taking in my formidable size, or maybe it was something else. He abruptly glanced away and tracked a man and woman who were walking down the hall past the rec room. The woman watched Dominic in return, and then she smiled at him. He sat taller and gave her a wave, keeping his focus on her until she and the man were out of sight.

I sat again. "Is that your girlfriend?"

He spun around. "No." His expression softened. "She likes Martin."

"Was that him with her?"

"Yeah."

"She wasn't looking at him. She was looking at you."

He said nothing to that.

"All right." I sat back and slapped my hands on the armrests of the chair in a resigned move. "I'll make you a deal. I'll tell you what you want to know, then you answer all my questions. Right now."

He met my stare and studied me for a long moment. Eventually he nodded.

"Okay," I said. "What would you like to know?"

"Have there been more break-ins?"

"No. Nothing's been reported. No signs of any problems."

He exhaled in relief. "Are you going to get the power turned on?"

"It's in the works."

"Is there any way you can put more security in place?"

"I'm working on that too."

He nodded again, and I took that to mean he was pleased with my responses. Then his gaze locked on the table between us. "What are you going to do with the house?"

"I'm going to restore it."

He raised his head. "You are?"

"Yes."

"To what? It's been renovated a number of times over the years. What will it look like when you're done?"

"What it was like when Griff Harrison lived there."

"Oh." Dominic's lower lip quivered. "It was beautiful then." He blinked and was back to the more stoic pose I was beginning to expect from him.

"Now tell me," I said. "Who wants to destroy the house? And why?"

He opened his mouth to speak but closed it just as quickly. He shook his head. "I have no reason to trust you."

"We had a deal."

He considered me for another moment. He seemed torn between

what he wanted to say and what he thought he should. Then he leaned in and whispered, "I am not supposed to tell anyone."

"And who told you that? Edward Harrison? I know you saw him before he died."

Dominic's mouth dropped open. He waited to answer, examining me once more like he was trying to make a decision that could forever alter things for him. "Edward just wanted to thank me for taking care of the place. He wanted to make certain that even though someone new owned it, that I would continue to keep an eye on the house after he was gone."

"To torment me, no doubt."

"Why would you say that?"

"Like I said, he didn't care for me." I still believed that, despite what Joe had said.

Dominic looked surprised but then said, "Edward told me he wasn't sure if the man who was buying the estate could be trusted. That it was up to me to save the house. That you might let in the people who want to destroy it. That you might even sell it to them."

That Edward Harrison had given me that much thought definitely added plausibility to the idea that he was actually behind everything.

"I'm not selling," I said. "Who are these people that Edward was worried about?"

Just then a woman entered the rec room and called out, "Time for dinner," as if the room was full of residents.

She went to the man watching the TV and without a word to him undid the brake on his chair and wheeled him away.

Dominic stood. "That's all I know, so I'm going to go eat now." He threw me another one of his annoyed expressions. "Or are you going to make an old man starve?" He didn't wait for an answer. He walked off, and I didn't try to stop him.

I wasn't sure I'd get anything more useful out of him right then anyway. Although I was sure there was more he wasn't saying. I got up and slid on my coat. My cell rang as I headed for the exit. Opening the door, I was hit with a blast of cold air, a perfect fit for the name that flashed across my phone's screen: *Perkins Federal Correctional Institution.*

I froze, the door still open, snow gusting in. The phone clutched in my hand rang again.

Another ring, and I answered as I took off for my car.

"Mr. Marshall?"

My skin crawled at the sound of that sanctimonious voice.

"*Mr.* Moore." I emphasized the Mr. He wasn't a senator any longer. No sense missing the opportunity to rub that in.

He responded with a laugh that was surprisingly warmer in tone than I would've expected from him. "I suppose that felt good to say."

"You bet your ass it did. The only other thing I have to say to you is that if you don't stop harassing Luke—"

"I'm not harassing him. And if you're blocking me from seeing my son—" Oddly he didn't finish the threat. Instead his voice softened as he said, "I'm sorry. That's not what I meant to say."

I got in my car and slammed the door shut. "Whether or not you see Luke is his decision. Not mine. And it's certainly not yours."

"But he values your opinion. If you could talk to him…"

Was he seriously asking for my endorsement?

He changed directions before he finished that thought. "I hear you've purchased the Harrison Estate and that you're having trouble finding investors to come on board."

That had me stopped with my hand on the key in the ignition. So maybe my recent problems weren't Edward Harrison after all. "You know, you really need to get a new MO. Fucking with my business is getting old, and it's not going to win you an early parole date."

"I'm not intervening in your business." More quietly he added, "Not this time."

Right. Although my instincts still told me he wasn't involved, that the more likely suspect was Edward Harrison.

When I said nothing, Luke's dad continued. "I don't expect you to believe me. All the same, I'd like to help. I have some available funds—"

"You've got to be kidding me." I let go of the key and dropped back in the driver's seat. "Do you honestly think I'd take money from you? You threatened to kill the men I love. You can go to hell for all I care. You had a good man for a son, and you lost him. That's on you. I'm not the person to help you get him back, so don't even try to play me. You just stay away from Luke, from Matthew, from all of us. That's your only shot at redemption."

"I need to talk to my son. One way or the other, I'm going to get him to listen to me." Then the line went dead.

That was it. He'd gone too far.

I scrolled through the contacts on my phone and found the name of the federal agent who'd been the lead investigator on the case against former Senator Moore.

Making threats from prison had to be good for adding a few years onto the man's sentence. I hit dial on the phone and started the car.

Checking the clock on the stereo, I took off while I waited for someone to answer the call.

Luke would be home soon. We needed to talk.

* * * *

"What happened?" I switched the phone to my other ear and shut the door to the town house, hoping I didn't have to head back out. The storm was set to keep dumping snow on the city throughout the night.

"We're not sure yet," the man from the security company said over the phone. "Someone was spotted on the property, but they took off before security got out of their car. The guards are searching the property now. If they find anyone still there, the police will be dispatched. Hang on for a moment, and I'll check to see if they've come across anyone."

I waited as I slid off my overcoat and suit jacket, then kicked off my shoes. The security company had their procedures to follow, but I had a strong hunch who had just trespassed onto the Harrison Estate. While I'd stopped off to talk to the FBI, Dominic very well might've been headed to the estate. Although I couldn't imagine he had gotten out of the nursing home in this weather. Or maybe that shouldn't have surprised me. If security didn't come across him on the property, I'd need to put in a call to make sure he'd made it back to the nursing home.

"Okay, Mr. Marshall," the man said when he came back on the line. "Security hasn't found anyone on the grounds or in the house. But they did find another open window at the rear of the home. Could be more kids or some homeless trying to get out of the weather. Would you like us to report this to the police?"

"No, that's okay. I'll have someone out there tomorrow to take a look at securing the windows."

"All right. The guards will circle the perimeter one more time to make certain whoever it was is long gone. I'll be in touch if they discover anything."

I thanked him and hung up.

Teenagers again? What were the odds? Especially considering Dominic's persistence. Or had there been something to his warnings?

I loosened my tie as I pondered that, making my way into the living room.

Luke sat on the couch. He didn't have his computer on his lap, and he wasn't watching TV. He just stared off across the room at the window. The drapes were drawn closed, so he wasn't interested in the storm. The living room and the entire first floor were dark except for the lone light beside him.

Without looking at me, he asked, "Everything okay?"

"Yeah. Someone was spotted at the estate again, but they took off when security got there."

"You have to head over?"

"Not this time. Where's Matthew?"

"At the library. He went to get some work done after dinner with his mom. I got a text from him an hour ago. He said he'd already stopped here to feed the puppies."

I took a seat in the chair across from him.

Luke gave up on staring at the drapes and eyed me in that way he always did when he was trying to figure out how to say something, or how to avoid saying it. But then he looked away, shifting his focus to the lighthouse painting that hung over the fireplace. He studied that picture like it had the answers to all his problems.

The choppy waves of the sea and the storm rolling in toward the lighthouse reminded me of my life right then. A storm brewing and no way to stop its assault.

But maybe I could shed some light on it.

I leaned forward, my elbows on my knees. "Listen, there's something I have to tell you—"

"About dear old dad?"

I shouldn't have been surprised by that. Luke had gotten pretty good at reading me, reading my every hesitation and shift in my voice.

"He called me today." I relayed the conversation, including his determination to speak to Luke. "He offered to fund the renovations for the Harrison Estate. Most likely so I'd get you to meet with him."

"What did you say?"

"I told him to go to hell."

That brought out a grin. Then Luke grew serious again. "He must have someone watching us."

"Maybe not. It's been on the news that I bought the estate. And I'm sure he still has connections."

"I guess." He met my stare once more, his eyes scanning mine. "What else happened?"

"It's not related to your dad. Not this time."

"What did he do?"

"Did you hear me say it's not him?"

"Tell me."

"Everyone who was interested in funding the restorations has backed out. It's probably too early to assume anything, but it—"

Luke flung his head back to the couch behind him. "Fuck."

I couldn't stand how defeated he looked. I went to sit next to him. "I don't think it's your father."

"Right. Then who?"

"Edward Harrison."

Luke lifted his head and considered me like I'd lost my mind. "Richard, Edward Harrison is dead. My father's not."

"All right. For argument sake, let's say it's your dad. Do you think I give a fuck?" I reached out and laid a hand on his thigh, caressing the side of his leg with the pad of my thumb. "He's screwing himself by repeating some of the same mistakes that landed him in prison."

Luke must've seen something in my expression. "What did you do?"

"I talked to the feds." I stilled my hand. I didn't want to tell him the rest.

"And?"

"There's not much they or the local police can do until there's more calls. Then they can establish a pattern. Nothing he said was an outright threat. Though they did suggest you keep a record of the calls, and if they don't stop, you can file for a restraining order. There's enough history, it'd be a no-brainer for a judge. We should talk to your lawyer."

He gave a nod. "I'll call tomorrow."

I was glad I didn't have to push him on it. "Thank you."

He shook his head and laughed.

I wrapped an arm around him, pressing my lips to the hair above his ear. "Even if it is him who's messing with me, it doesn't matter. Nothing means more to me than your safety."

He jerked away from me. "Don't shrug this off. Not this time. I can see how much that estate means to you." He let out an exasperated breath. "I need this shit with him to be over. Now." There was a degree of desperation in his voice and his demeanor. He wanted something he knew I'd never go for.

And I was certain of what that was. I'd known when he'd first told me his dad had called that he'd eventually come to this decision, but I wasn't ready to have that talk.

Just then the wind outside picked up speed, and the ominous howling matched the conversation we were having—or more precisely, not having just yet.

I gestured toward the window. "It's getting bad out there."

Luke pulled his phone out of his pants pocket. "I'll text him and tell him to get his ass home."

A minute or two ticked by as we waited, not saying anything.

When Luke didn't get a reply from Matthew, he said, "I don't like this. He usually answers."

I wasn't liking it either. Not after the call from his dad. "Come on." I got up and went for our coats by the door.

We weren't waiting any longer.

Chapter Eight

"Any idea where to look?" I asked Luke as I glanced around the library's first floor. We stood near the circulation desk, scanning the crowd of students at the computer stations and the public study areas. There was no sign of Matthew.

With the storm worsening the way it had been for the past several hours, I had expected the place to be nearly empty. It wasn't. The large open room near the front desk was packed with students and staff, all focused on their phones, computer tablets, or laptops, and not a single one of them reading a physical book. Matthew went to a community college that shared a library with its affiliated university. The building was massive and would take us forever to search.

"He'd be off somewhere by himself," Luke said. "Where it's quiet."

I pointed to another section with rows of long tables and not as many students. We wove in and out of the tables and chairs, but Matthew wasn't there either.

We moved on to check the other open study areas and any individual cubicles we came across as we made our way through the first floor, but we still couldn't find him. Anxiety had settled in my chest and was kicking up a notch with each minute that ticked by.

"Try texting him again," I said as I got out my phone and dialed our home line. There was no answer.

Luke shook his head when he got nothing in response. "Maybe he headed home already."

"Then why isn't he answering?"

We exchanged a look. A combination of anger and panic was visible in Luke's eyes, and I knew he didn't want to put words to the fear any more than I did.

"Let's go check out the other floors," I suggested. "Maybe his phone can't get a signal up there."

Whereas the first floor had been all about computers, the second floor was packed with shelf after shelf of books, and there weren't as many students or library staff in those aisles.

We continued on to the third floor. As we exited the elevator, Luke pointed at a sign indicating the location of periodicals and reference materials.

Only three people browsed those stacks. I was about to tell Luke we needed to try something else when I reached the last row and found someone with wavy dark hair sprawled on the floor halfway down the aisle.

Matthew.

He lay on his stomach, his arms limp at his sides, his cheek pressed flat against a stack of books on the floor, his lips parted, and his face paler than normal.

I sprinted for him. "Luke! He's here." I hit my knees. "Matthew."

Luke was at my side as I rolled Matthew onto his back.

Matthew's eyes fluttered for a moment, then opened. "What?" He looked up at me, then at Luke as he started to sit up. "What are you doing here?"

"Take it easy," I said as I helped him. The rush of adrenaline had my heartbeat thundering in my ears. I checked Matthew over for any sign someone had struck him. "Are you okay?"

"Sure. Guess I fell asleep."

"You were sleeping?" Luke slid off his knees and dropped to his ass, slumping back against the shelves.

I did the same across from him. "You fell asleep?"

"Yeah," Matthew said.

"While you were searching for a book?"

"No. I was sitting here reading. Just got really tired and thought I'd close my eyes for a minute."

Luke let out a sigh of relief, then asked Matthew, "Are you sick?"

"No. I'm fine."

I reached out and cupped the back of his head. "You're studying too hard. You need to get more sleep at night."

In an instant Luke went tense. "It's not the schoolwork keeping him up at night." He eyed me again, and I knew what he was thinking, what he wanted to do to end the nightmares he'd been having. I didn't want to have that discussion right there on the library floor.

I shook my head and refocused on Matthew. "What were you doing studying here?"

"It's quiet on this floor." He wiped the sleep from his eyes. "And I wasn't studying anything for school." He picked up the top hardback book that contained several bound issues of *LIFE* magazine and set it in his lap. It was open to an old black-and-white picture of the Harrison Estate. Books and printouts lay all around Matthew. Biographies about Griff's life, scanned newspaper articles, and additional magazines featuring the Harrison family and their famous property.

Matthew glanced up from the book. "Why are you guys here?"

"The storm's getting worse, and we couldn't get ahold of you." I shifted to find a more comfortable position and settled against the shelves again, biting back the wince as my hip throbbed. Now that the adrenaline had passed, the slight twinge of pain I'd been feeling all day had returned with a vengeance.

Maybe it was those aches, or maybe it was all the students on the campus or sitting on the damn floor, but I felt like I'd aged ten years in the past two months. I gestured to the book on Matthew's lap. "You were looking up stuff about the estate?"

"I thought maybe I could find something that would encourage Dominic to talk to you."

"And you were also curious to learn more about Griff and his life."

"Yeah. Most of the articles are about his career and the parties he used to throw. There were a lot of pictures with his fiancée, the princess." He turned the page to a photo of a man with a woman. Matthew grew quiet as he stared at the picture.

"What's wrong?" I asked.

He shook his head. "Nothing."

I wanted to encourage him to say more but opted for waiting until we got home. "We should head out before the storm gets any worse."

Matthew got on his knees and started to gather the books and papers and pack everything into his backpack. His mood seemed to lighten with an immediacy that had me wondering if I'd missed him doing that at other times lately. He flashed Luke a huge grin like he had the best secret he couldn't wait to spill.

"What?" Luke asked.

Matthew halted his packing. "My mom told me something funny at dinner tonight."

I leaned back against the bookshelf and watched them. This could be interesting.

Matthew sat on his heels and cocked his head to the side, like a puppy trying to assess Luke. "Although I'm not sure how funny you'll find it." He laughed again despite what he'd said.

Luke rolled his eyes. "Great."

"My mom called your mom a few weeks ago."

"Oh God. Why?"

"My mom wanted to see how she was handling everything. She wanted to let your mom know there was someone she could talk to if she needed a friend." Matthew bit his bottom lip. He released it, and his next words poured out. "They've been doing stuff together."

"Stuff?"

"Yeah." Matthew looked to me and then back to Luke, his delight seeping out despite his attempt to hold it in. "They went to a PFLAG meeting."

Luke's mouth dropped open. "Are you kidding me?"

"Nope. My mom's been going for years, and she suggested it one day when they had lunch." Matthew paused, an amused glint in his eyes, even though he was desperately attempting to keep a straight face. "And the group was just starting to plan the pride parade for this summer. They want us to walk with them." Matthew spun toward me, and his forehead hit my shoulder. The laughter came pouring out full force, his body trembling against mine. I joined him in laughing at Luke, who glared back at us.

"A fucking parade?"

Matthew finally quieted and lifted his head. "She's just trying to make up for everything."

"I know. It's just... I went from having no parents to having this supportive mom who accepts her son's two lovers, has a rainbow sticker on her car, and now wants to be in a parade where there'll be men wearing leather jockstraps and collars. It's a lot to get used to."

Matthew gripped my arm as if that was all that would keep more laughter at bay. "Your mom was nominated chapter secretary."

Luke flung his hands in the air, and they landed on his thighs with a loud *slap*. "Great."

"Better than the alternative," I offered.

He gave a nod. "I suppose so."

"I like that they're talking." Matthew grew quiet after that. He reached for another book on the floor and set it on his lap. He opened and closed it at the corner as he spoke again. "They're acting like real in-laws."

"In-laws?" Luke scoffed, then grew serious as Matthew nodded, keeping his focus on the book he held.

I hadn't seen that embarrassed expression from him in months.

"I just mean"—he shrugged—"our moms are... you know... It's like we're married or something."

Luke threw me a startled *what the fuck do we say to that?* look.

I cleared my throat. "Kid, you just brought out the old Luke and scared the crap out of him."

Luke bumped my leg with the side of his shoe. "Jerk."

Matthew didn't laugh or say anything more.

I encouraged him to face me. "Do you want to get married?" When he didn't answer, I kissed him and asked again, "Matthew, do you want to get married?"

He glimpsed something over my shoulder, and I turned to see what had caught his attention. A young woman stood at the far end of the aisle. She looked even younger than Matthew and had blond hair streaked with purple and a silver bar piercing her right eyebrow. She wore wedge heels and shorts with tights underneath. Who wore shorts in the middle of a blizzard, even with the tights? She was smiling, her eyes wide, and then she spun around and took off.

I turned back. "Matthew."

He shook his head. "We can't get married."

"I know. But if three men could legally marry, would you want to? Is that something you'd like for us?"

"I guess... I guess that'd be nice. To make it official."

"It would. But I think we all know we're in this for the long run."

"Yeah."

"What am I missing here? What's the matter?"

"My mom asked about it tonight."

"About you getting married?"

He nodded. "She's sad. Especially now that more and more states are legalizing gay marriage. She's done a lot for the cause and now..."

"You can't actually get married."

He shrugged again. "It's not a big deal. I was just wondering what you guys thought. If it bothered you."

It was about killing me that this was something I couldn't give him, that he'd never able to tell his mom he would have a legal, official wedding.

Maybe I wasn't the only one. Luke raised his knees toward his chest and propped an arm on each kneecap. "What if..." He gestured between Matthew and me. "What if the two of you—"

"No," I said. That was not even an option.

"No," Matthew echoed. "That's not—" He moved to kneel between Luke's legs. "I don't want that. I just felt bad about my mom."

I pushed onto my knees behind him and kissed the side of his neck. "You can't live for her."

"I know. I just want us all to be together no matter what."

In a rare declaration, Luke held Matthew's face in his hands and said, "We will be. Always." He leaned in and pressed his lips to the other side of Matthew's neck, and I wound my arms around them both.

Matthew sighed like that had made all the difference.

A pair of giggles floated our way from farther down the stacks. The girl in the shorts was back, and she'd brought a couple of friends, dressed equally as weather inappropriate. Apparently we were the night's study-break entertainment.

"We should get home," I said, although I was finding it hard to let go of them. "The roads are only going to get worse until morning."

"Okay." Matthew was breathless as Luke continued to sweep his lips along Matthew's skin, going lower and lower. "Let me run to the bathroom quick, and then I want to check out these books."

Luke stopped the teasing, and reluctantly I separated myself from them and returned to sit on the floor against the shelves opposite Luke. Matthew stood and took off for the end of the aisle, squeezing by the girls who were still there gawking at us. Then all three of them scrambled to follow Matthew as he headed toward the nearby restrooms.

One asked, "Are those your boyfriends?"

Matthew mumbled something in reply. The only word I could make out was *partners*.

The full meaning of what we'd been talking about hit me. He'd never get to say he had a husband. Not in a legal sense. That was just the kind of thing to bother him when he really thought about it—or when his mom made him feel bad about it. I adored Lydia, but right then I wanted to give her a piece of my mind, and it wouldn't come out anywhere close to the polite, respectful tone I'd always used with her.

Luke stared off toward where Matthew had walked away. His thoughtful expression mirrored how I imagined I looked.

I tapped the side of his foot with my own. "What are you thinking?"

He shrugged. "I don't know."

I kept my gaze locked on him until he said more.

"Sometimes I wonder if he just tells us what he thinks we want to hear."

I joined him in watching where Matthew had gone. "He's come a long way from that insecure young man we first met."

"Sure. But…"

"What?"

"I'm pretty sure it doesn't take much, and he's back to feeling lost like he was then."

I was torn between elation at Luke sharing his thoughts so easily, and heartsick at the truth behind his words. "Because I haven't been home." It wasn't a question.

Luke nodded but then said, "I don't know. Maybe that's not it."

"It's not the same as before we met. He hasn't been alone. He's had you."

Luke shook his head in exasperation. "Don't you get it? When you're not around, he and I aren't—" He stopped as if he'd just realized he'd said that aloud.

"Go on."

He stood. "Forget it."

I snorted out a laugh as I got off the floor.

He got the message and continued. "It's like we're waiting for something. It's the same thing when it's just you and me. It's fine, great, in fact. But it's not... right. It's not us. And I think that's been getting to him."

"Do you—" I started, but the ring of my phone cut me off. I checked the display. "It's Dominic's nursing home." I hurried to answer the call.

"Mr. Marshall?" A woman asked.

"Yes. Is everything okay with Mr. Pesaro?"

"We're not sure. He's left our facility."

"When?"

"He wasn't here for dinner."

Which meant he'd left the nursing home right after I had. Just as I'd feared.

"I might know where he is. Let me check, and I'll get back to you."

She offered her thanks and hung up.

Matthew had returned and caught most of the call. He was slipping on his coat as he asked, "Dominic's escaped again?"

"Yeah." I looked to Luke. "I'm guessing that open window at the estate earlier tonight had nothing to do with any kids."

"He seems stubborn enough to head out in this storm. Why'd the nursing home call you?"

"I asked them to let me know if he took off or if anything else happened to him."

"Maybe you should just let the cops deal with him."

"Nah, it's okay. I'll head over to the estate and see if he's there."

Luke studied me, but he didn't ask anything more.

"I don't want to get him in trouble," I said. "I had Walter do a quick background check today. Seems like everything Dominic said was true. He lived at the estate since the time he was born, and he was the Harrisons' butler for fifty years until Edward moved out. So I have no doubt he's just going to keep on showing up there until I at least get a new security system installed."

Luke zipped up his coat. "We can stop and see if he's there on our way home."

The library's loudspeaker cracked. Then a man spoke, announcing that the library would be closing in fifteen minutes due to a countywide snow emergency.

"No," I said. "You guys head home."

Luke sported that unwavering, hard look that said arguing with him would take longer than a slow drive through the storm to the Harrison Estate. "We're going with you." He held a hand out and took a stack of books Matthew was trying to cram into his bag.

I hesitated, then nodded. "All right."

It was clear to me. There were things that needed to be said, things we needed to discuss. We'd been growing apart. Maybe only in subtle ways, but enough that it bothered the hell out of me that I hadn't even seen it.

If I kept them closer than we'd been for the past few weeks, maybe they would open up more.

Matthew slid his stuffed backpack onto his shoulders and picked up the last of the bound magazines. "Do you believe what Dominic said about someone wanting to destroy the house?"

"Here." I took the extra books and carried them for him as we headed down the aisle. "I'm beginning to believe there might be something to it. And I think it might be related to why no one wants to invest in the property."

Luke stopped, and Matthew and I did the same.

"What's your drop-dead date to begin the restorations?" Luke asked. "When will you start losing money?"

"I'm already losing money." More than I wanted to admit. To them. To myself. To anyone.

"Shit. You should've said something."

"I'm taking care of it. I'll eventually get someone to invest. Just have to find the right person."

He gave a nod, and we started moving again.

After we entered the elevator and the door closed, I looked to Luke. "What do you think? Do you believe Dominic?"

"I don't know. I still think your investor problems are my dad again, but I'm probably not seeing things too objectively on that front."

"Well, either way, I'm not sure Dominic is telling us the whole story."

"How do you mean?" he asked.

"Maybe there's more than merely the house at stake."

"More? Like there's something else he's protecting?"

"What?" Matthew asked. "Something inside the house?"

"Possibly," I said. The elevator doors opened, and we headed for the circulation desk. "All I know is that a lot of people made offers on the property when Edward Harrison first listed it for sale. Offers that far exceeded mine, and yet he agreed to sell to me. I'm starting to wonder if that was because he wanted to mess with me, that he's still messing with me."

Matthew stopped that time. "Uh, Richard, he's dead."

"Yeah, but he could've set all this in motion months ago, so I'd lose everything. The estate. My business. Everything." And maybe Dominic was there to make certain it all went as planned. Or maybe Dominic had been duped as much as I had.

Luke and Matthew both sported puzzled expressions.

Luke said, "That's crazy. Why would Edward Harrison do that? Wouldn't keeping you from buying the place have been enough to have fun at your expense while he was still alive? Then he could've witnessed your frustration. Why go to all this trouble?"

I gave him a long look. "Why did your father?"

He snorted out a laugh. "To show he could. To show me he had all the control."

"Right." Edward Harrison and Luke's dad were a lot alike. If they had known each other, they probably would have been best friends. Or mortal enemies.

After Matthew had his books checked out and we were in the car heading for the parking lot exit, Luke spoke again from the passenger seat beside me. "No matter what, I think Dominic's obsessed. And obsessed people are dangerous."

I was starting to believe he was right. On both counts.

Chapter Nine

"Are those crosses?" Luke had his flashlight pointed at the massive chandelier that hung in the entranceway of the Harrison Estate. Strung amid the crystal pendants were dozens of beaded rosaries. Light from the flashlight projected the dangling crucifixes on the walls all around us.

"It looks like they're Catholic rosaries," I said as I closed the front door.

Luke kept the light directed at the chandelier. "That's a lot of dead Jesuses just hanging there. Why the hell would someone want that in their house, welcoming their guests?"

"Who knows? Edward Harrison was a crackpot." I pointed at the chandelier. "He probably had that specially made."

"Make sense," Matthew said from where he stood at my other side. "The Harrisons were heavily involved with the Catholic Church."

"That they were," came a voice from above.

Dominic was standing on the second-floor landing. He wore another of his cardigan sweaters, this one black-and-white checkered. He held an oil lantern in the air. One side of his face was lit with a brilliance that showcased every wrinkle and age spot, even with the distance between us. The other side of him was cast in deep shadows. The effect mirrored what I thought of the man: he was an odd mix of innocence and deception. I still couldn't decide whether to trust him or not.

Then he spoke again, the lantern swaying in the air with his words. "Edward was a close personal friend of the bishop. They'd have dinner here together once a month."

I pointed at him. "You are not supposed to be here."

He started down the steps, the ancient lantern creaking as he moved. "I told you, I'm going to protect this house."

"And you didn't tell me from who."

"You think those rent-a-cops you hired to drive by here a couple of times a day are going to stop the people who want to get inside?"

"What people?"

"If you don't know, you don't deserve this house." He reached the bottom of the steps and paused on the last one. "I want to know the truth. What are you going to do with this place after you renovate it?"

I ignored the question. "I want you to stop breaking in." Despite my words, I was fairly sure he wasn't going to do that. Even if I got him to strike another deal with me. He was stubborn as hell. I gave in and said, "I'm going to open a resort."

He smiled, more to himself than to me. "A resort? That's…" He seemed to be pondering the idea. "This house should be full of people, activity, life. I've hated that it sat empty all these years." Then his expression turned skeptical once again. He refocused on me. "You're really not going to sell it, even when you're done with the work?"

"As long as I can swing the finances, I'd like to keep it."

He held the lantern higher, examining my face in great detail. "Don't lie to an old man."

"I'm not. You have my word on that."

"How do I know what your word is worth? Maybe you lie to everybody." He pointed at Luke and Matthew. "Swear on their lives."

"I won't do that for anyone, about anything."

"Aha!" He moved off the bottom step and came at me, jabbing a finger my way. "You're lying."

"You're a nut, old man."

He stopped and studied me again for a long moment. His eyes squinted until they nearly closed, and his bushy silver eyebrows drew together. Without another word, he took off, moving past me, out of the foyer and farther into the house.

"What's he doing?" Matthew asked.

"Apparently whatever the hell he wants."

"Are we supposed to follow him?"

"I guess."

Luke threw me a wry smile. "Maybe it's just me, but I'm really starting to like this guy."

I was too. Although I probably shouldn't have been, considering everything Dominic was telling me—or not telling me.

We followed him through room after room and eventually into the solarium on the far end of the first floor. He said nothing as he set the lantern on one of the four round metal patio tables, then crossed the room to stare outside at the back of the property.

The exterior walls of the solarium, along with a good portion of the ceiling, were made entirely of windows, each window with a shade that could be pulled down for privacy. Every shade was rolled to the top. The floor was covered in small octagon tiles in various shades of blues that mimicked a crystal-clear tropical sea.

Along the three outer walls, situated under the windows, sat large elaborately sculpted terra-cotta flower pots, each with the head of a different animal protruding out the side of the pot facing us. The most disturbing was a rattlesnake, his jaws open, his three-inch-long fangs jutting out as if he'd already sprung to strike his prey.

"Let me guess." I pointed to the pot with the snake. "Edward picked those out."

Dominic just grinned at that.

All the pots were empty and looked like they had been washed clean of any dirt or the remnants of long-ago-dead plants. Most likely the result of Dominic's handiwork.

The wind made an eerie whistle as it blew through crevices in the frames of the old windows. Outside, the storm tossed around the falling and drifting snow to the point where visibility was down to nothing. I was doubting we'd make it home that night, let alone to the nursing home to drop off Dominic.

I was also beginning to think Dominic wouldn't say anything more, and then he finally spoke again. Just not about what I wanted to hear.

"After his father died, Griff had this solarium added on to the house. He loved to lounge in the sun, but he felt too exposed outside by the pool. The price of being a celebrity, I guess. So he drew up the plans for this room. It was a pet project for him. He took such care picking out everything. The floor tiles were handcrafted to match the colors of the Pacific Ocean at his favorite beach in Hawaii."

"It's gorgeous," Matthew said.

"Yeah." Dominic nodded. "I've always loved it. But it's a bitch to clean," he added with a laugh. Then he grew thoughtful. "I've tried to keep up with the place over the years, but it's too much for me now."

Matthew stepped closer to him. "You did a really good job."

"You did," I said. "I expected the house to be in much worse shape."

Without turning away from the window, Dominic gave another nod. "Thank you."

"But I'm curious. The ballroom doesn't look like you've cleaned in there as much as the other rooms."

"I try not to go in there very often. I hate that room."

"Why?"

He shrugged. "It's just too big." He spun around, went to the table with the lamp, and sat.

His rapid movements told me there was more to that answer, but I decided not to push it. Instead I asked, "But you did clean up after the party? All the dinnerware and the glasses?"

"Someone had to. There was booze and food left on almost every table. I couldn't let the place get overrun with bugs and rats."

"So when you were doing all this cleaning, why didn't you pack up the items that the Harrisons left behind in the rest of the house?"

He shook his head. "I didn't want to hide it all away like no one had ever lived here."

I was curious how he'd been getting into the house all these years with Edward's security in place, but held back on asking that too. Dominic had said that Edward had wanted him to continue keeping an eye on the house, which meant Edward had probably given Dominic access after everyone had moved out. More evidence that Dominic was still working for Edward. Although I was having a hard time believing that now, and I wasn't sure why.

Matthew joined Dominic at the table, sitting beside him. "Do you mind if I ask a question about Griff?"

"Not at all."

"Did he kill himself?"

"No! Absolutely not. He was murdered." Dominic scooted his chair closer to Matthew, taking care not to scratch the floor tiles with the chair's metal legs. "The police never even searched for his killer. But Griff would never have taken his life. I knew that without a doubt. Because I knew him better than anyone. Well…" He paused as if he was unsure if he should say more. "Not better than his lover."

"The princess?" Matthew asked.

Dominic turned away and stared off into the storm again.

"He wasn't in love with her, was he?" Matthew's expression turned hopeful. "He was gay, wasn't he?" He chewed on his lower lip as he waited for a reply.

Dominic kept his gaze locked on the blowing snow. In the light of the lantern, he appeared more vulnerable than he had before, even at the nursing home. He seemed to be carefully considering Matthew's words, or maybe what he wanted to say in return.

Luke went to sit on Dominic's other side, as engrossed in what his answer would be as Matthew.

Hell, I was too. I took a step forward.

Dominic finally nodded. "I guess he's been gone long enough

now. I don't really need to keep his secrets any longer." He looked to Matthew. "It's not like you'll judge him, right?"

"We'd never do that."

"So all those rumors were true?" Luke's voice contained genuine surprise.

"No, not all the rumors. Not the ones about all those secret male lovers he had. Those were all lies. I was one of the few who knew the real truth."

"Which was?" I asked.

Everyone turned to me, evidently shocked at my interest in hearing about Griff's life. I rolled my eyes and moved in to join them, grabbing a chair from a nearby table and sitting across from Dominic. "Well?"

A grin hit Dominic's lips. He was enjoying that he'd captured my attention. "Griff was madly, passionately in love with one man."

Matthew bounced in his chair. "I knew it!"

I reached out and ran a hand over the warm skin at the back of his neck.

He threw me a smile, then asked Dominic, "Who was he?"

"An actor. Oliver Nash. He never became nearly as famous as Griff. In fact, he's no one you'd even know today. He had a bit part in Griff's first movie. A western called *One Last Go*. They played gunslingers in a gang that robbed stagecoaches. The entire gang decided to hang up their life of crime, but no one believed they were done with that life, and they kept getting dragged back in. Griff and Oliver fell for each other on the set, and they were together from then on. Until Griff died."

"Wow." Matthew leaned forward so his elbows rested on the table, his chin propped in his hands. "They had to keep it a secret for so long, but they stayed together anyway."

Luke laughed. "Told ya. You're such a sap."

I placed my hand at Matthew's nape again, this time keeping the contact going. "There's nothing wrong with that."

Dominic watched us for a moment, then focused on the light flickering in the lantern as if it was hypnotizing him, sending him back fifty years. "It was romantic, that's for sure. Which is partly why I agreed to help them hide their relationship. It wasn't all about doing whatever my boss asked of me. He was a good man, and he deserved to be happy. I used to sneak Oliver in here at night so none of the staff would see him. And I would help them meet when Griff was in Hollywood working on a movie. They were kind of amazing together. I just knew I had to help them. The way Griff looked at Oliver was…"

Dominic glanced up and met my stare. He studied me as if trying to decide if he should say more. "It's the same way you look at them."

It was nice to hear that it was evident to someone on the outside how I felt about Matthew and Luke, especially considering how much I'd been gone lately, and how close Luke and Matthew were growing.

Matthew focused on Dominic again. "What happened the night Griff died?"

"He and Oliver were here at the house." He shook his head. "It was awful. They had a horrible fight. I was in the kitchen and heard them yelling at each other. Then Griff sent me out on an errand, and I was gone when he—" Dominic stopped, clearly choked up over what had happened that night, no matter how long ago it had been. "If I hadn't left, maybe I could've done something to save him. But instead, I found him in his room, lying on the floor, the gun in his hand. I knew the moment I saw that gun, that someone had planted it there."

When he didn't say more, I started to ask, "Could it have been Oliver who—"

"No. He wouldn't. But someone did. I tried to find out who it was, so everyone would know Griff didn't kill himself. It wasn't fair that people thought he did that. But I couldn't figure out who it might've been." He looked frustrated with himself. Furious even.

I felt for him. He'd been unable to prevent someone from hurting his boss—his friend—and that had eaten away at him all these years. Now it was probably too late. If Griff had been killed, the person responsible could very well be long dead by now.

The howling grew louder outside, and the lantern flickered faster as if the wind had blasted right through the windows.

"I've got to get more oil for this." Dominic braced himself on the arms of the chair so he could stand, but surprisingly, his body fought him on the action, and he had to rock a bit to get moving.

"Wait." I held up a hand. While we had him talking... "I want to know what you mean about the people who are after this house."

He sighed and settled into the chair again. "Just what I said. There are people who are going to try to force you to sell. Or do whatever necessary to get inside. If they haven't already."

"Why didn't they just buy the estate from Edward?"

"He didn't *want* to sell. To anyone. But he was dying. He didn't want his grandson to make the decision on who would get the house, so he *had* to sell. He was trying to get it wrapped up before he passed away." Dominic stood then with surprising deftness. He shoved his chair in, the metal legs scraping along the tiled floor. The chair slammed into the edge of the table, and the resulting rattle echoed off the glass windows of the solarium. "Edward knew there were people who wouldn't care about this place, who would destroy everything, and he didn't want that."

"That's what happens sometimes when a property this old is purchased. It gets gutted or torn down. There are no guarantees."

"I'm not talking about real estate developers. These people have another agenda."

"What agenda?"

He pointed a shaking finger my way, his previous frustration now directed at me. "I don't trust you enough to tell you that. You'll just end up wanting what they want."

The lantern flickered again and then went still. Dominic's anger seemed to dissipate with the shift in light.

"What do they want?" I asked.

He evaded the question and returned to the wall of windows. The snow whipped through the air and smacked into the window pane directly in front of him, and he flinched.

I got up and moved to stand beside him. "You can trust me. I will not hurt this house."

He kept focused on the snow for another moment, then spoke without looking at me. "Edward mentioned you before he died."

I snorted out a laugh. "I can only imagine what he said."

"He asked me to give you something, but only if you admitted you weren't going to turn around and sell the house."

"I won't."

Dominic removed his wallet from his pants and fumbled with it, pulling out a business card. "You're supposed to call that number if you need help with anything."

I examined the card, front and back. There was no name, no description, just a ten-digit local phone number. "Whose number is this?"

"I don't know. He wouldn't tell me. All he said was that it was an unlisted number."

"Is this your idea of a joke?"

His more innocent expression returned. "It's no joke. He gave me that card to give to you."

I studied the card again. Despite my curiosity, there was no way in hell I would give Edward Harrison the satisfaction of calling the number. Even if he *was* dead. I asked, "If Edward cared so much about this place, why did he walk out fifteen years ago and leave it empty?"

"He was trying to reconnect with his grandson."

"What does that have to do with the house?"

"Edward had lost everything. His wife, his only son. I know he was an asshole to most people, but all that was really to hide how scared he was, how lonely. I could relate to what he was going through."

Which gave even more credence to the idea that Dominic might still be working for Edward, doing him this one last favor by screwing me over.

Dominic continued. "All Edward had left in his personal life was his grandson. But that boy hated his grandfather, hated being a Harrison, hated living in Griff's shadow all the time. The estate connected Edward to all that. He figured if he left this place behind, his grandson might be more willing to come see him. That's why he didn't take anything with him. He wanted to start over for the boy. No one wants to grow old all alone, with no family or friends to care about what happens to you. All the money in the world can't diminish that kind of loneliness." Dominic looked away. With his forefinger, he traced a line of frozen snow that clung to the other side of the window.

The wind picked up speed again, and the howling grew more incessant. If he wasn't going to tell me more, then... I sighed, feeling shitty about what had to come next. "Listen, we better get going. It'll take us a while to get to the nursing home in this weather."

Before I'd even finished speaking, Dominic was backing up, shaking his head.

"You have to go back," I said.

"No. I'm not leaving here."

At his words, an enormous spiral of snow slammed into the side of the house, rattling the wall of windows.

Luke stood. "Shit. That's not good."

"Yeah," I agreed. "Guess we better wait until morning to head out."

Dominic smiled. He clapped his hands. "My first guests in fifteen years. I'll make up a room for you." He spun around, his body cooperating more than earlier. Then he abruptly came to a halt and faced us. "You all sleep together, yes?"

I gave a nod. "We do."

"Okay. Give me a few minutes." He turned to leave again.

"Take the light," I told him. "We've got our flashlights."

"No worries. I can walk through this house with my eyes closed. I won't be long." He waved a hand through the air. "Make yourselves at home, and I'll come get you when your room is ready." He headed for the doorway into the main house.

I called after him. "You don't have to do anything special for us."

He didn't stop as he shouted back, "Nonsense. It's my job."

Except no one was actually paying him to do it.

"Hold up." I went to him where he had stopped in the doorway. "I'll make you another deal, but I want your word this time that you won't break it."

"What's the deal?"

"I'll call the nursing home and tell them you're staying with us here tonight. In the morning you go back and remain there until our friend finds your granddaughter. In return, I promise not to let anyone hurt this house. The power will be on shortly, and I'll have a new top-of-the-line security system installed. I'll also keep you apprised of everything." I held out a hand. "Deal?"

Dominic hesitated, staring at my outstretched hand. "Deal." We shook, and he added, "Thank you." He took off again, moving faster than most men his age could manage.

I returned to the table and sat between Luke and Matthew.

"Yeah," Luke said. "He's really growing on me."

Matthew laughed at that.

I didn't.

Luke studied me with curiosity. "He's harmless."

Was he? I'd believe that when I could get a straight answer from him. "Thought you said he was obsessed, and obsessed people are dangerous?"

"Yeah, but he's more the quirky, harmless kind of obsessed."

"You might be right." I looked to Matthew and asked, "Have you ever spent the night in a haunted house?"

"Nope. But it's not so scary when you've talked to the guy who's been haunting the place."

"True."

His expression grew concerned. "Do you think the puppies will be okay until the morning?"

"Sure. You already fed them tonight, yeah?"

"What if they get out of the pen?"

"We'll just clean up whatever disasters the little rascals make. It'll be fine."

He leaned into my side and rested his head on my shoulder. "Thanks."

We sat quietly, waiting, watching the storm outside. With the vast windows, it was almost like we were out in the snowstorm, but it also felt like we were protected from it, as if more than the glass separated us.

A few minutes later Dominic returned. "All set. It's not what I would've done years ago, but it'll do for tonight. This way."

He led us to a room near the staircase on the top floor, at the opposite end of the hall from the master suite. He had a new lantern filled with oil. It was lit and sitting on one of the bedside tables. A fire glowed in the fireplace. The room was cozy with a double bed, a cheery color of yellow adorning the walls, and a series of wooden shelves that lined one side of the room and were covered in books.

Dominic pointed to an open door that led to a bathroom. "The water's still shut off, so I put a couple of jugs of water in the washroom."

The bed had a blue blanket covering the mattress. It looked like the one from the nursing home we'd found the night we'd met Dominic. There were two more blankets folded at the foot of the bed. This room seemed less dusty than the rest of the house, and I was impressed with just how much cleaning up he had managed to get done in the amount of time he'd been gone.

The bed was significantly smaller than ours at home, but we'd make do.

Dominic turned to leave but stopped short. "Richard." His voice was low, like he was again reluctant to mention what was on his mind.

"Yeah?"

"I'm sorry I can't trust you yet. It's just…" He shook his head. "I've known men like you all my life." He eyed Matthew and Luke over my shoulder where they checked out the books on the shelves.

"You can say whatever you want to in front of them."

He waited a long beat, then said, "You hide behind your success and your money. You think if no one looks beyond all that, they won't see how scared you are. How small and unnecessary you feel. But it's there. You can't hide it from everyone. And if you try… Well, that could make you a very dangerous man, one who has to win at all costs, to keep people from seeing you fail, from seeing how scared you really are. I can't trust that kind of man." He stared me down for another moment, then left, closing the door after him.

"Yeah," Luke said from where he was casually leaning back against the bookshelves. "He's definitely growing on me."

Matthew chuckled. He was now sprawled out on his stomach across the bed, his chin propped on his folded arms.

Luke approached me then. Slowly, like he thought I might take the opportunity to get back at him for pinning me to the mattress in the basement the other day. He stopped a step away from me. "I think he's got you pegged."

I was speechless as I considered Luke. I had no idea he saw me like that.

Matthew eyed us with curiosity. He didn't see me that way, and I wasn't sure which realization about them was more disturbing.

"I'm not hiding anything." When I was afraid of something, I dealt with it. Period.

With harsh swiftness I went to the other side of the room and checked the fire. The fireplace seemed to be in good working order, which had me more impressed with Dominic's efforts.

Luke came up behind me. "What he said really bothers you."

"No." Or did it? I turned and stared at the bed beside where Matthew lay. He was still intently watching me. I added, "I'm just not sure why I'm doing this anymore."

Matthew scrambled onto his knees. "Doing what?"

"My business." I moved to the window that overlooked the back of the property. The snow swirled its way across the courtyard, and the eagle statue looked small and frail in the storm. I kept my focus on that statue, trying to ignore that I didn't want to see their reactions when I said the rest. "I used to like the chase, the thrill of going after a deal, landing it over everyone else. I liked getting people excited about a project. But lately, it seems... empty. Meaningless."

"Since my dad fucked with you." Luke's words weren't a question.

I turned back to him. "No. This has nothing to do with your father. It just happens to be how I've been feeling since then."

Matthew shifted to sit on the edge of the mattress. "You could always do something else." The bed was so tall that his feet weren't able to touch the floor. He'd taken off his shoes, and one of his socks hung off the ends of his toes. Despite how young that pose had him looking, there was a hopeful wisdom to his expression. It astounded me how he'd managed to stay so unjaded, to keep his optimistic outlook about life after everything he'd been through—his father's abuse, his loser ex-boyfriend who'd taken him for granted, and all the men at the Haven who'd used him and discarded him like he was trash. He made me want to be a better man.

I held his wide-eyed stare and let the words pour out without giving it too much thought. "I'd like to be more hands-on with this place. Maybe handle some investments on the side, but put more of my focus into getting this place up and going, help run the business side of things when it's open."

Matthew grinned at that.

Luke stepped forward and shrugged. "So, do it."

"You don't care?"

"What the fuck you do for a living? Absolutely not."

Matthew nodded in agreement. "We just want you to be happy."

"Right." Luke pointed at Matthew. "What he said." He hesitated, and then he threw me a smirk. "Well, if you became a prison guard at the Perkins Federal Correctional Institution, I might worry you had another motive."

"If I had a plan to hurt your father, he'd already be hurting."

Luke laughed. "Right."

Matthew had an entirely different reaction. He jumped off the bed and came to me. Wrapping his arms around my middle, he laid his head against my chest. "Don't even joke about that."

I held him close. "I'm not going anywhere near him." Over his head, I gave Luke a pointed look. "None of us are."

Chapter Ten

Luke eyed me for a long while as I held Matthew.

Finally he came to us. He gave me a quick kiss and said nothing more on the subject of his father. Instead he grinned and pulled Matthew backward toward the bed with him. "I'm beat. Let's see if we can all fit or if we gotta sleep on the damn floor."

We made the bed work. It was actually pretty comfortable, even without pillows. Yet, despite that, sometime in the middle of the night I was startled awake, my heart thundering away like someone had been attacking me in my sleep. It took me a minute to remember where we were and why the bed was smaller than usual.

The fire was crackling, burning low in the fireplace, and beams of moonlight lit the room and the lower half of the bed with a subtle glow that gave the moment a serene, romantic vibe that was in direct contrast to the tension I'd awoken with.

Matthew lay asleep on his stomach beside me, his arm draped across my middle, his head turned away from me toward Luke. Even with the fire, the room had been chilly when we went to bed so we'd slept in our clothes.

I remained still and waited, trying to decide if I'd been dreaming or if I'd actually heard something that had awoken me.

Then the bed shifted, and the blue blanket was yanked off Matthew and me.

Luke was lying on his back, breathing heavily, kicking at the blanket that was now bunched up at his feet. "No. Stop!" He bolted upright with a start.

I sat up and reached for him, laying a hand on his shoulder. "You okay?"

Matthew stirred. "Luke?"

"Yeah. Yeah, I'm fine." He shrugged off my touch, got up, and darted for the window. He jerked it open and braced himself on the frame, breathing deep as the crisp, fresh air assaulted the room.

I gave him a moment and was just about to go to him when he spoke, his back to us.

"I called the prison today. To ask about the procedure for visitation. The prisoner has to put all visitors' names on a list, which my father already did for me. Each visitor then has to be approved. I got the ball rolling on my approval, just in case."

"Luke." I swung my legs off the side of the bed and moved toward him, stopping at the foot of the bed. "No."

"I have to do this."

"It's only a way for him to stay in your life. To force you to keep in contact."

"That's just it." He faced me. "What if I need to see him? To see the truth."

"What truth?"

"If he's really trying. If he's different."

"Too bad if he is. He fucking wanted to kill you. There's no making up for that. Even if he hadn't pulled a gun on you, the way he's treated you all your life proves he doesn't deserve another shot at being your father. No matter what he says or does now, that doesn't mean he should be forgiven."

"That's not true." Matthew slid off the side of the bed closest to Luke. "If someone is trying to do the right thing, to make up for their mistakes, isn't that better than if he did nothing? If my dad came back—"

I jabbed a finger at him. "That fucker wouldn't be allowed near you." He'd have to come through me first.

Matthew's eyes widened. He stared at me, his mouth gaping. "He's not going to come see me. But I think I'd have to hear him out if he did."

"He had his chance to be your dad, and instead he beat you. Why don't the two of you get this?"

Matthew spoke with more force than he'd ever used with me. "I know what he did to me. I was there." He swallowed stiffly, and when he said the rest, he talked in a more subdued tone. "I'm just saying, I might have to see him. Not for him. For me."

These two were seriously attempting to kill me. I ran my hands over the top of my head and set to pacing the length of the bed opposite them, then forced myself to come to a standstill.

Luke sat on the edge of the windowsill, his arms folded across his chest. "That's why I have to do this. For me. And for you guys. Not for him. I have to be the one to tell him to leave us alone, to stop contacting me."

"You confronted him once before, and look where we are. Right back to him fucking with you. And that time you had FBI surveillance surrounding the place."

"He's in prison. I'm pretty sure he won't have a gun this time." He laughed, but when he saw Matthew and I weren't joining in, he stopped. He stood and struggled with the window a moment to get it closed. Then he faced us again. "I need closure."

"You think the dreams will just disappear because you talk to him?"

"If they don't, I'll go see someone. But this is what I have to do first."

I scrubbed a hand over the lower half of my face, searching for the right words. "I cannot tell you how much I hate this idea." I dropped to sit on the end of the bed. A part of me wanted to keep fighting him on it, but I also knew I had to let him make his own choices. I had learned my lesson the last time he went to see his father. "If you seriously think this is your only option…" I breathed deep. "I won't stand in the way of that." It was the best I could give him.

He didn't say anything. He just took off, rounded the bed, and went to the bathroom, slamming the door shut behind him. I heard the splashing of water.

"That's not what he wanted to hear." Matthew came to stand between my legs. With both thumbs he traced a path from the middle of my forehead outward as if wiping away the worry lines, and then he held my face in his hands. "He may not be able to put into words why, but he needs you on board with this. He needs you to believe it's a good idea."

I shook my head. "I can't do that."

Before Matthew could say anything more, Luke stormed into the room and stopped, closer to me this time, but he kept distance between us that I was not comfortable with. Matthew stepped aside and watched Luke, then me. I could practically feel the unease zipping through the air between the three of us.

I gripped Luke's hand and tugged on him until he sat beside me on the bed. "I don't want to see you make the wrong decision. What if he takes this as a sign to torment you even more? To torment us? Matthew? What if he sends someone after us again and this time the guy doesn't just hold a knife to Matthew's throat? Once you do this, you can't take it back. I don't want you to have to live with that kind of mistake, that kind of regret."

He jerked his hand away from me. "What do you know about

regrets? The kinds of mistakes you make don't even show up on most people's radar."

"What does that mean?"

"Everything you say and do comes out like you've practiced for that one moment your entire life."

That had me speechless. When I looked Matthew's way, he didn't say anything.

I turned back to Luke. "You don't think I'm genuine?"

"That's not what—" He waved a hand in the air like he was dismissing the entire conversation, but then he said, "You don't understand what it's like to regret something so bad, you'd do anything—*anything*—to take it back."

I wanted to tell them about Anne and what I'd let happen to her, but this was about Luke. He had to know I was behind him if he really felt he needed to go see his father, but I was struggling to find a way to say that without lying to him.

Before I could formulate the words, Luke stood and traversed the room once more. He stared out the window, his body held tight. It was a stoic stance mixed with that vulnerability he rarely let out.

I went to him, wrapped both arms around him, and held him from behind, my chin resting on his shoulder. When he didn't respond or relax, I shifted to stand between him and the window. "Luke."

"It's okay. I get it." Suddenly, and with urgency, he grabbed me by the hips and pulled me to him. It was a long, drawn-out kiss that wasn't about passion, but about saying more than either of us had managed to get out that night.

Yet I needed to give him more.

With my forehead against his temple, I said, "I can't lie about what I feel. I don't want you to see your dad, but I get that you have to make your own decision on this."

He shook his head as if that still wasn't enough.

I tightened my grip on his waist and gave him a slight shake. "Hey."

He stepped out of my touch and moved away from me, heading for the bed. "Let's just get some sleep."

He wasn't hearing me, wasn't getting what I was trying to tell him.

I charged forward and spun him to face me, then turned us and backed him to the narrow space between the fireplace and the window so he had nowhere to go, so he had to focus on me.

"I just don't want him to hurt you. You and Matthew, happy and safe. That's all that matters to me."

"He won't hurt me. Because this time I'm not waiting to see what he'll try next."

"Right. Because you're in control of your life now." I tilted my head back in exasperation and then tossed him a smile. "You're so damn stubborn."

His eyes went wide. "Me?"

That had Matthew laughing. We both looked at him, and he fell backward onto the middle of the bed and laughed harder.

I eyed Luke again.

The look on his face lightened as he watched Matthew over my shoulder. Then he asked, "What's he find so funny?"

"I have no idea."

"I'm glad we can amuse him."

"Yeah." I shot another glance at Matthew over my shoulder. "He's awfully sexy when he laughs like that."

That had Matthew quiet. He rolled onto his side and stared at us in return.

I turned back to Luke, bent forward, and whispered against his ear. "We're damn lucky he's ours."

"We are."

I held him tighter. "I'm behind you, no matter what you want to do."

He nodded, gripped the back of my head, and brought our lips together again. This kiss was soft and slow and seemed to be about Luke speaking to me with his mouth in a way he was far more comfortable with, and I accepted it, accepted him as he needed to be right then. But when we parted, he said, "I'm not sure what I want to do yet. I don't *want* to play into his hand."

"You'll know when you've made the right decision for you. When you can honestly say it has nothing to do with him." Precisely what Luke had been saying, and the exact opposite of what I'd been telling him. I wanted him to stay away from his father *because* of his dad and what he might do.

A grin formed on Luke's face that indicated he had come to the same conclusion.

"See?" I said. "I don't always get everything right the first time."

The grin grew, and his body relaxed. He looked so damn beautiful, so sexy leaning there against the wall in the moonlight, a bit of dark stubble on his face, an undeniable strength and passion in those blue eyes.

"God, I love you." I came forward, pressing him to the wall with the weight of my body, and he held me in return. His breath hitched as

I kissed a line up the side of his neck. Without delay he arched against me, his body begging for more of my touch.

Another kiss, and another, and I worked my way toward his mouth. "You want to know a secret?"

"Tell me." His breath caressed my lips. The look on his face held a note of desperation, like there was something he needed to hear, needed to feel, or maybe something he wanted to ask me. Before I could say anything, he clutched at me, pulling me even closer as if he knew what I was about to tell him. "I need you," he whispered. From that first night we'd met, he'd always heard me best with my touch, more than my words.

I offered him a smile and said, "I have waited fifteen years to have sex in this house."

"You have, huh?" He arched into my touch again, keeping the fierce hold on me.

"I have. And I wasn't just waiting until I owned the place. I was waiting for the right person."

Luke licked his lips, and without turning away I called Matthew to us.

But Matthew remained quiet, and there was no sound of him moving toward us. Without seeing him, though, I knew we had his full attention. "Touch yourself," I said and then leaned in and kissed Luke. On the mouth that time. The stubble on his chin scraped my own, and the dual masculinity of that contact kicked my desire up another notch. I dropped a kiss on the tip of that sexy chin, then went lower, enjoying the catch of his breath once more with my tongue's touch to the base of his throat. I kissed lower and lower, eventually sliding to my knees before him. He gripped the back of my head and gave me one last long look, then focused his attention across the room to Matthew. I could only imagine the delicious things he was witnessing.

When I asked Matthew to do something in bed, he did it.

I slipped my hands under Luke's shirt and pushed it up, massaging his chest. "Take this off."

He did, all without looking away from Matthew.

I got the zipper down on Luke's jeans next. "You too cold for this?"

He shook his head and helped me strip away his jeans and underwear.

Still on my knees, I gazed up at him. "You know what Edward Harrison said to me that night I came here for his last party, when I told him I hoped to buy this house? He said he was disgusted thinking about what a faggot like me could do in his family's home."

Luke shifted his attention to me. He caressed my cheek with his thumb. "Then I can see why you were so determined to have this place."

I heard Matthew move off the bed. He came up alongside us, one hand running over my nape, the other stroking Luke's bare arm. Matthew was wearing his underwear and nothing else, the front of the fabric already moist with his arousal. He said, "I say we show him what three men can do." He bent down and kissed me, his lips parting as soon as we made contact, and then he offered the same to Luke.

I wanted nothing more than to shove them onto the bed and fuck them both, but I was never a fan of going at it with just a little spit to smooth the way.

That didn't mean I couldn't give us all a night to remember.

After all, I was a damn talented faggot.

I met Luke's gaze again. "You might not want to be standing for this." I didn't give him time to react. I lifted one of his legs over my shoulder, slicked a finger with my spit, and swept it along the skin behind his balls while I took his cock into my mouth.

"Holy shit." His body shook immediately and with urgency as I swallowed him down.

Matthew slid in between the wall and Luke, then eased them to the floor so Luke was leaning back between Matthew's spread legs. I upped the intensity, stroking and sucking, and they watched me go to town on Luke's cock, all while Matthew ran his hands over Luke's bare chest, tweaking his nipples just how Luke liked whenever he was getting blown or fucked. With Luke's leg still over my shoulder, I kept my finger moving along his sensitive skin, teasing him, torturing him with that one touch. I wanted to fuck that gorgeous ass of his, but I remained focused on his dick.

"Oh man... that's... beautiful." Matthew's words were punctuated by ragged inhales.

I released Luke's prick. "You think that's good? Watch him when I do this." I took Luke deep again and glided my finger farther back, over and around his opening. With one quick movement, I drove inside his ass and pegged his gland. Luke arched and groaned a long series of guttural noises, gripping Matthew's bare thighs in both hands.

"Oh God." That was Matthew. I would've thought it was his ass and dick I worked over by the way he sounded, like he was about ready to explode. It was moments like that when I wished I had more hands, another mouth. It was frustrating as hell not being able to suck them both off, to at least touch Matthew.

Then Matthew, in his infinite wisdom, made contact with me. As if he'd read my mind, he placed a hand at the back of my head. He was barely able to reach, but it was enough I could feel him, feel them both. It was like walking through that spot on the beach where the sea and land came together in a beautiful roll of the surf.

It wasn't long and Matthew's hand trembled. He moaned and thrust his hips forward, and I knew he was coming just from watching us as he moved against Luke.

Then it was Luke's turn. He was close. I was intimately familiar with his every sound, with every shift of his body. I continued pegging his prostate, stroking his shaft with my hand as I swept my mouth along him. He shuddered, and that was it. He was climaxing, spurting into me, and I swallowed it down, not stopping until he had given over the last drop of his release.

Only then did I let him go. I fell back onto my heels and rushed to get my dick out, fumbling with my pants until I grasped my aching erection. I hauled Luke toward me by the back of his neck, stroked myself, my hand flying over my flesh, and came on him, painting his lips with my cum.

When I'd wrung myself dry, Luke collapsed back against Matthew, and Matthew turned Luke's head to the side to kiss him, hard and deep. The kiss was sloppy, all tongue and passion, despite that they'd both already gotten off, like just tasting my release between them was enough to get them going again.

But then as they parted, Luke drifted into that after-climax fog of his. I leaned forward and kissed Matthew, loving the taste of both Luke and me on him.

He said, "That was amazing."

"Yeah? You liked watching that?"

"Uh-huh."

When Luke returned to us from that sated place he'd gone, he glanced down at himself. He was slumped against Matthew, naked, cum on his chin and chest. He looked debauched and thoroughly fucked. "How the hell am I naked and you two are still dressed?"

I laughed. "It's okay. I'm pretty sure Matthew's gotta ditch the underwear and go commando in the morning."

That had Matthew laughing with me.

Luke too. But then he grew serious. That desperate expression was back on his face, in his blue eyes. When he spoke, his voice was unsteady, and he held his entire body perfectly still. "You ever regret walking over to our table that first night at the Haven? Knowing what you do now? About my father? About everything?"

It wasn't like him to ask something like that, to sound so insecure.

Maybe he did need more than my touch. Maybe he needed the words, needed to know that we wouldn't lose this connection between us.

"Never," I said and cupped his cheek. "No matter what your dad has done, or what he might do." I drew him into my arms, then tugged on Matthew until it was the three of us together, sprawled on the floor as one. "There has not been one moment that I've regretted that night at the Haven."

* * * *

I awoke the next morning to the warm glow of the early sun cascading over the blankets that lay across the three of us. Arching my spine, I stretched, and Matthew shifted his head my way. He continued sleeping, though, even as a soft rap sounded on the bedroom door. I slipped out of bed and took a quick look out the window. The snow had stopped coming down, but the wind whipped the remaining white stuff around like mad, which meant we probably wouldn't be going anywhere right away. I crossed the room and opened the door to find Dominic waiting in the hall.

"Mr. Marshall, you have a visitor."

The formality with which he spoke caught me off guard, and then his words sank in. "Someone's here?"

"A Mr. Terence Kinkaid is waiting for you downstairs."

"He specifically asked for me? Like he knew I was here?"

"Yes," Dominic said. "Is he the same Kinkaid who owns half this city?"

"That's him."

"He has two men with him. They're outside waiting."

"In the snow?"

He nodded. "They look like bodyguards."

"I'm sure they are. Could you tell him I'll be down shortly?"

"Certainly." Dominic went to leave but then stopped. "He wants the estate, doesn't he?"

"Yes."

The nervous disappointment on Dominic's face wasn't hard to miss. He gave a nod and dashed off.

I closed the door, woke Luke and Matthew, and once they were up and out of bed, I filled them in on the details.

Luke tugged one of the blankets off the bed and wound it into a ball. "Isn't this the guy who's always stealing deals out from under you?"

"That's the one."

He chucked the blanket onto the bed. "I don't like this. How did he know he'd find you here? Especially in this weather?"

"I don't know." There was no reason for Kinkaid to assume I'd be staying at the estate.

"What does he want?" Matthew asked. He already stood by the door, like he wanted me to understand he had every intention of going down there with me. "To invest in the restorations?"

"No. Kinkaid never comes on board someone else's project."

"So what's his agenda?" Luke asked.

"He's the one who made the offer to buy me out, but I've told him no. On several occasions. I doubt I'm going to want to hear what he's offering this time."

A few minutes later we headed downstairs, the oil lantern I carried lighting the way down the dark staircase. Dominic waited at the bottom of the stairs. He gestured to the double doors across the foyer. "He's in the library."

"Thank you." I turned to Luke and Matthew. "Why don't you all go wait in the solarium? This won't take long."

Luke gave me an exasperated look. He gestured for Matthew to follow with a tip of his head. "Come on."

I eyed him sharply as they proceeded by me toward the library.

"Don't worry," Luke added. "We'll wait outside the door."

A moment later they did just that as I stepped into the library. The drapes on the two windows had been pulled back so more light bathed that room than any other, and a fire was going in the fireplace. Kinkaid was examining the leather-bound books on the shelves. He moved in a slow sideways step, taking in the titles, and didn't glance my way as I closed the door. He had his overcoat draped across one arm. His dark hair was slicked back, and he appeared remarkably crisp and unaffected by the storm outside. The charcoal-gray three-piece suit with a purple tie and a matching silk scarf around his neck made him look as if he was heading to a wedding. Or a runway during Paris Fashion Week.

Standing there in the library, he had a blasé demeanor about him that unnerved me more than his showing up unannounced and uninvited.

I set the oil lamp on the desk. "Terence, it's nice to see you."

Without turning to face me, he said, "I'm sure it is."

Asshole. "Can I ask how you knew I'd be here?"

"There's not much I don't know." He rounded to face me, an amused grin on his lips. "And the fact that you don't realize that proves just why I've always liked you. You are one smart businessman, Richard, but you're not ruthless. You care. Maybe too much. But that's made you an interesting"—he tipped his head back and tapped a finger to his lips as if searching for the right word—"adversary. You never bore me like so many others."

"I'm glad I could amuse you." *Asshole* wasn't feeling like a strong enough descriptor. "Now what can I do for you?"

He returned to examining the books and ran the tips of his fingers along the spines as if appreciating the collection, which was odd. He was more the type to admire a restored 1957 Chevrolet Bel Air than a leather-bound copy of *A Christmas Carol* by Charles Dickens. "I'd like to discuss why you won't accept my latest offer. It was quite generous."

It had been. Twenty percent above what I'd paid for the place. "As I said before, the estate is not for sale."

He turned to face me, and with his arms out at his sides, he gestured to nothing in particular. "Everything's for sale."

"Not everything."

He laughed at that. "See? Right there." He pointed at me. "Most men know that's not true. But not you." He paused and lowered his hand, almost as if he realized he wasn't going about this the right way. "Can I be frank?"

"I'd prefer it."

His arrogance slipped away, and he seemed genuine for the first time since I'd met him. He gestured at the chairs by the desk, and we sat across from each other.

"Listen," he started, "I can be a jackass. I won't even try to deny that, but I was sincere when I said I've always liked you, and not just because you *amuse* me. You're a good guy, Richard. So let me turn off my competitor mode and give you some friendly advice." He laid his coat over the arm of the chair and sat back, his legs crossed. "There are others who are going to do whatever they have to in order to get their hands on this estate, and they will not take no for an answer. They will not be as patient as I've been."

I considered him. He *was* being sincere. "Why this house? What are they after? What are *you* after?"

"It's not the house." He picked a piece of lint off the knee of one pant leg and flicked the speck onto the floor. Was he stalling? Pondering what he should—or should not—say? He uncrossed his legs, leaned in, and spoke low as if telling me the next part would get him kicked out of some secret club for arrogant millionaires. "It's one specific item that's on the property. An item I've wanted for a very long time. I—and I'm sure the others—only recently learned it was in Griff Harrison's possession at the time he died, or I would've made an offer to Edward years ago. I'm willing to give you far above what you paid so long as you leave everything here and sell me the property, the house, and all its contents."

I didn't want him to realize I was unaware of what the item could be. If I asked, he wouldn't tell me anyway. He'd keep the upper hand for as long as he could. I decided to play the odds. "Since we're being frank. You and I both know your offer wouldn't come close to covering what I'd be giving up."

For the first time since we'd started talking, and despite his earlier words, he studied me as if I were a smarter foe than he'd expected. Or maybe he was trying to figure out what I did or did not know.

He said, "Then you realize that it should not be hidden away. The world needs to know about it. It's not meant to be a secret. It never should've been."

I kept quiet.

"Okay," he said. "I'll give you thirty percent over your purchase price."

I stared back at him, said nothing.

"Forty."

I held still, not wanting to show any reaction.

He sat back and confidently eyed me as if what he was about to say would change my mind. "The others will use whatever means necessary to acquire the item. Including getting *you* out of the way."

When I still said nothing, he slapped his hands on his thighs and rose. "All right, then." The arrogance was back. It radiated off him. Was this how I looked to people who turned me down? He laid the coat over his arm and smoothed the fabric. Perhaps waiting for me to change my mind. When I didn't, he met my stare. "Don't say I didn't warn you." He headed for the door and didn't wait for me. He moved out into the entryway and kept on going.

I got up and followed, with Luke and Matthew stepping in beside me once I passed where they'd been waiting by the door.

"Did you get all that?" I asked in a whisper low enough Kinkaid wouldn't overhear.

Luke gave a nod.

Kinkaid had stopped in the center of the foyer. He had his overcoat on and he was staring at Dominic, who stood halfway up the main staircase. Kinkaid spoke to him as if he knew him. "You should encourage him to listen to me, to take my deal." Then he stalked off, not even bothering to close the front door behind him. Like a ghost, he disappeared into the whirl of snow, his men in tow. The howl of wind rushing through the open door penetrated the silence left in his wake.

I went to the door and slammed it shut, then spun around and pointed up at Dominic. "You. Start talking. What's he after?"

"I don't know what he wants, what any of them want." He looked—and sounded—about ready to panic. "But they will do anything to get it. They'll destroy this place. And you if they have to."

I threw my hands up. "You're full of useful information."

Matthew gave me a quizzical look. He offered the same to Dominic. "If you don't know what they want, how did you even know they're coming for it?"

Dominic didn't say anything.

I took a step closer to the staircase. "Because Edward Harrison told you so before he died."

Dominic's lips quivered like he wasn't sure what to say to get out of having to admit the truth. He finally nodded. "Edward said people connected with the men who killed Griff would be coming to find whatever it was that Griff hid from them, and that they would destroy the house trying to find it. He said I would be the only one left who could protect this place."

"So Griff…" Matthew started.

When he didn't finish, Luke added, "He was killed because he hid something that didn't belong to him?"

"No. Whatever he hid, it was his. According to Edward the men who killed Griff had been threatening him. But he wouldn't give them what they wanted. Not long before he died, he confided in Edward about whatever it was he had, and he said that no matter what, he wouldn't sell it to anyone."

I shook my head in exasperation. "And you still want me to believe you don't know what it is?"

"I don't."

Matthew glanced my way, and I gave him a nod, encouraging him to ask his next question.

"Why didn't anyone come looking for whatever Griff hid after he died? Why wait so long to try to find it?"

"Edward said everyone who knew of its existence assumed Griff must not have had it since he never gave it to those men. I guess they didn't think he'd die to protect it. They assumed the item had been sold to someone else, and they've been combing the world for it. Then before Edward died, he found out someone named Fitzwater was getting close to learning the truth. If one person knew, it was bound to get out, and everyone would know."

Everyone but me—the guy who owned the place.

"What truth?" I asked.

"That whatever Griff had was still here at the estate. But Edward was dying. He knew he couldn't do anything about it. That's why he said I had to be the one to keep the house safe."

"So if he thought these people might destroy the estate to get at whatever Griff hid, why didn't Edward just give them what they wanted, or sell it to them so they'd leave the house alone?"

"I asked him the same thing." Dominic gripped the banister before him in both hands. "I begged him to tell me what it was that Griff had so I could get rid of it, but he wouldn't. He said no one was getting their hands on it."

"Sounds like Edward Harrison," Luke offered. "So how did this Fitzwater person figure out that the item was here?"

Dominic shook his head. "I don't know."

I laughed. It was exactly as I'd imagined. "Fitzwater found out from Edward."

Dominic started down the steps, shaking his head as he went. "No. Edward wouldn't do that. He was trying to keep it a secret."

"Right. Until he was near death. Then he made sure I got the house, and he let certain people in on the fact that what Griff hid before he died was still here. So they'd come after this place, come after me. Because whatever Griff had…"

When I didn't finish, Dominic spoke again, looking very resigned. "It's yours now. You bought the house. Everything here is yours."

"Hey." Luke came to me and elbowed me in the arm. "You own something worth killing someone for, only you don't know what the hell it is."

"Or where it's at," Matthew said.

I nodded. "Or who all's coming for it."

Matthew and Luke watched me as I contemplated that, and it hit me then what I needed to do. No matter what was really going on, I would not bring any sort of danger into their lives.

I had two choices. Sell the house to Kinkaid and get Matthew and Luke away from the estate. Or find whatever it was that Griff hid and get it out of the house, sell it to the highest bidder in a public way so everyone would know it was long gone from the Harrison Estate.

Luke must've been thinking along the same lines. "We've got to find whatever it was that Griff had. Before they try to *force* you to sell."

Matthew came to stand beside Luke. "But how do we figure out what they want? Or where it's at?"

Luke glanced around the entranceway, at the doors to the library, then down the main hall. "We should take a look, inventory what's here—"

"I want you two to head home."

Luke recoiled at my words. I'd hurt his feelings. One look at Matthew's equally wounded expression, and I knew they didn't want me tackling this on my own.

I hated that, but I wasn't about to get them involved, and if they weren't leaving me to handle this alone, then... "Why don't we all get out of here? Kinkaid's new offer is at least worth considering."

There was no missing the disappointment on their faces.

Dominic had grown quiet again, arms folded across his chest as he took in our exchange, and then he said, "I'm beginning to see how it is with you three."

I glared at him. "What does that mean?"

"You know..." He gestured between the three of us. "Your roles in your relationship." He pointed at me. "You've always gotta be the one in charge. Don't you ever let them make a decision on their own? Don't you ever take their thoughts or feelings into consideration? Don't you ever listen to their advice? Or are they just your playthings?"

"Watch it, old man. You have no idea what you're talking about."

He raised his bushy eyebrows. "Looks like I hit a nerve."

Matthew was shaking his head. "That's not true. He always listens to us."

Dominic's smirk faded. He came at me with such force I wasn't convinced of his eighty-five years. He stopped short of making contact and jabbed a finger at me. "If you really wanted to know what Kinkaid and the others are after, you'd be able to figure it out."

I was catching on now. He was hoping to piss me off so I'd feel backed into a corner and come out fighting. He was manipulating me, and he was succeeding.

Luke chuckled. "Man, he's got your number."

I frowned at him.

He just kept on grinning. "Well, it's working, isn't it? Don't tell me all this doesn't piss you off? People trying to force you into doing something you don't want to do? There's no way you want to give up.

You don't want to sell to Kinkaid just because he tells you to. You want to be the one to find out what Griff hid in this house."

Apparently I was obvious to everyone.

I moved toward the main hallway and stopped, my back to them. "You three are driving me nuts."

Luke came up behind me and wrapped an arm around my waist. That touch alone had the frustration dissipating. He said, "That's because we're right." He kissed my cheek. "Come on. Let's figure out where Griff might've stashed this secret item."

I turned and held his gaze for a moment. I desperately wanted to leave them out of this, but he was right. I wasn't about to sell because some asshole walked onto my property and tried to coerce me into it.

"Okay. We'll have a look before we leave." I faced Dominic. "Guess it's time for you to give us the grand tour."

Chapter Eleven

"This is stupid." Dominic came to a stop in the middle of the enormous kitchen and glared down at the marble countertop of the center island. An iron pot rack hung directly overhead, a pot on every hook. The frustration rolled off Dominic, and I thought he might grab one of those pots and take a swing at me. Instead he sighed and said, "You're wasting your time. There's so much left in this house. You'll never know what they want by just looking around."

Probably. But I said, "It's my time to waste."

We had planned to begin our search in the basement since Dominic had said that Griff had stored a lot of items down there, but before we'd left the foyer, Dominic stubbornly refused to move or answer more questions until I promised I wouldn't go breaking down the house's walls or tearing up the floors. I assured him I just wanted to do as thorough a search as I could manage, focusing on Griff's personal effects, and then go through the house, room by room, checking every possible hiding place Dominic could think of. He'd silently agreed, grumbling under his breath as he headed for the kitchen.

Now frozen in place again, he said, "You should get Kinkaid and any others to back off some other way."

"With or without your help, I'm searching this house."

"Fine. But we're not going to be able to figure anything out like this."

"It's a place to start."

He studied me. "You don't believe any of this, do you?" He seemed hurt by that. "Kinkaid is not lying. He will not stop. None of them will."

Maybe. But I just wasn't one hundred percent convinced that what they were after was actually in the house. It could still be a part of Edward's plan.

I told Dominic, "It's nothing personal. I trust what I can see. So why don't we have a look?"

He harrumphed but got moving again, going for the far side of the kitchen.

Luke followed, and Matthew went to do the same, but then he stopped beside me and slipped a hand into mine. "I can't wait to see what's left from Griff's life."

I gave him a nod. "I'm kinda curious myself."

I had been all through the estate when I'd first toured the property after Edward listed it for sale, but I couldn't recall the specifics of the items in the basement. Just that it had been full of crates and trunks. I hadn't bothered to take a closer look.

Until now.

We advanced as a group down the narrow staircase off the kitchen, Dominic and the light from our flashlights guiding our way.

The basement contained a series of large stone rooms that covered the full length and width of the house. It was dark and cold but dry, with low ceilings. Even with our flashlights and the sporadic ground-level windows that ran along the top of the walls, it was difficult to see into the corners, and the scuffling of our feet echoed as we progressed farther into the abyss.

The first room contained two pairs of industrial washers and dryers and a worktable, bracketed by a set of freestanding wooden shelves. The laundry machines were modern enough they had to have been installed no more than a few years before Edward moved out. The table was positioned directly under an opening for a laundry chute. There wasn't much else to the space. All the shelves were bare. Dust was the only thing that covered every surface.

We filed into the next room and found it the exact opposite of the one before. A narrow walkway provided the only access through the maze of trunks and wooden crates. Cloth tarps draped several pieces of furniture. The taller items stood like ghosts guarding the sea of treasures.

"Is this all Griff's?" Matthew asked.

"Almost all of it." Trepidation filled Dominic's voice, like he dreaded the task of going through everything.

Matthew got on his knees and opened the closest trunk, dust wafting up as the lid was disturbed for what was probably the first time in decades. He tugged out a leather gun belt with double holsters that housed two revolvers and bullets in the loops on the belt. The entire thing looked like it could've been straight out of an old western. "Is this from one of his movies?"

Dominic nodded. "A lot of this is. He usually got to keep a few props from each film. Back then the studios didn't auction off every last item for a buck like they do now."

Matthew pulled open a second trunk, and Luke did the same beside him, while I found a crowbar on a nearby shelf and pried open a crate. Inside were several swords, an FBI badge, three passports, a bundle of fake cash, and clothing from various time periods, including a uniform for a World War II US Army officer.

Luke held up a tattered red, white, and blue flag that had only thirteen stars and had bullet holes riddling much of the fabric. "I bet this is from that Revolutionary War movie he made. Damn, some of this shit should be in a film museum or something." He put the flag back and inspected another garment. "Some of this could be worth a lot of money."

"Could be," I said. "But..."

"What?"

"Whatever Kinkaid's after has to be worth a lot more than a prop from a movie made in the fifties or sixties." I glanced at the flag Luke had returned to the trunk. "Maybe something in here isn't really a prop. Maybe it's the real deal."

Matthew had continued on to another trunk. "How are we going to know?"

"I'll have to get an appraiser to take a look. Here in the basement and throughout the rest of the house."

"No." Dominic still stood in the corner of the room near the open doorway. "No one else is going through all this. It's staying here."

I hated having to tell him. He seemed so genuinely upset by the idea. "You do realize I can't keep all this down here forever, right?"

"No." He shook his head, coming farther into the room, reaching out as if he could gather all the crates and trunks into his arms. "It stays here."

"Hold on." I gestured for him to take it easy. "I'm not just going to toss it out. I can see if there's a museum that's interested." I indicated the crates beside me. "And you can let me know what you'd like to keep."

He said nothing to that, but it seemed to calm him some.

I moved on to one of the trunks. More movie props and costumes. Despite what I'd said about having everything evaluated, I thought it unlikely that something valuable would've been left unlocked down in the basement with Griff's other items.

Just then a cool draft blew across the back of my neck. A scratching sound followed. I turned, but there was nothing there, just another tarp-covered piece of furniture. Something narrow and tall. Maybe an elaborate coat rack.

The scratching started again. Louder this time. It was definitely coming from behind the tarp. I raised my flashlight, but I couldn't see through the thick material.

"Shhh," Matthew said from where he and Luke were searching a trunk together. "Do you hear that?"

Luke stopped digging through the items.

I gestured with the flashlight. "It's coming from over here."

The scratching continued.

Luke stood and was beside me in an instant. He grabbed my arm, like he wanted to keep me from moving closer to the sound. But I had to take a look.

I yanked down the dust-covered tarp. Underneath was a man my height, his arms folded across his chest, eyes open and locked on me. Luke and I both recoiled a step, until I realized the man wasn't moving. He was frozen in that pose, those brown eyes never blinking.

I reached out and felt the back of his hand. "It's a wax figure."

"Now…" Luke pointed at it. "That's just spooky."

Matthew rushed toward us. "That's Griff."

"Really?" I studied the figure closely and recognized Griff from the few movies I'd seen. He had dark brown hair, cropped close, and an intense but warm look in his eyes. Like a combination of Luke's and Matthew's eyes. The representation of Griff wore a similar WWII uniform as the one I'd seen earlier. His chin was lifted, and his entire posture radiated a man in command. Of himself and his troops.

"That's him," Dominic said softly from behind us. "There are two more of those wax figures down here somewhere. Wearing costumes from different movies, but they're all Griff."

The scratching sound, which had stopped when I'd tossed aside the fabric, began again.

Luke gripped my arm once more and jerked me back a step. "What is that?"

"Just the wind." I pointed to the window above us. There was a gap along the outer edge of the warped wooden frame, and behind the figure of Griff hung a Native American dream catcher. Suspended on a nail, it rubbed against the stone wall with each gust of air.

"Jesus." Luke practically breathed the word.

"That scare you?"

"Shit, yeah."

And yet he'd stayed with me, to protect me. I grasped him by the back of the neck and planted a hard, chaste kiss on his lips.

"What was that for?"

"You being you."

I caught Dominic watching us with marked curiosity.

"What?" I asked.

"So the three of you… you know…" He waggled his eyebrows. "All together?"

"Yeah."

"How does that work?"

"Quite nicely." When he gave me another inquisitive look, I added, "I fell in love with both of them. There was no other option for me."

"No," he said. "I meant the sex."

Matthew chuckled from where he had returned to kneeling on the floor before a trunk.

Luke went to speak, and I held up a hand. "Don't." Who knew how detailed he'd get? "It's none of your business," I told Dominic.

"I didn't mean to offend you. I just… A lot of people have trouble imagining two men together. I'm not entirely sure I get how three guys can…" His eyes widened, and he gestured with a hand between Luke and Matthew and me. "All at once."

Luke went to say something again, but I beat him to it.

"We're done with this conversation. Let's get back to the search." I moved on to another crate, and Luke joined me.

Matthew opened the trunk before him. "It'll take forever to go through all this."

He was right. I returned the lid to the crate when I found more movie memorabilia inside. "Let's go have a look at the rest of the house and see if we can find any hiding places where something could've been stashed away for fifty years."

"Uh, Richard," Luke said. "This place is beautiful, but it's also a creepy old mansion. I'm pretty sure there's a ton of places like that."

"And," Dominic said, "we don't know how big it is. It could be the size of a coin. Or even smaller."

Matthew stood. "Maybe we'll get lucky."

I offered him a smile in thanks, and we made our way back up the staircase by the kitchen. We paused the search long enough for a quick bite to eat when Dominic said he could scrounge together something from his stash of canned goods. Matthew also took the time to make a phone call. He wanted to see if Walter and his boyfriend Kevin could head to our house and check in on the puppies. Once Walter had Matthew convinced the roads had been cleared enough that they could safely head over to our town house, we continued our search, proceeding through the rest of the estate room by room, Dominic directing us to obscure storage spaces and closets. We looked through additional trunks and on shelves. We checked for loose boards in the floors and hidden compartments in the built-in bookshelves. We inspected the stairs for treads that could be lifted up. Luke even examined the numerous fireplaces, using his phone's camera to get a peek farther inside.

With Griff's items in the basement, the tapestries on the walls, the slew of china in the kitchen, and the various knickknacks all over the house, I was beginning to wonder if perhaps Griff had hidden the object in plain sight. A lot of items in the house could be worth more than they appeared at first glance. I would definitely have to get someone to review everything.

As we searched, Dominic watched our interactions more than he helped. I tried to imagine how he saw us. He didn't seem to be judging our relationship. He was more curious than anything else.

When we finished with the last room on the third floor, I asked him, "What's in the attic? More movie stuff?"

"No. Personal items from the Harrison family. Some of it's Griff's. Most of his stuff from the master suite was moved up there after his funeral."

"All right. Let's take a look, and then we're calling it a day."

Dominic led us to a closet at the end of the hall. Inside was an access door. We made our way up the steps and into the attic.

The space was roomy enough we could stand comfortably, but it was even colder than the basement. And dustier. The entire attic smelled of stale air and something like incense.

There were stacks of crates, suitcases, and more trunks. Nothing looked like it had been disturbed in a very long time. The crates we opened contained primarily clothes and books, and the trunks were the same, with family scrapbooks and photo albums mixed in. Along the back wall of the attic were several framed paintings, mostly portraits and landscapes.

I pointed to the paintings, and Dominic said, "Those aren't worth much. That's why Edward had them taken down. Griff liked to support local unknown artists. He'd buy a few each year and hang the pieces all over the house."

But maybe one of them was worth something in today's market. Another thing to have checked out.

We continued searching. Dominic chatted as we worked, telling Matthew story after story about the Harrisons and their eccentric parties, about the ones Griff threw that were elaborate yet intimate. Eventually he grew quiet.

I turned to see what was up. He was intently studying Luke and Matthew.

The two of them were wearing sunglasses they'd found in one of the trunks. The aviator pair Matthew had on was too large for his face and made him look like a kid trying on his dad's glasses. Luke was laughing at him, and I knew what Matthew was about to do in return.

He lunged for Luke and tickled his sides, and that had Luke squirming to get away from him. They leaped to their feet, and Matthew chased Luke, both of them circling the section of trunks they'd been searching through.

"They do that a lot?" Dominic asked as I stepped up to him.

"What?"

"Take things so casually?"

I wouldn't have described it that way. If anything, the two of them took things too seriously sometimes.

I looked to Dominic. "They're not taking this lightly. None of us are."

He was quiet for another moment, then asked, "Do you think if you can figure out what everyone wants, you'd also be able to find out who killed Griff?"

"Don't you suppose whoever did would be long gone by now?"

Dominic held his arms out at his sides. "I'm still here."

"True. Maybe once we know what they were after that night, we can talk to the police."

"Hey," Matthew called out. "Check this out. There's something in here." He was back to kneeling on the floor. A section of the baseboard was missing, exposing a narrow hole that he'd probably only seen because he'd been crawling around from trunk to trunk. He reached in and pulled out a flat wooden box. He removed the lid, revealing dozens of envelopes. He slid a sheet of paper from one. "They're letters." After examining it more closely, he removed a second one. "They're for Griff." He read it aloud. "*Dearest Griff. I hate being away from you. I wish you were here. I wish I was holding you in my arms again. There is no one who eases the pain, who silences my fears the way you do. Please tell me you'll be coming back soon. I can't bear another long winter's night without you. I ache to touch you again, to kiss you once more. Always, your love.*" Matthew laid the letter on his lap. "Wow." He practically sighed the word.

"Told you," Dominic said. "They were amazing together. It was like a real-life version of his more romantic movies."

"I bet," Matthew said around another sigh.

Luke ruffled Matthew's hair from where he stood behind him. "What did I tell you? Such a sap."

"Shut up." Matthew swiped at Luke's hand that was still running through his dark hair.

"Our sap," I added, unable to keep the grin at bay.

"Yep." Luke tilted Matthew's head back and planted a kiss on his lips.

Dominic had grown quiet again as he watched our exchange. He looked tired and worn out. The search had taken hours and none of us had eaten anything since the rushed breakfast earlier. The entire day had probably been more physical activity than Dominic had done in a long while, even if he did get around better than people ten years younger.

He moved farther down the row of items where we'd already searched and sat on the edge of a trunk. He stared off at nothing in particular along the far wall, his face drawn with exhaustion and something like sadness. It had likely been our banter that had gotten to him. It had to be hard being alone for so many years after his wife and daughter had died.

I glanced at Luke and Matthew. "Let's call it a day. Dominic may be right. Whatever Griff had, it could be anywhere. It could be an item we've already seen. Or it could even be buried somewhere on the property. The only way we have a shot of finding it is if we know what we're looking for."

Matthew picked up the box of letters. "We should read through these." His expression turned sheepish, like he'd suggested digging up Griff's grave. "I mean, maybe there's something in here that'll help us figure out what he had."

"Sure," I said. "Sounds good."

Dominic was looking our way now. "Can you return them when you're done? If Griff wanted them hidden there, I think that's where they should stay."

I couldn't bring myself to remind him all the items we'd been going through would eventually have to be removed from the house, so I kept quiet.

"I will," Matthew said. "What do we do next?"

"I'll come back tomorrow with someone who can appraise everything in the house." I turned to Dominic. "Is there any place else you can think of to look?"

He seemed to be considering it. "No."

"Did Griff or the other Harrisons have a safe for their valuables?"

"There were three safes. Two of them were wall safes, but those were removed long ago. I don't know where the third one was located. I don't think I ever saw it, but it was added when Griff lived here." He had a frustrated, embarrassed look on his face, like he should've been able to remember more. He shook his head. "Edward probably had it torn out a long time ago."

"It's something to check into. Someone had to have installed it for Griff."

"I can dig into that," Luke offered. "I can also do some checking for building plans. See if any of the remodeling projects blocked off old hallways or closets that Griff might've been able to access back then."

"You know what we should do?" Matthew said. "Look into Griff's life. What he was doing right before he died, where he traveled, what major purchases he made, what other people he'd been spending time with, stuff like that." He glanced at Dominic.

"I..." Dominic dropped his head, shame radiating off him. "I can't remember those sorts of details. I'm sorry."

Understandable. It was several decades ago. Even someone younger would have trouble with that level of recall.

"It's okay," Matthew said. "I've got all the magazine articles and books about him from the library. And there were a lot more I haven't looked at yet."

Luke nodded. "I bet there's a ton of information online too."

I wanted to tell them I was doing the rest of this on my own, especially with Kinkaid's predictions of more people coming for whatever Griff had, but one look at Luke and Matthew, and I knew that's what they expected me to say. I shot Dominic a sideways glance. He thought the same, which reinforced his earlier comments about me having to be in control and not considering their opinions.

"Okay," I said. "Let's see what we can find out about Griff's life."

Matthew flashed a smile. Surprisingly, the one Luke sported was almost as wide.

In a tired, drawn-out gait, Dominic moved in the direction of the stairs. I stepped into his path before he could get by me. "You have to go home tonight."

"I am—"

"To the nursing home."

"Fine." He continued on and stopped beside the staircase, waiting there for us.

I went to Matthew and Luke. "Thanks for helping me with this."

Luke glared at me like he didn't quite believe my words, or was waiting for me to say I didn't want—or need—their help.

"I mean it," I added.

Matthew came to stand between Luke and me and gave Luke a quick kiss. "He means it."

Luke searched Matthew's face, then met my stare. His expression softened. "Okay."

With that, Matthew turned toward the stairs, but then he came to an abrupt halt. "Hey, look at this." He handed Luke the box of letters and headed around behind the opening that led downstairs. He stopped before a large armoire made of a deep brown wood with red inlays. A gorgeous piece of furniture. He went for the iron handles on the intricately carved doors.

Before he had them open more than a crack, the double doors flew all the way open and a man wearing a black ski mask shot out. He grabbed Matthew by the neck and spun him around, shoving him hard and fast against one of the open armoire doors.

Luke and I rushed forward, but before we reached them, the man whipped Matthew around and slammed him down onto the floor. I lunged for the guy, and he hurdled over Matthew for the stairs. Dominic managed to dive out of the way in time for me to seize the man by the arm.

I tugged him backward and heaved him against the wall beside the stairs.

He threw a punch. I successfully dodged it, and he tossed out another that hit me square in the jaw. I stumbled backward, but I quickly recovered and got him flat to the wall again. "Who the hell are you?"

He grasped my throat and clenched down.

I dislodged his grip and doled out my own punch that had him slumping sideways. I got him by the throat that time. "Who are you?"

"Richard." I could hear the panic in Luke's voice. I expected him to be at my side any second. He never came. "Richard!"

I glanced back over my shoulder. Matthew lay on the floor, his eyes closed. Luke and Dominic were leaning over him.

I let go of the intruder and went to Matthew, dropping to my knees beside Luke. I heard the man in the ski mask take off down the stairs, but I couldn't care less right then.

Matthew lay still. So very still.

I laid a hand on his chest and put my ear to his lips. "He's breathing. Did he hit his head?"

"I don't know." Luke tapped Matthew's cheek with an open hand. "Matthew, wake up."

He didn't.

"Support his neck," I told Luke.

He did, and I lifted Matthew into my arms, standing at the same time. I rushed for the stairs, and Matthew's head lolled to the side and landed against my shoulder.

Chapter Twelve

"When did they say they'd have the results?"

Luke checked the time on his phone. "An hour ago."

"Goddammit." I dropped my head back to the wall behind me and stared at the stark white ceiling tiles. We were seated in a cramped cordoned-off area of the emergency room with Matthew lying in a bed beside us as we waited for the results of his CT scan. So far all we knew was he had a concussion.

By the time I'd gotten him down to the first floor of the Harrison Estate, he had awoken and said he was okay. I could breathe a little easier at that, but I had continued on to my car just as quickly as I'd been moving with him before he came to.

When we'd gotten to the ER, the doctor had asked him several questions like his name and the date and what he could remember of what happened to him, and then she'd checked Matthew's coordination and reflexes and ordered the scan to rule out anything serious since he'd lost consciousness.

"In about a minute," I said, "I'm going out there to find the results myself."

Luke nodded. "I hear ya." He folded his arms across his chest again, just as he'd been sitting for the past hour.

Matthew turned his head our way and reached a hand out for me. "I'm okay. I feel fine now."

I interlaced my fingers with his. "Are you sure?"

"Yeah. They just wanted to keep an eye on me for a little longer. The scan isn't gonna show anything."

Luke stood and went around to the other side of the bed. "You still sick to your stomach?"

Matthew sat up taller. "No. I'm all right now. I just want to go home."

Luke remained standing beside the bed, the tension visible in the tight clench of his jaw and those arms back across his chest. He tipped his head to me. "I think that sounds good to the big guy too." Then he let go of his rigid posture and brushed a lock of Matthew's dark hair off his forehead. "And me too."

I stroked the back of Matthew's hand with my thumb. "I'm—"

"Stop." His voice was full of exasperation.

I stopped, mostly because that was a new tone for him.

"Don't say you're sorry again. This wasn't your fault."

The hell it wasn't.

"Richard."

I met his gaze, and he said, "We're going to find whatever it is they want, you're going to keep the estate, and no one else is getting hurt in the process."

That sounded just about perfect to me but... "Listen—"

"Don't." Luke shot me a look that would send a death row inmate running in fear.

"What?"

Before he could say another word, the curtain was drawn open, and the doctor from earlier entered. "Mr. Stewart, how are you feeling?"

"Fine."

I stood, and Luke and I waited near the opening of the curtain to give the doctor room to work. She checked Matthew's eyes and reflexes again. "You look good. The symptoms seem to have dissipated. I'd say you're ready to go home."

"He's okay?" I asked.

"Yes. The results of the scan were normal." She looked to Matthew again. "If the symptoms return or you feel worse, I want you to come back in. And I want you to take it easy for the rest of today. Nothing strenuous. Someone should also stay with you for the next twenty-four hours."

Matthew nodded and shook the doctor's hand. She left, drawing the curtain closed behind her, and Luke moved to sit on the edge of the bed. He patted Matthew's calf. "Told ya you were fine."

Matthew smacked his arm. "*I* told you guys."

Watching them together, I felt like a weight had been lifted from my chest. Like I'd been holding my breath underwater for far too long, and I'd just managed to breach the surface. I returned to stand beside the bed.

Matthew swung his legs over the edge so he faced me. "Let's go home. We've got a lot of research to do."

I couldn't help but smile at that. I reached out and held his face in my hands. "I'm completely in love with you, and it means a lot to me that you want to help." I placed a kiss on his forehead. "But you are not doing any research tonight."

He pouted, then drew in a deep, frustrated breath. "Okay." He hopped off the bed. "I'll watch you guys do it."

Luke laughed. "Sounds good to me." He winked at me from across the bed and lowered his voice so no one outside the curtain would hear. "I mean, how much longer is a man supposed to wait for you to fuck him?"

"No way." Matthew shook his head a little too adamantly for just having had a concussion. "There's a rule. Not unless it's all three of us."

"You'll be there watching, remember?"

"You're mean." Matthew glared at him. "I meant watching you guys do research. Not each other."

Luke feigned shock at that. "I didn't say you couldn't get off while you're watching. Just try not to move around a lot or do anything strenuous."

I hung my head and sighed. "You two are going to be the death of me. No sex after a concussion. For any of us. Period."

Matthew rounded the end of the bed and pointed at Luke. "Ha!"

The genuine confusion on Luke's face was priceless. "You're happy about no sex? Dude, that's just not right."

Matthew elbowed Luke in the side as he slid past to retrieve his clothes from the chair beside the bed. While he got dressed, we moved out into the main aisleway so he'd have more room to maneuver.

I held out my car keys for Luke. "Here. Take him home and stay with him. I'll catch a cab and be home as soon as I can." I turned to leave.

"Wait." Luke grabbed my arm, stopping me. "Where are you going?"

"I won't be long."

"You're going after someone, aren't you? Who do you think sent that man to the estate?"

"I don't know. It's gotta be someone who wants the property, though. Probably someone who made an offer to Edward before he died. I'm going to start with Kinkaid and work my way down the list."

"You don't know that for sure. It could be my dad. Maybe he sent that man there for us. Maybe it has nothing to do with the estate."

I scoffed. "It's not your father. Whoever it is, they want what Griff had."

"Then let's let the police handle this. They jotted down all the names you gave them. If these people are dangerous, I don't want you anywhere near them."

"You do realize you sound like a hypocrite?"

He seemed surprised by that, and then he got my meaning. Perhaps now he'd better understand my stance when it came to his father.

"All right," he said. "I get what you're saying. But why not try to find out what they could be after before you approach anyone? At least you'll have more info than the nothing you've got now."

He was right about that. Logically, it made sense. It took my brain a minute to convince the rest of me to back off on the burning need to hurt someone for what had happened to Matthew. "Okay. I'll wait and see if the police find out anything."

Luke came to me and whispered his next words, keeping his back to the curtain. "And you have to let him help you."

I shook my head and barely found my voice. "I can't." I gestured toward where Matthew dressed behind the curtain. "Not after this."

"He's really into all this about the estate and Griff Harrison. It means a lot to him. Don't tell him he can't be a part of it. He wants to know that you need him, that you'll let him in when you need help."

Luke voicing Matthew's feelings wasn't something I was used to. Then it hit me what he was actually saying, and it had little to do with how Matthew felt.

As if confirming that, Luke wouldn't make eye contact. What he'd said was a lot for him to admit. Even if he *was* using Matthew to do it.

I bent my head until he met my stare. "I do need him. And you."

At those words, Matthew stepped out from behind the curtain. "All set." He looked apprehensive, like he knew I planned to keep him and Luke away from what was going on with the Harrison Estate.

Everything in me was shouting to do just that. I hesitated. Luke steadily watched me.

At least if they helped with the research, they wouldn't have to actually be at the estate. That was something. "Okay," I said. "Come on. We gotta get you home and get some rest so we can start looking into Griff's life."

The tension seemed to instantly fade from Matthew. "I've still got all those magazines and the books I checked out of the library. And the letters from Oliver."

He and Luke took off down the hall as Luke said, "I'll get started with some online searches about the renovations that were done after Griff's death."

I was left staring at their backs as they headed for the ER's checkout window, their heads together, making plans.

It meant the world to me that this was important to them, and I didn't want to push them away. Not now. Not with how much I'd been letting them down lately.

But I also would do whatever it took to protect them. And to find out who had come into the estate and hurt Matthew.

Because nothing more was happening to anyone I cared about.

* * * *

I flipped the page of the magazine and scanned the rest of the article I'd been reading. It—and every other one I'd read—painted my rival Terence Kinkaid as an eccentric millionaire who blew cash on real estate, sports cars, and women the way regular people paid for a movie and popcorn. The majority of the current article focused on his two latest conquests: his new girlfriend, the twenty-five-year-old daughter of a notorious rapper and producer whose music empire was worth billions, and a 147-foot Mondo Marine Explorer, a luxury yacht he kept docked in the Cayman Islands.

None of that surprised me.

A week had gone by since the three of us spent the night at the estate. The winter storm had passed, leaving behind frigid temperatures and snowdrifts several feet high, and we were no closer to figuring out what someone would want from the house, which had me frustrated as hell. It also didn't help that the police hadn't been able to figure out who broke in and gave Matthew the concussion. I'd mentioned Kinkaid's name to them, along with everyone else who'd made offers on the house, but there had been no evidence Kinkaid or anyone else had hired someone to search the property. But like Luke had suggested, I was waiting to approach anyone until I learned more. Although my patience was running thin, and Luke knew it.

I tossed the magazine aside, sank into the couch, and let my eyes fall shut.

A warm hand landed at the back of my neck and began rubbing.

Without opening my eyes, I groaned. "God, that feels great."

Luke kept the touch going from where he sat on the couch beside me.

We'd been researching for hours now and had read nearly everything we could locate on Griff, his death, the Harrison Estate, Kinkaid, and the other men and women who'd made offers on the property. Every flat surface of our living room was covered in newspaper clippings, printouts, and magazines. Both Luke and Matthew had their laptops open to web searches and media archives. I had gathered as much information as I could from the local history section of the public library, and Matthew had visited three university libraries in the city, tracking down whatever was available on Griff Harrison and his family's estate. Meanwhile Luke had contacted several local companies specializing in safes to see if any of them had installed one at the estate fifty years ago, but that was a dead end.

As was everything else. So far we hadn't learned much. Except that there had been no witnesses and no real evidence collected from the night Griff died. All accounts of his death had stated that he was home alone and had shot himself in the head, and that his butler found his body in the master suite on the top floor.

Suicide. Case closed.

During the past week, I had also fielded a half dozen more calls from individual investors and corporations who wanted to purchase the Harrison Estate. It seemed no one was interested in investing in the place so long as I was the owner, but they were desperate to buy the property, and the offers were substantial.

At least with the added security, there had been no signs of additional break-ins. All I'd managed to accomplish with the house was to have the electrical inspected, the power turned on, and the high-end security alarm system installed. Anything more than that would have to wait for me to acquire the necessary financial backing.

Which I *was* going to do. I had every intention of finishing the project. On my own terms.

While Luke continued rubbing my neck, I reached out to Matthew where he sat on the floor before us. He had his back against the couch cushion, and I ran my hand through the dark wavy hair above his nape. Luke and I had been taking turns combing our fingers through his hair, caressing the back of his neck and shoulders, anywhere we could reach, as we pored over the articles and search results. It seemed neither of us could stand to go very long without touching him. Even a week after the concussion.

Luke leaned into my side. "You okay?"

"Yeah." I opened my eyes. "Just a long week."

"Oh, man." Matthew waved his hand in the air above his head. "I found a picture of him."

"Who?" Luke asked as he peeked over Matthew's shoulder to view the book on his lap.

"Griff's lover." Matthew kept his concentration focused on the bound book before him, which featured several back issues of *LIFE* magazine. He scanned the page for another moment, then said, "It's an article about Griff's career after he won the Oscar. There's a picture of him and Oliver at a wrap party for Griff's first movie, the one they were in together." He held up the book for us to see.

Griff Harrison was pictured with two men. All three were standing side by side, relaxed grins on their faces, glasses of champagne raised. Their appearances fit the typical movie stars of that time period. Sophisticated, clean-cut good looks blended with a trace of that bad-boy attitude that seemed to radiate off them. Griff had the same short dark hair as his wax figure, and there was a glint in his eye like he had the best secret. Or maybe I was seeing things.

Matthew gave me the book, and I asked, "Which one's Oliver?"

He got on his knees facing us and pointed over the top of the book. "On the right."

Oliver was a hint shorter than Griff, with similar dark hair.

The two men stood a few inches farther apart than Griff and the other man, which in those days was probably more telling than if they'd been outwardly touching at a public event. They'd likely made every effort to appear as though nothing was going on between them.

"Good-looking couple," I said. Griff looked… happy. So did Oliver. I couldn't imagine how hard it had been for him when Griff had died. "What ever happened to him?"

"Oliver?" Matthew shook his head. "I don't know. He stopped acting not long after that movie. I couldn't find a recent address or phone number for him. I'm guessing he passed away."

"Damn." It would've been helpful to talk to someone else who was there the night Griff died.

Matthew continued. "I couldn't locate his obituary or any family, but I did find a Hollywood trivia site that had a bio about him. It said he had been friends with Griff, and that he lived here in the city following Griff's funeral. It also mentioned he was never married." Matthew's voice had grown somber on the last word.

I handed the book back to him. "You okay?"

"Yeah." He turned to sit on the floor again and examined the picture more closely. "It's just so sad. They always had to hide their feelings, and they never had a chance to build a life together, to grow old with each other."

Something about how he'd said the words had it sounding a little too personal, like he could relate to Griff's life.

No matter how many people were now more accepting of gay men and women, the three of us was something few could—or would want to—understand.

"We're not hiding, Matthew."

"I know." But he didn't so much as glance my way. Luke and I exchanged a look. Neither one of us was buying that.

I asked, "Do you feel like we are?"

"No." Matthew shrugged. "Not anymore."

"Then what's wrong?"

He didn't say anything right away. I was about to push when he asked, "Will you be upset when you're older?"

"Upset about what?"

"That we're not married."

I thought about why he might be asking. If this was about his mom. Or if he was asking for himself. Or for me.

"Do you mean for legal reasons or sentimental ones?"

"Both, I guess."

"I don't need a piece of paper to tell me we're a family. I only care that we're together. The legal stuff... We can take care of that as much as possible with lawyers and paperwork."

He must've liked that answer. He turned and smiled at me, then looked Luke's way.

Luke pointed at me. "What he said."

"Does that help?" I asked.

"Yeah." Matthew turned back to the book.

"Good." I dropped a kiss on the top of his head and spoke against his ear. "I always want to know what you're thinking. Okay?"

He nodded, grabbed another book of bound magazines, and began reviewing them. A minute later, he said, "It says here Griff was single at the time of this interview, so this was before he was engaged to the princess. They asked him if he was hoping to find love."

When Matthew didn't offer more, Luke asked, "And what did he say?"

"Huh," I teased. "Look who's the sap now."

"Shut up."

"You think I mind? There's nothing more intense than a horny, romantic Luke."

Matthew laughed and tipped his head back to look up at Luke. "That's true."

Luke just rolled his eyes. "So what did Griff say?"

Matthew read from the article. "*Of course I want love. Who doesn't? I want love and commitment and passion. All of it. I want that comforting companionship that comes from being with someone for years. Where you just know by loving them that you're a better person. I want a family, a home, and even a dog to greet me at the door.*"

"That sounds about right." I raked my fingers through Matthew's hair again and waited for him to mention keeping one of the puppies, but he returned to silently reading the interview. I wanted to give him time to bring it up on his own, so despite how tough it was to do, I let the topic go.

Luke and I returned to our individual searches of Kinkaid. Several minutes later Luke sat taller. "Here's something new. It's from a feature article about Kinkaid and his lavish lifestyle." He scanned the page. "In addition to all the cars and houses, Kinkaid also collects art. Mostly Renaissance paintings. They say his collection is worth millions."

Luke silently read more, then said, "This part summarizes something that happened a few years ago." He read from the page. *"Terence Kinkaid was briefly a suspect for arson and burglary after he was found in possession of a painting that was thought to have been destroyed in a fire at a private residence. One man was reportedly killed in the fire. Kinkaid claimed he'd purchased the painting from an art dealer, then surrendered the painting to the police and was never charged for possession of stolen property or further investigated for arson."* Luke sat back and pointed to his laptop screen. "This could be it. Maybe he's after a painting."

That could definitely be it. "Although," I said, "the appraisers I had go over everything confirmed that the paintings we'd seen at the estate weren't worth much." They had reviewed the entire contents of the house, including all the movie stuff, the artwork, and the various trinkets, and they had priced nothing at more than a few thousand dollars. Not substantial enough to warrant the offers from Kinkaid.

Matthew held up a hand. "Wait. I think I saw something." He reached beside him on the floor for the box of letters he'd uncovered at the estate. He turned to face us and sifted through the box. "Here it is. I didn't get a chance to read it all the way through yet, but there was something about Griff going to an auction. Maybe it was for a painting." Matthew reviewed the letter and then said, "Oliver called it a private auction. It was held in New York City the same day he wrote this letter. It sounds like Griff went to a lot of trouble to get invited, and he had to unexpectedly leave for it when he and Oliver were spending the weekend together. I don't think Oliver was happy about that. He said…"

Matthew read from the letter. *"I wish you hadn't gone to that auction. I wish you'd stayed here with me. We get so little time alone. I hate watching you leave our bed for any reason."* Matthew stopped reading and scanned the rest of the letter. "Oliver mentioned the name of the guy who hosted the auction. It sounds like he was a mutual friend." Matthew gave the name, but it didn't ring any bells with me. He said, "I'll search for him and the date of the auction online." Matthew pulled his computer onto his lap and entered the info. He clicked several times, then paused to review a page, his eyes widening as he read the text.

"What?" Luke asked.

Matthew kept reading to himself, his mouth gaping. "Wow." He blinked and looked up at us. "There's a blogger who writes about all kinds of conspiracy-type stuff, cover-ups, that kind of thing. He referred to a secret auction in New York City, held on the date of Oliver's letter."

"What were they auctioning off?" I asked.

"There are rumors that one of the items was a secret sixteenth-century painting by Silvio Lombardi."

Luke whistled. "*The* Silvio Lombardi?"

"Yeah."

"I'm no art expert," Luke added, "but if I'm remembering things correctly, wasn't he one of Leonardo da Vinci's students?"

"That's right," I said. "He only did twelve paintings, and they're all worth a fortune."

"And they're all owned by museums," Luke said. "I remember that from my intro to art history course in college. There's nothing in a private collection."

"What else does it say?" I asked Matthew.

He read more. "*Some believe the auction was private because of a secret item: a painting by Silvio Lombardi that has never before been seen in any gallery or public showing. Rumors abound, the most interesting perhaps, is the idea that the Catholic Church has been hiding the painting for centuries because of its—*" He stopped reading again. "Oh my God."

I shifted forward to the edge of the couch cushion. "What?"

"Oh. My. God."

"What?" Luke and I said in unison.

Matthew looked up. "Because of its homosexual content."

"That's it." Luke jabbed a finger toward Matthew's laptop. "Griff Harrison bought that painting."

Matthew nodded. "And it's somewhere at the estate." He set his laptop aside and got on his knees before me. He rested both hands on my kneecaps, and I could feel the excitement radiating off him. "This makes sense. A lot of people think Lombardi was gay. And Dominic did say Griff bought a lot of art."

"Oh man." Luke was shaking his head in disbelief. He stilled and added, "I buy that the Catholic Church would make a painting like that disappear." He spoke to Matthew but gestured to me. "We thought he had some secret stash of money before. He's really fucking rich now."

I scoffed at them. I hadn't been keeping the total sum of my investments a secret on purpose.

"Yeah." Matthew met my gaze, the animated expression in his dark eyes growing more pronounced. "Forget needing investors for the restorations. You find that paining, and you're all set."

"I don't know." I would believe that such a painting existed when I saw it with my own eyes. I wasn't about to fall victim to a scam perpetrated by one dead Edward Harrison. I gestured to Matthew's laptop. "Let me see that website."

Matthew handed the computer to me and moved to sit with his back to the couch again, leaning against my leg. I read the full article about the auction and the rumors of the painting. The blogger had no idea who'd been in attendance or if the auction had even been real.

I went back to the search results for the date of the auction and the name of the man who'd held it. Another blog came up, referring to the private auction. That blogger indicated that a man named Mark Smith had been in attendance. He didn't buy anything, but there was a rumor that a week later, he purchased a secret painting that had originally been sold to someone else the night of the auction. Although that post indicated that no one knew the identity of the secret painting's artist.

If Griff did acquire that Lombardi painting, did he turn around and sell it to a man named Mark Smith? And why?

I relayed the information to Luke and Matthew, and Luke said, "Search for Griff's name and the date of the auction."

I ran the search. "Nothing."

"Try each day for the next week after."

I did, and I got a hit for a scanned magazine article on a website about the history of celebrities and their fans. The story was a feature about the rise of stalking cases.

Griff was mentioned in the article. He'd been stalked by a man who broke into the Harrison Estate on several occasions. The first break-in was four days after the auction, and there were many more following that. All by a young man named Charles Fitzwater.

"Son of a bitch."

Chapter Thirteen

Edward Harrison had said someone named Fitzwater was close to learning the truth about what Griff hid the night he died. And now, Griff's stalker had the same last name.

No way was that a coincidence.

Matthew and Luke were watching me. I held up a hand, indicating I needed a minute, and silently read more of the article.

The stalker hadn't stolen anything, but he'd rifled through the dressers and the two closets in the master suite. He'd even taken several of Griff's suit jackets off the hangers as if he'd tried them on, which was what led the police to consider the man a crazed fan stalking Griff. The supposed stalker had been arrested several times for trespassing on the property, but Griff had never pressed charges. And no one had been able to determine how Charles Fitzwater had been getting in or out of the estate.

"Get this." I told Matthew and Luke about the stalker and the Fitzwater connection.

"What do you think it means?" Luke asked.

"Maybe, if there really is a painting, this Charles Fitzwater guy got wind that it was at the house and kept coming back to try to find it, and then when he was discovered inside the house one night, he ended up killing Griff. Or he told others about the painting, and they killed Griff to get their hands on it." I paused and considered my options. "I need to have another talk with Dominic."

Luke asked, "You think he knows about the painting?"

"I'd bet my ass on it. He knew everything that went on in that house. But if not, it's at least a topic to get him back to talking about Griff and the house and where a painting might be hidden."

Luke threw me a concerned look. "What if Dominic was involved with Griff's death? He was there the night Griff died. Maybe someone paid him to get that painting for them."

"Thought you said he was harmless."

"He is," Matthew said.

I nodded. "I think so too. But he's not telling me everything."

Matthew shook his head. "Dominic would've said something if he knew about that painting."

I wasn't so sure about that. I reviewed the article again to see if there was anything else I needed to know, but there wasn't.

A few minutes later Matthew yawned, and his head landed on my knee.

I tapped him on the shoulder. "Let's head up and get some sleep."

"Okay." He started gathering the magazines and printouts he'd been looking through.

Luke and I helped, and when we had the living room back in order, Luke dragged Matthew off the floor. "Come on, kid."

I gave a nod toward the stairs. "Go on up. I've got to shut down the computer in my office."

They headed for the stairs right as my cell phone rang. A number I didn't recognize flashed on the screen, and when I answered, a woman I didn't know asked, "Mr. Marshall?"

"Yes."

"I'm calling from the Clark County Historical Society. I'm sorry to call so late, but I just learned that you've acquired the old Harrison Estate."

I turned off the lights in the living room and moved through the dark house for my office. "That's right."

"Oh, how wonderful." The lilt of her voice had me picturing exaggerated clapping and jumping to go along with the verbal reaction. "We are delighted that someone has taken over the historic home, and we would love to discuss your plans for the estate."

"Why are you asking?" I left the lights off in my office and sat behind my desk.

"Our members would surely be interested in a house designed by the late Clyde Urbanski. Plus, it was the home of Griff Harrison. We'd love to do a feature for our newsletter. Something on you and what you hope to do with the house."

When I didn't say anything right away, she spoke again.

"We'd also be interested to hear about the contents of the estate. I hear Edward Harrison left it almost exactly as he'd had it when he lived there."

"Pretty close." I wasn't giving anything away with that. It was well-known how Harrison had walked out that night of his last party and had never returned.

The woman asked, "Do you know if there are any of Griff Harrison's personal items left in the house?"

That had the hairs on the back of my neck standing up. I didn't want to brush this woman off—I needed any PR I could get about my plans for the house—but I wasn't about to say too much. Or trust anyone at this point.

"Listen," I said, "things are a little crazy right now. If I could get your number, I'd be happy to give you a call in a few weeks when I have more definite plans in place."

"That would be fantastic." She rattled off her number. I switched on the desk lamp and grabbed a pen to jot it down. "Oh, and silly me," she added. "I don't think I gave you my name. I'm Judy Fitzwater."

I dropped the pen and sank back in the chair. *Fitzwater.* I carefully chose my next words. "Well, Ms. Fitzwater, I know you're not calling for your newsletter, so you can cut the charade." I paused for emphasis. "I know exactly what you're after."

"Excuse me?"

"You're not interested in the house. You want what's inside. Did you send that man wearing the ski mask to get it? He hurt someone very important to me."

"No. That was not me. But I hear your man's doing fine. Just a concussion."

I slammed my hand down on the desk. "If I find out you had anything to do with hurting him, you are going to pay."

She had the nerve to laugh at that. "I'll tell you what I will pay for. The house. I'll give you a fair price for the Harrison Estate if you promise to leave it as is and never set foot on the property again."

"It's not for sale. So you might as well give up. You're not going to get what you want."

"Oh, Mr. Marshall." Her voice had grown cold, calculating. "I think I am."

"Is that a threat?"

"Certainly not. It's a promise." The line went dead.

Dread engulfed me as I stared at the number I'd written down. I reached for the keyboard sitting on my desk and ran a search for Judy Fitzwater. The first result was for the Clark County Historical Society. She'd served as the director for the past five years. So at least that appeared to be on the up-and-up. I tried several of the other results and found additional mentions of her work as a member of the society.

I clicked more results and scanned the pages. Finally I came across one that included the name of her grandfather, Charles Fitzwater, Griff's stalker.

Just how long had the Fitzwater family been after the secret Lombardi painting? Had Charles Fitzwater killed Griff?

And how far would his granddaughter go to acquire what her grandfather never could?

Just then a low bang came from somewhere in the house. The front foyer. Or maybe the kitchen. I hadn't heard Luke or Matthew come downstairs. I held still and listened. Then came a faint tapping. Nothing I would've noticed had I not been concentrating for the smallest of sounds.

Definitely the kitchen.

Despite that the house alarm hadn't been triggered, I bounded to my feet and grabbed the only item nearby, a stapler. Not much of a weapon, but it could do damage to someone's face. I quietly but quickly moved through the office, the living room, and on into the kitchen.

Low light from the streetlamps seeped in through the window above the sink and offered enough light I could see there was no one there. I rounded the counter that divided the room but found nothing and no one there either.

Then something rubbed against my leg.

I went for the light switch next to the sink and flipped it on. One of the pups sat at my feet, her head cocked to the side as she stared up at me. Behind her I spotted where she'd knocked over the trash can.

She and her littermates had grown in the few days they'd been staying with us, and apparently they could now traverse the steps without assistance.

I pointed at her. "You're supposed to be in the basement."

Her head cocked to the other side, and I had to admit, she was pretty damn cute. They all were.

I set down the stapler, scooped her up, and carried her downstairs. A section of the makeshift pen we'd constructed near the washing machine was shifted sideways, creating a tiny opening at the base. All the rest of the puppies were gone. I set the one from the kitchen inside the pen, then moved the fencing back into place and secured it with a new zip tie, then added another tie for good measure. Once we got them all back inside, I didn't want anything to happen to the little furballs.

The door to the basement bedroom was open. I found Matthew lying on the bed with the other puppies. They were all nipping at him as he wiggled his fingers and sock-covered toes for their benefit.

I said, "Thought you were going up to bed."

He halted the playing. "Just wanted to check on these guys again and take them outside for a bit."

"Where's Luke?"

"He's taking a shower." Matthew sat up against the headboard and gathered the pups so they were all on or near his lap.

I sat facing him on the edge of the bed. "You're doing a great job with them."

"Thanks."

I reached out and petted the closest puppy. "Do we still need to keep them locked up?" They seemed too small to be out on their own, but if we made sure the basement door was shut, they couldn't get into too much trouble. Although what I knew about taking care of puppies I could fit on the tip of my pinkie finger.

"Yeah," he said. "They're still too young. They need the training pads. They'll have accidents yet for a while. Plus they'll chew on everything."

The puppies climbed over him to swat and bite at each other. He kept stroking them, one at a time, never giving more attention to any specific puppy.

He'd been coming home at least twice during the day to take care of them, and he did it several more times in the evening. I had a hunch he also woke up during the night to look in on them then too. I wasn't sure how he kept track of all seven when he took them outside. Good thing we had a fenced-in yard. All but one of the pups were now tumbling their way down the sides of the bed. The last one stayed on Matthew's lap. She was the runt of the litter with white on the tips of her paws and an equally white stripe along her belly. She was Matthew's favorite, whether he wanted to admit it or not.

I gave her head a pat. "Aren't you afraid of losing them in the snow?"

He laughed. "They do okay. They like to jump in the snowdrifts. They were all out of the pen when I came down here. One of the sections is loose."

"I secured it. Should hold this time until they get big enough to jump over it."

When he didn't say anything more, just kept petting the pup on his lap, I took the dog and set her on the floor. I moved to lie at his side and lifted his shirt. I kissed my way across his abs as I waited. I wanted to encourage him to admit he was interested in keeping her, but I also needed him to accept that he was as much a part of deciding about our future as Luke or I was.

"Richard?"

"Yeah?" I kissed his bare stomach again, this time gliding my lips along the dark patch of hair that disappeared beneath his jeans.

He ran a hand over the top of my head. "Do you want kids?"

I froze.

Here I'd expected a conversation about a puppy, and he'd brought up children. Nothing meant more to me than giving him and Luke everything they wanted, but… *kids*?

Was this another topic his mom had mentioned?

I was still disappointed I couldn't offer him a legal marriage.

I would never lie to him, though. I gave the warm skin of his abs one more kiss and looked up at him. "No. It's never been something I've felt compelled to do."

He shrugged. "I was just curious."

I got up and turned to sit beside him. "If that's something you want, then we need to talk about it."

"No. I don't. Not really." He stopped for a moment like he was trying to find the right words or was giving the topic considerable thought. "I just… I realized I never asked you guys. We never talked about it."

It had never even occurred to me to ask them. "I should've brought that up when we started seeing each other."

He smiled. "That sounds stupid. We didn't really date, did we? We sort of just fucked and moved in here."

"Does that bother you?"

He was serious again as if he was contemplating that too. Then he leaned his head back against the headboard to look up at me, and another slow grin formed. "No."

I bent down and kissed him.

When I pulled back he said, "I hadn't ever really thought about having kids. It wasn't even on my radar, you know? I just don't want you guys to give up something you've always wanted because there are three of us."

"Are you thinking Luke's got some burning need to be a dad?"

Matthew laughed at that. "No." His laughter cut off when he glanced across the room.

Luke stood in the doorway, a shocked, panicked expression on his face that was very reminiscent of the man he'd been when we first met him.

Matthew slid off the bed and went to him. "It's okay. I was just curious." He tugged Luke to the bench beside the bed and sat with him so they faced me.

Luke said nothing, just stared off at the opposite wall, his eyes wide, his body held so tight I figured he might never be able to move again.

Matthew took Luke's face in his hands and encouraged him to turn his way. "Luke?"

"Kids?"

Matthew shook his head. "I was only wondering if Richard ever thought about it."

Luke's mouth opened, closed again. He finally whispered, "He'll give you whatever you want."

Matthew studied him, then looked at me. He seemed to be carefully pondering that. "That's not true. He's not giving me everything I want."

Chapter Fourteen

Matthew had said the words in a lighthearted tone, but they still sent me reeling, had me stunned into silence.

Luke contemplated Matthew for a moment. Then his lips turned up in that teasing grin of his. He obviously understood something I didn't.

"You're right, kid. How much longer do you think we have to wait?"

"Hmm." The glint in Matthew's eyes was almost a match for Luke's expression. "I'm guessing not much longer now." In an entirely erotic move, he stood and crawled up the bed toward me on all fours. He straddled my lap and made a hungry sound deep in his throat as our bodies connected. He bit his lower lip, kept those dark eyes fixated on me, and leaned in.

The shock that I'd somehow let them down faded, and I gave myself over to the moment with him. The press of his lips to mine had an instantaneous jolt of desire racing through me. He kissed me wildly, wantonly, then more slowly, drawing out every sensation as our lips brushed, as our warm, moist tongues made contact again and again.

When the kiss ended, he shifted his hips, rubbing himself over my cock, all while his heavy, hot breaths struck my lips.

I gripped his hips and encouraged him to keep moving. Then I forced him to stop. Because I had to know.

"You sure you're feeling up to this? Your head doesn't hurt?"

"It hasn't hurt all week."

Every time I thought about how he'd gotten that damn concussion because he'd gone to the estate with me, I wanted to pummel the guy who'd hurt him. And maybe myself for taking him there. Matthew could've been seriously injured, and I couldn't shake the image of him lying in that hospital bed.

"God." I ran the tips of my fingers along his cheek and shook my head in agitation. "I want to know who hurt you."

"Please don't worry about it." He traced my lower lip with both thumbs. "I don't want anything to happen to you." He kissed me once more, his tongue searching out mine with soft, lingering swipes that drove me crazy with the need to be with him—to thrust inside him until we both came. All week it had taken considerable self-control to keep from offering him more than a kiss, a caress, but I wasn't about to chance anything where his head injury was concerned.

"You keep doing that," I said, "and I'll give you whatever you want."

"Doing what? This?" He swept his lithe body over mine, his ass dragging over my groin, increasing the delicious ache in my cock.

I grasped his hips tighter and grunted in response.

"Or this?" He braced his hands on the headboard on each side of me and slowly, teasingly came forward until our lips met again. Then nothing about it was slow. It was a deep, passionate kiss that I didn't want to end. I wanted to hold his head in my palm and keep us connected in that ravenous moment until all he could feel, all he could breathe in was me.

But then he pulled back. "Please." The raw, raging desire in those dark eyes was intoxicating. "Fuck me."

Who could resist that?

Who'd want to?

I flipped us around and pinned him to the mattress. Immediately he spread his legs under me, and I slipped in between his thighs. With hard, heavy thrusts, I humped at him, kissing along his neck as I moved against him.

It all felt amazing, and we still had our clothes on.

But we were also missing something.

Someone.

Then Luke was at my back, running his hand over my thighs, my ass, then between my ass cheeks.

Goddamn clothes.

He bent over me. "You're wearing too many clothes."

Glad we were on the same page.

I clutched the bottom of Matthew's shirt, hauled it off him, and stripped him of his jeans and underwear while Luke got rid of his own clothes. Then they were taking care of mine until we were all naked, touching, my mouth on Matthew's lips, then Luke's. Back and forth, one man, then the other.

I moved in between Matthew's thighs again, this time skin to skin, relishing the sweet slide of our erections. Luke reached for the lube and with clever, slick fingers got us ready.

Then Matthew raised his legs in the most blatant, beautiful move. I caressed my dick with my palm as I stared down at him.

This… would never get old.

I gripped my cock and slapped the tip against his ass. The tantalizing vibrations along my shaft encouraged me to do it again, and his breath hitched with each contact.

"You're gorgeous, kid."

He shook his head.

Did he still not get it?

I let go of myself and, with a hand to his chin, compelled him to look at me. "You're beautiful, Matthew. Inside and out."

His lips parted, but no words formed. Those wide eyes were begging me for more. I gradually, with unbelievable restraint, pressed inside him, and he whimpered. The slow drag of his body over the head of my dick was torture—pure blissful torture that I never wanted to end.

Out of the corner of my eye, I could see Luke leave the bed to sit on the bench and watch us, his hand sensually working his cock.

With Matthew's legs draped over my shoulders, I leaned in and kissed him again, torn between wanting to remain close, every part of us connected, and wanting to pull back so I could ram into him again and again until we both fell onto the bed in a mass of sweaty, sticky limbs and sated, limp bodies.

The heat of us coming together drew me farther inside him. I drove against him harder, faster. His eyes met mine, and we didn't need words. He clung to me like if he let go he'd lose everything—his entire world. Nothing matched the intensity of knowing I meant to him the same as he did to me.

I kissed him once more, then pulled back and drove into him, really fucking him for the first time in weeks. The bed shifted with each thrust, and the headboard slammed into the wall, a perfect match for the slap of skin as I moved against him, inside him. Matthew arched his body and reached up for the headboard, the pillow, the edge of the mattress, something other than me.

"No." Despite how good it all felt, I forced myself to stop. "Touch me."

He met my stare, then wrapped his arms around me and tugged me closer. The warmth of his chest on mine, his ragged breaths pouring out against my ear, the way he pressed into each thrust like he wanted to get me deeper inside him and hold me there all night—it all drove my desire higher, had my rhythm faltering.

I moved inside him with more speed and strength. Luke was there with us again. He lay on the bed and inched closer to Matthew, then whispered, "Tell me."

I had no idea what he meant by that.

Matthew glanced Luke's way, confusion evident on his face. Then, as if just looking at Luke had clued him in, Matthew stared up at me and said, "He feels huge… Bigger than he looks… Strong… Powerful." Groans punctuated his words as I kept moving in him. "It feels like every muscle in his body… every part of him… is fucking me." Another low, desperate sound tore out of Matthew. "I feel like I'm flying, like I'm—" He arched and groaned as I plowed into him faster, my body no longer under my control. Carnal need led the way.

Luke turned Matthew's head so they were eye to eye. "Like you what?"

"Like I'm going to explode into a million pieces. Oh God." He threw his head back again.

Luke reached between us and stroked Matthew's shaft.

"Don't let him come." I told Luke. "Not yet."

Luke nodded, and he slowed his hand.

I tilted forward and whispered to Matthew. "I want to feel you. Inside me." It took every ounce of control I had left, but I slid off him and onto all fours over Luke. Who was such a wise man. By the time I'd gotten into position, he had the lube in hand and was slicking his cock, then his ass.

He swiped some of the lube on my dick, then tossed the bottle to Matthew, and once again the smoothness of their actions had me imagining they'd been practicing these moves for weeks, like they planned to enter a synchronized sex marathon.

Not in my lifetime. Unless it was a marathon with just the three of us in the privacy of our own home.

That, I could totally get on board with.

I spread my legs for Matthew and waited.

Luke tugged me down by the back of my neck and lifted his legs higher, tilting his ass up. "Now, Richard."

I shook my head and held still, the tip of my dick barely making contact with him. I breathed deep, trying to cool down before I shot all over his ass without ever getting inside him.

I had been waiting too long to do this again. One on me. One in me.

Luke laughed, but it came out like a desperate groan. "What are you waiting for?" He released me and clenched the sheet beside him on each side. Those intense blue eyes of his begged me for more, and I almost gave in. But I kept motionless, kept waiting.

Then Matthew pressed in close at my back. He kissed along my spine until he was draped over me. And as he buried himself in my ass, I slid into Luke, the three of us coming together as one. Finally.

"This," I said. "I've been waiting for this."

They didn't really fuck me. I was so far gone, I rocked back and forth, sinking into Luke and sliding back on Matthew, taking control of their pleasure and my own, and together we fell into the sweet abyss.

"Luke," I said. "Stroke yourself."

He did, his cock slick from the lube.

"Faster."

He quickened his pace.

"Now slow down."

He sucked his bottom lip in between his teeth and did what I asked.

"Let go and pinch your nipples."

He kept his hand on his cock and tweaked one side of his chest.

Matthew gripped my hips tighter, and his pace quickened. He always loved hearing me tell Luke what to do.

"Two hands, Luke."

Luke grunted like that suggestion alone was pure torture, but he let go of his dick and went for his other nipple, pinching and tugging as I snapped my hips faster. He arched his back but kept those hands on his chest, groaning with each thrust. The sound of our bodies coming together and the squeak of the bed filled the room.

Matthew moaned again. He was close. His hips slammed against me over and over.

I paused with my cock buried in Luke and let Matthew lead the way. He plunged into me with abandon, and that had my shaft swelling inside Luke.

Then Matthew came, his body trembling with release. "Oh God." As he stilled he kissed my back between my shoulder blades again and again, and I wound my arm around behind him and held him to me.

When he could catch his breath, he pulled out and shifted to lie beside us. Without delay he reached for Luke and started jerking him off, kissing him at the same time. Just watching them together kicked everything up another notch for me. I fucked Luke again, even harder than before, finesse long gone from my movements. He groaned once more and threw an arm over his head to keep from slamming into the headboard. Matthew picked up the pace on his dick, and Luke's stomach muscles tightened. He shot, his cum arcing up onto his own chest.

"Fuck." I thrust once, twice more, falling onto Luke, my hips jerking against him as I came.

When I'd given him all that I had, I stayed right there, lying over Luke, my arm draped over Matthew. We were all sweaty and sated, deep exhales and sighs sporadically escaping our lips.

"Damn." Luke huffed out another heavy breath. "That was…"

When he didn't say more, Matthew added, "Intense."

I raised my head. The fitted sheet was no longer stretched over the mattress. The blankets were gone, and the top mattress had skidded sideways so it was half off the bed. It had also shoved both the nightstand and the lamp over onto the floor. When the hell had that happened?

Who cared?

I grasped Luke by the back of the head and kissed him. Without breaking the contact, I swung off him and reached across his body for Matthew. Then we all had our lips pressed together. A sweet, lazy kiss of three men coming together in pliant, sated bliss.

Just then barking started in the other room. Reluctantly I let go of them and shifted to lie on my stomach beside Luke. "I think we scared the pups away."

Matthew laughed with me. "They can climb the stairs now. I better go check on them." But he didn't make a move. He lay there with his head on Luke's chest, a hand moving over my shoulder. There had been a time when Luke lying between us like that would've had him tense and nervous as hell. I was relieved to see our distance lately hadn't brought out those old instincts.

I lifted up and caressed his cheek with mine, and in that moment I felt closer to him than I had since I returned from my business trip. The night spent with them, their help with the research, the intense sex afterward, the intimacy of lying there touching them both—it all gave me a sense of peace, a serenity nothing else matched. No matter what happened with the estate, I'd have Luke and Matthew and that was ultimately all that mattered to me. Anything else I could live without. But not them.

Another puppy barked from the other room. I sighed and sat up. "I'll go see if they're okay." I grabbed a towel out of the cabinet, got marginally cleaned up and dressed in a pair of jeans. In the outer room, all but one of the puppies played near the fenced-in area. One by one I returned them to the kennel and then went searching for the runt. She was curled up inside a laundry basket filled with Matthew's T-shirts. I scooped her up, and when I had her inside the pen, all the others clamored around her and settled into a single pile of fur. The runt was at the bottom with only her head poking out. She looked uncomfortable. I shimmied her out from under her brothers and sisters and held her to me. Instantly she nestled against my chest.

Such a small thing. Young and innocent. She'd never survive outside in the winter weather on her own.

Matthew came to stand beside me. He wore jeans and nothing else. His curly hair was sticking up all over.

I wrapped my free arm around him and kissed the side of his head. "You smell good." He smelled like sex and sweat and Luke and me— the way he hadn't nearly enough lately.

Luke staggered by, dressed similar to Matthew. "I need a shower." He stumbled up the basement stairs. Sex always knocked him out like he'd downed a couple of sleeping pills.

I asked Matthew, "You think he'll make it to the bathroom?"

He snuggled into my side, his arms enveloping me. "Doubt it."

We stood there for a while, watching the pups in the pen as the one slept against my chest, Matthew practically asleep at my side.

I bumped him with my hip. "Come on. Let's go see if he fell asleep in the shower."

Matthew nodded and let go of me.

I returned the runt to the pile. Right as she'd gotten settled again, a text came through on my phone. I tugged it out of my pocket and checked the display.

This is Simon Security Systems. An alarm has been triggered at your home address. Emergency personnel are being dispatched.

"Shit."

Matthew's head jerked up. "What is it?"

"The silent alarm."

"Here?" Matthew whipped his gaze in the direction of the stairs. "Luke." There was panic in his voice.

"I know." I had to get to Luke. I wasn't waiting for the cops. I also wasn't leaving Matthew alone. I grabbed his hand and started climbing the stairs.

Keeping Matthew behind me, I slowly moved us through the kitchen, spotting no one and nothing out of the ordinary. As we reached the staircase leading to the second floor, I heard the click of the door to my office as it was shut.

I stopped. Everything in me wanted to go see who was trespassing on my property, who was invading my home and my personal space. I didn't get a chance to decide on a course of action. Matthew yanked on my hand. He mouthed the word *no* and dragged me up the stairs with him.

In our bedroom, I shut and locked the door.

Luke was coming out of the bathroom. His hair was wet, and he wore only a pair of underwear.

Speaking low I said, "Someone's in the house. In my office." I gestured to the bedside phone. "Matthew, call 911 and make sure they're coming."

He went to the phone.

Luke wrenched on a pair of jeans. He zipped them up but stopped before he got the button closed. "My dad. He sent someone here." He headed for the door, but I stepped into his path.

"We're waiting for the cops."

He shook his head. "I need to see who it is."

I braced an arm across the door, blocking his way. "No. You are not going down there."

He grabbed my arm and tugged. The force of his action almost had me letting go, but I held my ground. Then he shoved at my chest, and when that didn't work, he gave in and backed off.

Matthew hung up the phone. "They're coming."

I took a step toward Luke. "The cops will catch whoever it is."

He nodded. He looked so resigned to waiting there with us, his next move completely caught me off guard. He was by me and out the door in a heartbeat.

"Goddammit." I sprinted after him. "Stay here," I called back to Matthew.

He didn't. I heard him on the steps, barreling down after me.

Luke sprinted through the house, and by the time I caught up with him, he had the office door open.

Behind the desk sat Dominic.

His right cheek was red and swollen. The skin below his left eye was already sporting a bruise, and there was a cut on his lower lip.

What kind of scum would beat on a man his age?

Matthew gasped when he reached my side. "Dominic. Are you okay?"

Dominic offered Matthew an appreciative smile, gave a nod, and then he met my shocked stare. "They came into the house tonight. The house where my father died, where my family and I lived, where my daughter took her first steps, where she spoke her first words. It's all I have left of them, and if you don't do something soon, they will destroy everything to find what they're after."

Chapter Fifteen

I hung up the phone, and Luke approached where I stood in the kitchen doorway.

"What did they say?" he asked.

I kept my gaze locked on Dominic who sat on a stool at our kitchen counter holding one of the puppies in his arms. The little thing had been barking like crazy so Matthew had brought him upstairs, and Dominic had been loving on the dog since, while I had phoned the police to cancel the call from our home security company and to get them to check out the Harrison Estate instead. After that, I put a call in to Simon Security Systems to verify if someone had entered the estate earlier that night.

Apparently Dominic had gotten into our house through a window he found unlocked in my office. He had figured we were already asleep for the night, so he was planning to eventually find his way to the living room and crash on the couch until morning.

Now Matthew was heating water on the stove as he chatted with Dominic.

"The police are on their way to the estate," I told Luke. "But from what Dominic described I'm guessing whoever was there took off after getting in a few swings at him." He also told us how he'd seen them ransacking the rooms upstairs right before he went to hide in the master suite.

"You think it was the same guy who was there the other day?" Luke asked.

"Who knows at this point?"

I was starting to think any number of people had been strolling in and out of the house without my knowledge since the day I bought the place. I gestured with a tilt of my head toward Dominic. "I'll take him to the hospital and get him checked out after I talk with the police at the estate."

"We'll go with you."

I shook my head. "No. Stay here. I'll be late." I went to move into the kitchen, but Luke grabbed me by the arm and yanked me to a stop.

"Why won't you let us help you? You keep pushing us away."

Pushing them away? Hardly. Despite my better judgment, I'd let them into this entire thing, and Matthew had gotten hurt in the process. I wasn't sure I'd ever forgive myself for that. I thought I had learned my lesson years ago with Anne.

Luke squared his shoulders and stared me down. "If this was about me and someone breaking into a property I owned, no way in hell you'd let me head over there on my own. Cops or no cops."

He was right about that.

But until I knew more, I wasn't about to chance anything else happening to either of them.

Luke was still glaring at me. He wasn't about to back down, and I didn't want to fight him on this. Not with things starting to get back to normal between us.

I watched him for another moment, and he didn't waver.

I gave a reluctant nod. "All right. We'll all go talk to the police, but we're not staying long."

"Fine." His expression softened, and he moved past me into the kitchen.

I followed and went straight to Dominic. "You broke our deal again. You were supposed to stay at the nursing home." I couldn't stand seeing the bruises on his face, couldn't stand that someone else had gotten hurt over that damn house.

He kept stroking the puppy and spoke in a calm, neutral tone that was more unnerving than his usual aggravation toward me. "So did you. You said you'd keep the place safe. They came at me in the master suite. They were *inside* my house."

"Your house?"

He scowled up at me like he was daring me to challenge him on that point, despite that I had all the paperwork to prove otherwise.

I let out an amused chuckle. There was something about him I liked. He had a determined strength to him. The fact that he'd been cryptic as hell about everything wasn't as irritating as when I first met him. I was beginning to understand he had his reasons for holding back.

If what he'd told us about his family was true—and I was starting to believe it was, despite a lack of evidence to back that up—I could relate to his situation. He had failed to protect the family he loved, and he'd do anything to erase that feeling, or come up with a way to live with it. Protecting the Harrison Estate seemed to be all he had left, and even his control over that was slipping away.

I gestured at the bruises on his face. "Who did this to you? Who was at the house?"

When he didn't respond, I changed gears. "How many were there?"

"Four." He gave another pat to the puppy and then nodded. "At least four."

"Did you recognize them?"

He said nothing.

"Who were they?"

His hand stilled on the dog. He glared at me again, then looked to Matthew and Luke, and back at me. "The men who killed Griff."

Okay, so maybe his cryptic ways *were* still annoying.

Matthew set a mug of steaming cocoa in front of Dominic. "They couldn't be the same guys, right?"

"They're not." I glanced Luke's way. "And none of this is your dad."

He gave me a nod like he was starting to get that.

Dominic went back to petting the pup. "Well, I know it's not the *exact* same men. They'd be older than me. But they're connected to them."

"To who?"

He threw me another look like I was the stupidest person he'd ever met. "The ones who want to destroy the house."

"You're talking in circles again." And my patience was running out. "Speaking of the estate, how did you get in? Every window and door is secured with the new alarm system." The installation had added a significant chunk of money to my debt, but I hadn't wanted to take any more chances.

Dominic shook his head. "I know a way inside that doesn't require your security code." He sipped the cocoa. "This is good." He drank more.

"And what way is that?"

He set the mug down and studied me. Something shifted in his expression. His eyes softened and they held a certain degree of trust I hadn't yet seen him direct at me. "There's an old storm cellar that hasn't been used in decades. No one who lived at the house when I did knew about it. Not even Edward. The cellar entrance is well concealed, even without the snow. There's an opening in the cellar that leads to the basement. Griff had that opening installed so Oliver could come and go without alerting the other staff." He stopped talking, and he grew concerned, then panicked. All of a sudden he stood, unsteady on his feet. "Oh God." He nearly dropped the puppy.

Luke moved in and retrieved the dog. He steadied Dominic with a hand on his arm. "What is it?"

"They're following me. That's how they got in tonight."

I stepped closer. "They weren't following you. My security company said someone entered a valid code tonight. Which means they either hacked their way in or bribed someone at the security company." A big part of me wanted to trust Dominic. But I wasn't ready to let him in on the fact that I knew about the painting. Instead I said, "You know what they're after, don't you? And you know where it is."

"No." He shook his head so emphatically he was going to hurt himself. Or pass out, what with how beat up he was.

"Easy does it." I encouraged him to sit on the stool again. I gave him a minute to calm down and then said, "Judy Fitzwater from the historical society called me tonight. She asked questions about the house and Griff's personal items left inside."

Dominic nodded like he'd expected that. "She was the one Edward mentioned was close to learning the truth. She came to the estate on the night Edward died."

"You talked to her?"

"Yes. No one had knocked on the front door for so long, I almost didn't answer. When I did, I could tell she knew she'd find me there." He drank from the mug once more, taking several slow sips that lasted so long I thought he might not share more. Then he spoke again. "I never told anyone I'd been going there."

"Edward knew."

"Yes."

Which gave credence to the theory that Edward Harrison was behind everything. I was back to wondering if there even was a painting—or anything else—hidden at the estate.

"What did Fitzwater want?" I asked.

"To take some pictures. She said she was doing a story for the historical society on the person who was buying the house. In fact, I think she said your name." Dominic grew quiet, contemplative. "Do you think she knows who killed Griff?"

"Maybe." I filled him in on the prowler who was related to Judy Fitzwater. "You ever heard of him?"

"Sort of. A man had been coming into the house, going through Griff's things. The staff was asked to watch out for him, but I never heard his name. The police and Griff didn't say who it was." He stared off past Matthew toward the doorway leading to the basement like he was trying to force a memory to the surface. "Or maybe Griff did say. Maybe I forgot." Dominic smacked a palm on the counter. The mug of cocoa teetered but stayed upright. "Dammit. I should've known he was involved."

We were all quiet for a moment. Then I asked Dominic, "Did you let Fitzwater in the day she came to the house?"

"Not after Edward told me about her. I told her no and shut the door in her face."

I braced a hand on the counter beside him so I was invading his space. "Have you heard of the painter Silvio Lombardi?"

"Sure. Who hasn't?"

"Did you know it was one of his paintings that Griff had?"

Dominic stared up at me, eyes wide.

I stared back.

"No." His mouth dropped open. "You're lying."

I told him about the rumors of the painting's existence, about the auction, and what we'd learned from our research of Kinkaid and his interest in Renaissance art. "Are you familiar with that auction or the painting?"

He didn't look like he wanted to answer.

I straightened to my full height, folded my arms over my chest, and kept silent, hoping he'd eventually fill the void with the truth. The puppy squirmed and whined, trying to get out of Luke's arms and back to Dominic's lap. Dominic held out a hand for him, and Luke passed him over. The dog quieted again and set about licking Dominic's fingers.

"Yes," he finally said as he kept his focus on the dog. "Griff went to that auction." He shook his head with even more vigor this time. "But he didn't buy anything. If he had gotten that painting I would've known. He'd been searching for that secret Lombardi painting for years, and he would've told me if he'd succeeded."

"Why did he want that Lombardi so badly?"

Dominic was quiet for a long moment, stroking one of the pup's ears. Then he said, softly, warily, "Oliver was a fan. He had several prints, but Griff wanted to get him an original, no matter what it cost him. When Oliver heard a rumor about an unknown Lombardi painting, he was so excited about it, reading everything about Lombardi he could get his hands on. From then on Griff was determined to find that painting for him." Dominic's hand abruptly halted on the dog's back. "Oh God. All Griff's inquiries about

Lombardi's work, going to that auction, people must've assumed he had the painting. That's why they came to the house that night."

I was getting good at reading Dominic, knowing when he was lying. I was also beginning to understand that he didn't really like to lie to me. He was offering the truth, so far as he knew it.

But maybe Griff did have the painting from the auction and decided not to tell Dominic for some reason. Or he'd eventually acquired it another way. In either case, I was starting to accept that the painting might just be at the estate. I also knew that Judy Fitzwater believed that too, and she was not going to back down. Her family had likely been after that Lombardi for decades. What had Luke said?

"Obsessed people are dangerous."

Then another thought hit me.

Luke eyed me with concern. "What are you thinking?"

I looked to Dominic. "Is Oliver Nash still alive?"

"Yeah, I believe so. Why?"

"Maybe he's come to get what he thinks is his. Maybe he's the one who sent that man into the house the other day, sent those men tonight who attacked you."

Dominic shifted on the stool so his whole body faced me. "No."

"Why not?"

"Oliver wouldn't be involved with something like that. He would just come to me and ask for whatever he wanted from the house."

"Perhaps he didn't want you to know about the Lombardi. Or he's got another agenda. Maybe he heard about this Fitzwater woman coming for the painting and is taking the opportunity to exact revenge."

"For what?" Luke asked.

"For Griff's death. Oliver was there that night, but the police didn't know that. They never questioned him. Maybe he witnessed the murder but knew he had to hide or he'd be next. And now he's going to use the painting for leverage, to finally uncover the truth." I turned to Dominic again. "Do you know where Oliver lives or how we could get in touch with him?"

"No. I haven't talked with him since the funeral."

Which was probably for the best. If Oliver was in this for revenge, fueled by fifty years of anger and grief, approaching him could bring even more trouble into our lives. I asked Dominic, "Do you believe Griff would've died to protect that painting?"

He considered that. "No. Not something like a painting. Not even a Lombardi." He stopped. His face held a note of shock, then sadness as realization hit him. "But he would've done anything to protect Oliver."

Maybe that's what he'd been doing that night. If any of this were true. I crossed the room and paused at the kitchen doorway.

Charles Fitzwater had most likely murdered Griff while trying to get his hands on that painting. I wasn't about to let that family—or Oliver Nash—hurt anyone else.

From behind me Luke asked, "What are you going to do?"

I faced them. "I'm finding that painting before anyone else does." I pulled out my phone. "I just need to buy some time."

Matthew came around the kitchen counter. "How?"

By doing the one thing I had sworn I'd never do.

I brought up my contacts and scrolled through them, looking for one name.

Chapter Sixteen

"Mr. Marshall, you can go in now."

I tossed aside the copy of *Sports Illustrated* I'd been thumbing through for the past forty minutes that I'd been forced to wait, stood, and gave the receptionist a nod in thanks.

Kinkaid's office was decked out in dark carpeting and wood panels, and in the middle of everything sat a mammoth mahogany desk accented with carved pillars that made the whole thing look like it belonged in a museum. Perhaps it had been, and he'd spent a fortune to acquire the desk, whether it was for sale or not.

The entire office featured nothing plush or upholstered to give the space even the appearance of offering comfort to visitors. Neither did the man standing behind the desk.

Kinkaid had his arms folded across his chest and looked as hard as the room. "Hello, Richard." He offered his hand, but he didn't move. He was waiting for me to come to him. He knew how to make any other person in the room feel inferior.

It wasn't working with me. Although I did opt for polite professionalism and went to shake hands with him. I was, after all, there to make a deal. "Terence."

He held my gaze for a moment. Then he sauntered out from behind his desk and went to an antique world globe. He folded back the top half, revealing glasses and decanters of booze. "Can I get you something to drink? Scotch?"

"Nothing for me."

"Ah. You're one of those." He poured himself a glass and knocked it back. "You don't like to break the rules? Have some fun?"

"I have quite a lot of fun, actually. But when it comes to my business, I prefer a clear head."

He poured another and returned to his desk, glass in hand. "Good to know. Have a seat." He didn't wait for me to sit, though. He set the glass on the desk and ensconced himself in his chair, elbows on the armrests, hands folded in front of him. He stared at me again, and then his mouth turned up in a knowing grin, the mirth in his eyes a little too familiar. The same way Edward Harrison had looked at me when I told him I'd one day own his estate.

I took the seat across from Kinkaid, and he kept the stare—and the silence—going. He wasn't trying to read me or figure out what to say. It was his way of making me feel uncomfortable, of trying to force me to show my hand.

I had no intention of letting him do either.

I remained motionless, saying nothing. The seconds ticked by on the pendulum clock that hung on the wall beside us.

Finally he spoke. "I've heard you've been having some break-ins at the estate. Have you decided to take my advice and sell?"

"No." I paused, giving him a pointed look, showing him without words that I was in control of what happened next. "But I will sell you the painting you're after."

"Ah." Despite the verbal reaction, his face showed no sign of surprise at my admission that I knew about the painting's existence.

"Tell me," I said, "Why do you want it so badly? It's not the money."

"No, it's not." He leaned forward and rested his elbows on the desk. "It's no secret I'm not a fan of organized religion. I believe the churches hold too much power, and the Catholic Church exerted theirs for far too long hiding that painting. They had no right to do that. It's time for it to be seen, appreciated." He hesitated, then offered a quick grin. "Besides… a secret Lombardi painting that no one knew for sure existed all these years? Forget the *Mona Lisa*. That Lombardi will be the most famous painting in the world."

I gave a nod. It would be one hell of a discovery. But in spite of understanding where he was coming from, I wanted—needed—to keep away the kind of trouble that painting and people like Fitzwater could bring down on us. I waited a moment before saying more. Just because I was going to give Kinkaid what he wanted, didn't mean I had to make this easy for him. I studied the walls of his office. Every one of them featured framed awards, newspaper clippings about his business and personal life, and photos of him with racing cars, yachts, and celebrities. Who constructed a shrine to himself like that? In his own office?

A man who was insecure, who needed to show people: *look at everything I do, everything I have, everyone I know.*

I'd made the right choice picking him. He'd want the world to hear that he had acquired the secret Lombardi. He'd be photographed with it in every newspaper and magazine. The online art community and every social network would explode with the news.

I focused on him again. "If the painting is really at the estate, I'll sell it to you for double what you previously offered for the property, but only if you give me the time to see if the painting's there myself, and if you also..." I matched his pose, my elbows on the edges of the armrest. "Leave me alone, and get everyone else to do the same, including a woman named Judy Fitzwater. You put some of your high-priced security personnel on the estate and at my house twenty-four hours a day, and I'll get you that painting. That's the deal."

Without hesitating he lifted his glass and tilted it my way. "I'll give you what I originally offered, no more. That's a decent finder's fee." He drank from the glass, then clanked it down on the desk but didn't give up his hold on the scotch.

"No," I said. "It's double or nothing."

He seemed to be pondering that, tapping his thumb against the side of the glass. "We both know what I offered is far above what you'll need for your restoration project."

"Double. Take it or leave it."

He sat back and eyed me for another minute. "You're lucky I've always liked you."

That right there—the arrogance—pissed me off, and confirmed why I had never wanted to work with him. I hated that I was making this deal with him, but I'd do anything to keep Matthew and Luke safe.

"All right," he said.

"You'll make certain there's no more trouble at the estate, and for me and the people I care about?"

He gave a nod. "I'll have my security get right on it." He pointed at me. "But I want it in writing that you guarantee to sell the painting to me for the price we agreed as soon as you find it. No matter what other offers you get."

"I can do that."

"Then you have yourself a deal. Members of my staff will be at the estate within the hour to help you with your security problem." He paused, then stood and swiped the glass off the desk, a gloating grin on his face. "I never thought I'd see the day when you'd sell me something. I think this calls for a toast." He returned to the bar in the globe, his back to me.

"That's not necessary."

He didn't stop pouring the drinks.

I took the opportunity to stand and have a closer look at the framed photos and newspaper articles tacked to the walls.

Without turning my way, he said, "Those are from my charity work."

I stopped at one article that included a photo of Kinkaid at a charity art auction. The caption read: *In attendance were several members of the founding families of the Clark County Historical Society, including Terence Kinkaid and Judy Fitzwater.*

I zeroed in on the photo. The woman the caption identified as Fitzwater stood beside Kinkaid, both smiling, arms around each other like they'd posed for similar pictures together a thousand times.

Goddammit. I clenched my hands into fists at my sides and held very still.

I should have known.

I sucked in an agitated breath and moved on to a nearby photo. I didn't want Kinkaid to see what I'd been looking at or to get that I knew he was involved. Not yet. Information was power, and I had every intention of keeping the upper hand. I stayed focused on the image of Kinkaid at the finish line of a Motocross track. He was standing with his hand on the seat of a sleek Kawasaki motorcycle tricked out in the stars and stripes of the American flag like he was some kind of daredevil. A blue helmet was tucked under his arm, mud covering him from head to toe. He had a smooth grin plastered on his face, and I wanted to punch him right in the polished, perfect fucking teeth.

Kinkaid joined me and offered a glass. "I'll have the intent-to-sell paperwork drawn up today."

I clasped the drink.

He wore that calm, almost amused expression he'd been sporting since I'd gotten there. Asshole thought he'd beaten me.

I downed the drink to keep from pummeling that look off his face.

He held out his hand. "I'm glad we could come to an arrangement that worked for both of us."

Staring at his outstretched arm, I was momentarily frozen. This bastard had fucked with my business. He'd sent his men into the estate. They'd hurt Dominic. Attacked Matthew.

It took everything I had to calmly shake hands with him. I ditched the glass on a side table, and when I turned to leave, he stopped me with his next words.

"Oh, Richard, before you go. Let me show you something."

I forced myself to face him. Kinkaid stood on the other side of his desk again. He set his drink down, returned to his chair, and reached into a side drawer. He pulled out a thick manila envelope, dropped the envelope onto the desk, then gestured to the newspaper clipping I'd been looking at on the wall. "I should've taken that photo down as soon as I had Fitzwater call you."

I glared at him. "And I should've known you were behind everything." But I'd been too focused on one very dead Edward Harrison.

Kinkaid laughed. "My grandfather began searching for the missing Lombardi decades before I was born, then my father took over, and now it's my turn. I will be the one who owns it next. Make no mistake about that."

"Was it your grandfather who killed Griff Harrison? Or was it Charles Fitzwater?"

"*Charles*? He didn't have the guts for something like that. He never made a move without a word from my grandpa. They were friends from the time they were kids, when my grandfather kept the bullies away from little, weak Charles Fitzwater." Kinkaid laughed again but said nothing more.

So I did. "I know the police investigated you for arson. Did you kill that man who died in the house fire just to get his painting?"

Again, nothing from him but that self-righteous stare.

I kept my distance, afraid of what I might do if I got any closer. "I've gone over the entire property. The painting's not there, so you can continue your search somewhere else."

"Then you missed it."

"Trust me, I've looked everywhere. Griff never had that painting."

"Oh, he did. And you haven't looked hard enough because the place is still standing. That house has been remodeled several times since Griff lived there, and from what I hear, you haven't torn up the floors, you haven't knocked down a single wall." He paused, examining me again. "I would seriously rethink my original offer to buy the house." The anger had faded, and that smug grin of his had returned. He reached for the glass of scotch and took a swig. Nonchalantly he swirled the remaining amber liquid. "Or it might not be just the estate you lose." He tipped the glass my way, then set it down and picked up the envelope. He slid out a stack of papers and tossed the top one onto his desk. "Take a look."

I stepped forward and scanned the paper. A copy of Matthew's class schedule. Kinkaid tossed out an 8x10 photo on top of that. The exterior of our town house.

He threw out another. Luke inside the house, lying back on the couch. That picture looked like it had been taken through the front window of the living room. Then another photo. Matthew in the hospital while being transported for his CT scan. Another. Luke heading into the front door at his work. Another. This one from inside the house. In the basement. Matthew sleeping in the bedroom with the puppies lying all around him.

I moved on instinct and had Kinkaid out of his chair and against the wall behind his desk in a heartbeat, his throat clenched in my hands. I drove the back of his head into the wall and one of his precious framed photos showcasing him while skydiving clattered to the floor, the glass shattering on impact. I slammed him again and got farther in his face. "You lay one hand on them, and I will end you."

That smirk was back. "It's your choice. You can make this all go away. Just give up the Harrison Estate."

The office door burst open, and two men grabbed me by the arms. They tore me away from Kinkaid and had me flattened face-first on the carpet in seconds. More men surrounded me, held me down.

"You okay, Mr. Kinkaid?" one of the men asked.

"I'm fine."

I heard him come in closer. He pressed a foot into the middle of my back. "You have three days to work out the details." He jammed his heel harder into my spine. "But you *will* sell me that property." Then he bent down over me and spoke low. "Seventy-two hours, Richard."

His men lugged me off the floor but kept hold of me.

Casually—much too calmly—Kinkaid came forward and got in my face. "And don't even think of involving the authorities, or like I said, you will lose more than the estate. Much more."

* * * *

I raced home and found the first floor of our house dark and empty. When I left Kinkaid's office earlier, I had rushed to text Matthew and Luke on the way to my car. I didn't want to alarm them with the panicked sound of my voice. I had tried to keep calm with my messages, just telling them my meeting had ended, and they'd both responded with see-you-at-home type replies, so I knew they were okay.

It was late. They'd probably had dinner and gone upstairs, but I couldn't stand the sight of the empty house.

I chucked off my coat and sprinted up the stairs to our bedroom, needing to see them, to make sure they were safe.

A lone light was on, and Matthew lay on his stomach in the middle of the mattress with his head at the foot of the bed, his laptop beside him. Textbooks and papers were spread out all around him, but he wasn't paying attention to the books or the laptop. He had the box of letters from the estate open and was reading one of them. His phone sat near his elbow, "At Last" by Etta James pouring out the tiny speaker. Not Matthew's usual style of music. Maybe he'd purposely looked into songs from the 1960s.

Despite the surge of panic that I hadn't discovered Luke there with him, I went to Matthew and gingerly sat on the edge of the bed so as not to startle him. I ran a hand down his back. "Hey."

He rolled onto his side. "Hey."

That smile… It called to me even more than that first night I shook his hand at the Haven.

"Where's Luke?" I asked.

Matthew reached for his phone and cut off the music right as Etta James was belting out the last soulful note. "He said he'd be late. He had a big programming project he had to get wrapped up today."

Luke's IT consulting firm had substantial security at the building where he worked, mostly for the servers and pricey computer equipment they had on site, but at least that had me feeling a little better.

"Were you studying?" I asked.

"Trying to."

I gestured to the box on the bed with a tilt of my head. "But you couldn't stop thinking about those?"

He glanced at the letters and pinched his bottom lip between his teeth, answering my question with barely a nod of his head.

"Don't." With a hand on his chin, I forced him to turn to me again. "Don't ever feel stupid about something like that. I like the way you care about people, the way you feel things. It's part of why I fell in love with you."

That got me another smile. I leaned in and kissed him.

His lips parted under mine, and he slid closer, grasping on to me. Then suddenly he jerked back. "Wait. How'd it go with Kinkaid?"

"Do tell," came a voice from across the room. Luke was leaning against the doorjamb. He wore dress slacks and a tie and seemed both aroused at watching us and curious to hear more about my meeting.

The tension in my chest fled at the sight of him. I got off the bed and headed across the room. "Missed you today." After finally getting to fuck them, I was feeling like I had that second night we'd spent together at the Haven, like I could never get enough of them.

Luke shook his head and retreated a step. "Don't think you can just give me that look and I'll drop to my knees anytime, anywhere." Despite his words, he couldn't hide that he was definitely interested in doing that exact thing.

"Oh, you won't?" I teased. I gripped him by the waist and tugged him to me.

He laughed in mock exasperation. "You think you got me all figured out, don't you?"

I offered him a soft, chaste kiss. "Uh-huh." I turned him to face the bed and pulled him to me so his back was tight to my chest, then spoke against his ear. "I had you figured out that first night at the club when I made you look at me while I fucked you."

He grunted an amused agreement.

I reached around and stroked him through his pants until his cock grew hard from my touch.

From where Matthew sat on the bed, he had a look of frustrated disappointment etched on his face. I was about to ask him what was the matter when Luke's breathing picked up speed, and his head dropped to my shoulder. "God, don't stop."

I kept my hand moving over him. With desperate urgency, he spun to face me and kissed me again. I wasn't sure why, but he needed this—needed me. I had no intention of letting him down. I backed him toward the bed, and we tumbled onto the mattress at Matthew's feet, Luke tugging on my shirt as we went down. I held him tighter to me and deepened the kiss. The clothes would have to wait. I wanted more of his mouth, of his talented tongue.

But in a flash Matthew was yanking me off Luke with determined fierceness. "No. No. No," he chanted as he rolled me to my side.

Poor Luke was left lying there, a confused expression on his face.

Matthew climbed over me and squeezed in between us until we had made enough room for him. He sat with his legs tucked under him and raised his hands out between us like a referee holding back two boxers. "You two are insatiable. No one touches again until we talk." He looked my way. "What happened today with Kinkaid?"

I laughed as I got off the bed. "All right." The humor died off fast, though, as I headed for the closet, undoing my shirt cuffs, stripping off my tie and the shirt as I went. I had no desire to tell them about Kinkaid's threats, but I wouldn't lie to them. I swapped my dress clothes for jeans and a T-shirt, and when I exited the closet, the two of them were sitting with their backs to the headboard, both silent, waiting for me to say more.

They remained quiet as I gave them the rundown of my conversation with Kinkaid. I held nothing back. I told them about the connection between him and Fitzwater, about the photos Kinkaid had shown me, and his threats if I went to the police.

When I stopped, Luke swung off the side of the bed. He set to pacing the length of the room. "Remember when my dad was fucking with us and you had that idea about moving away?" He froze, then jabbed his right forefinger in the air. "One more fucking person stalks us, and we're outta here."

"I'm with you on that." I waited until he seemed to calm down and had returned to sit beside Matthew. Then I went to stand at the foot of the bed facing them. "I'm going to sell. To Kinkaid."

Matthew sat taller. "No."

Luke shot off the bed again. "No way. You really wanted that house."

I did. I'd wanted it almost more than anything. But not them. And that was the reason behind the decision. Nothing mattered if there was a chance it could hurt them in any way. I said simply, but with absolute resolve, "It's not worth it."

Luke waved an arm in the air. "Just because Kinkaid threatens you, doesn't mean he's going to go through with it."

"He's not threatening me." The words had come out with more anger than I'd intended.

Luke stepped forward. "But why sell to him? If he's behind all this, he's the one who hurt Matthew. And Dominic."

I gave a good rub to the back of my neck and sighed. It was hard to admit, even to myself, but I was no match for Kinkaid and his available resources. "This guy's a closer. He always, *always* gets what he wants, and he's been trying to find that Lombardi painting for a long time. If it were just my business he was going after, that'd be different. I will not take chances when it comes to the two of you."

Matthew spoke then. "Maybe if we find the painting, you could—"

"No." I looked to Luke. I knew he'd get it. He'd seen Matthew and me repeatedly tortured in his dreams. I said again, "It's not worth it."

Luke dropped onto the bed, slapping both hands on his thighs in a gesture of resignation. "All right. It's your decision."

I glanced Matthew's way. I needed him on board.

Eventually he nodded his agreement. That didn't feel like enough, but I wasn't going to leave this open for debate. It was finished for me. I was selling.

I gestured to the box of letters sitting on the bed. "Anything interesting in those?"

Matthew shifted to lie on his stomach facing the foot of the bed, just as I'd found him when I'd gotten home. "Nothing about the painting." He scooped up the letter he'd been reading and stared at it as if lost in thought.

"What then?" Luke asked as he ran a hand over the back of Matthew's jean-covered thigh.

"It's just..." Matthew gingerly refolded the letter. "They had to hide all the time. They had to sneak around just to even be able to touch each other in Griff's own home." He kept his focus on the folded letter. "Griff took Oliver on a trip to Hawaii once. They rented a private villa on Maui and spent the entire week there. Just the two of them. It meant a lot to Oliver. Griff too. I think that's why he ordered those tiles for the solarium and had the murals painted in the ballroom and in the master bath, to remember that week by. Listen to what Oliver said..." He opened the letter again and read aloud. "*I awoke that last morning to the sound of the waves crashing on the beach and the whoosh of the ceiling fan over the bed.*"

I moved to sit on Matthew's other side and joined Luke in touching him, massaging up the back of his other thigh as he continued to read from the letter.

"*You were in my arms, your head on my chest, and I imagined what it would be like to wake up every morning like that, to take a walk along Kaanapali Beach with you every night as the sun sets, to make love with you as the stars come out and the moonlight hits the surf. I will never forget those days alone with you. I will treasure them forever.*"

Matthew sighed when he finished. "I can't imagine..." He paused, then spoke again with more certainty. "I'm glad we don't have to hide. I know it can be hard. Being three. But—"

"Hey." I encouraged him to roll over. "It's not hard. Hard would be without you."

He threw me that look that said he was amazed I wanted him, and it floored me that he still had no idea what I saw in him.

I drew him up and into my arms so he was straddling my lap. "Nothing about being with you is hard."

Luke moved in behind him so we were both holding Matthew, and he whispered in his ear. "Nothing."

A pleased grin hit Matthew's lips. He leaned back against Luke and at the same time embraced me tighter.

That connection—the three of us together—that was why I *had* to sell the estate.

I'd made the right decision. There was no other choice for me.

* * * *

It had taken me two hours to fall asleep that night, but sometime after I did, I awoke to the sound of low moans coming from the other side of the bed, then...

"No. No. Matthew!"

I turned and found Matthew rushing to sit up. He reached for Luke, who lay on the bed thrashing from side to side, clutching at the empty air above him.

"Luke," Matthew pleaded. "Wake up."

Luke shot up and swung his arm out wide. His elbow struck Matthew in the face, and Matthew fell back against me. Then Luke lunged at us, his hands wrapping around Matthew's throat, sending us all sailing backward, flying over the edge of the bed and landing in a heap on the floor, which brought Luke all the way awake.

In a heartbeat he let go of Matthew. "Oh God." He scrambled away from us and staggered to his feet. He had a hand clasped over his mouth as he stared down at us. "Oh God." Heavy breaths surged out of him, and he looked ready to run. Like he did after that first night we slept together, like he wished with everything he was that he could take back what he'd done—and what he felt about it.

"Easy, Luke," I said. "It was just a nightmare." I didn't want him to completely lose it and take off before I could get out from under Matthew.

With the way Matthew's dad had beat on him when he was a teenager, I knew how shitty Luke had to be feeling. It didn't matter that what had happened was an accident, the result of a nightmare.

He looked toward the bedroom door like he couldn't face either of us. "I'm sorry. I—"

"It's okay." Matthew rushed to stand, his right hand covering his cheek and eye.

I waited, afraid if I moved I'd disrupt what needed to happen between them.

"I—" Luke held a hand out for Matthew, then dropped it just as quickly.

Matthew stepped forward and reached for that hand. "It's okay."

Luke met his stare and leaned in to rest his forehead against Matthew's, gripping Matthew's hand in return. "God, I'm sorry." Then with urgency he jerked back and took off, fleeing into the bathroom. He had the door slammed shut by the time I was on my feet.

I wasn't sure who needed me more right then, but when I spotted

Matthew's trembling lower lip, my decision was made. I drew him into my arms.

He shook his head but didn't fight me on the embrace. "Go talk to him."

"In a minute. Are you okay?"

"Yes. Just go." He tried to pull away.

"Wait. Let me see you first." I examined his face. His upper cheek was red, and it was starting to swell. The eye looked worse. "You need ice on that."

"I'll get it. Just go see if he's okay."

I brushed the tip of my thumb under the reddening skin.

He shoved my hand away. "Please."

"Okay. Get some ice. But come right back."

He nodded and crossed the room, his gaze on the door of the bathroom until he walked out into the hall.

I went to the bathroom door and knocked. "Luke."

The faint sounds of vomiting came from inside, and then the toilet flushed.

I gave him a minute before I opened the door. When I did, he was staring in the mirror at himself, his hands braced on the glass, his every muscle tense, like he was about to puke again. Or hit something.

Without looking my way he asked, "Is he okay?" His voice wavered with the words.

"He's fine. He's more worried about you than anything."

"Fuck." Luke slapped at the mirror with both hands. "I'm calling the prison tomorrow and setting up a time."

"Okay." I moved in behind him and laid a hand in the middle of his back. "I think you should."

He met my stare in the mirror. "You're not going to give me any shit about it?"

"No." If this was what he needed to do, then he had to do it. I got that now.

"Good," he said. "And I need to do this on my own."

"All right."

His gaze locked on mine in the mirror again as the emotion threatened to burst from him. He slapped the mirror once more. "Fuck."

"It's okay." I ran my hand down his back and eased in closer. "What happened in the dream?"

He closed his eyes as if he didn't want to relive it, but he spoke anyway. "My dad showed up at the Harrison Estate when we were there. He came at Matthew, and this time he—" His throat worked as he swallowed hard. "He killed him. Pushed him over the railing on the second floor. Matthew just fucking lay there at my feet in the foyer, his eyes open, blood pouring out from under him. I sprinted up the stairs, lunged for my dad, and then—"

Matthew had awoken him.

I folded my arms around Luke and pulled him to me until he leaned back against me. "He's all right. He's here with us and he's fine." I did not want to mention anything else, but I had to tell him, while I could be there for him. With my lips at his temple, I whispered, "He's going to have a bruise. Probably a black eye."

"Goddammit." Luke tensed in my arms, and I sensed him closing off, condemning himself all over again.

"It was an accident."

He turned and shoved at me. "I hit him. Just like his goddamn father. I had my hands around his fucking neck."

"Stop." Matthew stood in the bathroom doorway. He came in and squeezed in between us, facing Luke. "You didn't hit me. You were lashing out at your dad. I accidentally got in the way. That's it. Please don't make this out to be something bigger than it is."

Luke stared at Matthew, and I could tell he was taking in the damage on the pale skin. With a hand at Matthew's nape, he drew him forward so they had their foreheads pressed together once more. "I'm so sorry."

"It's okay." Matthew ran his hands up and down Luke's arms. "Please don't be upset. I'm fine. All right?"

Luke pulled back and searched Matthew's eyes. Eventually he must've seen something that convinced him he had no other choice. He nodded.

That seemed to appease Matthew. He laid his head against Luke's shoulder and held on to him.

I knew better. This wasn't over for Luke. Not by a long shot. And to prove my point, Luke told Matthew, "I'm going to see my dad."

"Okay," Matthew said without letting go of him. "You'll go see him, say whatever you need to, and everything will be fine. You'll see."

I wasn't so sure.

What would it take for everything to be fine for Luke?

Maybe telling his dad to back off would help. Or maybe it wouldn't. But I had to let him do this. He had to be in control of this, had to be the one who made sure nothing more happened to us when it came to his father.

I got that.

Logically.

But I also felt like I was losing control of everything. It wasn't a feeling I was used to, or one I wanted to examine too closely, and I wasn't sure what that said about me.

Chapter Seventeen

"Yeah. Just like that, Matthew." I shifted my ass on the couch, trying to fend off my orgasm, desperately wanting the sensations to go on and on. There was nothing better than this after a long day. There was also nothing more beautiful than a focused Matthew going to town on my dick.

He lay on his stomach across the couch, his head in my lap, his lips wrapped around me. I had my hand resting on the back of his head, his dark hair brushing against my palm as he moved along my shaft. I glided my other hand down his back to his jean-covered ass, grasping one cheek in my hand. At my touch, he curled a leg beneath him, giving my fingers access to stroke his asshole. If only he'd taken the pants off before we got started.

"Almost," I said through gritted teeth.

Matthew bobbed his head faster, working me with both hand and mouth, and that was it. I came between his lips with a groan.

When I had given him everything I had, he looked up at me, a drop of cum on his bottom lip.

I wiped it away. "Come up here." I shifted us until he sat where I'd been. Kneeling before him, I opened his pants. He was still flaccid, but that wouldn't last long. Not after he blew me.

I grasped his shaft and wet the tip, swirling my tongue over and around the head, aching to feel the resulting rush of blood as desire surged through him. I wrapped my lips around him and sucked hard. With that, he grasped the couch cushions in his fists on each side of him. I reached out for his hand, and he frantically clasped mine in his.

That reaction couldn't be from the blowjob, though. He wasn't getting hard. Not so much as a twinge.

I pulled off but continued to stroke him with my hand. I kissed his hip, then his stomach, pushing his shirt out of the way as I trailed my lips toward a nipple.

He smiled down at me—a forced smile I didn't like the looks of. I also hated seeing the purple bruises he still had on his cheek and around his eye, no matter how much of an accident it had been.

"Are you okay?" I asked.

"Yeah. Just… maybe not in the mood. I'm sorry."

He'd always come once we got going. Always. "You don't have to be sorry." I let go of his dick but stayed draped over him. "If you weren't in the mood, you should've said something."

He shrugged. "It's okay. I like doing that for you." He regarded the hallway over my shoulder. "I should take the dogs out." Tugging his T-shirt down, he eased along the couch until he was out from under me. The shirt he wore featured an album cover for what I assumed was a band called OneRepublic. I had no idea who they were, but the various colored blobs on the shirt looked like sperm making their way up his torso. How fitting. Or not, since he was standing, doing up his jeans at the same time. Then he moved away, leaving me kneeling there on the floor before the couch, my pants open, my dick hanging out.

How often had he given me a blowjob when he hadn't been all that into it?

"Matthew—"

"It's okay." He stopped before leaving the room. "I'm just… I'm worried about Luke."

I got that. Luke had left hours ago to see his dad, and I was trying very hard not to let the worry carve its way into my every thought.

But there was something else going on with Matthew.

I couldn't stand the idea that he'd given me head when his mind was elsewhere. I stood and adjusted my clothes. "Tell me what you're thinking."

He shook his head, evaded my gaze. As if that would make me leave it alone.

One of the puppies began whining, and that got the others started.

"I'm gonna go take them out." Without another word, he left the room.

A chorus of high-pitched barks rang through the house as he led the dogs upstairs and outside into the backyard. I made my way into the hall and found his coat hanging by the door. I grabbed it and slipped on my own.

By the time I got out there, the pups were jumping in the drifts, and Matthew was kneeling in the snow, petting each one that came to him for a brief bit of love before taking off again. He had slipped on a sweatshirt, but he was still shivering, and his jeans had to be soaked through.

"Here." I handed him the coat.

He swiped it out of my hands and shrugged it on. It was impossible to ignore the anger in that move. Especially from him.

"What's the matter?"

"Nothing." In contrast to that he added, "If I wanted my coat, I would've worn it."

"It's too cold out here not to."

"It's my body. I know whether I'm cold or not."

I nearly recoiled at his tone.

The pups must've been getting cold. They were slowing down, gathering around Matthew.

I reached for him, cupped his cheek, and tilted his head back so he was looking up at me. "When we get back inside, you are telling me what's wrong."

There was no missing the moment his frustrated expression changed, the moment he gave himself over to what he really wanted to do. He leaned into my touch and nodded.

I let go of him, and he started encouraging the dogs toward the door. I left him to it and went after the runt who was sniffing along the fence at the rear of the yard.

When I got to the basement, Matthew had the others in the enclosure. I set the runt inside with them and didn't say anything, just went into our playroom, sat on the bench, and waited for him.

Matthew came to stand at the door.

I still said nothing, wanting him to speak without more encouragement.

He finally entered the room and took a seat on the bed facing me. "I don't like it."

"What?"

"That you're selling the estate. You're giving up, and that's not you. You don't back down from a fight."

That wasn't what I expected. Although I wasn't certain what had been on his mind, and that fact alone bothered me beyond words.

"He's right about that," Luke said as he stepped into the room, looking more at ease than I'd seen him lately.

"Hey." I gave him a halfhearted smile. "How did it go?"

"Well, I'm pretty sure I never want to step foot inside a federal prison again. There's nothing quite as bad as being sealed behind a series of locked doors and not being able to leave without someone else's okay."

"Being locked in there with your father?"

"Touché." He breathed deep and spoke again. "He said he'd stop calling. Said he'd back off until I came to him. No matter how long I needed. Even if he's an old man before I'm ready."

"You believe him?"

"I don't know. There's something different about him, that's for sure. But it felt good—really damn good—to tell him what I'd do if he didn't leave us alone, that I was calling the shots this time. If he doesn't keep his word, I'll file the restraining order. But... a part of me thinks he was sincere."

I'd believe that when I saw it.

Luke continued. "He wants to start a scholarship for gay youth. Named after that guy he was in love with in college, the one who killed himself, Danny Conner."

I gave a nod, signaling I remembered the name, not that I approved of whatever was coming next.

"He wants me to manage it." Luke gestured to me. "He wants you to handle the financial side of things."

"You get that he's just trying to buy you off, right?"

"That's a definite possibility. But if he wants to put his money toward a meaningful cause, I don't want to be what gets in the way of that."

"So you're really thinking about doing this?"

"No. At least not right now. I need some distance from him before I can even think about something like that." He pointedly looked at me. "But if I ever decide to do it, it'll be my decision to make."

"What are you saying? You want to let your dad back into our lives, and I'm not supposed to have an issue with that?"

"I'm saying it would be nice if you trust me, trust that I know what I'm doing. After everything we've been through, I think I deserve at least that much."

Matthew was intently watching me, waiting for my response.

A heavy silence descended, and my reply got locked in my throat. I knew what Luke needed me to say, what he wanted to hear, and I even knew what was the right move, but I couldn't force the words out.

He took an agitated step backward. "Just say it. You actually believe I'm gonna get lost again. That I'll end up taking off when I can't handle things with him."

"You almost did once." I'd meant it as a joke, but it was clear by the instantaneous drop of his jaw, he hadn't taken it that way.

"That's low."

I stood and shortened the distance between us. I didn't touch him, though. Despite that every part of me was aching to. He'd just shrug me off, and we needed to talk this out. So I simply kept focused on that stunned look in his eyes. He actually thought I didn't trust him, that I believed he would fuck things up somewhere along the way.

I said, "You don't get it, do you? I know you, maybe better than you know yourself. I saw that you were ready for this relationship before you even understood what you were feeling for us. I trusted you with my heart, with Matthew's. What we're talking about here isn't about trust. I'm just never going to want you to spend time with a man who held a loaded gun on you. *Twice.* I can't change that. But I do respect what you need."

Luke snorted out a frustrated exhale. He glanced away, but he couldn't keep the grin hidden. "Asshole." Then in an unexpected, sudden move, he gripped me by the back of the neck and tugged me in for a long, deep kiss, and when that kiss ended, he still didn't let go of me. He stared me down with an intensity that told me he was feeling things he didn't have words for. Or maybe he did. He held my face in both hands. "I fucking love you."

That wasn't something Luke said every day. Hell, it didn't even require all the fingers on one hand to count the number of times I'd heard it from him.

"I know you do, and that's why I *know* you won't run."

His expression lightened, and he kissed me again. "Thanks."

Reluctantly I stepped back. "Don't thank me yet." I gestured to the bed. "We need to talk."

"Weren't we just doing that?"

"There's more." I returned to sit on the bench, and Luke went to take a seat on the bed next to Matthew.

Matthew bumped shoulders with him. "You glad you went?"

"Yeah. I don't exactly trust anything he says, but it felt like closure telling him to back off or else." Luke hesitated for a moment as he searched Matthew's face. He raised a hand to Matthew's cheek, brushing the pad of his thumb under the bruised flesh. "I was thinking on the way home... I want to sleep on the couch. Until I'm sure the dreams are over."

"No," Matthew got out before I could offer the same. He gripped Luke's hand and held on to it on his lap. "It was an accident. If you wake up like that again, I know now not to get in your face. I want you there with us. I don't want you anywhere else."

Luke kept his focus on their combined hands. Eventually he said, "Okay."

I breathed deep in relief. There weren't words for how much I hated the idea of one of them not being in our bed every night.

We were all quiet for several moments.

"Matthew—" I started.

But he spoke at the same time. "I've been thinking about something."

When he didn't say more, I prompted with, "About what?"

"Maybe I should try to find my dad."

If he was attempting to get a reaction out of me, he'd found the right topic.

I leaned forward, elbows propped on my knees. "That's not going to happen."

I expected him to get angry like he'd done at the Harrison Estate when he mentioned his father. He didn't.

He got up and came to the bench, moving in between my legs, forcing me to sit up to make room for him. He rested his hands on my shoulders. "What if I need to? What if I need closure like Luke did?"

"Don't. Not *your* dad. I can't…"

When I didn't say more, he shifted back so I'd look at him. "Let me?"

Those were loaded words. The same words I'd said to Luke about confronting his dad the first time. When I'd said them to Luke, I couldn't have meant them more.

Until now.

I tugged Matthew to me and buried my face in his chest.

He held me in return, stroking my nape and my left shoulder. "I'm not saying I'm going to do it. It was just a thought I had."

I got up and stormed across the room. "Are you trying to make me angry?"

When Matthew didn't respond, Luke stood. "What's going on?"

Matthew bit his lip, but his gaze remained locked on mine. There was truth in what I'd said.

"Matthew's not happy with me right now." I returned to him and ran a thumb over that lower lip. He released it with my touch, his lips parting. Threading my fingers through his dark hair, I cupped the back of his head. "Talk to us. Tell us what you're really thinking."

"You can't give up on the Harrison Estate. You've wanted it for too long."

"It's just a house, Matthew."

"You didn't even talk to the police about Kinkaid's threats."

"I wasn't going to take that risk. It's a *house*. It's just money. It doesn't matter to me."

"That's not true. This is about more than the money. If you give up without a fight, it's going to eat away at you. Maybe not right away, but it will bother you more than you'll be able to stand." He clamped his mouth shut but then added, "What if you resent—"

"Wait." I shifted a step backward. "If you say I'll resent you—" I shook my head. "That is not possible."

"Are you sure?"

"Absolutely."

He didn't look like he believed me. "If that painting exists and it's at the estate, it's worth millions."

"I don't care."

"Yes, you do."

I threw my hands in the air and charged around the bed to the opposite side of the room. Did he really think money—or anything else—mattered to me over him and Luke? Did he think I was that callous? That hard? Questions I never imagined I'd ask myself about him. Not Matthew. With my back to him, I said, "Nothing will stop me from taking care of you. When you need me, I have to be there. If you're in danger, I have to do whatever I can to keep you safe. That comes first. Always."

"I know. I wouldn't want you to be any other way, but…"

When he didn't say more, I faced him. "What?"

"You can't be everything. You can't fix everything. And you certainly can't prevent everything. Some things are out of your control."

"But I will not do anything to knowingly put you in danger."

Matthew glanced away, worrying his lower lip between his teeth in frustration as if he still wasn't getting what I was saying. Or I wasn't getting what he was trying to say.

A ding sounded, and Luke tugged his phone out of his pocket. He didn't explain what it said, but it was clear from the look on his face that he thought he should tell us.

"What?" I asked.

"It's Walter. He's found Dominic's granddaughter. She says she'll meet with us tonight if we can make it." His phone signaled another new message. He read the text. "And she's not alone."

* * * *

Two hours later Matthew, Luke, and I waited in the hallway outside Dominic's room at the nursing home, while inside Dominic met with his granddaughter, her husband, and their newborn baby.

When we first entered the room and introduced everyone to Dominic, there'd been a litany of tears. First from Dominic, then

Isabella, then her baby as she handed over the little guy to meet his great-grandfather. Dominic had just laughed at the squirming, crying infant and held him close.

It was a beautiful moment, and it felt good to see Dominic that happy after the beating he'd taken the other night.

When we'd first met with Isabella earlier and told her about her grandfather, she'd wanted to go talk to him right away. She had grown up knowing nothing about him. Her father had told her that her mother and her mother's parents were all deceased. She was estranged from her father now. It was obvious the thought that she had one remaining family member who might care about her had her feeling more than a little emotional.

So once all the introductions had been made, I said, "We'll let you guys talk," and we stepped out into the hall.

There was an awkward, palpable silence between the three of us as we waited there in the vacant hallway.

"Come on." I gestured toward the exit and got moving.

"Where are we going?" Matthew asked as he and Luke followed. "Thought you said in the car you were going to explain to Dominic about selling the estate."

"That can wait." I had something else to take care of first, and besides, I wasn't about to ruin the moment for Dominic with news like that.

We exited the nursing home into the dimly lit parking lot. The dusting of new snow covered the older, dirty slush in a sparkling white blanket. It gave the one-story meager nursing home an almost magical quality that was a perfect fit for what had taken place inside with Dominic and his family, but not what would happen outside for me.

We filed into my car. I turned on the engine and cranked up the heat but didn't shift the car into drive. From the passenger seat, Luke watched me with that knowing, uneasy look he sported whenever he knew things were about to get serious.

And yet... I couldn't say it.

I stared out the front window. Fresh snowflakes hit the ground and disappeared into the existing layer of snow, becoming more than they'd been as lone flakes.

Like my life. Like the three of us.

Matthew moved from where he sat behind me to the middle of the backseat. He rested his forearms on the seat backs. "Richard..."

"Yeah."

"What are we waiting for?"

What *was* I waiting for?

I rotated in my seat so I could look at both of them. "There's something I need to tell you."

Luke groaned and dropped his head back to the headrest.

I laughed at that, and it felt good to let go of some of the tension. "This one isn't about you, so stop worrying. You don't have to say anything." But despite my words, I grew quiet again. I never talked about this with anyone. Except Anne. And even then, we didn't go into the details. I wouldn't do that to her.

But I needed to tell them. I wanted to. It was a big part of what I'd been trying to say to Matthew.

Yet I still couldn't find the words.

Matthew reached over the seat, gripped my hand in his, and gave a squeeze.

I nodded but remained quiet.

"Hey." Luke was studying me with concern, and it hit me then how odd my not talking must've seemed to them. He laid his hand on top of Matthew's so together they held mine on my thigh. "Just say it."

"Okay." I dislodged my hand from theirs and turned to look out the front window at the falling snow again. This time the flakes floated in the light breeze that had kicked up. Like they had no hurry to get where they were going. The door to the nursing home opened, and two elderly women with scarves covering half their faces stepped out. It occurred to me then how few people had been coming or going since we arrived. The snowfall wasn't significant enough to keep them away.

Sadness overwhelmed me. For Dominic and his friends in the nursing home. And for Matthew. If he outlived Luke and me, what would his final years be like? Would he have anywhere to go? Would he end up at someplace like Legacy Village?

Not if I could help it. If nothing else, I'd leave him a stockpile of cash. There had to be a number of nicer nursing and retirement homes in the city.

Could money buy the kind of security I wanted for him? It hadn't done anything to protect Anne. And neither had I.

Without looking their way, I finally started. "When I was twelve years old and my sister was five, she was abducted. She was gone for six days before someone found her." I drew in a deep gulp of air and forged on. "The day she was taken, my mom had left to go grocery shopping, leaving us in the backyard to play. I was supposed to watch Anne, but she was always annoying me, messing with my stuff. I was busy setting up this massive domino course on the sidewalk that led to the back gate. I'd been planning the course on paper for days, and I didn't want her touching it before I was ready to set it off. So after Mom left, I yelled at Anne to leave me alone and go play on the other side of the yard. Then…" My voice cracked on the word. I swallowed down the reaction and pressed on. "Then when Mom came home, she couldn't find Anne. I had no idea where she'd gone or when she'd left the yard."

I stopped. So had the snow. A thin layer had formed on the lower half of the windshield. I felt compelled to turn on the wipers to brush away the remnants, but I remained motionless. I might not be able to go on if I so much as moved an inch.

"A delivery man bringing a package to the wrong address by mistake found her. She was in an isolated house in a wooded area ten miles from our home. The delivery guy heard her sobbing through a window that was open a crack. He knocked and when there was no answer, he phoned for help. The police came, got her out of there, and they were able to stake out the place and catch the guy. But not before she spent six days in that house with him. He kept her locked in a room, her ankle chained to a bedpost while he was gone."

"Did he—" Luke didn't say more.

"Yeah." I nearly choked on the word. I had to force the rest out around the lump that had formed in my throat. "What you can imagine a sick fuck would do to a little girl, he did."

Matthew sucked in a sharp breath. "Oh God."

I grabbed the top of the steering wheel in both hands. "She was young and he had her heavily drugged the entire time, so she barely remembers anything. Mostly just the part when he first took her and when she was in the hospital after. Not much in between. The psychologist had said some of it might come back to her, or she might have triggers that affect her or her reactions to intimacy without her really understanding why or remembering the specifics. But she says she's okay, that nothing like that happened. The authorities only knew what he'd done to her from…" I stopped again, unsure if I could say the rest.

Luke reached across the space between us in the front seat and placed a hand at the back of my neck, his warm thumb stroking the skin below my ear.

I nodded and continued. "From the exam they gave her, and because the guy confessed to everything after they arrested him. He'd said he came into our yard, slipped a hand over her mouth, and dragged her away. All while I sat right there, messing with those stupid fucking dominoes." I gripped the steering wheel tighter. "I live with the regret of what I let happen to her every day."

"Jesus, Richard," Luke said. "You were just a kid."

"But it doesn't change that it was my fault."

Before the words had finished leaving my lips, Matthew was climbing over the seat. He sat half on my lap, half on the center console. He laid his head on my shoulder and wrapped his arms around me. "The only person who's to blame for what happened to Anne is the sick fuck who took her. I can't stand that you think you have to shoulder any of that."

"I didn't tell you so you could feel sorry for me or so you could say how wrong I am to feel this way. I wanted you to know about that part of my past. I was hoping you'd understand why I have to sell the estate. I don't want to hold on to it and regret that decision later. For any reason."

Matthew hugged me tighter and kissed the side of my neck. "I understand."

"Yeah," Luke offered. "You do what you gotta do, and we'll be right there with you."

I met his stare over Matthew's head. "The same goes for you."

He gave a nod in understanding.

Yet somehow I couldn't help but feel like I was letting them down, letting myself down.

I forced aside that reaction.

I'd do whatever I had to, to keep them safe.

Chapter Eighteen

The next day after work, when Dominic spotted me standing in the doorway of his room at the nursing home, he pointed down to the bed on both sides of him. "Look. I'm still here."

I laughed. "I came to see if you want to go to the estate with me."

"Yeah?" He was already working his legs over the edge of the bed. "What for?"

"I wanted to talk with you about something." And I wanted to give him a chance to say good-bye to the place, but I kept that to myself for now.

He grabbed a cardigan sweater off the end of his bed. This one was white with a florescent green-and-purple Aztec design that resembled what a child would draw with finger paints. Where did he get those sweaters? The nursing home's lost-and-found box? This one definitely looked like the kind of thing someone would intentionally lose. Maybe there was truth in that scenario. He'd likely spent a great deal of money on supplies to take care of the estate. There had probably been little left for himself. And it wasn't like he'd had any visitors bringing him birthday and holiday gifts over the past few years. Although maybe he would now that Isabella was back in his life.

His right arm got stuck in the sweater, and he flapped the sleeve in the air, trying to get it to cooperate. I stepped forward and helped him untangle it.

When he was situated, he said, "Thank you."

Those two words stung to hear. He wouldn't be thanking me for long.

A half hour later, we entered the Harrison Estate. The grand foyer looked much the same as it had the night we stayed there, except this time the power was on and the furnace was running, removing the sharp chill from the air. The chandelier adorned with rosaries lit the entryway with a brilliance that made it difficult to imagine Dominic had been attacked inside the house just days before.

Much of the dust on the staircase had been tracked around by us, the electrician, and the furnace people well before the attack, and the house had another set of stairs leading to the floors above, so there was no telling if the intruders had gone upstairs via the main staircase or not.

For some reason I was feeling the need to have a last look at the house before I gave Dominic the news about selling to Kinkaid. A part of me knew once I told him, it would feel official. Finished.

As we made our way through the house, I got what Dominic had meant about the ransacked state of it.

The library was our first stop. All the reading chairs had been knocked over, the books swiped off the shelves where they now lay in a jumble on the floor, many of the books splayed open with their pages torn.

Dominic knelt by a pile near the corner of the room and reverently ran the tips of his fingers over destroyed copies of *The Great Gatsby* and *A Tale of Two Cities*. His favorites? I couldn't bring myself to ask.

I felt for him. He may not have been able to keep up with the mounting dust, but he'd done a good job saving the place from complete disarray in the fifteen years it had sat vacant.

We moved on and surveyed the rest of the house. The ballroom on the second floor had clearly been gone through, but it wasn't as wrecked as the bedrooms. They'd been searched similarly to the library. More books had been tossed around, drapes ripped from their rods, and furniture toppled over into the middle of the rooms.

The master suite was the only location left undisturbed, but that had probably been because there wasn't much there.

A thought occurred to me then. "If Edward never used this room why did he remove the furniture?"

Dominic stopped in the middle of the bedroom. "Edward had every intention of sleeping in here. His staff took out Griff's bed, the dressers, all his personal items, but that's when the noises started. It spooked the staff. Edward too. So he told them to quit, and everyone left this room alone after that."

I flashed him a quick grin. "So that's when the ghost rumors began?"

"Yep." The corners of Dominic's lips turned up in a slight smirk, and then he grew somber again. As we had looked over the house's damage—and even more so standing there in the bedroom—his focus seemed to be more on me than the house. As if he knew what I was about to tell him.

Only, there was something else I needed to share first. "I know who killed Griff."

Dominic's eyes widened. "Who?"

"Terence Kinkaid all but admitted that his grandfather did it."

"He killed him because of the painting?"

"Yeah, probably to cover up that he'd broken in, and why. But his grandfather died several years ago, so there'll be nothing the police can do."

Still standing in the middle of the room, Dominic spoke, and his voice sounded all the more subdued. "But at least we know the truth now." He moved to the fireplace and rested a hand on the mantel. He stayed like that for a minute, then looked back at me. "Years ago there was this young man who lived here at the estate. He worked as an assistant for Edward. He hated the job, hated how Edward spoke to him when he ordered him around, but he needed the money. He was alone and miserable, and I always feared I'd wake up some morning and find out that he'd hanged himself in the night. Or had downed a bottle of pills. That young assistant was the only staff member who was supposed to move to the new house Edward had purchased, and I was worried that without the rest of us there with him, that young man really would take his life one day. But after that last party Edward hosted, the assistant quit, said he'd had a better job offer." Dominic eyed me with a new expression for him. Admiration, maybe.

I knew which young man he was talking about. The one I'd found a job for fifteen years earlier.

Dominic continued. "The night of that party, I stood on the second-floor landing when you left and I saw you give him your business card. I heard what you said to him too. At first when you showed up here with Matthew and Luke, I didn't recognize that you were the same man. I only put it together when I saw you in the attic with Matthew when he was hurt. Very few men who have the kind of tenacity and drive you do also care the way you do." He stopped as if he regretted saying that to me. Or maybe not, considering his next words. "This business of yours… You may get a rush from it, you may enjoy it, but you do know you are destined for more, right?"

I studied him. My gut reaction was to tell him he didn't know me as well as he assumed, but I stopped short of saying anything. Perhaps he saw me in a way I should've been looking at myself long before then.

Dominic gestured at the room around us. "I ran in here after I spotted the men who broke in the other night." He shook his head as if he didn't want to relive it.

"Why didn't you call the police?"

"What would they have done? File a report?" He focused on me. "I knew you'd be more motivated to help." All at once he seemed unsteady. He gripped the fireplace mantel in both hands.

I went to him and held his arm. "You okay?"

"Yeah." He shrugged. "It's just... They came at me in the place where I..." He pointed to the hardwood floor before the fireplace. "Where I found Griff."

That solidified my decision. The best thing for all of us was to let the property go. "Listen..."

Dominic considered me again. This time there was no trace of anger or frustration or sadness.

I told him about my conversation with Kinkaid and the threats against Luke and Matthew, and he listened quietly, carefully.

I ended with, "I have to sell. I can't put them at risk. And I can't chance going to the police. It's not worth it to me."

"I understand." He glanced around the nearly empty room once more, and I did too. There wasn't much for anyone to see, but for the two of us, there was a lot to take in. His past. My lost future. I pictured the room as I would've loved to have seen it after the restorations, with the new furnishings in place. It would've been something else.

Dominic was back to watching me. "You were really excited about your plans for this place."

"I was."

He nodded but didn't look away. "Investing other people's money doesn't give you the thrill that it used to, does it?"

I examined him, unsure how he was so good at reading people and yet so difficult for me to read. "No, it doesn't."

"That happened with Griff and his acting. When he was younger, it was such a high for him—getting a movie deal, the fans—but then it became what he thought he needed, not what he wanted."

He'd accurately described how I'd been feeling for a while, even with landing the Harrison Estate.

We were quiet again, back to looking around the nearly empty room.

His next words came in a cautious, gentle tone, like he was afraid of how I'd react. "There's something wrong with you and your men, isn't there?"

My entire body tensed, and I moved several steps away from him. "We're going to be fine."

"I didn't mean to imply you wouldn't."

"I've just been working a lot lately. I hadn't realized how that's been affecting them, affecting us."

"You expect too much."

I thought he'd meant from Matthew and Luke until he said more.

"Those two men don't want perfect. They want you. If you try for perfect, you'll fail every single time."

That pissed me off at first, but... He was right. I'd been trying too hard. Afraid of losing them since the minute they walked through my front door with their bags packed, all set to move in.

Dominic continued. "You don't give them enough credit. They both have a lot of strength."

"I know exactly who they are and how strong they are."

"Do you? What the three of you have, it grounds them. A relationship like that—a love like that—it gives a person the courage to be himself, to find out who he is. Which means they may not end up as the same men they were when you met them."

My gut churned at that.

Would those men still want me? Need me?

Or was that my fear talking?

I wasn't a man who let fear rule my life, but wasn't that what I'd been doing? About so many things.

As if reading my thoughts, Dominic added, "You have to trust them, trust that they're strong enough to handle whatever it is that comes up. And that you're strong enough to love them as they grow and change throughout the rest of their lives."

I scoffed at that. But oddly, he was making more sense than he had since I met him.

Dominic studied the room, this time with obvious resignation. "What will Kinkaid do with this place once he finds the painting?"

"I have no idea. But he'll go through everything and gut the house to find it if he has to."

Dominic turned toward the fireplace and didn't say anything for a moment. Then he spoke again, barely above a whisper, his back to me. "What if *we* find the painting? Tonight."

I took a cautious step toward him. "How would we do that exactly?"

He still wouldn't look at me. "You could give it to Kinkaid. Then you'd get to keep the house, and Kinkaid would leave you and Luke and Matthew alone, right?"

Another slow step. "Dominic, do you know where it is?"

Again he said nothing right away, but there was no missing the desperation in his eyes as he faced me. "I wish I did, but—" He shook his head. His eyes grew moist, and I couldn't grasp what had made him so upset. "I trust you now, Richard. That's why I want you to have this." He gave one last glance at the fireplace, the door, the bare room behind me as if he had to check for someone who might be listening in. Or as if Griff's ghost was really there with us and could hear him.

Dominic reached for a chain fastened around his neck and slid the other end out from under the collar of his shirt. Dangling off the chain was a gold key. "It's to the missing safe. Griff had tucked this key under the handset of the phone by his bed the night I found him. The key was inside a folded piece of paper that had my name on it. He knew I'd use that phone if anything happened to him and I had to call for help. On the paper he'd written that the key was to a hidden safe and asked me not to tell anyone about it."

"You knew all this time that whatever Griff hid, it was probably in that safe and you didn't say anything?"

"I don't know where the safe is. Until that night with Griff I didn't even know it existed." He paused and hung his head. "When I met you, I didn't think I could trust you. Then you said it might be a Lombardi painting, and I wasn't sure I wanted you to find it."

"And now?"

"I'm trusting you with the last thing Griff asked of me. I kept this a secret from everyone for him." He held the key out for me.

"And you never looked for the safe or told anyone about the key?"

"No. I thought if he wanted someone to have what was inside, he would've told me where the safe was located, told me what was in there and what to do with it."

"Maybe he didn't have time to write all that down. Or he didn't want to put too much information in writing in case someone else discovered the note. Maybe he figured you'd go find the safe, that you'd know where to look."

"But I don't."

Oddly, I believed him. I was also guessing Kinkaid knew there was a hidden safe, or he was hoping there was one. That's why he'd mentioned tearing up the house to find the painting. I checked my watch. "Well, we've got less than twenty-four hours to figure out where it's at before I have to meet Kinkaid and sign the paperwork to sell the house."

Dominic nodded. "I'll help in any way I can."

I tugged out my phone.

It took everything I had in me to fight against what I wanted to do: leave Luke and Matthew out of this. But they'd been right. I didn't want to let the house go. I didn't want to allow Kinkaid to push me around. They deserved to hear that from me.

When Luke answered, I asked, "Can you come to the estate?"

* * * *

Dominic and I made our way into the foyer and waited. The knock came a few minutes later.

I opened the front door for Luke and Matthew. "Come on in. We've got a painting to find."

They both appeared apprehensive until I filled them in on the safe and the key Dominic had given me.

"You were right about me not wanting to give up. I've got to take this last shot at keeping the estate, and I wanted you here with me."

Matthew rushed forward and flung his arms around my neck. I wasn't sure if the reaction was because I was going to look for the painting or because I had asked them to be a part of it.

Before I could get clarification, Luke spoke as he handed me the work gloves I'd asked them to bring. "So where do we start? We've already searched every room."

"I'm not sure yet."

"Should we get a metal detector, scan the walls and floors? The opening for the safe could've been concealed during one of the remodeling projects."

"Maybe." But that would probably give us a good number of false hits, and we'd be needlessly tearing up a lot of the house in the process.

I'd been giving it thought since I called them, trying to figure out where Griff could've quickly accessed a safe that night, where such a safe could be hidden that no one would've stumbled across it in fifty years.

I was certain Dominic was the answer.

What did he know about that no one else did? I could think of only one thing.

I turned to him. "Show me the hidden entrance that you've been using to get inside the house."

"There's no safe there. It's just an opening in the basement wall."

"You were the only person other than Oliver who knew about it, right?"

"Yeah."

"Okay. Then let's take a look."

We followed him to the stairs off the kitchen and into the basement, winding through the various rooms in a single line, past the crates and trunks filled with Griff's movie memorabilia, and into a narrow room at the far end of the house. The space was nearly empty with just a lone cot sitting in the corner. No windows. No doors. One of the solid stone walls appeared only slightly newer than the others in the basement, but it had no sign of any opening.

Dominic walked across the room and stood facing that wall. "There." He pointed to the chipped, soiled surface a few feet farther down from him. "To come in from the outside, you have to use that entrance. It moves inward and can be closed from behind. But when you're already inside the house, you have to use this side." He pointed directly in front of him at the stone wall. "Griff would've used this one that night if he did hide the painting in here."

But there was no sign of where a section of the stone wall could be removed or could pivot either in or out to form an opening.

Disappointment hit as I realized that Dominic was perhaps more senile than I'd considered before and that he'd made up the entire story of the secret opening.

"Dominic, there's nothing there."

He threw me a smug, annoyed expression over his shoulder. Then he turned, laid both palms on the wall, and pushed his weight against it. He was gonna strain a muscle. Or ten.

I advanced and laid a hand on his shoulder. "Stop."

He didn't, and half the wall began to move, separating it from the remainder of the surface, creating an uneven edge that followed the line of mortar between the stones, which was how the seam had remained invisible.

Luke came to stand beside me. "Holy shit."

He and I hurried to help Dominic, who seemed irritated as he stepped aside. "I've done this countless times over the years."

The wall glided with surprising ease. It sat on a thin wheeled track, and in no time we were able to squeeze through the opening and into the storm cellar.

Matthew followed. "It's empty. Except for this." He picked up a rusted crowbar that was covered in cobwebs and had been leaning against the base of one wall.

"It's here," I said. It had to be. I went back to the opening and inspected the wall on both sides of the gap we'd made. I pushed on the stone surface in several places but found nothing.

That entire wall was definitely newer than the rest of the basement, but what about the floor? Had Griff installed a new one of those too? I examined the floor inside the basement, but everything seemed normal. I did the same with the dirt floor in the storm cellar, pushing at the dirt with the side of my shoe to see if I could find anything underneath. Matthew and Luke joined in. It was a small space, and it didn't take long to search. We neared the opposite corner when Matthew stopped.

"Here. There's something here." He dropped to his knees and put on a pair of gloves. He shoveled handfuls of dirt aside. I joined him.

When we had the top layer of dirt cleared off, we had exposed a three-foot square concrete slab. I carved out a trench along the edges. "It's a lid."

Luke retrieved the crowbar. "Use this."

I offered him a warm look in thanks and gave the same to Matthew beside me. No matter what, I had definitely made the right decision in having them there with me.

I painstakingly pried up the lid, and with their help, shifted it to the side, revealing a top-loading safe. Despite having been installed inside a concrete enclosure, there had been some water damage. The lid and edges of the safe had rusted a bit. Even with the key, getting it open took effort with the crowbar.

As I unsealed the lid and got it flipped open, everyone grew silent.

The safe was narrow but deep, and inside was a thin wood frame, the face of it pressed against the side of the safe so we couldn't see the front.

Dominic sucked in a deep breath. "It's really here."

I yanked off the gloves and pulled out the frame. Surprisingly, the safe had protected it well. Not as well as proper storage in climate-controlled conditions would have done, but the frame didn't appear as if it had gotten wet or was otherwise damaged. Still kneeling on the floor, I turned the frame over.

"Wow," Matthew said from beside me. "It's beautiful."

It was. *She* was.

"But," Luke said, "not what we were thinking."

The woman in the painting wore only a sheer cloth draped around her. A single bare shoulder and an ankle were all that were visible of her body, but the cloth clung to her in a way that beautifully accentuated her female form. I said, "It resembles a Lombardi, though."

"Yes," Dominic offered. "And it's painted on a wood panel."

I glanced up, and Luke nodded from where he stood beside

Dominic. "I did some checking. All Lombardi's paintings were on wood, and none of his other work was ever transferred to canvas."

Dominic added, "And this is not one of his known pieces. This one's more..."

"Provocative," I finished for him. Which was probably why the Catholic Church had initially concealed it.

"So..." Matthew grinned. "It's definitely the secret painting everyone's after."

"Right." I pointed across the room to the doorway in the wall. "Griff must have hidden it in here that night. Or maybe it was already here. That's why he'd had the safe installed in the first place. Then he went to the farthest room from this location, his bedroom, and that's where they found him." I got off the floor, carefully holding on to the painting. "It looks like I've got a call to make."

Luke gripped my arm. "You sure you want to do this?"

"Absolutely. We get this painting out of the house, then I can focus on the restorations. And the three of us."

He gave a nod that said a lot. At least to me. He needed that focus, needed the three of us to be together—to be *right*—again.

We all did.

Chapter Nineteen

"Matthew." I kept my voice low but spoke his name with a harsh tone I rarely used where he was concerned. "If you don't keep your head down, I'm driving you home right now."

I watched in the rearview mirror as Luke reached up from the floor of the backseat and tugged Matthew down by the back of the neck. That was followed by a surge of laughter from Matthew. Then from Luke.

Damn, those two.

Bringing them with me went against every instinct I had. This could go badly, could end with the very thing I was trying desperately to avoid. But I had known with one look from Luke there was no way he was letting me go to this meeting alone, and I couldn't keep pushing them away, as Luke had described it.

With how things had been between us lately, I was worried if I pressed this, it might just be too far. Almost losing him because his dad had been tormenting him was bad enough. I couldn't take seeing him walk away now because of my own decisions.

"Richard." Matthew's voice was cautious as if he knew I wouldn't like what he was about to say. "How are we going to watch your back when we can't look out the windows?"

"You didn't come to watch my back." I was handing over the painting, taking the money, and that was it. "Nothing's going to happen."

Having a conversation with them tucked behind the front seats as I drove was starting to feel ridiculous, but we were almost there, and I wasn't taking chances.

"Nothing, huh?" Luke let out an exasperated snort as if he'd decide for himself whether I was safe or not while making the exchange with Kinkaid.

Matthew laughed again. He could interpret Luke's reactions even better than I could.

I pulled into the parking garage and drove to the fifth floor, then cut the engine. The ungodly early hour and the dark, nearly abandoned garage weren't easing my concerns. I'd have given anything to be home in bed, Matthew's head on my chest, Luke's arm draped across both of us.

I sighed and lifted the painting from where I had it propped on the front seat beside me. We had wrapped the frame in one of Dominic's blue blankets at the estate. I opened the car door. "Don't you two move. If something happens, I'll hit your number on speed dial, and you can call in the cavalry."

"Yes, sir." That was Luke. I pictured the salute he'd probably used along with the sarcastic tone. Then came the resulting laughter from Matthew. It cut short, though, as I stepped out of the car.

"Please be careful." The words rushed out of Matthew.

"I will."

Luke added, "Crack the window so we can hear."

I started the car again and did as he'd asked, then shut the door. The frigid air tore through me, chilling me to the bone. I raised the collar on my coat and headed to where the three of us had discussed stashing the painting. Kinkaid had selected the parking garage for our meeting, but I wasn't about to give him all the advantages.

When I had the painting taken care of, I surveyed the vast, empty concrete space around me. When the hell had our lives transformed into some kind of suspense movie Matthew would rent for us to watch on a Friday night?

I heard the faint sounds of footsteps, but I couldn't tell from which direction.

"Mr. Marshall."

I turned toward the voice.

Three men approached, their footfalls growing louder as they shortened the distance between us. All were tall and broad and fastidiously groomed, dressed in identical suits with dark glasses so I couldn't see which way they were glancing, like they were agents in the Secret Service. Was the ensemble by choice or a team uniform Kinkaid enforced on his employees? Did these guys in their suits and shades follow Kinkaid around on the Lakeview Country Club's golf course every morning? I grinned, holding back the chuckle at the ridiculous spectacle he must've made everywhere he went.

Speaking of Kinkaid, though. He was nowhere in sight.

The bodyguard in the middle said, "I need to search you for a weapon."

"I'm not carrying anything."

It didn't seem he cared. He stared me down, and I gave in, raising my arms straight out at my sides. He slipped on a pair of driving gloves like he might contract a disease just by touching me, and then he patted me down. When he found no gun or other weapon, he signaled to someone behind me.

I spun around. A black Cadillac Escalade with tinted windows inched toward us. It came to a stop beside my car. The driver—wearing the same suit and glasses as the others, even though it was still dark—got out and opened the back door. Kinkaid and a woman exited. From the picture I'd seen in his office, I knew his companion was Judy Fitzwater.

Before I could say anything, the man who'd searched me said, "He's clear."

"Where is it?" Kinkaid asked.

"The money first," I countered.

He scrutinized me for another minute, then removed an envelope from his inside jacket pocket. He handed the envelope to Fitzwater but spoke to me. "I'll need you to sign the paperwork in that envelope. It states that you found the painting on your property and are selling it to me, and that the sale is final no matter what I find out about the authenticity of the painting."

The smug bastard assumed the authenticity would work in his favor, not the opposite.

"I'll sign," I said, "but only if you announce publically that you now have the painting, that it's no longer at the estate." I didn't want anyone else coming for it.

"Of course."

Right. Just as I'd imagined. He couldn't wait to tell the world what he was about to acquire.

Fitzwater brought the envelope to me. Inside was the paperwork, as well as a cashier's check for the amount we'd agreed on. More than enough for the restorations. I read through the paperwork, and with my phone, I snapped a picture of each page and the check, and e-mailed everything to my attorney. She was standing by to approve the deal. I had no intention of trusting Kinkaid. I slid the check into my inside jacket pocket and said, "As soon as my lawyer gives the okay, you'll get the painting."

Everyone grew quiet as we waited. The occasional honk of a car on the city streets below indicated the time for rush hour traffic was drawing near. The open space of the vacant garage seemed to shrink in size with each minute that ticked by, and with each lingering stare from Kinkaid's uniformed lackeys.

My phone signaled a new e-mail message with the go-ahead from my attorney.

"Everything looks in order," I said.

"The painting." Kinkaid's impatient tone echoed off the concrete floor and ceiling.

I gestured to the bank of elevators off to the side. "In the trash can. It's wrapped in a blanket." Kinkaid signaled with a nod, and Fitzwater went to retrieve it.

He'd donned white gloves by the time she brought him the covered painting. Kinkaid carefully removed the blanket from around the frame. His jaw dropped. "Well, would you look at that?" He examined the painting with painstaking concentration, then did the same with me as if he knew something I didn't. Or thought I knew more than I was saying.

He held up the painting for Fitzwater to see. They exchanged a look I also couldn't read.

Kinkaid tucked the painting in the blanket again. "You sign those papers, and we have a deal."

I signed. It was easier than I'd imagined. The painting wasn't meant to be mine anyway, and if I could use it to get this man out of our lives and get on with the restorations, I was more than happy to let the Lombardi go.

Kinkaid handed the painting to Fitzwater, and he came toward me. He took the paperwork and said, "Walk with me for a minute."

I hesitated, but a part of me wanted to know what he wasn't saying. I stepped in beside him, and we moved several yards away from his men, stopping once we reached the short wall at the edge of the parking garage. Kinkaid stared out over the city, and I faced the other way, keeping my gaze locked on my car—where Matthew and Luke waited.

Kinkaid spoke without looking at me. "Can I ask how you found it, *where* you found it?"

I had no intention of mentioning Dominic's involvement. I didn't want to offer any details at all, but it wasn't like I would be revealing something he could use against me now. "It was in a safe in the house."

"Ah." He didn't press for more. Although he seemed to want to. He was studying my profile, still trying to read me as if I had additional information that he needed.

I was missing something here.

I forced aside the curiosity. I was done with him, and I was leaving with Matthew and Luke. I started to move, but someone grabbed me by the upper arm and spun me around. One of Kinkaid's men, the one who'd frisked me earlier. He'd approached on my other side while I'd been paying attention to Kinkaid. And my car.

I blocked the first punch, but the second came faster than I'd expected.

I took two more hits to the face before I got in a good punch to his. His next jab to my ribs hit me hard, and I slammed against the concrete wall behind me, the top edge ramming into the middle of my back. This guy was no bigger than me, but he was ten years younger and had obviously done some boxing. He was a trained fighter.

I recovered fast and got in several solid punches before he had me on the ground. He pinned me there for a moment, his knee digging into my back, hands braced on my shoulder blades. Then without warning, he backed off, and I struggled to my feet as he sprinted for a stairwell door.

Kinkaid was long gone, and so were his other men, his car, and Fitzwater.

There was also no sign of Luke and Matthew.

Despite my instructions that they keep their heads down, there was no way they hadn't taken a peek once they heard the scuffles and groans of the fight.

My car looked disturbingly tranquil.

Holding my side, I rushed forward. "Matthew! Luke!"

The door behind the driver's side flew open. Matthew shot out, then Luke, and I felt like I could breathe again, despite the lingering pain.

"Are you okay?" Matthew hurried to my side and wrapped an arm around my waist, steadying me.

"Yeah. Probably looks worse than it is." I felt the blood dripping down my face from a cut above my eye.

Luke held me up on my other side. "We couldn't hear a thing once that car drove up. The engine drowned out what you guys were saying." He helped me lean against the side of my car. "They beat you up and took the painting?"

"Yeah, but he paid me first."

"Then why the fists to your face?"

"I have no idea. I thought they were distracting me to get to you. I figured he spotted you in the car."

Matthew shook his head. "Why would he want to get to us now? You gave him the painting."

"I don't know, but there's something else going on here, something he wasn't telling me."

"How can you find out?" Luke asked.

"You know what? I don't give a fuck. Let him take that painting and do whatever the hell he wants with it. So long as he leaves us alone."

"Sounds good."

"Yeah," Matthew added.

Luke helped me into the backseat of the car, then drove us home while Matthew sat beside me and spent the entire drive using the first aid kit from my glove box to clean up the blood and add a bandage to my forehead. He kept asking if I needed to see a doctor, but it wasn't bad. I'd felt worse when Dominic had thrown the fireplace pokers at me.

I was quiet as we stepped into our house. The adrenaline from the fight—and from thinking something had happened to Luke and Matthew—was dissipating, frustration and anger replacing it. Despite my earlier words, everything in me wanted to march into Kinkaid's office and get in a few good damaging punches before his men could drag me off him, then figure out what he was up to and come up with a way to stop him.

I set the cashier's check on the kitchen counter and stared at it, my complete focus on that need to get back at Kinkaid. Then a hand enfolded one of my clenched fists. Matthew's hand.

The complete support and devotion in his dark eyes had the anger and frustration fading away. I opened my hand and held his in mine. If anything had happened to him, to either of them—

"It's okay," he said. "Luke and I are fine."

I'd been noticing how good Luke was getting at reading me, but it was really Matthew who'd always seen the truth.

Luke came up behind us and pressed into my back, his chin on my shoulder. "Try not to do that worry thing you've perfected. The painting's gone, and you've got the estate. I think that means we can celebrate."

I kept my gaze locked on Matthew but spoke to Luke. "And I'm sure I know exactly how *you* want to celebrate."

He snorted out a laugh. "Well, what better way is there?" He turned his head and kissed the side of my neck, then upward toward my ear, his breath warming my skin. "Remember that night my dad crashed one of your parties?"

"Yeah." Although I wasn't sure why he felt the need to bring his dad into this.

"Remember what we did in your office afterward?"

Ah. Now it was making sense. "How could I forget?" I had fisted him while Matthew blew him, and the fact that Luke had trusted me enough to go there with me had meant more than any words. That night had solidified things for us. A ceremony of sorts.

"Well," Luke said, his voice filled with mirth and growing lust. "I'm thinking it's Matthew's turn."

Matthew's eyes widened.

I cupped his chin. "I like the sound of that."

He bit his lower lip and nodded. He did too. But then he said, "You're hurt."

"I can't even feel it." I stroked the side of his face with my palm. "But I want to feel you."

All at once the puppies began barking in the basement.

Matthew was breathless when he said, "I better check on them first."

"I'll help." Luke started to walk away but stopped and came back to me. "You get everything ready upstairs." He patted my ass, and together they took off for the basement.

I went upstairs and got towels and extra lube from the bathroom, my cock growing hard at just the idea of what we were about to do. Leaving my clothes on, I spread out on the bed to wait. I wanted to take things slowly, build up the anticipation, work Matthew into a frenzy, hear him moaning and pleading for me to give him more and more. I imagined what he'd look like all splayed out before me, heavy breaths pouring out of him, his lips parted, his body arching, every part of him begging me to fuck him, to move my hand inside him. I rubbed myself through my pants, then forced myself to lie still, tucked my hands behind my head, and focused on the open doorway of our bedroom. Only, no one came through the door.

It had been almost twenty minutes now. Reluctantly I got up to see what was keeping them, imagining Matthew and Luke trying to clean up some disaster the pups had created in the basement.

Whatever it was, they were leaving it and getting their asses upstairs.

But when I stepped into the basement, I found the large open room empty. All the lights were on and the pups were calm, sleeping in a pile. I checked the bedroom, but no Matthew and Luke.

I headed back up the stairs and called out for them.

There was no answer.

When I saw the cashier's check was gone from the kitchen counter, and spotted what was sitting there in its place, I stopped, stared, the breath catching in my chest. Then I rushed for the counter.

Matthew's and Luke's phones sat side by side. The phones hadn't been on the counter when they went downstairs. Matthew might've set his down, but not Luke. He was never without his phone unless we were sleeping or fucking. And neither one of them would've taken that check.

I swiped Luke's phone off the counter, and it rang. No name flashed on the display. Just a number I didn't recognize. I answered.

"You missing something, Richard?"

Kinkaid.

"Where are they?"

"I was willing to let you and your men walk away, no trouble, and you just had to go and fuck with me. Did you really think I'd fall for it?"

"Fall for what?"

"What you gave me is worth quite a significant fortune, but it's not the one I wanted, and we both know it."

The one he wanted?

I gripped Matthew's phone in my other hand. "What have you done to them?"

"You have an hour and a half to bring me the other Lombardi."

"There is no other one."

"Don't play stupid with me."

I had no idea what he was going on about, but I wasn't risking Matthew's and Luke's lives by trying to figure it out. I dropped Matthew's phone onto the counter and pulled mine out of my pocket. I searched my contacts for Luke's friend Walter. I sent him a text message. *I need your help.* "I'm not playing," I said into the phone. "There's no other Lombardi painting at the estate."

"Oh, there is." Kinkaid paused like his focus was distracted. "And I said no cops. Not even retired ones. Text him back. Tell him never mind, everything's fine, that you got it figured out on your own. Now, or you'll see how far I'm willing to take my methods of persuasion."

Without delay I did as Kinkaid instructed. Forget that he was monitoring my phone. It was beyond disturbing that he knew Walter was Luke's friend and that he'd been a cop. It proved how much Kinkaid had been looking into our lives, and how desperate he was to get what he wanted.

I had no intention of pushing that desperation too far. Not when he had Matthew and Luke.

Kinkaid spoke again. "Get me that Lombardi painting or you'll *never* see them again. I'll meet you at the estate in ninety minutes. Do not involve the police, the feds, anyone. You contact another person, and one of them will have a very serious accident. I'll let you imagine which one."

"If you fucking touch—"

"You're not calling the shots today. You will do as I say, and then you'll see your men. That's the deal this time. An hour and a half, Richard." The line went dead.

I stared at the phone—Luke's phone—and scrambled to figure out what Kinkaid had been talking about. But I couldn't focus on anything except…

I hadn't set the house alarm when we'd gotten home earlier. I'd been so distracted by what Kinkaid might be up to, and I let someone come into our home and take them, while I was fucking around with towels and lube and my dick.

"Fuck!" The rage came pouring out, and I flung Luke's phone across the room. It bounced off the far wall and thudded onto the kitchen table. The table where we'd had our first date, where I'd known, even then, that I was falling in love with them.

I was immobile. I couldn't move. Couldn't breathe. I slid down the side of the kitchen cabinet and landed on my ass. My head hit the door behind me, and my phone slipped from my hand.

I felt as helpless as the twelve-year-old boy I'd once been, listening to my mom sob in the next room, her and I both imagining we'd never see my sister again.

If anything happened to either—

No. They were going to be fine.

A lone pup started whining downstairs. That snapped me out of the panic and despair.

I had to get back to the estate, take a closer look in the safe. There had to be a second painting. Probably the gay painting the rumors had indicated, which would be worth much more than any of Lombardi's other work, simply because it would confirm the rumors about him.

Maybe I'd somehow missed it in the safe. Maybe Dominic could offer more information, or had another secret he'd been keeping from me. This time I was shaking the old man until he spilled everything he knew. Because nothing more was happening to the men I loved. I'd do *anything* to protect them.

With that, a thought hit me.

That was what Griff had been doing that night, like we'd assumed. He hadn't been protecting the painting. He'd been trying to keep the man he loved safe. The man he shared his heart with, his life with, his bed with.

At that, it all became so clear to me.

What I hadn't seen. What I should've known from the start.
I stood. "Fucking son of a bitch."
He'd been lying to me the entire time.

Chapter Twenty

I sped through the city streets, and when I pulled up in front of the Harrison Estate, I shot out before the car stopped rocking, then stormed in the front door of the house. "Dominic!"

He had wanted to stay there overnight one last time before the renovations began, and I'd agreed, leaving him there while we left with the painting.

Dominic came rushing down the main stairs. He caught a look at me and drew up short. "What's wrong?"

"Kinkaid's got Luke and Matthew."

"What do you mean?"

"I don't have time to give you a play-by-play. Where is the second Lombardi painting? I have less than ninety minutes to find it or Kinkaid's going to hurt them."

Dominic started down the staircase again, coming to a halt at the bottom. "Second painting? I had no idea about the first one until you told me. I don't know where—"

"Bullshit. Don't even try to lie to me. I know the whole truth now." I charged forward and jabbed a finger at him. "I know who you really are."

He shook his head and backed up until his heel hit the first stair. Then he spun around and darted up the staircase again.

"Stop!"

He didn't.

"Griff Harrison."

That did it. He came to a halt.

Then, as if that moment would change his entire life, he slowly turned my way.

I pointed at him again. "He wasn't in love with some actor named Oliver Nash. He was in love with you."

Resignation washed over Dominic. He tilted his head back and stared at the chandelier that hung like a crystal guardian over the foyer. Finally he lowered his head, tears in his eyes. "Yes."

"And you loved him?"

"I did."

Looking back on everything he'd said and done, it was obvious. Why the house meant so much to him, why he'd been staying in Griff's old room, why he'd begun "haunting" the place to keep Edward from taking over that bedroom, why he loved the solarium floor, and why he'd reacted the way he had when Matthew found the old letters hidden in the attic. Dominic was the one who'd spent that week with Griff in Hawaii. The one who cleared the snow off Griff's grave. The one who'd fought with Griff the night he died.

Every time Dominic had mentioned Oliver, he'd been talking about himself.

I had a lot of questions, but right then I *had* to find that painting.

"So he bought those Lombardi paintings for you?"

Dominic nodded. "Griff knew how much I loved his work. He'd seen how obsessed I'd gotten about the rumor there'd been a secret painting."

"Where is the second one?"

"I don't know."

I moved in closer. "Bullshit."

"Richard, I don't. I would never put your family in jeopardy over a painting. No matter what it would mean to have something Griff bought for me."

I believed him. Despite everything, I did. In fact, he'd given no indication he'd wanted to keep the first painting rather than use it to ensure Kinkaid's threats didn't come to light.

I gestured toward the back of the house. "Let's check the safe again." I headed for the basement stairs, and Dominic fell into step behind me.

We searched the safe and its concrete encasing but found nothing. I checked my watch.

Sixty minutes left.

"Tell me what happened that night."

"We were all alone in the house. I had given the rest of the staff the night off, and Griff was in the kitchen cooking. We were going to have a candlelit dinner in the dining room, something we'd never done before."

"He was going to give you the Lombardi paintings that night?"

"Maybe. But he got a call and then…" He stopped. "I've been thinking about it, how we argued that night. I think he knew they were coming for the painting—the two paintings, I guess—and he fought with me so I'd leave."

"To keep you safe."

"Yes. We never argued before that night. He pushed me away on purpose."

What I should've done with Matthew and Luke.

"And after you left, he hid the paintings. One in the safe. And the other…" Where? "Griff was desperate to keep you safe, but he also didn't want to just give them the paintings."

"No." Dominic marched across the storm cellar toward the basement opening but halted before going inside. "Griff would not have risked himself over something like that. He wouldn't have left me alone just so I could have an original Lombardi."

"You're right." If Griff loved Dominic—*really* loved him—he would never have put anything above the two of them being together.

I considered what I would've done in the same situation. I gestured toward the safe and worked through my thoughts aloud. "Griff was planning to give them one of the paintings. The one with the woman. That's why he left it in here and why he had the key in his room. He figured if he resisted a little, then eventually gave them the painting of the woman, he could tell them that was the only Lombardi he had. He could keep the second painting for you. Or if need be, he could use it as leverage to make sure you were safe."

"Oh God." Dominic stumbled backward a step and propped himself against the opening in the stone wall. He looked ready to be sick. I wanted to ease up for his sake, but I had to figure this out.

I continued, thinking out loud again. "But he didn't have time to mention the safe to them. Or give them the key. Or he decided not to."

"Why would he have done that? Why would he have put himself at risk? He *wanted* to be with me."

"Maybe he ran out of time. You said it yourself. He was protecting you. He knew you'd be back soon. The two of you never fought and you would've wanted to find out what was wrong with him. He was running out of time. He realized those men wouldn't be able to get to the safe and leave with the painting before you showed up. And once they got the painting, the two of you were dead. That would be the only way they could get away with it free and clear. So he lied, gave them a fake name of someone else he said was at the auction." The fictional Mark Smith, the name we'd found online. "Griff told them he'd sold the paintings to Smith, and they shot him and left."

Dominic's lower lip quivered as he stared at the wall behind me.

I eyed him for a moment more to make certain he wasn't actually going to get sick, or pass out. Then I asked, "How long were you gone that night?"

"Thirty minutes, tops."

"That didn't give him a lot of time to retrieve the second painting from the safe and then hide it somewhere." I kept working through it in my mind. Griff was desperate to keep the man he loved from getting hurt. But the painting also meant a lot to him.

An idea hit me. "Come on."

Dominic followed. "Where are we going?"

"The solarium."

We raced up the stairs and when we got to the solarium, Dominic asked, "Why here?"

"You said he loved this room."

"He did."

"So maybe he came to his favorite place that night. It felt comfortable to him. On instinct he would've thought of this room." I looked around. There was nothing. Just the empty pots. "Those weren't here then, right?"

"Right. Edward replaced everything Griff had in this room."

Except the tiled floor. I pointed to it. "Are there any loose sections of the floor?"

"No."

Nevertheless, I was convinced I was on the right track. I glanced at my watch.

Forty-five minutes.

Softly Dominic said, "This wasn't his favorite room."

"What?"

"You said he would've come to his favorite place. This wasn't it. He loved this room, but..." Dominic pointed to the windows. "He and I could never touch in here. I was his butler in this room."

"Okay. What about the ballroom? He'd had that mural painted on the ceiling to remind him of the ocean and the week he spent in Hawaii with you, right?"

"Yes, but..." Dominic shook his head. "I was his butler even more in that room, especially when he had his parties. All those people... Griff wasn't himself then. He was an actor. He hid everything he felt for me, and I couldn't even look at him. I was so afraid someone would see the truth."

Which explained why Dominic hated the ballroom. "Where then?"

Dominic hesitated, his gaze locked on the floor before him like he was sorting through the memories, trying to get the right ones to surface.

I was about to jog the thoughts from him with a good shake when he spoke again. "Our bedroom." He lifted his head. "*His* bedroom. It was the only place where we had complete privacy, where we could really be together."

That was it. It had to be.

I said, "Right after he hid the painting there, the men who broke in found him in that room. Once he told them who he'd sold the paintings to, they killed him, making it look like a suicide so no one would know they were at the estate or why."

"But there's nothing in that room. There's no place he could've hidden it."

I started for the hall. "It has to be there."

Dominic scrambled to follow me out of the solarium and up the stairs. He was out of breath when we reached the master suite.

I scanned the room. Just the love seat and the fireplace. I inspected the surface of the mantel and pushed on the bricks, hoping to locate a hidden compartment. I gave up and moved on to the two walk-in closets but found nothing in those.

He was right. There was nowhere to hide a wood-panel painting, even if it was smaller than the one we'd discovered in the safe.

I went to the bathroom, checking my watch on my way.

Thirty minutes.

The bathroom walls and cabinets were almost entirely white, and the space was even emptier than the outer bedroom. The wall behind the massive tub featured the only color. A mural of a long stretch of beach and the ocean beyond with the sun setting in the distance, casting an orange glow over the surf and the sand. Maui. Another reminder of when Griff and Oliver—no, Griff and Dominic—had stayed there.

Anguish overwhelmed me. Matthew hadn't had a chance to see that second mural yet. He'd mentioned wanting to take a look when we first came to the house.

What was happening to him right then? To both of them? Were they together? Alone? Scared? Hurt?

Despite the bare state of the room, I frantically tugged open the doors and drawers of the vanity.

Nothing.

Then I saw it in the mirror. A door for a laundry chute on the wall behind me. I spun around. The opening was large enough that a painting similar in size to the one we'd already found might fit on an angle. I called to Dominic, "No one used this bathroom after Griff?"

"No." He stood at the open door. "No one."

I went to the laundry chute and grabbed the handle. The door wouldn't budge. I yanked harder. It finally gave way, tipping toward me. It was dark inside the chute, and I couldn't see far. If the painting had fit—and if Griff had put it in there—it would've just ended up in the basement laundry area. Unless…

I stuck a hand inside and searched around. At first there was nothing but the interior walls. I leaned in as far as possible. My hand came across some kind of soft fabric. I gripped the edge between two fingers and carefully maneuvered the object toward the opening. When I had a better hold, I could feel that it was something hard wrapped in the fabric, like a thin piece of wood. Slowly as not to risk dropping it, I pulled the cloth and the item out through the opening.

Dominic's breath hitched as he stepped forward. "That's Griff's quilt. His mom made that for him when he was a child. He usually kept it draped across the foot of the bed. I forgot all about it."

The painting, if that was what we were about to see, had been the right size that Griff had been able to wedge it diagonally inside the chute. The fabric of the quilt was a bit worn, but it didn't look like it had sustained much damage. I knelt on the tiled floor and laid the blanket before me. I folded back the edges and spread it open, revealing the back side of a wood panel, which at one point had been attached to a brace but other than that was without a frame. Tucked into the wooden brace was a piece of creased, aged paper. One name was handwritten on the front. *Dominic.*

"Is that for me?" Dominic asked.

"Yes."

He sucked in another sharp breath. Then he forced down a swallow. "Would you mind?" He nodded to the paper.

I unfolded it and read the short, hastily scrawled note aloud.

"*I love you, Dom. I always will. I bought this painting for you because I wanted you to have something that would remind you of how beautiful our love is. No matter what happens, no matter what anyone says, never forget that it was beautiful. I should've told the world that.*"

That had me nearly choked up, but I didn't have time to process anything other than the fear and panic racing through me. I refolded the paper and handed it to Dominic. He clasped the note in a shaking hand and clutched it to his chest.

I returned my attention to the painting and turned it over, feeling guilty touching it with my bare hands.

That time it was *my* breath that caught.

The painting featured two nude men on a bed, embracing, their limbs mingling, both draped in a single cloth as if they'd just made love, a look of passion and longing and love passing between them.

"It's gorgeous." And was in excellent condition, even without the presence of a frame. If the Catholic Church had hidden it away for centuries as the rumors suggested, they'd done a good job preserving the piece.

"Yes," Dominic said. "It is beautiful." Still holding the note to his chest, he pulled out a phone from his pocket. "Isabella gave this to me. She says it has a camera. Would you mind taking a picture before you give the painting to Kinkaid?"

"Are you sure you're okay with me doing that?"

He stood taller and looked offended for a brief moment, and then his expression transformed into one of complete conviction. "Absolutely. No one else is losing someone they love because of that painting."

"Okay." I took the photo for him. Then I stared at the wood panel. I imagined what Griff must have felt that night, realizing that a man named Kinkaid might kill him over a painting, that he had only minutes to do whatever he could to keep the man he loved safe.

I sank back on my heels. "He's going to kill them."

"What?"

"He's not going to let any of us out of here."

Dominic shook his head. "That's crazy. Why would he do that if you're giving him what he wants?"

"You, me, Matthew, and Luke. We all know what his grandfather did to Griff. And he kidnapped Luke and Matthew. He has to know I won't let that go. That I'll go to the police after they're safe."

"What's he going to do? Kill four people? He can't be that certifiable. He can't think he'll get away with that."

Obsessed people are dangerous.

"I think you were right all along, Dominic. He's going to destroy this house. With us in it."

"How?"

"A fire. He's done it before. For another painting. He killed someone to get it. Just like he'll do to us. Maybe he'll have his security force take us out first or tie us up, but in any case, he'll burn the place down with us in it."

I checked the time.

Twenty minutes.

I needed help. But who? And how? I couldn't use my phone. I also wouldn't be surprised if Kinkaid was monitoring more than my phone, that he'd somehow know if I contacted the police in any way.

I removed my wallet from my back pocket and slid out the business card Dominic had given me the night we stayed at the estate. I stared at the number on the card. Matthew's words raced through my mind. *You can't be everything. You can't fix everything. And you certainly can't prevent everything. Some things are out of your control.*

"Dominic, mind if I use that new phone of yours?"

There were only two things—two people—I cared about having with me when I walked away from this.

Fuck my pride, my business, the estate, all of it.

I took the phone from Dominic and dialed.

* * * *

Kinkaid sauntered through the estate's front door, looking smug and arrogant. I wanted to pummel that expression right off his goddamn face.

I held that instinct in check and waited near the entrance to the main hallway. I watched as four men and Fitzwater filed in behind Kinkaid. There was no sign of Luke or Matthew.

"Where are they?" I demanded.

Kinkaid stopped, a suave grin turning up the corners of his mouth. He was fucking enjoying this. Fitzwater and the others halted beside him so he was flanked by his hired guns.

"Where's the painting?" he asked.

"I have it."

"I have them."

"You're not getting it until I see they're okay, until they're standing beside me."

He studied me for a moment, and there was something intensely desperate behind the arrogance. Had I been right about how far he'd go? He gave a nod to Fitzwater. She pulled out her phone and spoke to someone as Kinkaid and I kept the stare going.

A minute later the front door opened, and two of Kinkaid's armed men entered, wearing those damn dark glasses and tugging Matthew and Luke in by their arms. Both of my men looked wary and cold— neither was wearing his jacket—but they were alive and unharmed.

They'd never looked better.

Luke met my stare. "Richard…"

Without more than that, I knew he was asking me what I wanted him to do. If only I knew what that was. I was playing a lot of this by ear.

"You both okay?"

He nodded.

Kinkaid scoffed. "Nobody laid a hand on them. But that's going to change quickly if you don't get me what I want."

"Send them to me, and I'll tell you where you can find it."

He gave another nod to Fitzwater, and she gestured to Luke and Matthew. "Go on."

Luke grabbed Matthew's hand, and they started toward me. Then Luke's steps faltered, the wet soles of his shoes slipping on the marble floor. I braced myself, ready to make a dash for them if I needed to, but I didn't want to give Kinkaid or his henchmen any reason to think I was screwing with them so I held still. When Luke moved on sure footing again, I breathed easier.

I kept my gaze locked on Kinkaid as Luke and Matthew came the rest of the way. Despite the fact that Kinkaid was the only one of them unarmed, he was the most dangerous.

When Luke and Matthew were at my side, I asked again, "You okay?"

Matthew answered that time. "Yeah."

I gripped his hand in mine and hauled him behind me. I tried to do the same with Luke, but he wasn't having any of that. He stood his ground shoulder to shoulder with me.

I longed to take them both into my arms, feel how alive and breathing they were, then get us the hell out of that house, but there was still the matter of several hired guns and one crazy son of a bitch staring us down.

"As you can see," Kinkaid said, "they're fine." His voice no longer possessed that cool, controlled arrogance. He was coming unhinged. "My patience is about gone. The painting. Or you'll only get to take one of them home with you."

"You'd really kill someone over a piece of art? Like your grandfather killed Griff Harrison?"

"My grandfather did what he had to do when confronted with a difficult man who got in his way. Just like I will. The painting. Now."

There was no more hedging. Or else I might push him too far. I only had to hope I'd given them enough time. "It's upstairs. On a table in the ballroom." It wasn't, but if I could stall a little longer...

I had given Dominic my phone and sent him to hide in the basement with the painting, telling him to wait by the secret entrance. Partly to keep him safe, so he could get away if need be, but also so he could bring me the painting if the original plan failed.

I'd hand over that second Lombardi in a heartbeat to save Matthew and Luke.

Kinkaid signaled to Fitzwater, and she bounded up the stairs.

I spoke to Kinkaid, trying to keep him distracted. "You don't have paperwork for me to sign this time?"

He laughed. "We both know we're beyond that."

Which meant I'd been right about his plans. He knew I was going to turn him in, and he wasn't letting me walk out of the estate.

"Let me ask you," I said. "How did you find out the painting was here?"

He seemed overly amused by that. Or with himself and his twisted accomplishments. "The night Griff died, he told Charles Fitzwater and my grandfather he'd sold the paintings."

"You mean the night your grandfather *murdered* Griff."

The bastard actually snickered at that. "For fifty years our families have been following the wild-goose chase Griff sent us on. We tracked down every Mark Smith in the world to no avail. It was my idea to look into Griff's life again. Judy found out he had a safe delivered to the estate the day after he supposedly sold the paintings, and I knew they were here the night my grandfather came for them. That they were still here. Even if the safe was long gone, those paintings never left this house."

Fitzwater appeared at the top of the stairs right as Dominic's phone vibrated in my pocket. That was the signal. They were outside.

I reached for Luke and didn't let him shrug me off that time. I tugged him behind me.

"It's not there," Fitzwater shouted down to Kinkaid.

With that, the front door burst in, and several SWAT team members barreled inside. More appeared on the second-floor landing and even more alongside us in the hallway leading to the kitchen.

Kinkaid stumbled backward, the fury evident in the murderous look he darted my way.

I kept him in my sights and didn't miss when he lunged sideways and stole the gun from one of his men beside him.

Shoving Matthew and Luke toward the open library doors, I got us moving before Kinkaid had the gun aimed. There were commands to halt from the SWAT team, and then multiple shots rang out. A barrage of bullets smacked into the wall next to us, and I heard the chandelier—with its crucified Jesuses—hit the floor.

Luke tripped and fell against me. I grabbed his arm, then Matthew's, and kept us going until we were out of the crossfire and behind the closed door of the library.

I dragged them with me into the dark room, and we hunkered down with the desk between us and the firefight. With the moonlight coming in through the windows, there was a serenity to our surroundings that directly contrasted with the violence that continued in the foyer.

Then in an instant, the blaze of gunfire ceased. Several lingering shouts rang out and then silence.

I turned to Matthew. "You hurt?"

"No. That was…"

Fucking unbelievable, but neither of us voiced that thought.

We were all breathing heavily.

Matthew's eyes widened as he glanced over my shoulder. "Luke?"

I spun around. Luke had his head bent, a hand raised in front of him. His fingers were covered in blood. "My side." He looked up and must've seen the terror in my face. "It's not bad."

It was blood.

It was bad.

Chapter Twenty-One

"Richard..."

I heard the resolve in Matthew's voice, but I didn't turn to face him.

He spoke again. "He's going to be fine. It wasn't bad at all."

The same thing Luke had said. And it hadn't been. A minor flesh wound, they'd called it. But one that had involved far too much blood for my liking.

It also could've been much, much worse. Either one of them could've been killed. Right in front of me.

I kept my gaze focused on the white curtain around the emergency room bed. If I never saw another of those damn curtains again, it would be too soon.

Matthew said again with undeniable sadness, "He's fine."

"I know." No serious damage. No surgery. No sutures. The doc they had working on him—who looked like he should still be in high school—just had to finish cleaning the wound and bandage Luke up, and then we could take him home.

With that, Matthew went back to the eerie silence that had lingered between us during the drive to the hospital. I hated when he was quiet. Almost as much as I hated how he'd sounded so despondent.

So many things about that moment were wrong.

When we first arrived at the hospital and were waiting in the ER for the doctor, I had filled Matthew and Luke in on what I'd learned about Dominic and Griff—that Dominic had actually been Griff's lover—and I was surprised that Matthew wasn't asking a dozen questions on that topic alone.

I returned to staring at the curtain. A minute later it opened and the doc came out. "He's all set. The nurse will be in with the paperwork."

Matthew was on his feet and beside Luke's bed in an instant.

Luke reached a hand out and gripped Matthew's. "I'm okay. Just gotta keep an eye on it and make sure it stays clean."

Matthew nodded.

I watched the exchange from where I had remained in the chair a few feet from the foot of his bed. The images of Luke in that bed and Matthew in a similar one when he'd had the concussion were burned into my memory. I knew I'd carry them with me forever. Alongside the one of Anne being pulled from the ambulance as my parents and I waited by the door leading to the hospital. She had looked so small and frail.

Lying in the bed before me, Luke didn't appear either small or frail. But he did seem vulnerable. In a way I'd never thought of him before. Not even when his dad had threatened to kill him.

This time he'd been in danger because of me.

Matthew rubbed the top of Luke's thigh in a comforting touch, and Luke stared across the length of the bed at me. "You gonna let all that incredible guilt you love to lay on yourself keep you from coming over here and seeing that I'm okay?"

"I can see you from here."

"Richard—"

I sat back. The chair slammed against the wall behind me. "I was no better than Kinkaid. I was obsessed with keeping that estate, with building the most famous resort in the city, and look what it cost you."

"It's nothing. I didn't lose an arm."

I shook my head. "I never should've let you—"

"Don't." Matthew spoke with such force, it had me quiet in a heartbeat. "Please don't do that."

"Do what?"

"Push us away. Say you should've done it sooner."

But I should have.

Matthew's next words had him sounding even more frustrated. "If it hadn't been for our help, I don't think Dominic would've ever opened up to you. He didn't exactly trust you at first."

"Mr. Marshall?" A woman approached from down the hall. She wore a plain dark pantsuit and had her blond hair pulled back in a ponytail. She had introduced herself to me at the estate, but I'd been completely focused on Luke and hadn't heard much of what she'd said. Other than her name. She was the woman who had answered the phone when I called the number on the business card Edward Harrison had left for me.

I stood and held out a hand for her. "Detective Saunders. Thank you for everything."

We shook, and she said, "Well, Edward Harrison insisted if I ever got a call from you that I was to take it very seriously. I see how right he was about that." She gestured for me to sit, and she settled in the chair beside me. "I wanted to stop by and let you know it looks like Kinkaid is going to survive, and we have Fitzwater and all the others in custody."

Kinkaid had been shot during the gunfire exchange with the SWAT team, and several of his goons had made a run for it. It was nice to know none of them were out there, waiting to follow through on some twisted alternate plan Kinkaid might've put in place.

Saunders continued. "Kinkaid and two of his hired men are still in surgery, but they'll all pull through barring any complications. We'll need to get your official statements and ask some additional questions, but that can wait until tomorrow after you all get some rest." She smiled at Luke and Matthew and then turned to me again. "It was a good thing you called me directly. Kinkaid's been under investigation by the feds for fraud and art theft for a while now, and I'm sorry to say, we believe he has a couple of our police detectives on his payroll."

I was glad for the confirmation that I'd made the right call in taking a chance contacting her—not that I knew it was her I was calling when I dialed. "Why was it your number Edward left for me?"

"He thought things might turn ugly once the rumors started about an old Renaissance painting hidden inside the house. He wanted someone from the force in the loop, to help if you needed it. He said people like Kinkaid would probably come after the estate and try to extort the painting from you, whether it really existed or not. Edward told me that was why he sold the property to you. He knew you'd do right by the place. No matter what."

I threw her a skeptical look.

She laughed. "Edward Harrison may have been a complete asshole most of the time, but he quite liked you, Mr. Marshall. The more he learned about you, the more he respected you."

"Well, that doesn't make me feel better about taking the homophobic bastard's help."

"Oh, he wasn't homophobic. He just liked to use whatever he could to rattle people's cages. He knew Griff was gay, and he was fine with that, even back then. In fact, he was awfully fond of his cousin. Edward believed that painting existed, and he wanted to protect it for Griff, keep it out of the hands of whoever killed him."

"If that were true, how come Edward never looked for the painting himself?"

"I think he did, at first. I'm just not sure he wanted to admit to anyone that he couldn't find it, which is probably why he never told you about it."

"So before Edward died, he paid a cop to help me?"

"Not exactly. He didn't hire me. My grandfather and he were old friends. Well, my grandfather was more Griff's friend, but they all knew each other."

"Who's your grandfather?"

"Oliver Nash. He was an actor Griff met in Hollywood. In fact, my grandpa met my grandmother at one of Griff's parties at the estate. She was with the catering company, and it was love at first sight. He even gave up acting and moved here to be closer to her. They were never married. My grandmother was quite the feminist, and she vowed when she was younger that she'd never legally tie herself to any man." Saunders smiled at that. "Grandpa was very supportive of her beliefs, but it was like they were married to our family. They were together until she died eight years ago." She grew quiet, a sadness engulfing her. Then she drew in a deep breath, and the grief dissipated. "I was happy to assist Edward, give him a sense of relief in his final days with the knowledge I'd be here to help if you needed it." She paused like she was carefully considering her next words. "You should know. Edward tried very hard to find evidence to prove who killed Griff. He'd be incredibly grateful to you for finally bringing that truth to light."

It *was* one of the good things that had come out of everything that had happened in connection with the Harrison Estate—if I could go so far as to say any of it had ended with a positive result.

She stood, and I joined her. Then she hesitated again as if she were deciding if she ought to say more. "You should also know. Edward didn't just give you my number. He asked me to keep an eye on you and the estate. I was not to intervene unless you or the house were in serious danger. Or if things got to the point where you were financially in trouble and were going to lose the property. Then I was to approach and give you this." She removed a piece of paper from her inside jacket pocket and handed it to me. It had a list of twenty names. "Those are some of Edward's friends and associates who would be interested in investing in the estate, no matter what your plans for the place."

I took the list. "Thank you." What I didn't tell her was that I was fairly certain none of Edward's rich friends would be willing to invest in what I now wanted to do with the property. Sitting there in the hospital, waiting for Luke to get checked out, I had settled on a new idea as so many things became clear to me.

I spotted Dominic coming down the hall behind Saunders. I gestured for him to step forward and pointed to Luke. "He's okay."

Relief flashed across Dominic's face.

"I'm sorry about the house," I said.

He waved that off, but he wasn't fooling me. The foyer, the staircase, the wooden banister, part of the main hallway, and the doors leading to the library had all been riddled with bullet holes, and the chandelier had come crashing down, shattering into hundreds of pieces, which had to have damaged the formerly pristine marble flooring.

It would now cost more than I'd planned to renovate, and I no longer had the money Kinkaid had offered for the first painting.

Dominic shrugged. "It's just a building. I'm glad Luke and Matthew are okay."

Detective Saunders spoke again. "Maybe once you get started with the restorations, you'll find that secret painting Kinkaid was after. It sounds like it would be worth a fortune."

Dominic's eyes widened at her words.

Saunders offered her hand, and we shook again. "I'll give you a call tomorrow so we can set up a time to get the rest of your statements."

Dominic was intently studying me, and when Saunders was gone, he asked in a hushed whisper, "You didn't tell them you found it?"

"It's your painting, Dominic. It was always meant to be yours."

Tears filled his eyes, and he tipped his head back for a moment. "Griff loved me." He pointedly met my stare. "And I loved him. It feels good to admit that, to say it out loud. Finally."

I went to him and laid a hand on his shoulder. He gripped my hand in return.

When the rush of emotion seemed to have passed, I encouraged him to sit with me. "Why did you say he was in love with Oliver?"

Matthew sat on the edge of Luke's bed. All of us had our complete attention on Dominic.

"No one—*no one*—ever knew the truth about the two of us. It's difficult to admit something you've hid for so long."

"So Oliver and Griff were friends?"

"Yes. In those days, Oliver was one of only three people who knew about Griff's sexuality. But..."

"But what?"

He rubbed the back of his hand over his chin, his hand shaking with the move. "Oliver didn't know about me."

"Because Griff hid you? Like his dirty secret?"

"No. It wasn't like that. It was a decision we made together. If anything, he wanted to tell the truth, give up his career and live openly at the house with me. But it was a different time then. With his fame and his family's status, it would've been nearly impossible, unsafe for him."

"So if Oliver wasn't meeting with Griff at the house, why the secret opening in the basement?"

"Griff had it installed for us. We'd meet down there when the house was full of people. I'd pretend to be heading out shopping or on an errand, and I'd slip back inside through that opening. Or he'd use it to sneak home when he was supposed to be on a movie set. That way we could spend the night alone and no one would know he was there."

I couldn't imagine how difficult it had been for Dominic. And Griff. Having to hide that they were gay from almost everyone, pretending to be something they weren't for their entire lives. Matthew had been right. We were beyond lucky that we didn't have to hide. Even if many people didn't get the three of us together, we were living in a more open and tolerant time.

"So Edward also knew about Griff," I said. "Who was the other person?"

"Griff's fiancée. She was a friend who agreed to the engagement to help him hide the truth."

"And Isabella's grandmother? She wasn't your wife, was she?"

"No. We were never married. I was in love with Griff even when I met her. He and I had grown up together, but he was my boss and he was away a lot. His career was taking off, and I thought he was straight then. So I tried to pretend I could be something else. In the end, I told her the truth. About me. But not about what I felt for Griff. She lived at the estate for a while so we could raise our daughter together, but eventually, we both realized she needed to go live her own life."

"And when your son-in-law found out about you, that you were gay…"

"He took my granddaughter away. But thanks to you and Luke's friend, I have her back." He smiled at that, then grew serious again. "What will you do now?"

I knew what he was really asking me.

"I'm not going to open the resort."

Matthew and Luke stared at me, their shocked expressions a match for Dominic's. Although his was laced with disappointment.

"I'm keeping the house, and I'm going ahead with the restorations, but I'd like to turn it into something else. I might end up adding a couple more buildings to the property, but I'll leave the pond and the gardens, maybe add walking paths."

"Walking paths? For who?"

"You. And people like you. I want to turn the estate into an assisted-living facility. The main house and other buildings could be used for housing. The ballroom would be good for all kinds of activities. We could bus in residents from other nursing and retirement homes so they could spend the day there. I'll set up a company to handle outside investments to cover the operational costs so it won't be expensive for the residents." The more I talked about it, the more excited I got. And Dominic's lighthearted, eager expression matched how I felt.

I was beyond relieved he liked the idea.

I stared at the paper in my hand with the list of names from Detective Saunders. "But don't get your hopes up. I'm going to have to take on investors to get the place up and going, and I was having trouble getting people to sign on before, when it was going to be a posh resort." But with Kinkaid out of the way maybe things would improve on that front.

Dominic grinned at me. "You can do it. I know you can. People like you. They trust you."

"Thanks for that." I paused, hoping I was making the right choice with my next words. "I'm going to need to bring some experts on hand. Nurses, doctors, specialists. People who'd know what the residents would want and need. But I'd also like to include someone who has an understanding of the house, someone who could help me oversee the renovations. You game?"

"Really?" He eagerly scrutinized me and grinned again. That was only the second time I'd seen him that happy. The first being the night we introduced him to his granddaughter and his great-grandson. "Yeah, I am."

"Good. I'd like you to be the first resident too."

"Live there again?" He blinked back the tears forming in his eyes once more. "I'd love that, but I don't know…" He dropped his head, then lifted it just as quickly. "I have a friend." He cleared his throat. "A male friend. Martin."

"Why, Dominic, are you dating someone?"

He laughed. "We're just… very good friends. You saw him at the nursing home. He was with the woman you assumed I was interested in, but it wasn't her I had my eye on."

"I see. Well then, he's more than welcome at the estate."

Dominic eyed me for a long moment, then reached out and gripped my forearm. "Thank you." There was a level of sincerity to his tone I hadn't heard from him before.

"Thank *you*," I said in return. "For everything." I looked to Matthew and Luke. "What do you think of the plan?"

Luke's blue eyes held a new expression. Something I couldn't quite put a word to. Pride, maybe. "Sounds just about perfect coming from you."

Matthew nodded but didn't say anything, and he wouldn't look at me. I had no idea what he was thinking, but I sure as hell hoped I was reading that look wrong. Because if anything, he seemed angry with me. And not about the estate.

We needed to talk. But not there.

"How long until you can leave, Luke?"

"Not long. They just gotta get the paperwork together."

"Good." We needed to be home.

The three of us alone together.

* * * *

When we finally arrived home two hours later, we all just stood in our living room, staring at each other, me on one side of the room, Matthew on the far end, and Luke near the couch. No one said a word, and the distance between us felt like we were strangers waiting for the next available teller at a bank.

I breathed deep and broke the silence. "I'm sorry I brought all this into our lives."

Matthew was shaking his head before I even stopped speaking, but he didn't offer anything more.

"Everything is fine now," Luke said. "We're all fine. So you can stop feeling guilty and stop with this holding-back thing you're doing."

I scrutinized him. "You could've been killed. Because of *me*."

"A little scrape on my side does not come close to almost being killed."

I scoffed at that. Leave it to Luke to make light of everything.

"Besides," he continued, "it was not because of you. You weren't the one with the gun."

When I still said nothing, still remained motionless, Luke spoke again. "Jesus, Richard. Fucking come over here and touch me. See if I'm okay, tell me you love me. Something. This isn't like you."

He was right about that. I went to him and drew him into my arms, pressing my lips to the side of his head, and I held on like I might never let go. "If you'd been hurt worse…"

He ran both hands down my back. "I'm fine."

I shook my head and hugged him tighter. "God, I never should've involved you in this."

"Just stop!" Matthew's voice was so full of frustration and anger, Luke and I jerked apart and both gaped at him. I'd never heard him talk to either of us like that. He added, "Nothing that happened was your fault."

I hated how he sounded, how he stood there like he was made of marble, so stoic, so unhappy, so not like him.

Cautiously I said, "I just want you guys to understand that I would not have done any of this if I'd known it would put you in danger."

"We know that. Do you think we'd actually believe you were expecting something to happen to us?"

It did sound stupid when he put it that way.

"No," I said. Our eyes locked, and we said more without words. About what we meant to each other, about how sorry I was, how scared I'd been that something more could've happened to him or Luke.

I started toward him, and he met me halfway. He laid his head against my chest and held on to me, his arms locked around my middle like a vise. I embraced him in return, my chin resting on the top of his head. I couldn't let go. I wanted to get closer, and for once, I wasn't sure how to do that. We stayed joined in that pose for several breaths, and the longer we remained like that, the more the tension in his body seemed to fade away.

When we eventually parted, Luke stood there watching us with longing in those expressive eyes.

I gave him a pointed look in return. "Don't even think about it." Even if his injury wasn't serious, he wasn't supposed to put pressure on it. In addition to that, we were all exhausted. It was only late afternoon, but it had been one hell of a long day. "You're in no condition for anything."

He shook his head. "Not that." He stepped up behind Matthew, then came forward like he meant to kiss me over Matthew's shoulder, but instead he whispered, "At least not for me." He caressed the length of Matthew's arms, kept his gaze on me. "We were rudely interrupted before."

He was talking about what Matthew and I had been about to do before Kinkaid's men took them. At Luke's words, Matthew's lips parted and he sucked in a sharp breath, his eyes wide. He nodded.

I wanted nothing more than to bring us all together again, for the night to be something special. I longed to show them with my touch what I'd been trying to say.

I reached for Matthew's hand, and he grasped mine in return. Keeping hold of him, I silently led the way upstairs.

We needed this connection.

We needed to be *right* again.

In the bedroom, Matthew went to stand at the foot of the bed and waited. He eyed my every step, a nervous, excited anticipation radiating off him.

Yeah, we needed this.

I told Luke, "You just lie back and watch."

"In a minute."

Slowly, sensually he helped me get Matthew undressed, both Luke and me kissing along Matthew's skin as we stripped away his clothes. Then Matthew and I were naked and on the bed, Luke lying next to us in his underwear and a T-shirt that covered the bandage at his side.

"Lie still," I told him again.

"Uh-huh." He licked his lips, his gaze still locked on me where I was kneeling between Matthew's spread thighs.

Matthew watched me too, never looking away as I leaned in and teased his bare flesh with my lips and tongue. His neck, an earlobe, the base of his throat, a nipple, the side of his abs—which made him laugh and wiggle—then his hip, the inside of one thigh, the top of his pubic hair, his balls. All the while, I held his cock and caressed the tip with my thumb.

Then I released him and sat back on my heels again. I ran both hands up the insides of his thighs, loving the goose bumps that followed my touch. I kept the contact light as my palm brushed his balls. His every breathless reaction, every ragged, pleasure-filled sigh drove me on. With my focus on Matthew's face, I didn't notice what Luke was up to until my fingers came in contact with his hand on Matthew's cock, intent on giving him pleasure in the same way. Luke stroked him from the base to the tip, then teased the slit with his thumb. All the while, Matthew let out little murmurs of appreciation, his head shifting back and forth on the mattress.

Luke leaned in and gave the top of Matthew's cock a kiss before taking the head into his mouth, offering moist sweeps of his tongue that spread his spit and Matthew's precum around the sensitive head. I almost told him to stop and go back to lying beside us, but I had to trust he'd know not to take things too far and hurt himself.

I repositioned myself down the mattress and joined him, licking up

Matthew's length, gliding my tongue along his shaft, never letting go of his balls.

Matthew's head lifted off the pillow. "Oh my fucking God. I love when you guys do that."

His cock grew harder with each touch, each flick of our tongues. He moaned and then whimpered, his body shifting on the bed as he rocked under the erotic attention of two mouths, two sets of hands. Arching his back, he reached over his head to grab the headboard. "Oh, oh God."

Careful to avoid smacking our heads together, Luke and I met at the tip of Matthew's cock. We kissed, our tongues tasting each other with the head of his erection between us. Matthew's stomach muscles tightened, and his body shook. It was an uncontrollable action that meant he was close.

I pulled off and held out one finger. "Get it wet."

Luke let go of Matthew and sucked on my index finger like he could make Matthew come with his mouth on me. And maybe he could. What with the way Matthew watched us.

I let my finger slip from Luke's mouth, resituated both myself and Matthew so the backs of Matthew's thighs lay over the front of mine. I angled his hips and ran that wet finger along the crease of his ass while Luke drew Matthew's dick back in, going farther this time, deep throating in the way that always had Matthew losing control. His ass surged off the bed again and again.

"Take it easy," I said. "We don't want this over before we really get going."

Luke let go of him. He nodded and moved to lie beside us. Matthew was once more intently staring at me with those wide, dark eyes. Every time he looked at me like that, I felt like a damn superhero. A king. A god.

And wrapped up in that admiration and desire was his love for me.

I was one very lucky man.

I went for the lube and sat it closer to us, got the towel situated under him. I bent over him and spoke with my lips touching his. "I love you."

"I love you," he said. "So much I get scared."

"Of what?"

"I don't want to lose you."

"Aw babe, I'm not going anywhere. We're here together. With Luke. Always."

He nodded, and I kissed him, deeply, fervently, offering him all my desire, all my devotion, and he clung to me in return. There was an undeniable spark to the moment. Like the first night we spent together at the Haven. Something exciting and alive and scorching passing between us that none of us could ignore.

Keeping close enough I could feel his heated breath on my lips, I held his gaze as I reached for his cock. Only…

I'd been wrong about everything.

He was growing soft, and when my hand made contact with him he flinched.

Fucking *flinched.*

I sank back on my heels. "Matthew?"

Then the truth hit me. The wide eyes, the repeated licking of his lips, how he'd tracked my every move, and the words he'd just whispered.

He was no longer turned on.

He was scared. And not just about losing me.

"Matthew?"

"I…" He didn't say more.

And I didn't need him to.

He didn't want me to fist him, to touch him like that. He never had.

I flew off the bed and tugged on my briefs and jeans, then a T-shirt. I was surprised when they didn't immediately follow me out of the bedroom. I'd probably shocked the hell out of them by walking away.

I raced down the stairs and into the kitchen, rounded the counter with the stools, and stopped before the sink. Bracing my hands on either side, I stared down at the drain like focusing on that one thing would keep the bile from making its way into my throat.

I could hear Matthew's footfalls as he entered the kitchen behind me. Slow. Cautious.

Without turning around, I said, "If you ever do anything like that again—" I couldn't say more, wasn't even sure what I wanted to say.

"You'll what?"

When I didn't respond to that, Matthew spoke again, his voice unsteady. "I wanted to do something for you. What's so bad about that?"

I spun to face him. He was dressed again, looking frightened and confused. My instinct was to go to him, but I couldn't. I was frozen in place. "Because it's a lie. Don't you get that?"

He shook his head.

"How can I trust that everything I've done to you—every time I've touched you— that it was something *you* wanted, not something you were doing for me?"

His eyes were wide again. "I wanted everything we've ever done. From the moment I saw you, I wanted whatever you'd let me have, whatever you wanted from me."

I ran a hand over my hair. "Jesus, Matthew."

"What?"

"That's not—" I stopped, again unsure of what to say, or what I could trust myself to say right then.

When I didn't offer anything more, he came closer. "Richard... what have I done wrong?"

The confusion on his face made me angrier, and I hated that feeling, hated that it was directed at him. "I never thought you'd lie to me."

Matthew's gaze dropped to the floor before him.

Just then Luke entered the kitchen. He leaned against the doorway, arms folded over his chest, and the silence stretched on between us.

I turned my back to them, but not before I spotted the shaking in Matthew's shoulders. "Luke, do me a favor."

"Yeah?"

"Hold him."

"It's not me he needs."

I forced myself to look at Matthew again. He had the same expression on his face as the night we'd gone to the Haven to get Luke, not knowing whether Luke had fucked someone else or not. Only this time, that hurt, terrified look was even more pronounced.

Because of me.

No matter how angry I was, I couldn't keep away. I crossed the distance in two steps and gathered him into my arms.

Matthew just stood there, arms at his sides, tense for several achingly long seconds. Then his arms came around me, and he buried his face in my chest. He shook more.

I'd never felt like a bigger ass. Even if I'd meant what I'd said to him, even if my feelings were hurt.

Luke watched us from across the room. There was a new sadness etched on his face, like witnessing this moment between us was breaking a part of him.

I expected him to come to us and try to get us fucking again, to distract us with kisses and touches and moving us toward the bedroom.

He didn't. He continued leaning against the doorway, that disturbing heartache in his eyes.

All my confidence was gone, shattered. I didn't know what to say or do to make Matthew feel better, didn't know if I trusted myself to speak at all. I might make the situation worse if I said anything, considering how frustrated I was. I continued to hold him and looked to Luke again, almost wishing he'd take that step forward to get us back to the fucking. I'd never been at such a loss for words. Panic gripped my chest. I was hurting Matthew more the longer I stood there like that, saying nothing.

The sorrow on Luke's face eased, and his expression softened. He gave a nod as if he understood what I needed more than I did.

"Matthew," he said, "look at me."

Slowly Matthew turned, and I let go of him. He didn't move away, though. He leaned back against me. Maybe he thought if we discontinued the contact, we might never touch again. Which was bullshit.

Yet a part of me *was* finding it hard to put my hands on him. Logically I knew that every time I'd held him, kissed him, caressed him, stroked him, fucked him hadn't been a lie, but I couldn't seem to make myself stop the absurd reaction.

My touch had scared him upstairs, and all I could see—and feel—was that flinch.

Whatever Luke saw in Matthew had him moving toward us. He cupped Matthew's face and brought his head up. "It's going to be okay."

That snapped me out of whatever fucked-up trance I'd been in. I bent so my lips were pressed to Matthew's ear and folded my arms around his chest. "It is. It's going to be all right. I was angry with you, but that doesn't mean we can't talk our way through this."

He nodded.

"It makes me sick thinking I almost did something you didn't want. Matthew, I could've *hurt* you, damaged you. Emotionally. Physically. I could've seriously injured you if I had continued with that if you didn't want it, if you weren't relaxed and open to it. How could you ever think I'd want that?"

He lifted both hands to his face and wiped at his eyes, and I hated that I couldn't immediately make this go away for him. Or me.

"Why would you agree to do that with me upstairs if you didn't want to? And don't give me that line about wanting to do something for me. Tell me *why* you wanted to do that for me."

He didn't say anything.

Luke searched Matthew's face. "I think… to make you happy."

I spun Matthew to face me. "Is that true?"

He nodded again.

I let go of him and staggered back until my ass hit the edge of the counter.

"It's just—" He started, then stopped.

"What?"

"I know you've been feeling like you were losing control of everything, with the estate and the break-ins and Kinkaid and Luke's dad. And maybe even us—the three of us. I didn't want you to feel that way. I wanted to give you something that would help you have some of that control back, something that would bring us closer. I don't want you to push us away because you're feeling guilty about what happened to me, to Luke. I don't want you to close yourself off from us."

So he'd almost let me...

I was suddenly finding it difficult to think, to breathe. I took off and headed past them for the hall.

Luke called after me. "You're going to walk out? That's not like you either."

It wasn't. But... "I just need a minute." I didn't want to talk to Matthew when I was that upset.

I made my way to my office, closed the door, and sank into the chair behind my desk, recalling again and again that moment when Matthew had flinched from my touch. Every single time it was like a dagger to my gut.

A half hour later the office door opened. Luke stood on the other side. He didn't enter the room, though. He just said, "He's gone."

"What?" I bounded to my feet. "Gone where?"

"To his mom's for dinner. He told me he needed some time by himself, and he went to the basement to wait for her. Since it's so cold out, he called her to pick him up. He never even said good-bye when he left."

I dropped back into the chair. That Matthew had chosen to call his mom for a ride rather than ask to borrow my car, let alone go to his mom's at all after the day we'd had, got the anger and exasperation bubbling up again.

When I said nothing, Luke pointedly glared at me. I knew what he was waiting for.

"I'll fix this," I said.

"Yeah, you will." He'd spoken the words in a more patient, understanding tone than I'd expected. "One thing's for sure," he added. "That man who walked out of this house is not the same kid with low self-esteem we met at the club, despite what he said and did tonight. He was trying to connect with you. He knows what he wants, and he's struggling to figure out how to tell us, how to show us. That's what tonight was about. Because he won't settle for anything less now."

Luke watched me for a little while longer. Eventually he came to stand beside my chair. He stroked my cheek, then tilted my head his way. "I love you." He gave me a quick kiss and left the room, and I sat there, working through how things had gotten so fucked up, how I'd almost hurt Matthew instead of seeing what he'd been trying to say, instead of seeing what he'd wanted and needed from me.

* * * *

Several hours later, as I waited for Matthew to get home from his mom's, I still sat in my office, thinking over the past few days, over every conversation.

He'd been right.

I had been feeling like I was losing control of everything, so I'd tried even harder to hold on to that control, and in the process I'd failed to keep them safe. I *was* feeling guilty about that, and I was also afraid I'd hurt them again someday. There was a good chance I would've put distance between us because of that guilt. I had done it with Anne. Hell, after college I'd moved hundreds of miles away from her and the rest of the family because it was too hard to see them all the time.

Matthew had sensed that, and he'd thought he had to do something drastic just to make me happy, to keep us close, to keep me from destroying us.

Or maybe there was more to his reasons than that.

I had to hear what else he was thinking.

And I needed to talk to him. Because no matter what, I wasn't letting myself ruin what we had.

To avoid chasing after him and making a scene at his mom's, I did research on nursing and retirement homes in the city. A futile distraction at best. By ten I was getting worried. Dinner with his mom never lasted that long.

By midnight I was beyond worried. I couldn't stand it any longer. I got up and went in search of Luke. He wasn't upstairs in his office or in our bedroom. I made my way into the main room of the basement, but he wasn't there either. Neither were the puppies. The makeshift kennel was open. The large carrier Matthew had brought the pups home in was gone.

Luke was sitting on the bed in our playroom, his back against the headboard, his legs out straight in front of him, his arms and ankles crossed like he'd been sitting there stewing for the past hour. Or longer.

I knocked on the open door.

He glanced up at me but didn't speak right away, just kept his lips pursed. Then he finally said, "After he was gone, I came down here and found it like this."

"He took the puppies with him?"

"I'm guessing so." Luke held up his phone. "He texted me an hour ago. Said he was helping his mom with something and might be a while. Said if it took him much longer, he'd spend the night there. I tried to call him, but he's not answering." Luke dumped his phone onto the mattress beside him and once again folded his arms over his chest.

I sat on the edge of the bed. "What do you think he did with the dogs?"

"He mentioned a couple of days ago that his friend Erika was home. He said he was going to keep them another week or so until she got settled in. I'm assuming he dropped them at her place." Luke quietly studied me for a moment. "He's not coming home tonight, is he?"

"I don't think so." I leaned forward and swiped a knotted rope off the floor, one of the numerous dog toys left in our basement. "He wanted to keep that little runt."

"Yep."

"I was waiting for him to say something about it, to say what he wanted on his own, but he wouldn't."

"Nope."

I turned to Luke, and he added, "Since you're so big on getting us to talk and asking us what we want…" He hesitated, his glare locked on me, his hands gripping his biceps. "Here's what I want. You to go get him and bring him home. And don't bother coming back until he's with you."

My Luke. So passionate and full of emotions he didn't know how to process or express. Although he was doing a damn good job of it right then.

I stood. "That's exactly what I'm going to do." I went to him and uncrossed his arms, then hauled him up. "And you're coming with me."

He shook his head. "I'm not who he needs to hear from."

"Yeah, but we're not *right* unless it's all of us." I purposely used the same words he'd said to me when I'd been worried they'd grown closer without me.

A grin tugged at his lips, and he finally gave in to it. "I don't know which one of you is more infuriating." He paused and then sighed in exasperation. "This is Matthew. All you have to do is talk to him, and he'll be fine."

He was right, but I still laughed at that. "Is that all I have to do?" We'd come a long way if Luke was the one frustrated with our lack of communication. I moved in and embraced him. "It's going to be okay. He's coming back home to us tonight."

Chapter Twenty-Two

Matthew's mom answered the apartment door sporting a terry-cloth robe over her flannel snowflake pajamas, and a scowl on her face. "It's one thirty in the morning."

"I'm sorry," I said. "But this can't wait."

She opened the door wider. "Damn straight it can't. I expected you *hours* ago." She stepped aside for Luke and me to enter, then gestured toward the bedrooms. "He's in his old room."

I started down the hall, Luke behind me. We both stopped when she spoke again. "I swear the three of you are more drama than teenagers." She went for a duffel bag that sat by the door. "You take care of my Matty or we're going to have words. I've never seen him so upset."

"We will," I said. "I promise."

She gave a nod. "I'm going to stay with my friend tonight. She lives here in the building." With a quick jab of her finger toward me, she added, "And when I get back in the morning, I expect you to have taken Matty back to his home where he belongs." She spun around and left.

Luke stared at the closed door. "Every gay man should have a mother like her."

I couldn't agree with him more. We got moving again and stopped outside Matthew's old room. The door was open a crack. I pushed it the rest of the way in. Matthew sat on a footstool at the window, blankly staring out at the city lights. A train blared its horn a block away, drowning out the traffic on the streets below.

His childhood room was small but tidy. He'd taken most everything with him when we moved in together, but despite the bare shelves, there were a few items still decorating the room. A blue striped comforter covered the bed, comic book posters featuring Spider-Man, Batman, and Wonder Woman adorned the walls, and all seven books of the Harry Potter series sat predominantly along the back of the desk, just as I imagined Matthew had kept them when he'd been a teenager. There was no dust, no other signs the room had sat vacant since Matthew moved in with us. Most likely his mom made a point of keeping it that way, despite that she didn't want him to return and instead wanted him to be happy with us in our home.

I motioned to Luke to go ahead with what we'd brought. He set the carrier on the floor beside him and opened the door. The puppy immediately barreled out. She was the runt with the white stripe along her belly. Without delay she scrambled to Matthew, bit down on his pant leg, and tugged.

That got his attention. "Hey, you." He scooped her up and looked toward the doorway at us. He didn't say anything right away, just held the puppy against his chest, scratching her behind one ear. Then he finally asked, "What's she doing here?"

"She's yours." I stripped off my coat and tossed it on the chair in the corner. "You can't just walk out on her. She needs you."

He turned and stared out the window again and continued stroking the dog's fur. "She's not mine."

"She most certainly is." I went to him, and with a hand under his chin I tipped his head back so he'd look up at me. "No matter what happens, no matter what you're feeling, you don't take off."

Luke snorted out a laugh from the doorway. "Well, that lasted thirty seconds."

Matthew glanced around me. "What did?"

"He's trying not to be so controlling."

Matthew gazed up at me again. "It wasn't about that."

"I think it was, at least partly." I went to sit on the edge of the bed facing him. "I know I made mistakes, didn't handle things the way I should have. That doesn't mean you walk away from us. That doesn't mean you spend the night somewhere else."

"I just…" He shrugged. "I needed time to think."

"I understand that. I needed the same thing. That's why I went to my office, to collect my thoughts." I paused, then asked, "What were you thinking about?"

"About what you said, about why you were so angry with me." He shook his head. "I didn't lie to you. I wanted to be with you like that—have you touch me like that. But…" He seemed to be running through it all in his mind, what he'd really felt and thought earlier. "Maybe my reasons weren't the right ones." He sat up straight and turned so his whole body faced me. "But I've always been honest with you."

"I know that."

The pup squirmed in his arms. He set her down, and she sniffed along the floor toward Luke.

"Do you?" Matthew asked barely above a whisper.

"I do."

"Because if you can't trust me, then I..." He trailed off as if he couldn't say the rest.

Sometimes I forgot how inexperienced he was when it came to long-term relationships. When I thought about which one of us had the least familiarity with commitment and monogamy, which one of us was still the most likely to run, it was always Luke. I never thought Matthew would try to leave us, even if just to his mom's. I never imagined I could say something to make him go, never imagined I'd lose my faith in the connection I had with him.

But I'd done both of those things.

"I do trust you, Matthew. Please talk to me. Tell me what you're thinking."

"I wanted us to do something special." Those wide dark eyes connected with mine. "You made it sound like you were bored with your life."

"Not with you. Maybe my work. But never with you. I love you. That has nothing to do with sex. The sex is just icing on the cake. Amazing icing. But being with you is not about the sex for me. It's the intimacy. It's being close to you. Emotionally. Physically. I get that by just talking with you, touching you. The specifics of how we get off don't matter to me."

He didn't respond. He looked to Luke, who scrutinized Matthew in return like he was attempting to read him again.

"No." I pointed at Matthew. "You talk. For yourself."

"You kept trying to push us away. Your instinct through this entire thing with the estate was to keep us out of it. And now you're feeling guilty about letting us in at all because we got hurt, because you're imagining how much worse it could've been. What if you never let us in again?"

"I was trying to keep you safe. Not keep you out."

"I know. You'd do anything to protect us."

What did he mean by that? He'd said he liked that about me.

Without me having to ask, he offered more. "You talk about keeping us safe like we're something you've collected, not like we're your partners who want to help you and be there for you."

I straightened. "That's not true."

"You didn't tell us you'd changed your mind about what you were going to do with the Harrison Estate."

"I just came up with that at the hospital."

"You make us talk all the time, but you haven't been. You only told us about what happened to your sister so we'd understand why you were selling the estate, not because you wanted to share that part of yourself with us."

I reached across the space between us and gripped his hand in mine. "I did want to share it with you. It just wasn't easy for me to do. I've never, *never* talked about it with anyone before you two. Not like that."

He stared at our combined hands.

I offered more. "I guess I didn't realize I wasn't communicating as effectively as I thought. I've always considered myself an open person. I figured that sharing my life with you, that getting you to talk, to open up to us, being there for you for whatever you needed, meant I was committing to this relationship. But I see now… You're right. I was holding back a piece of myself. I should've leaned on you more, let you in more, and I didn't."

"Huh," Luke said from where he still stood near the door. "Who knew?" He had the puppy in his arms. He stepped farther into the room, set her down, and closed the door before she could escape.

"What?" I asked.

"Who knew I was the expert at communicating in this family?" He moved to lie on his uninjured side across the bed beside me. "I mean, I was having nightmares, I told you guys about it, confronted my dad, and now the dreams have stopped. Easy breezy."

"Oh," I said. "Is that how it went?"

"Sure."

Matthew laughed, and it was good to hear that sound from him, good to see him smiling. He spotted me watching him.

I squeezed his hand. "I know I said I was trying to keep you safe, but the real reason I was holding back, not sharing with you as much as I should've—and maybe why I might've ended up pushing you away like you said—was because…" I hesitated and found the next two words difficult to articulate, even to him. I drew in a deep breath and whispered them as if I might hurt myself if I said them louder. "I'm afraid."

He searched my face. "Of what?"

"A lot of things. Hurting you most of all. Not being what you need. Losing you. Losing the estate. Not being able to find the investors I need. I hate the idea of failing at this—failing at anything."

He stroked the backs of my fingers with his thumb. "You won't lose me." He kept the contact going. "And you won't fail. No matter what happens. Because just trying to do the right thing—for yourself and for others, like you are with the estate—means you could never be a failure."

Years younger than me, and he was one of the smartest men I'd ever met. "You're something else, you know that?"

He shook his head.

I wanted to reach out, hold him in my arms, and love on him until he understood how special he was, until he understood what I felt for him, what he meant to me, but there was more I needed to say. "Now I'm also afraid of…" I focused on our joined hands and forced the next words out. "I'm afraid of touching you." I looked up at him.

He met my stare, and there was genuine fear in his eyes. He got up and came to stand between my legs. "I'm sorry. I should've told you how I was feeling, told you what I really wanted. And what I didn't."

I nodded. "You have to promise me that you'll never do anything with me that you don't want. Even if it's something I ask you to do. It has to be your choice. I can't be someone who takes advantage of you. Or hurts you."

"You would never do that. But I promise. I'll only do what we both want." He held very still, and the look in his dark eyes turned to that passionate, trusting expression he gave me whenever things got physical between us. "Please touch me."

That was all I needed.

I gripped him by the waist and hauled him forward between my legs until our lips met. He fell into the kiss, straddling my lap and holding me like he never wanted to let go.

When we parted for a breath, I said, "I won't shut you out or push you away. I swear, I won't."

He nodded. "I trust you." He traced my bottom lip with his thumb. "Just please don't stop touching me." Then he kissed me again. He moved over my body as he consumed me with the most powerful, passionate kiss I'd ever been a part of.

How could I be afraid of this?

I wanted all of him, all of Luke. I wanted every moment I could get with them for the rest of my life.

But I also knew I'd be watching Matthew's reactions, looking for the signs for a long time to come.

As if he'd read my thoughts, he gave me a clear signal, whispering in my ear. "I used to fantasize about this in high school. Being with a guy like you in this bed."

I closed my eyes and relished those words, the contact. "And now you have two." He was driving me crazy with the little nips and licks along the sensitive skin of my neck.

He sat up. "Yep. Two." He reached over my shoulder for Luke.

I felt the bed dip, and then Luke pressed into my side, he and Matthew kissing.

Just watching them together—safe and alive and loving on each other—was like coming home after being trapped in a long winter storm, and I knew, I'd do whatever I had to, to keep from losing this, losing them.

Matthew still had one hand at my nape. He encouraged me closer, and then I was a part of the moment with them, all of us coming together in those wet, silky kisses that left me breathless. Matthew leaned into me until we lay on the bed, Matthew on top of me, Luke there with us. They stripped me of my clothes with deft precision, and then they were naked too, save for the bandage on Luke's side.

"So this bed hasn't seen any action?" I asked as Matthew straddled me again, his thighs spread over mine, bare skin sliding over bare skin.

"Oh my God. It saw a lot. But it was just me and my hand."

"So you never—"

"Nothing. Not in here."

I rolled us until he lay on his back below me, my hips snug between his spread legs. "Time to remedy that."

He reached out with both arms and gripped the blanket beside him in his fists as if he needed something to hold on to, something to keep him from losing control.

Only, I *wanted* him to. It was a beautiful sight to see him lying before me, hard and wanting and needing me. Needing *my* touch.

I'd never longed to see that more—feel it more—than in that moment.

I couldn't resist. I scooted down and crouched over him, taking his cock in between my slick lips. A desperate groan tore out of him as I swallowed him down, his body arching up under me.

Then Luke moved around behind me and spread my legs apart. In a heartbeat he had his mouth on my ass. I forced myself to stop working the head of Matthew's cock. "Luke—" I groaned as his tongue darted inside me.

He swirled and stroked, and then I was the one who was losing control as he fucked my ass with his mouth. I returned my attention to Matthew's erection and took myself in hand. I heard Luke doing the same.

Matthew shifted under me, his body lost to the pleasure, my own lost to Luke's touches. Maybe I'd been wrong about this being icing on the cake. Right then, I needed this more than air. I needed to hear them and feel them when they came. I needed to know that I hadn't broken this for us.

As difficult as it was to think about Luke stopping that amazing rimming, I wanted him closer. "Luke, come here." Then I sucked harder on Matthew, pressed at his slit. I took him deep once more as Luke crawled up the bed to lie beside us. He was engrossed in my actions, as mesmerized by Matthew and me together as I always was with them. I reached over and gripped Luke's cock, stroking him at the same time as I kept my mouth moving on Matthew. I gave them no mercy, working them over just the way I knew they each loved.

It wasn't long and Luke groaned with his release. I kept going, racing my hand along his shaft until he moaned louder, his hips jerking faster, more cum arcing up and landing on his abs. Then he dropped back to the mattress. "Oh man. You always know just what the hell to do with those hands."

That's when Matthew's breathy moans started.

I let go of Luke, slid my hands under Matthew, and grabbed his ass, tugging him deeper into my mouth, encouraging him to let go, to thrust and fuck me. He did just that. His hands on the back of my head, he drilled up into me. "Oh God. I love you." With those words, he came, his ass clenching in my palms, his pelvis grinding against me in little spasms.

When he eventually sagged back to the bed, sated and quiet, I rushed to sit up and stroked myself until I shot, my release landing on the base of his dick and dripping down his sac. He had his fingers twisted in the blanket as he came down from the orgasm, and he'd never looked better. So open and sexy and completely gorgeous.

"Hey." I gathered him into my arms and sat back on my heels so he straddled my thighs once more. "Unless your mom's on her deathbed, you come home to our bed at night."

He nodded. "I will."

Luke sat up and whispered in my ear. "That would be one of those controlling things we talked about on the drive over here."

Matthew shook his head. "No. Please don't change." He held my face in his hands. "I like that you want me home with you."

"Me too," Luke offered. He leaned into us, and we kissed as one, the three of us tumbling onto the bed together.

We caressed and moved against one another, slower this time, savoring, stroking, tasting everywhere. I kissed Matthew's lower back and up his spine to his nape, then along the sensitive skin of Luke's neck and lower, down his chest, over his hip, and along the insides of his thighs. I felt like I touched them in ways I hadn't done in ages, or maybe like I'd never done before.

I wanted to show them—and myself—how *right* we were when we were all together. I wanted them to know that I would never try to push them away again.

* * * *

I awoke in Matthew's old room with someone pressing down on me. I opened my eyes and found a head of dark hair lying across my chest.

Matthew had an arm around my waist, a leg over both of mine. His hold was tight but not restraining. We both wore only our underwear beneath the white sheet that was draped over our lower halves. The fabric of that sheet was stretched across his firm ass cheeks. It was almost exactly the same way he'd fallen asleep after his shower the night before. Except the puppy was now curled up on the bed alongside his thigh.

I ran a hand through his wavy hair as I lifted my head and checked his other side for Luke.

What little was left of the small bed beside us was empty. A folded piece of paper sat on the pillow. I opened it and read Luke's handwriting.

Went out for coffee and breakfast and to run a quick errand. Won't be long. Will explain more later. I took the puppy out so she should be good for a while. Tell Matthew she needs a name.

"Is that from Luke?" Matthew asked without moving from where he lay sprawled across me.

"Yeah. He said he'd be right back. And that your dog needs a name."

Matthew lifted his head like he was considering that. Then he lowered his cheek to my chest and snuggled in, the rasp of his facial hair deliciously teasing my right nipple.

I heard the front door of the apartment open. A minute later Luke stood in the doorway of the bedroom. He carried a brown sack and three cups in a Starbucks takeout tray. When he saw I was awake, he whispered, "Doesn't look like you're going to be able to move right away."

Matthew shifted but didn't get up. "I'm not sleeping. I'm thinking."

"He's trying to come up with a name for the little furball." Who right then was attempting to climb down the side of the bed to get to Luke.

Matthew sighed, and his breath tickled as it swept through the hair on my chest. "I wasn't thinking about that. I already have a name. Trixie."

"That sounds like a hooker's name." Luke held up the bag he carried. "Pastries." He set everything on the nightstand.

I gave a nod in thanks for the food and asked, "How would you know what female hookers call themselves? You ever been with one?"

"No way." He took one of the coffees and sat at the foot of the bed facing us.

"A *male* prostitute?"

His answer could open up a can of worms where Luke was concerned, but I was curious.

"Nope," he said. "Never paid for sex. That's my dad's shtick."

It was good to see he could joke about it.

"You?" he asked.

"Never." I lifted one shoulder to get Matthew's attention. "How about you?"

"Me?" He raised his head and propped his chin on his hands directly over my heart. He seemed reluctant to say anything. His eyes revealed an embarrassment beyond what I'd ever witnessed from him. "Yeah." He chewed on his lower lip and then continued. "When I went to college the first time, there were these boys who came to campus every night, just looking to score some cash. I was so horny and lonely, I paid for this one guy three or four times a week. Until my Intro to Psych professor said he'd pay *me* for it." He sighed. "That was such a sweet deal. I was getting fucked regularly *and* getting paid for it too."

I would've thought he was joking, but he'd said the words so seriously.

Luke and I stared at him.

Then suddenly he rolled onto his back and busted out laughing in that signature giggle of his. "Oh man. You should see your faces. You actually believed me."

In a rush I moved onto him and tickled his sides. "Why, you little shit."

He squirmed and laughed more, and the last of the tension from the day before faded away.

"Hey, watch it, you two." Luke was struggling to keep his coffee from spilling with the shifting bed. When we looked his way, he added, "You want to know where I went this morning or not?" With that, he got up and stepped out into the hall. He came back with a large, thin box that had a note taped to the top. He returned to sit at the end of the bed and handed it to me. "It's for you."

Matthew and I sat up against the headboard, and I set the box on my lap, curious what Luke had gotten me. And why. I opened the note first. It wasn't from Luke but from Dominic. The sprawling, shaky handwriting gave away his age more than anything since I'd met him. I read it aloud.

"This is yours now. I know you'll do right by it. I don't need it to remember his love, and I don't want his money. I never did. Try not to forget, a man has never truly failed if he's surrounded by friends and family who love him. You're a good man, Richard Marshall. Tell Matthew thank-you for the puppy. My granddaughter loves him. I know my great-grandson will too."

I stared at the note for a moment more. Once again, it amazed me how good Dominic was at reading me. He'd understood me in a way I hadn't accepted about myself before I met him.

I handed Matthew the note and opened the box. Inside, wrapped in a white cloth, was the Lombardi.

Luke gestured to the painting. "Dominic texted me this morning and asked me to come get it."

Matthew leaned into my side. "Oh God, it's beautiful." He glanced up at me. "What are you going to do with it?"

I shook my head, completely astounded and honored that Dominic trusted me with the painting.

I knew what I had to do, though. What I was sure Dominic hoped I'd do.

"I'm going to find a reputable museum to sell it to. People should see this. A lot of people. Then I'll use the money from the sale to get the assisted-living center going."

Luke gave me a long, pleased look from across the length of the bed, and there was that pride in those blue eyes. "Dominic's right. You're a good man."

Matthew nodded. "Not many people would do what you're trying to do."

"Thanks. It means everything to me that you're on board with the idea." I took another long look at the painting, then covered it and closed the box.

We drank our coffee and ate pastries sitting on Matthew's old bed. As we finished eating, I bumped Matthew's shoulder with mine. "So what were you thinking about earlier?"

He shrugged. "Just stuff."

"Come on. Thought we were going to work on our communication?"

He sipped his coffee, then said, "Stuff I wanted to ask you guys about." Another shrug. "There's just a lot we haven't talked about."

"So ask."

"Now?"

"Yeah. We can stay here and talk until your mom kicks us out."

"Okay." Biting his lower lip once more, he looked to Luke and then back to me. He breathed deep, and the words came pouring out of him. "Do you really want to keep Trixie? Can she sleep in bed with us or will that bother you? What if she chews on everything? Will you want to get rid of her? Do you even like dogs? Are you going to let me pay you back for my school? Do you think a lot of people look at us and think there's something wrong with us? Do they think we're sinning? What happens if one of you decides you don't love us anymore? Do we all break up? Or do two of us stay together? Is that even an option?" He abruptly cut off and shook his head. "Forget it. They're stupid questions." He shot off the bed and went to stand before the window, still clad in only his underwear.

The way he'd rambled from one topic to another had my head spinning, but I slid off the bed and moved in behind him, placing my hands on his shoulders. "They're not stupid questions."

He turned to face me. "Obviously they are. Just look at him." He gestured to Luke who sat perfectly still on the edge of the bed, eyes wide. "He's not even blinking."

"You just threw a lot at him all at once. But if those are things you're wondering about, then they're valid questions."

Luke did blink then. He got up and moved in beside me. "He's right. You can always ask whatever you want."

I offered Luke a grin, then to Matthew said, "First off, I do like dogs, and Trixie's family now, so she can stay no matter what. Even if she chews the whole house apart. And she can sleep in our bed with us. Okay?"

He nodded.

"About the money for your school. Can't we just call it a gift? It means the world to me that I can help you reach one of your goals, and I would never think less of you for accepting it. I actually think you're incredibly brave for going back to school in the first place, and if you let me help you, then for me that means I'm your partner, that we're in everything together."

He searched my eyes. "Okay."

I threaded my fingers through his dark hair and drew him closer. "And we are *not* sinning. Fuck what anyone else says or thinks about that. In my opinion, we're luckier than most people *because* we're three."

"Yeah." Luke pointed at me. "What he said."

I glanced his way. "How long do you think you can keep getting away with that?"

Nonchalantly he looked to the ceiling like he was considering that. He shrugged. "As long as you guys continue to say shit better than I could."

I scoffed. He'd gotten damn good at expressing himself all on his own. Dominic had been right when he said Matthew and Luke wouldn't end up the same men I'd met. Luke definitely wasn't the man I'd first approached at the Haven, and I wasn't sorry about that in the least. I loved him more because of who he'd allowed himself to become, because he'd opened himself up to us despite his past.

And Matthew... he was trying very hard to get what he wanted and needed out of this relationship. I wasn't about to let him down.

I turned my focus back to him. "And no matter how much it kills me to say this, we are not an all-or-nothing thing here. If Luke gets some fucked-up idea in his head that he doesn't love us anymore, we'll do whatever we can to change that, but if he wants to go, we can't stop him. That, however, will not change how I feel about you." I leaned in and brushed my lips against his. "I won't leave you just because Luke walks out on us."

"Hey." Luke elbowed me in the side. "I'm right fucking here. I'm not going anywhere."

"Relax," I said. "It was hypothetical."

He threw his hands in the air. "Don't we talk enough about real shit? Now we've gotta talk about hypothetical shit?"

Matthew shook his head once more. "We don't have to talk about any of this."

Luke sighed and reached out for him. He tugged Matthew forward and into his arms. "I won't leave you. Even if the big guy here does something completely moronic like dump us, you'll still have me. Okay?"

"Okay."

"Although..." Luke pulled back. "We may have to find a new place to live. I'm thinking if he breaks up with us he's not going to want us hanging around, sleeping in his bed, fucking in his shower."

"Speaking of that," I said.

"You don't want us fucking in the shower anymore?"

"Don't be stupid." I went to get my coat off the chair and removed the paperwork I'd brought with me. "Here." I handed each of them an envelope.

"When did you do this?" Luke asked as he flipped through the papers.

"Right after we met Dominic. Your names are now on the deed for our town house, and if something happens to me, you'll also get my life insurance policy, my business, and any other investments I add to my personal portfolio, as well as the Harrison Estate. I also listed you both as my Health Care Power of Attorney so you can make decisions for me if I can't. There's no one I trust more than you two." I waited until Matthew looked my way. "We may not be able to legally get married, but we can set it up so it's as close to a marriage as we can manage. You two are it for me." I kissed him again and spoke one word against his lips. "Forever."

When Matthew still didn't say anything, Luke seized me by the hips and dragged me backward toward the bed. He shoved me down onto my back and straddled my thighs, then gestured to Matthew with a tilt of his head. "I think he's in shock. We better do something to snap him out of it."

"You got anything in mind?"

"Oh yeah. I got ideas."

"I'm sure you do."

Matthew laughed. He came and sat on the bed beside us. "I used to sit here when I was in high school and dream about what my life would be like when I was older. I never imagined it would be like this."

"Are you happy?" I asked. "Or do you want something more?"

He studied my face like that was the most ridiculous thing he'd ever heard. "Every day I wake up and I can't believe this is my life, that I get both of you. That's all that matters to me. I'm sorry I left last night."

"No. I'm sorry, Matthew." I sat up, holding on to Luke as I leaned to the side to kiss Matthew, and when the kiss ended, I kept contact with him, our foreheads pressed together. "I never should've gotten so angry with you. I should've handled it better. There's nothing we can't work through if we just talk to each other. I forgot that for a moment."

He nodded. "Me too."

Then without warning Luke's eyes went wide as he started to slide sideways off my lap. I tried to grab for him, and we toppled over onto Matthew. All three of us nearly slipped off the edge of the mattress and onto the floor. I caught them in time and held on. I wasn't about to let them fall.

Or let them go.

Luke chuckled as he helped shift us to the center of the mattress again. "This bed is way too small for three people." He moved off me and lay on my other side. "There should be a new rule. No matter how upset someone is, we don't just take off."

Both Matthew and I stared at him, speechless. I knew Matthew was thinking back to the same moment in time that I was. When Luke had left and gone to the Haven when he didn't want to talk about his father or admit he was falling for us.

Luke rolled his eyes at our reaction. "What? A man can't grow and change? Jeez."

I reached over and rubbed his dick through his jeans. "I love it when you grow."

Matthew snorted. "Oh man, that was bad." He laughed more, and that got Luke and me going.

Then with sudden urgency, Matthew got up and yanked on my arm. "Come on." He gripped Luke's arm too so he was pulling us off the bed at the same time.

When I was on my feet, I nabbed Matthew from behind, wrapping my arms around his waist, and kissed the side of his neck. "Where are we going, kid?"

He turned to face me, then waited until Luke was there with us. He embraced us both and said, "Home. To *our* home."

Damn, that sounded good.

It sounded *right*.

We were all at our best when we were together. No matter where we were. No matter what we were doing. Laughing, fucking, talking, or just living. We were stronger as three.

Stronger than any fear or doubt or worry.

I knew that now in a way I hadn't completely understood before.

"Yeah," I said. "Let's go home."

ABOUT THE AUTHOR

Sloan Parker writes passionate, dramatic stories about two men (or more) falling in love. She enjoys writing in the fictional world because in fiction you can be anything, do anything—even fall in love for the first time over and over again. Sloan lives in Ohio with her partner and their neurotic cats. Her greatest moments in life are spent with her family, her friends, and her characters.

To contact Sloan, find out about her other books that are available for purchase, and read free stories, visit: www.sloanparker.com. If you'd like to be notified of new releases and get exclusive sneak peeks, be sure to sign up to receive Sloan Parker's newsletter via her website.

OTHER TITLES BY SLOAN PARKER

More (More Book 1)
Breathe
Take Me Home
How to Save a Life (The Haven Book 1)
More Than Just a Good Book
Something to Believe In
I Swear to You
The Break-In
Swept Away
A Lesson in Truth

www.ingramcontent.com/pod-product-compliance
Lightning Source LLC
Chambersburg PA
CBHW050027180626
46810CB00002B/602